THE  Baldwin PORTOLANO

A NOVEL

SHARON O. LIGHTHOLDER

Also by the author:

The English Rendition

Every family has a secret. But when a well-intentioned lawyer discovers that violinist Emily Finch Montgomery is a victim of the Swiss banking fraud that hid dormant accounts from owners for decades, he threatens to unravel her lifetime of carefully crafted lies. She must decide if her legacy to her family is the comfortable lie or the truth of her escape from Prague when Hitler annexed Czechoslovakia.

Dedicated

To my father and those who serve.

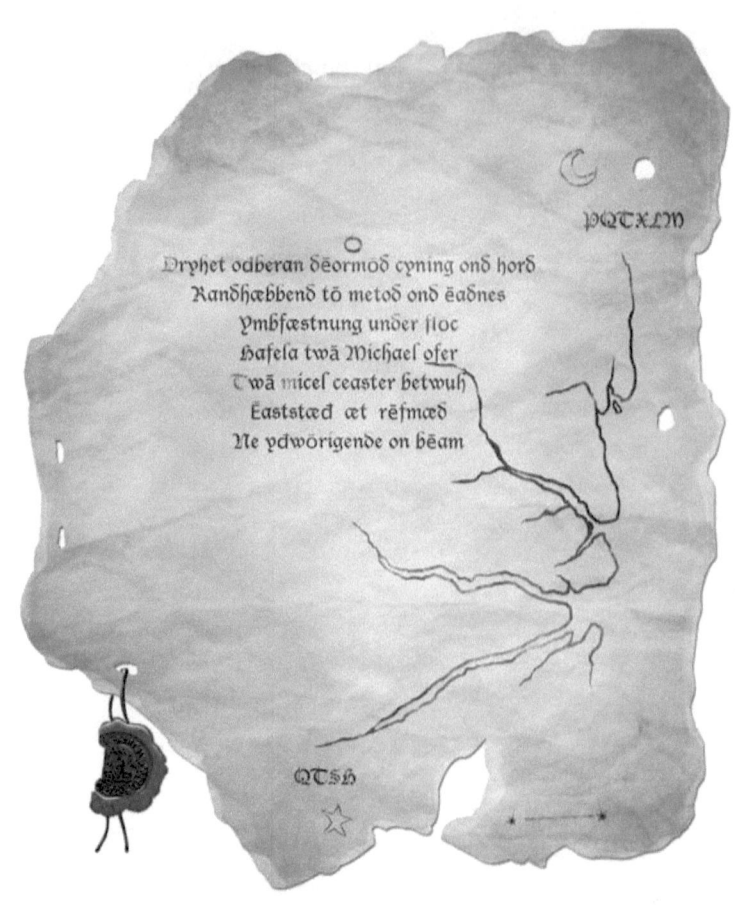

Dryhet odberan ðeormoð cyning ond hord
Randhæbbend to metoð ond eadnes
Ymbfæstnung under floc
Hafela twa Michael ofer
Twa micel ceaster betwuh
Eaststæd æt refmæd
Ne ydworigende on beam

ILLUSTRATION OF BALDWIN PORTOLANO
FRONT

ILLUSTRATION OF BALDWIN PORTOLANO
BACK

Chapter № 1

Wednesday
October 25, 1916
Whitehall, London, England

"What?" Captain Mansfield Smith-Cumming frowned at the static emanating from his new candlestick telephone and readjusted the earpiece. "Could you say that again?" His bushy eyebrows arched, and he sat straighter. "Do I understand correctly that you want Second Lieutenant Crispin transferred to *my* section?" He looked up as two pigeons landed on the wet limestone ledge outside his window. "Certainly, Prime Minister. If you will be kind enough to send Mister Meade around at one, I shall attend to the matter personally." He glanced at the boxed chronometer on his walnut desk as he returned the earpiece to its hook. Eleven forty-three. He pressed the buzzer on his desk before the earpiece had stopped swinging and smoothed his short silver mustache with the back of his thumb.

At fifty-seven years, the thickset Smith-Cumming was fitter than his silver hair or limp suggested. After returning to London from retirement, he adopted the required diplomatic frock coat and striped trousers expected of officials at Whitehall. However, he flaunted stylish cravats with jeweled stickpins, and insisted that his staff in the foreign section of Britain's military intelligence refer to him simply as "Cumming."

His assistant, Finley, entered the office and braced to attention. Finley had simply replaced his naval uniforms with dark suits, which hung poorly on his slim frame. "Sir?"

Cumming pulled a sheet of letterhead from the desk drawer and wrote as he spoke. "Finley, send a messenger over to the War Office to fetch the file on Crispin, double quick."

Finley took the page and read the green-inked words back to Cumming. "To confirm, you are requesting the complete military file of Second Lieutenant William...." He paused at the name before continuing slowly, "Bismarck Crispin."

"German middle name. Bad luck, that."

He saw that Cumming had signed with his customary single initial. Finley smiled, relishing how the simple green C converted a routine administrative request into a directive of the first order. He spun on his heel and returned in less than fifteen minutes carrying a thick paper file. "The Crispin file, sir."

"And? Have you had a squint at it?"

He placed the file on the blotter in front of Cumming. "A quick one, sir."

"Well? What do you make of him?"

Finley began slowly. "He's not one of us, but rather one of those university chaps who signed on after graduation. Just turned twenty-one. Assigned as the Communications and Signals Officer for–" He shook his head slowly. "Poor bastard has been in the trenches at the Somme since the first whistle in July and now with the new offensive they kicked off this morning, he's in the thick of it. If he is still–"

With a flick of his wrist, Cumming sent the file back across the desk. "Take another read while I look over the morning dispatches. Tell me why *he* would assign some pipsqueak to the Foreign Section?"

"Who, sir? The Admiral?"

"Higher. Mister Asquith himself."

The tin spiked fasteners at the top of the pages kept the contents from scattering as he snapped open the pale tan file folder, flipped through the thin onionskin pages, and reported. "Studied ancient languages. Took a first class degree in English. Entered the service promptly thereafter. Seems quite ordinary. Born in India...."

"Family?"

He turned two pages and cleared his throat. "Orphaned. Only child. Father was a minor clerk in some tea and spice company. Lived in South Africa for a spell. Father died when he was eight. Mother the year following. Parceled out to an elderly aunt near Cornwall for a year or so, then becomes a ward of the local parish priest and lives in a boarding house. Unmarried."

Cumming glanced at a typed report, inked a directive at the bottom, and picked up the dispatch. "So, he's been on his own since he was a small lad, yet he matriculated. How extraordinary."

"Oxford, no less."

Cumming muttered. "He is an *Oxonian?*"

"Seems that he showed a gift for language, specifically Old English. He speaks a dozen modern languages as well as Greek and Latin, sir. Odd notation this–" He squinted at the poor penmanship. "The summary atop his security packet notes that he wrote dictionaries of invented languages in school."

"Still, without family or fortune–" Cumming pushed the reviewed dispatches into a neat pile. "His German name will not serve him well in the coming years. What are his prospects after the war? Teaching village children their letters?"

"Parents were British, but–" He fanned the pages until he found Crispin's enlistment form. "Saxon. That's what he wrote for his mother's heritage."

Cumming chuckled. "Saxon? Cheeky lad! Probably thought he was too clever by half when he wrote that, rather than 'German' on the form. May have a relation or two in the old country." He sighed. "They may have been British, but they were not *English.*" He fingered the monogrammed fob on the heavy silver watch chain that crossed his barrel chest. "So, why then is the P.M. taking this lad out of the trenches when we need every man jack we can muster?"

Without looking up from the file, Finley said, louder than he intended, "Frocks! They haven't the foggiest notion of what it is like over—"

"Stand corrected. Mister Asquith is neither your average bumbling politician nor is he insensitive to how critical the Somme is to our plan of battle. Perhaps you were unaware that he lost his son, Raymond, just weeks ago in that very same offensive. Now, hand back that file and leave me to my reading."

Chapter № 2

Wednesday
October 25, 1916
London, England

Half a mile away from Cumming's office in Whitehall, Jack Meade exited the black door on Downing Street and squinted as a gust of winter wind ruffled his straight dark hair. The rain had stopped during his meeting. The streets had taken on the dull metallic look he associated with the wet misery of English winters. He put on his new brown fedora with the pinch front and center dent, tugged the brim down, and struck out at a fast pace. As he darted between pedestrians, he moved with the athletic grace that few tall men could manage. In less than a block, he crossed Whitehall Street, ignored the mosaic of imposing governmental buildings between Trafalgar Square and the Houses of Parliament, and made straight for his office near Victoria Station. He met with his office manager and provided instructions to his secretary on his travel plans while he ate a ham sandwich.

At a quarter before one, Meade left his office, crossed the bridge, and walked briskly toward Whitehall Street. He wove his way past men in bowler hats with closed umbrellas, soldiers in wet greatcoats, and frock-coated officials scuttling between buildings. He dodged the madly scurrying Boy Scouts pressed into service as messengers.

Meade hurried past the War Office, turned the corner at Whitehall Court, found Number 2, and rushed up the steps. The hem of his unbuttoned coat flapped behind him. As he passed a stout woman in a long black dress and veiled hat, he startled a small flock of pigeons.

They scattered and circled before finding refuge on the ledge outside Cumming's office.

"Damned pigeons again." Cumming looked out the window toward the street. "Look at him, taking the steps two at a time. Built like a distance runner, wouldn't you say?"

Finley looked past Cumming's shoulder. "My God, what university chap would have the brass to wear a tweed Norfolk suit to Whitehall?"

Cumming laughed. "Jack Meade, that's who. And he's no lad. Late forties, I'd guess. Fit, though."

"You know him, sir?"

"Indeed. I worked with him before you joined my staff. He is the American who helped Sidney Reilly map the oil reserves in Persia before the war. Resulting in the oil concessions—"

"Oh? I thought Reilly managed that alone."

When Meade entered the building, Cumming turned from the window and walked past Finley. "That is precisely what you were meant to think. But I am convinced that it was Meade, not Reilly, who brokered the agreement. Professional oilman, amateur antiquarian. Quite a large circle of acquaintances."

"Really?"

Dropping into his high-backed desk chair, Cumming said, "I tried to recruit him for the Cairo office before the war. He is the one who put me on to Miss Bell's astonishing new maps of Persia and Mesopotamia. Interesting fellow, he was the first to recognize that she knew more about those desert tribes than any Englishman."

"Didn't she recommend that Lawrence chap?"

"In actual fact, Meade did. But won't take the credit for it. I would not have thought Lawrence the right sort or vetted him but for Meade's assurance that he was a fine Arabist."

"Lawrence's negotiations with the tribal chiefs seem to be going well. Shifting some away from the Turks."

Cumming nodded toward the stack of papers on his desk. "Quite well, from his last dispatch. I don't want to think where we could be if Germany consolidates the support of the Ottoman's tribes."

"Could Meade be enticed to work for us now? On salary, with expenses, perhaps?"

Cumming laughed deeply. "My dear fellow, he *is* the Meade Oil Company. Millionaire before he was thirty." Ignoring Finley's blush, he said, "And he is certain to be at the front desk by now. Bring him in, will you?"

Finley returned promptly with Meade.

Standing behind his desk, Cumming extended his hand to Meade, who crossed the room with long strides. Meade's face was angular and tanned. His cool gray eyes had the level gaze of a hunter. Leaner than at their last meeting, he offered the impression of an outdoorsman rather than the shrewd businessman he was. Meade shook Cumming's hand as Finley left the room and closed the door.

Meade dropped his coat and fedora on the leather club chair closest to the window, settled into the chair facing the desk, and ran his hand straight back over his hair. "Thanks for seeing me. I can only imagine how busy you are."

"It is a pleasure to see you again, Mister Meade. I understand that–" The one chime from the regulator clock on the wall interrupted Cumming. Meade glanced around the office and surveyed the debris of a Naval career. A dented silver loving cup from a regatta and a cased brass sextant were centered on the credenza behind the desk under the portrait of King George V. The desk boasted an onyx pen set above the leather-framed blotter. The large cut-glass inkwell held green ink. Just enough clutter to make any posting seem like England, yet spare enough for sea duty.

Cumming reached for the lid of his glass humidor. "I understand that you wish to avail yourself of the services of Second Lieutenant Crispin."

"That's right."

"If I may inquire, Mister Meade, why ever would His Majesty's

Government release Crispin to you? We are at war, even if you Americans are not." Cumming removed the lid from the humidor. "Join me?"

"No, thanks."

After selecting a cigar, Cumming said, "I cannot see how a recent graduate in ancient languages, a junior officer at that, could assist the Meade Oil Company." He tapped the tan file folder next to his blotter. "Nothing here to suggest that he has any background at all in your industry."

"This isn't for my company."

Cumming carefully amputated the tip of the cigar with a silver clipper. "Personal? And just how could that possibly benefit His Majesty's Government?"

Measuring his words carefully, Meade said, "I have a portolano, a mariner's map of a coastline. Got it at an auction two weeks ago. I think it shows the location of a buried treasure somewhere in England."

Cumming suppressed a smile. "Surely your little treasure hunt can wait. As I tell the lads: it's duty first, self second."

"If I'm right, the map points to the most important archaeological find of our lifetime and a key to your history."

Cumming dropped the clipper back into the center drawer of his desk. "A map? Something out of *Treasure Island*, perhaps? Are there scalawags with wooden legs and parrots?"

Meade narrowed his eyes. "Not at all like *Treasure Island*. I bid on an uncatalogued collection of printed maps at auction and won. When I got back home, I discovered a rare portolano, on parchment, mixed in with the paper maps I expected to see."

"An error?"

"Either they didn't know what they had, or someone was using me to smuggle it out of the country."

Cumming frowned. "Why ever would you think that?"

"My apartment was broken into that night. They left the contents of the map box scattered on the floor."

"How did they overlook the portolano?"

Meade patted his chest. "It's not much larger than your hand. Had it with me in a pouch. I wanted to show it to an associate at Christie's, but he was not in his office."

"And what makes you think it wasn't a simple burglary?"

"They ignored a great deal of cash on the dresser, left the maps I had just bought alone, and took a fountain pen they couldn't sell."

Cumming nodded. "And you think someone is looking for this portolano now?"

"Yes. I've collected enough antiquities to know any map with Old English writing on it is really rare. Want to see it?"

Cumming frowned as he shook his head, put a match to his cigar, and was enveloped in a blue cloud. "Don't know a thing about old maps. What is so important about this one?"

"Anyone who collects maps has heard of the Baldwin Portolano. It's a rarity. The coastline is drawn in the Viking style, no inland detail at all, and there is a lengthy text on it. In Old English."

"How old would the map be?"

"No one knows, precisely, but the first record of it is in the diary of Baldwin, brother of Godfrey of Bouillon–"

Cumming tipped his head as though he had not heard properly. "First Crusade?"

"Yeah. About 1099, it shows up in Baldwin's diary while he was the King of Jerusalem. The Muslim cartographers drew their own maps of the territories they conquered from the 600s to the millennium. But many of their portolanos, their trading maps showing coastlines and ports of trade, were compiled from earlier maps drawn by others." Cumming leaned back and took a long draw on his cigar as Meade continued. "Given the age of this portolano, I'd guess that it was an older source map from the archives that Baldwin plundered in Jerusalem. He wrote a meticulous description of about a dozen maps in his diary. Some were Egyptian, on papyrus. Others were on paper. Five were portolanos. But only one had Old English writing on it." Meade shrugged. "But then this special portolano just vanished. The next trace of it is when it is listed in the sale catalogue of a Paris gallery of antiquities in 1597."

"Who bought it?"

"Nobody. It was stolen before the sale. It just disappeared. Until now."

"Tell me, Mister Meade. As rare as the Old English script and the age of the document may be, what proof have you that King Baldwin ever possessed your map?"

"Oh, didn't I mention his seal?"

"A royal seal?"

"Yeah. Small wax seal, no bigger than your thumbnail, on a thin leather ribbon that runs through a slit in the map. Half the wax has cracked off, but you can still see his face and crown in the center and his name on the edge. In Latin, of course."

Clearing his throat, Cumming said, "Of course. How may we assist you?"

"The translation is a problem. I need to know what the text means."

Cumming leaned on his desk and frowned at Meade. "But why Crispin? Our universities should offer several translators who are not in uniform–"

"I have a friend in Geneva, Somerset Maugham. I went to him for help. I thought that since he's a writer–"

"And?"

"He translated it, word for word." Meade chuckled. "It came out gibberish. Said that I needed more than just a translator. I needed someone who really knew the era as well as the language because it was coded in its references."

"Pardon?"

"The directions to the treasure depend on knowing England at that specific time. After he made a few calls for me to his contacts at universities, Maugham said that Crispin's unique imagination made him the only one for the job."

"Just to be clear, you want me to release a soldier for your material benefit?"

Recoiling slightly and frowning, Meade said, "No. I just want to find the treasure. It's England's, as far as I'm concerned."

"What you are describing sounds quite dear, but—"

"It's worth about eight million. That's in dollars."

Cumming abandoned his cigar in the cut-crystal ashtray and leaned forward. "I must have misunderstood you. Did you say 'eight million dollars'? What would that be in pounds sterling?"

Meade calculated quickly. "Today, we're at about a one-to-five exchange rate, so that's a million six hundred thousand pounds."

Cumming gently rolled the ash from his cigar into the crystal ashtray and took a puff. "How ever did you develop that estimate, Mister Meade?"

"There's a list on the back of the map. Mister Asquith was kind enough to ask someone from the British Museum to look at Maugham's translation of the items. He thinks they are funeral objects. Royal gold. Then he asked a friend of his at Christie's for an estimate. Between eight and ten million bucks at auction. Half that on the black market. Less still if all the gold were melted down."

Blinking rapidly, Cumming said, "I am having difficulty in grasping that value."

"I did, too. Then I remembered that during my last crossing, the Captain told me that the White Star Line spent a million and a half pounds building and fitting out the *Titanic*."

"You are telling me the treasure exceeds the cost of the *Titanic*!"

"Yeah. And that's not including whatever the portolano is worth as an antiquity. There is no comparison on which to base its value."

Cumming brushed his moustache with his thumb and frowned. "As rich a financial and historic find as this may be, I fear that it might be of equal interest to the Hun."

Meade frowned. "Why would the Germans care? It's English history."

"I don't care if it is nothing more than a fairground attraction. It is the value that concerns me. Over a million and a half pounds sterling? My God, man. That could put another battleship on the line or finance their war for months."

"Yeah, the money could–"

Cumming said quietly, "It is much worse than that. Your treasure could invigorate the flagging German morale."

"I don't see how."

Cumming examined the ember on his cigar before looking at Meade. "Mister Meade, the German Confederation lacks any sense of national unity although it was formed in 1871. Our sources tell us that the Kaiser has his inner circle working feverishly on what they call the *völkisch* to develop that national identity."

"I'm not following–"

"They are as desperate for a unifying history as they are for funds. They want to be an ancient civilized people with a common heritage. They want proof of their kingdom's historic reach."

"What could this do to–"

Meade watched the color drain from Cumming's face.

"Mister Meade. Your treasure could provide an excuse to invade England. Claim the history and gold as theirs."

Meade sat back into the deep chair and exhaled loudly.

Cumming leaned over his desk blotter. "How soon can you find the grave?"

"I don't know. It all depends on how bright Crispin is."

"Are you certain that he is the best man for the job? He barely made his security clearance."

Meade nodded quickly. "According to Maugham, Crispin is your most promising young scholar in the field of philology. After all, he mastered Greek and Latin as a boy, speaks several modern languages, translated the *Story of Frotho* from German and *Beowulf* from Old English on his own before he even went to college."

Cumming glanced at the closed file on his desk. "His record does indicate a facility with language."

"Maugham said the guy was so steeped in Old English it was like he'd been born in the wrong millennium."

"Somerset really said that?" Meade nodded as Cumming tapped the file and continued. "In that event, I shall have him recalled to England immediately."

"I have some work to do in France first. That's why Asquith sent me to you. I need the flexibility to go wherever this search takes me. And a letter of transit."

Sighing, Cumming asked, "What will you be doing in France?"

"What's that matter?"

"I shall not allow my other operations to be compromised by–"

Meade held up his hand to stop Cumming. "I just need a few days to look at a private map collection for a reference map."

"Why?"

"Coastlines change over time. I need a reference map to adjust the geography of the portolano to current conditions."

Cumming shrugged. "I'll write the orders now and have them personally conveyed to his commanding officer. Since you plan to be in France, I'll have him brought to you in Paris."

"Amiens. I need Crispin's help in Amiens."

Cumming looked startled. "But that is only a few miles from the front."

"I know. I can pick him up at his unit. We've got to hurry."

"Risky business, that. I can billet you on our next transport to Paris–"

With a crooked smile, Meade said, "No. Too many people know my face and would wonder why I was with the military."

"What do you propose?"

"I thought I'd just go to the Hôtel Ritz, like I do for other meetings when I can get a letter of transit. Let my secretary be open about it if I get any calls. From there, I'll just drop out of sight."

Cumming nodded and reached for his pen. "If you insist. You do realize that no one can know the particulars of his assignment. I'll concoct some tale to explain his absence. Illness. Perhaps trench fever."

Meade cleared his throat. "Besides a letter of transit, I'll need a courier. To get some antique maps to London –"

"Maps? Why should I help you move some maps?"

"You do not want to be the guy that lost this treasure for your country."

Cumming inspected the gold nib of his pen. "Well then. I am certain that we can find a way to transport a crate."

"Crates. I'll need a daily courier, until I have it all boxed up."

Cumming let out a sigh. "All that is within the realm of possibility. Do you want to review Crispin's service file before you decide?"

"I've made my decision, but I'd like to read it while you write up the orders."

Cumming slid the tan file across the desk. Meade read all of it while Cumming wrote a brief order in green ink on his letterhead and then rocked a silver blotter over the page.

Meade closed the file. "How soon can I have him?"

"He'll be ready for release by the time you get there. I'll have our man, Thompson will be his name, collect you from your hotel in Paris."

"Thompson."

"Right. How is your memory, Mister Meade?"

"Better than most for numbers. I'm okay with names if I see them written. Why?"

Cumming balanced his cigar on the crystal ashtray and took a small slip of onionskin paper from his drawer. His pen scratched across it. "These are your emergency contacts in Paris and London. Memorize their names and telephone numbers now."

He handed the paper to Meade and tapped the ash from his cigar.

Meade stared at the contact information as Cumming said, "Oh, should I dispatch anyone to meet with you or speak with you, you should challenge them by asking 'who sent you'. Am I clear?" Meade nodded as Cumming continued. "And the response will be the three letters 'RLS.'"

Frowning, Meade asked, "RLS?"

"Robert Louis Stevenson. The chap who wrote *Treasure Island*. Easy enough to remember for your treasure hunt, yet who would guess it?"

Creases formed at the edges of his eyes as Meade laughed. "I see. Thanks."

"Good luck to you, Mister Meade."

Cumming held out his hand for the frail onionskin. After Meade had relinquished it, Cumming blew gently on the cigar's ember until it shimmered crimson. When he pressed the ember against the paper, the onionskin curled and then flared. As it burned, Meade stood, scooped up his coat, and held his hat. Cumming examined the perfect ember on his cigar as he said, "Mister Meade, there is just one more thing."

"Yes?"

"You do know that you and Crispin will be bound by the Official Secrets Act. You may not discuss this mission with anyone. Ever."

"But–"

"*Semper Occultus!* 'Always secret'– that is our byword."

Chapter № 3

Wednesday
October 25, 1916
London, England

The Carlton Arms was but a staggering step above the customary London boarding house and struggled to retain the pretense of being a hotel. It served the minimal needs of men of commerce intending to do some business with His Majesty's Government, minor functionaries on temporary assignment, ill-advised travellers, and now, soldiers in transit or on leave.

The man who called himself Frederick Grimes selected it specifically for its proximity to Whitehall. Before he left Berlin, he had let his light brown hair grow longer than he preferred to emphasize the early gray at his temples. He had cultivated a beard to round his firm jaw and suggest a double chin. Steel-rimmed glasses shielded his brown eyes. His English clothing had been secured for him by others and offered a loose fit over his well-muscled frame. He slumped to appear less fit and shorter than his six feet.

Grimes soon became as unremarkable a fixture in the hotel as the dusty potted palms. He took the same corner table in the dining room for each meal and discreetly surveyed the other diners while appearing to read his book. Others saw precisely what he wanted them to see. A widower from the midlands. A salesman in a baggy black suit with frayed shirt cuffs who would disappear every now and again for a few days. A bumbling dumpy fellow eager to have the tales of others fill his empty hours. A sympathetic man more than willing to stand a returning soldier to another drink, applaud his exploits, offer stationery, and post a last letter home for a lad bound for France.

Grimes became a man of habit. After breakfast, he made his morning rounds. He began with the post office, where he read lovesick scrawls and tossed the unstamped love letters into the dustbin. He pocketed the envelopes with uncensored correspondence containing hints of troop movements or other valuable information. Then, he prowled antique shops and met with antiquarians. At eleven sharp, he visited the bookbinder with a loft of racing pigeons, passed off the letters of interest, and was back at the Carlton Arms by noon.

Lunch was well attended by public servants with limited income who made the rib-sticking shepherd's pie the main meal of their day. Only those dining at the Carlton Arms regularly would have recognized the similarity between lunch and the prior evening's offering. Grimes watched them shovel it in and rush off. He dawdled over his food and read his book through the noon hour. Often, he lingered late into the afternoon while nursing a gin and tonic with some weary traveler or soldier.

At dinner, Grimes would offer a nod or smile to the lost or lonely to pull up a chair. Just like fly-fishing in Bavaria. Tonight, however, he had shunned company and after dinner walked stiffly to his usual chair in the lobby. As he saw his reflection in the glass of the front door, he smiled. He no longer recognized himself as the tall and trim archaeologist who left a teaching position at the University at Heidelberg for a post on the Kaiser's personal staff.

The short balding waiter followed him and stood silently until he had settled into the creased leather chair. "A brandy tonight, sir?"

"Yes, thank you, Charles. Just a small one." Grimes smiled. He had struggled to master the midlands accent over the last year. Now it seemed so easy. When the waiter returned and placed a small snifter on the chipped table, Grimes noticed the fresh gravy stains on the waiter's white apron, quite unlike the spotless aprons of waiters in even the most modest German tavern.

Grimes absentmindedly tapped the book on his lap and watched the waiter shuffle back to the dining room. The drafty lobby suggested a clubby charm with deep reading chairs of chocolate leather and side tables. Occasional rugs, mimicking Oriental tapestries, had been placed over threadbare areas of the dark green carpet. Guests tended to linger in the ground floor dining room or in the lobby to delay retiring to the musty rabbit warren of rooms scented with memories of boiled cabbage and rancid roasted meats.

Fellow guest Samuel Morrison stumbled over Grimes' feet as he took the chair facing him. "Evening, Fred."

"Good evening, Mister Morrison." Grimes took a small sip of the fiery brandy, let the fumes cut through the pervasive scent of mold, and opened his book. After a few minutes, Morrison wandered off to seek other companionship.

The waiter passed through the lobby with his empty tray. "Another, sir?"

"Not just yet." Grimes offered a mock toast to the waiter.

At precisely half past eight, he glanced at the elderly desk clerk, who was making quick work of a registration. He seemed immune to time. Day after day, he appeared as the dining room was set for breakfast and departed at midnight, always dressed in what seemed to be the same black trousers, black bow tie, white shirt, and crimson vest. He had perpetual white stubble on his chin yet seemed as alert as the bright lights that glinted off his speckled head. He routinely tapped a small chromed bell to summon a waiter to carry a bag or offer a cigar or snifter of brandy to a guest in the lobby. As the hour grew later, he shooed away ladies of the evening, unless he knew them personally.

During his time at the Carlton Arms, Grimes had invented ways to remain relatively sober in spite of the river of drink he ordered. Some spirits watered the palm by his reading chair in the lobby. Others were abandoned at the table or around the hotel. He was developing his skills as a fraud and found the deception exhilarating.

He looked at the oak-cased clock above the desk clerk. It was five minutes after nine. Stahl was unacceptably late. He listened to the light rain against the tall windows and felt the draft crawl past the cracked glazing. He swirled his brandy and sighed.

The front door opened and a blast of damp air ruffled the palm fronds. A tall man in a gray overcoat entered. The door slammed behind him. He took off his hat and brushed his hand over his short blond hair while his coat dripped on the carpet. Grimes stared at Stahl and waved his book at the man who finally turned in his direction, nodded, and walked toward him.

"Ah. Mister Grimes. How are you tonight?"

Grimes quickly converted his glare into a smile. "It's a good night for a brandy. May I offer you one?"

"Yes. Thank you."

He hoisted himself from the chair with feigned difficulty, left his barely touched snifter on the side table, and shuffled toward the dining room. "We'll be more comfortable in there." He motioned to the waiter.

"Yes, Mister Grimes. What may I get you gentlemen?"

"A good snifter each. My friend has eaten already."

The slim man tossed his coat and hat on an empty chair and unbuttoned his suit coat as he sat. His powerful shoulders strained the gray wool when he moved. Grimes glared at his companion. "What the hell detained you?"

"I thought you were at the Carleton Hotel, not this hovel. What have you done to yourself?" His expression suggested a whiff of something unpleasant.

Grimes ignored him. "Did you bring it?"

"It was not there."

Staring at the man, Grimes whispered, "What?"

"Nothing like what you described was in there. Not a map on hide. Not the leather pouch you said it was in."

"I have antiquarians from Spain to the Sudan writing me of his inquiries about Old English on a parchment portolano. I am convinced he has the Baldwin. And I want it."

"I know you do. You should have won the bid."

Grimes sighed. "But I didn't, did I? I do not think you have any grasp of how important this is to...others."

Stahl's lips tightened into a thin pale line.

Grimes lowered his voice. "How difficult is it to rob his apartment?"

"It just wasn't there."

"You've been gone for days. How do I know you even—" He stopped short as the waiter approached.

Stahl's jaw muscle quivered. He watched the waiter place two globes of golden brandy on the table. When he had left, Stahl leaned back in his chair and reached into his suit coat. He tossed a slim pen case of black leather onto the table in front of Grimes.

Stahl smiled as he watched him open the case and gasp. Grimes picked up the pen and examined the delicately carved silver snake coiled around a large black fountain pen. He raised his eyebrows when he saw that the snake's eyes were emeralds.

Grimes returned the pen into the case and closed it. "It's a 1906 Parker Snake. Too rare to sell without undue attention. Why take it?"

"I wanted Meade to know I was there."

Grimes slipped the pen case into his coat pocket. "Flushing quail, were we?"

The man nodded. "He booked passage to Geneva. Spent a day visiting friends, it seemed. Lost him for a bit then picked up the trail back to here."

Grimes lurched forward. His elbows hit the table, and the brandy jumped in the glasses. "Meade? In London? Now? Why didn't you tell me straight away?"

Stahl took a long slow drink, almost taunting Grimes. "You said not to contact you except Wednesdays at nine."

Grimes shut his eyes. "My God! Use your head—"

"I did. I waited outside his London office. After I saw him leave, I telephoned for him. His secretary said he had just booked passage to France, and would be in Paris at the Hôtel Ritz for at least a week. There's only one boat this week, and I'll be on it as well."

"Then it is off to Paris with you. Don't disappoint me...a second time." Grimes tipped back his glass. He almost enjoyed the way the cheap brandy seared his throat.

Chapter № 4

Friday
October 27, 1916
British Expeditionary Force
The Somme Valley, France

Second Lieutenant William Bismarck Crispin began his day before dawn in a fetid command bunker in France. He gulped a bite of charred toast and looked up when Colonel Spaulding began pacing in front of the large situation map. Two helmeted officers hurried into the command bunker, the wet wool of their greatcoats adding to the persistent feral stench of latrine, mud, and rot. As the coated officers dropped into battered chairs in the middle of the ten-by-fifteen foot room, three desk officers, who were jammed against the walls, turned their chairs toward Spaulding.

A beefy white-haired major, carrying his flat helmet as though it were an empty pie tin, hesitated in the doorway. Spaulding noticed the newcomer and said, "Do come in, Major Rand! I'll have you shadow our signals officer during today's operation."

Swallowing the remainder of his toast, Crispin braced to attention and motioned to the empty signaler's chair beside his desk as Spaulding continued. "He's the linchpin for today's action against the Germans. He issues my directives and gets the field reports for all of us over the wire."

Rand stumbled into the chair. As Crispin shoved the empty saucer to the rear of the desk, he tried not to stare at the mustachioed relic from the India Campaign.

Rand leaned closer and asked, "What was your name again?" His uniform reeked of camphor mothballs and pinched at the neck.

Crispin brushed any lingering crumbs from his well-trimmed regimental moustache and said quietly, "Crispin, sir."

Squinting, the major glanced between Crispin and the other slim young officers in their winter wool uniforms at the briefing. Crispin's combination of fine features and light chestnut hair were what women might call classically handsome, possibly even dashing. No family signet ring. His blue eyes had an uncommon confidence.

The waxed tips of Rand's white moustache twitched as he confided in Crispin. "I am having a deuced time of it getting oriented. What with arriving in the dead of night. Seems quite higgledy-piggledy."

Crispin leaned forward and drew an arc like a rainbow in the dust on his desk. "We're dug into a hillside overlooking the valley, sir." As he swiped three parallel lines on the right side of the arc, he said, "We have three types of trenches spread over a couple hundred yards." He tapped the line closest to the top of the arc. "We are here in the reserve trench. Largest and best secured. We could fit the whole lot of us in here, should the need arise." Crispin tapped the middle line. "Next is the supply trench. That's where the men spend most of their time cleaning their gear, eating, picking lice, and clubbing rats. Dugouts are reinforced with timber."

Rand nodded as he watched Crispin's hand animate the diagram. "Near the base of the hill is the firing trench. Manned at dawn and dusk and now, when we are mounting an offensive. Then the coils of wire begin."

"Wouldn't our troops in the lower trenches be exposed to rifle fire from behind?"

Shaking his head, Crispin said, "Sandbags above the rear walls of all the trenches, called *parados*, protect them."

Four more helmeted officers slid past and took the last of the chairs facing Spaulding. The vinegar reek of fear-summoned sweat and rankness of the latrine followed them.

As he snorted, Rand's moustache quivered. "And the smell?"

"One becomes accustomed to it."

At the first electric hiss, Crispin grabbed a pencil from the stack be-side his helmet and began decoding the staccato dits and dahs, which pulsed from the telegraph and delayed the briefing. Colonel Spaulding aimed the tip of his pointer toward the noise. "Must we *all* listen to your telegraph?"

"A moment, sir. Station Sixteen is keying." Crispin had started to raise his hand to silence his new commanding officer and quickly thought better of the gesture. As Crispin converted the buzzes to letters on his notepad, he noticed that Spaulding's uniform had that freshness that Crispin had come to expect of the replacements. Green wool tunic and breeches were brushed. Leggings were wrapped tightly. His Sam Browne belt held a holstered Webley service revolver on one hip and a leather-cased gas mask on the other. All the leather was new and polished. All the brass was too bright.

When Crispin finished his transcription, he dropped the pencil and stood at the signals desk. At Spaulding's nod, he reported, loud enough for all to hear, "Signal from Station Sixteen, at our western gun emplace-ment. The Huns are positioning mortars in quadrant five three."

Lunging at the map like a fencer, Spaulding extended the pointer and planted its tip on a small block near the enemy trench. "Splendid. That is well to the west of today's objective." He looked at Crispin. "Have Sixteen inform us if they fire. Report his signal immediately." As Crispin sat down, the case on his belt tangled on the back of the chair. He quick-ly removed it and tossed it between his helmet and a wood-cased field telephone the size of a boot box on the right side of the desk.

After he attached the wires of his headset to the terminals of the Morse box so that he alone would hear incoming messages, he gripped the earpieces and tugged the band over the top of his head. Crispin pulled the Morse key toward him and tapped out Spaulding's directive before lifting the edge of the right earpiece to listen to the briefing.

Spaulding smacked the pointer against his palm like a riding crop.

"Our plan is to catch the Hun at his breakfast table." He smirked. "Or shortly thereafter. While indisposed." After waiting for the obligatory chuckle to subside, he turned toward the map on which the dark blue of the Somme River meandered like a lazy snake, crossing right to left. The green valley through which it undulated gave way on either side to gentle rolling hills of tan. Jagged trench lines, roughly parallel to each other, had been inked across the width of the map. British trenches were deep green-colored slices. Above them, red gashes marked the enemy trenches. Quadrant lines sectioned the Somme valley into numerically identified squares to avoid the ambiguity of words.

Slamming the tip of the pointer against a sharp bend in the green line, Spaulding said, "Here we are." He shoved the pointer up into the red line on the opposing hill. "There is the Hun's trench." He wagged the tip between the two points. "This passage is just over a half of a mile. Shortest route, but chockablock with wire coils. We shall take the offensive and pierce it." Spaulding pointed to a man in the front row. "Artillery status? Captain James! Let them in on our good news."

A ruddy-faced captain stood. "We are going to suppress their machine guns with an ongoing, targeted cannon barrage from the French 75s and then pound a line of shells through the wire, to allow—"

Several officers groaned. One shouted, "Old news, Freddy! You're peddling old news." Another said, "That creeping barrage with the whizbangs works grand in open terrain when we can march into a village behind your shelling, but the coils of barbed wire—"

The captain scowled at him. "I'm not suggesting we blow it up! Any fool knows that the coils just jump about and come down in a bigger tangle." He paused before continuing. "We're going to blow a pathway *under* the wire for your lads with our new Mark I howitzer."

Crispin heard a whining buzz in the earpiece, clapped it tight against his head, and leaned over the Morse box. He waved at Spaulding and shouted, "Sir! Moaning Minnie coming our way."

When Rand looked puzzled, Crispin said, "*Minenwerfer.*" When he saw no reaction in the man's startled face, he added, "German mortar. Hang on."

The bare bulbs in the command bunker flickered a moment before the explosion rippled through the trenched hill. The officers grimaced and flinched as the timbers groaned and a fine dust sifted through the ceiling planks.

After the officers sat straight again, the artillery captain shouted, "Hear me out! The Mark I is *very* heavy artillery. Its craters are almost two hundred feet across and ten to twenty feet deep." When the chatter had subsided, he said, "We'll pop off a long-round, well over our trenches. Your forward observer will call back the impact coordinates so we can register it and then adjust our aim." Crispin listened to the Morse code in his headset and wrote as the captain continued. "After fifteen or twenty rounds, they'll be inviting you in for tea."

Spaulding slapped the pointer against his palm. "Here's the schedule. Artillery begins zero seven hundred. Once range is registered, they automatically ratchet back a hundred feet and fire off again. When the pathway is sufficient, I will order a cease-fire and move our troops forward." He pointed to the signal's desk. "Crispin? Communications status?"

Crispin remained at his desk, completing his transcription. When called a second time, Rand nudged him. He pulled off his earphones and stood. "All communications are in place. I watched the signaler lay the new cable to the forward observer about midnight and tested the telephone just before the briefing. I'll have two signalers: one on the telephone and the other on the Morse. Runners are at the ready, but the communications trench was so packed with men as I made my way back that—"

Spaulding tossed his pointer on his desk and muttered, "Noted."

"Sir?" Crispin held a slip of paper at shoulder height.

Spaulding frowned. "Yes? What is it?"

"They just signaled that the rain has stopped."

"That's a bit of good news. Gentlemen!" Spaulding opened his pocket watch and held his hand above his head, as though starting a footrace at school. He cleared his throat before saying, "At my mark. Synchronize at zero six four zero." The officers sat as silent as prayer until he barked, "Now!" He glanced at Rand. "Gentlemen! Let me introduce Major Rand, who joined us last night." He marched from the room saying, "Anyone care for tea before we get to it?"

The beefy major stood as straight as a ruler. He gave a nod to each of the departing officers and shook the hand of the few who lingered to offer theirs. When the others had left, two helmeted corporals with side arms marched toward the signals desk. Each carried a bulky canvas satchel on a webbed strap. They saluted in unison. After Crispin and the major returned the salutes, Crispin motioned the shorter man into his desk chair.

After the corporals secured their gun belts and helmets on the desk, the shorter man adjusted the earpieces on the headphones while the taller one tested the wires on the field telephone. Rand turned to Crispin. "Where's our artillery posted?"

"Five miles to the rear, sir. The forward observer has a direct line to them. The set on my desk is spliced into that line to allow Spaulding to speak to the FO or artillery directly. Today, for example, that is how Colonel Spaulding will direct orders to the artillery."

Rand nodded vigorously, stood, and leaned close enough for Crispin to smell his stale breath as he said, "I see." The bunker rocked violently, and the lights flickered.

Holding the telephone receiver toward Crispin, the corporal shouted, "It's dead, sir!"

Crispin shouted, "Bloody hell!" When Rand frowned, Crispin shouted over the din. "Don't you see? The commander has them firing closer and closer to us until they receive his order to cease. With communications out, our own chaps will shell us!" Crispin took the handset and tested the connection on the box before shouting into the handset.

"Station One to Forward Observer! One calling FO? HQ to Reggie? Are you there?" Crispin threw down the handset and turned to the corporals. "Lads? What sport did you play in school?"

The seated man frowned before answering. "Cricket, sir."

The taller of the two tapped a bend at the bridge of his nose. "Rugby!"

Crispin pointed to the tall grinning man. "Grab your helmet and both bags." To the shorter, he barked, "Signal Sixteen that we're going out!"

As the Morse key buzzed under the corporal's touch, Rand clutched Crispin's elbow. "You are the signals officer. You can't leave the bunker!"

He shook free and grabbed his helmet. "For God's sake! The artillery is lighting off in just minutes. If I don't get the cable fixed, we may all be dead within the hour! Tell Spaulding I'm going out." Rand stood frozen until Crispin shouted, "Now!"

Rand turned toward the door and trotted toward the officer's mess.

The corporal with the satchels searched Crispin's eyes. "Think we can get through the trench in time, sir?"

"No. That's why we shall go over them." Crispin sprinted down the trench toward the rear of the hill. The corporal was at his heels.

Crispin raced past the sentries into the darkness. He stopped and glanced at the line of ambulances that had assembled behind the hill after midnight. The new ones had arrived, replacing the slower horse-drawn wagons. When the corporal caught up with him, Crispin took one of the satchels, looped the webbed strap across his chest, and slid the satchel to his back. "What position?"

The corporal cinched his helmet strap tighter and squinted into the darkness. "Flanker, sir."

"Go-getter, are you?" Crispin grinned and started up the dark hill at a measured pace. He stumbled, righted himself quickly, and wiped his wet hands on his breeches. When he heard the corporal panting and starting to pass him, Crispin whispered, "Easy. Keep it at a trot while we get our night eyes. Stop before the hill crests."

"Yes, sir."

Halfway up the back of the hill, they were drenched in sweat but moving easily at a brisk pace. Just before the top, Crispin stopped. "Take a good look out there." He pointed a pathway past one of their Vickers machine gun emplacements. "We'll cut left. Past Sixteen."

Fogged breath swirled around the corporal as he panted. "Hope he got the signal so's we won't get shot in the arse."

Crispin looked at his watch. The radium dots glowed distinctly.

The corporal glanced at him. "The time, sir?"

"Fourteen minutes before seven." He loosened the leather band, pushed it above his wrist, and pulled his wool cuff over it. Below them, the hill rolled down into a dark valley covered with scribbled coiled wire. There was a hint of gray from the shadowed sandbags along the rim of the trenches. "Anything moving?"

"No, sir. I've never jumped over a trench, do you really think—"

Crispin made an upward arc with his hand. "Just spring off the top bag on the *parados*. You'll be fine."

A sharp boom announced a mortar launching from the west. They dropped to the wet grass. The shell moaned as it fell toward the tangle of wire midway between the two hills. When it hit, earth and mud splashed up like a wave into a seawall and the earth shook under them. Before the sound had stopped ringing, Crispin balanced on his fingertips and dug the toes of his boots into the wet turf, like a sprinter at his blocks. He launched himself down the hill at breakneck speed. The corporal chased after him.

Crispin sprang from the top of a sandbag on the rear of the reserve trench and sailed over the chasm. He landed flatfooted and skidded sideways just as the corporal flung himself into the air. Both regained their footing and raced, shoulder to shoulder, toward the supply trench, which they hurdled in unison.

What little grass remained on the muddy hillside clotted to the hobnails of their boots as they landed. The corporal slowed. He saw Crispin shorten his stride and increase his speed and followed his form. Fifty feet shy of the firing trench, Crispin's right boot dropped into a small hole. He hopped a step and pumped his elbows to regain speed. He flew over the entrenchment just inches above the fixed bayonets. His toe snagged on a sandbag at the front of the firing trench. He corkscrewed, landed on his right shoulder, tucked in like a hedgehog, and rolled twenty feet into the muddy field at the base of the hill. The corporal belly-flopped into the mud beside him. The two lay on their stomachs, panting, chests heaving, unable to speak.

Crispin searched along the six-foot-tall coils of barbed wire for the post to which the signaler had anchored the telephone cable. New craters had altered the pockmarked moonscape.

The corporal wheezed as he whispered, "Which way, sir?"

When Crispin saw a ragged stump with a glowing ember and a twist of smoke curling from it, he pointed. "There. It was there." A German mortar shell moaned and landed far to their right. Crispin said, "The break has to be just past the first row of wire. See it? About two hundred yards, straight on." He elbowed his way forward, looking for the cable that ran back to the command bunker. When he found it, he let his hand slip along it as he crawled toward the wall of barbed wire.

The corporal belly-crawled past him using toes and elbows, wiggling like a fish on the beach. Crispin put his head down and followed the sound of the corporal grunting down the pathway flanked by wire strung on timbered Xs.

When they came to the barbed wire obstacle, the corporal slipped off the satchel and snaked under the wire. He reached back for the satchels that Crispin shoved toward him and dragged the bags another ten feet into the still-warm shell hole.

Arriving at the crater, Crispin rolled over the rim and slid to the bottom, splashing knee-deep in water. He handed the frayed end of the telephone cable to the corporal and whispered, "Start your splice." He motioned for the corporal to stay below the rim of the crater as he clawed his way over the stew of mud, twisted metal, and charred wood. He climbed to the rim facing no man's land.

Crispin ran his hands along the freshly tossed dirt at the lip, found the cable, and tugged on it. A ten-foot section came loose and whipped back at him, peppering his face with mud. Two rats squealed, jumped in the air, and bolted away from him.

Something moved beyond the rats. Crispin ducked, blinked, and wiped dirt from his eye with the back of his hand. He waved at the corporal, who was joining the cables and did not see him. Smearing mud over his clean helmet, Crispin began a slow ascent to peer over the rim.

Dull steel. A dark German bucket helmet. Inert. Crispin sighed. Probably just rats running over the debris. Just as Crispin started to climb over the rim onto the flat for the end of the cable, the steel tortoise moved. A second helmet was beside it. Plumes of breath floated up, shifted, and disappeared. Germans. Crossing perpendicular to him. Only twenty yards off. Something small was in front of the tortoises, like an insect they were tracking. The sight at the tip of the rifle barrel. The German snipers were crawling toward where the forward observer had dug into the muck.

Crispin dropped back into the shell hole, grabbed a clot of mud, and threw it at the corporal, who turned and scrambled around the inside of the hole. When he held up two fingers and pointed over the rim, the corporal glanced over the edge and pulled back quickly. Crispin opened the flap of his holster, drew his Webley, and crawled up to the rim. As he aimed, the corporal put his hand over the pistol and whispered. "It'll give us up."

Giving the corporal a brief nod, he started to squeeze the trigger. The Vickers machine gun on the hill behind them began its distinctive chirping tata tata tata. The corporal pulled Crispin down. After a quick burst, it stopped. Crispin heard brass casings ringing like cheap bells as they bounced on the concrete floor of the gun emplacement. Distant groaning. Another burst. A sound like a swarm of bees roared above them. Casings ringing. Crispin looked over the rim and holstered his pistol. He slithered out fifteen feet before he found the frayed end of the cable. When he tugged, it had plenty of slack but was connected. He clamped it in his teeth and elbowed his way back to the hole. The corporal took the cable from Crispin before he slid back into the crater.

Pulling the wire snips from his satchel, Crispin made a clean cut and stripped three inches of insulation from the damaged cable while the corporal prepared the cable from the reel he had strung around the rim.

Crispin handed the snips to the corporal and twisted the strands together.

The corporal whispered, "Bless that gunner. Might name my first-born Vickers. After the gun…or after you, sir."

Crispin chuckled. The corporal asked, "With permission, sir. What's your Christian name?"

"William. Not much of a moniker if you have a girl."

"Then your wife's name?"

As he finished the splice, Crispin grinned, ignoring the sudden pang and whispered, "Not married. Mother's name was Maude. She'd have been honored."

The corporal buckled his satchel and looked up at the sound of another mortar arcing in their direction. As the whining shell got louder and shrieked like the whistle on a teakettle past boil, the corporal splashed into the bottom of the shell hole and shouted, "Mother of God! Take cover, sir!" Crispin slammed his body against the wall of the crater and put his hands over the back of his neck. The shell landed less than a hundred feet from them. When the thunderclap of the explosion had rolled past, Crispin spun toward where the corporal had been and saw that the far wall of the crater had collapsed on him.

Only the heel of his boot protruded from the water at the base of the mudslide. Crispin jumped down and tugged at it. Unable to move it, Crispin shoved his hands into the mud. Something metallic jammed against the tip of his finger. He probed deeper into the mud and grabbed it. It moved slightly. When he yanked on it with all of his strength, it came up from the mud with a sucking sound.

He held a scorched rag of summer khaki tangled around a leather watchband and fell across the remains of a charred hand. He gagged, threw it to the side, and clawed at the mud just under the waterline. Then, holding his breath, he dove to the bottom of the black water and probed the slurry.

When his knuckle glanced off flat steel, Crispin dug like a terrier around the helmet, not knowing if it was the corporal or another part of some nameless soldier long buried in the muck. Once he found the helmet strap, he grabbed for the neck. It was warm. He tugged at the corporal's collar, struggling to get them both above the muddy water. They both sputtered as Crispin held the corporal's face above the water. When they had stopped gasping, Crispin pawed mud away from the corporal until he was able to move on his own.

When he turned, the corporal winced, grabbed his forearm, and held it against his chest. Crispin pushed the corporal's shoulders against the dirt wall and saw blood darkening the man's cuff and fingers. Crispin quickly unbuttoned the jacket and pulled the sleeve down his arm, searching for the shrapnel wound. He exhaled loudly. "You're not hit." When he saw that the corporal could not yet hear him, he pasted on a grin.

The young man's arm was broken in three places and the raw milk-white bone poked through his shirtsleeve just below the elbow. Crispin pulled a handkerchief from his breeches pocket, tied it around the bleeding, positioned the broken arm over the corporal's stomach, and buttoned the jacket. Crispin cupped his hands beside the corporal's ears and said, as loudly as he dared, "Don't move it or you might sever the artery. Understand?"

After the corporal nodded, Crispin tugged the man's necktie off and wrapped it around the post above the corporal's head. "That ought to let them find this crater."

The corporal pointed toward Crispin's Webley with his left hand. "Could I trouble you to leave your pistol with me, sir? If they fire off gas before the stretcher-bearers can get to me, I'll–"

Crispin pulled away, jettisoned the reel of cable from his satchel, and hooked the two webbed straps together. "Don't go chumpy on me. I'm leaving the marker so they can recover that lad down there. You are going out with me. No argument. You were hurt worse than this when you broke your nose in a scrim." He held the strap in front of the corporal. "Get the loop over your good shoulder."

Crispin tugged on the spliced cable. It was intact. He boosted the corporal over the rim and whispered, "Stay flat on your back. Don't push with your legs or they'll shoot your knees." He shoved the corporal under the wire. As he inched past, Crispin hooked the webbed strap to the D-ring on his Sam Browne belt and began crawling toward the trench. Grunting, Crispin began framing an apology to Rand sufficient to avoid charges for insubordination and get his ass out of the wringer.

After several minutes, the corporal whispered, "How much further, sir?"

As the French 75 whiz-bangs rained on the German machine gun emplacements, Crispin turned and shouted, "It is about a hundred yards." He resumed dragging his charge and muttered, "It's *farther; not further!*"

Chapter № 5

Friday
October 27, 1916
Paris, France

M eade ate a hearty breakfast at a small gilded Louis XV writing desk in his room at the Hôtel Ritz. He left his dark blue silk pajamas crumpled on the unmade bed and returned his matching leather suitcases to the wardrobe. After dressing in charcoal trousers with a black sweater over a white shirt, he holstered a compact blued Smith & Wesson .38 special at the small of his back. He shrugged into his salt-and-pepper tweed jacket and heavy black overcoat, threw the strap of his brown leather briefcase over his shoulder, and picked up his small brown Gladstone bag. He carried his well-used black fedora.

Taking the stairs to the lobby, he strode to the desk, picked up a small package that a messenger had left for him, and made dinner reservations. After glancing around the lobby, he selected a red leather armchair near the window, dropped the package into his briefcase, and pulled out yesterday's *Times*. Once positioned to watch the street entrance, he read the *Times* and glanced up whenever a vehicle stopped.

Small black Renault taxicabs with hoods like inverted bathtubs darted like mayflies around the Place de Vendôme before stopping at the entrance. Each carried one or two passengers to or from the hotel. One taxicab was followed closely by a light truck with a wooden deck resembling a farmer's open wagon. The back of the truck was filled with steamer trunks and luggage which had been tied down.

A long dark limousine stopped and a chauffeur wearing ivory livery opened the rear door for an elderly couple wearing ankle-length sable coats. As Meade watched them cross the lobby, he heard the rattle of another vehicle slowing on the cobblestones.

A large Renault pulled in front of the limousine and stopped. Golden oak coachwork formed the sides of the vehicle and the struts holding the solid roof. The metal hood and fenders were painted a light cream color. The isinglass curtains had been rolled down and secured. Meade looked through the wet isinglass and saw that the two upholstered benches were unoccupied, and the rear third of the enclosed cabin was empty.

He watched the door over the edge of his newspaper. A stocky dark-haired man in a blue suit and black overcoat entered, glanced around the lobby, and walked past Meade to the chair beside him. After a moment, he said, "Mister Meade?"

Meade nodded toward the enclosed Renault. "Yours?"

"Ours."

"Who—"

"Keep reading. I'm Thompson. I'll be outside. Wait a minute before you leave."

As Meade approached the Renault, Thompson leaned over and opened the passenger door. After tossing his bag and briefcase onto the floor, Meade slid in and stared at Thompson. "Who sent you?"

Thompson turned and said very softly, "RLS would have been my reply, had I not interrupted you in there."

Meade's shoulders relaxed. "Thanks. I'm new at this."

"You are keeping your room, aren't you?"

Meade nodded. "Booked it for a week. They expect me for dinner tonight. Left the room in shambles for the maid."

Thompson engaged the gear, and the Renault jolted forward. He braked quickly as a man with a black portfolio under his arm darted in front of the car and ran toward the hotel entrance. The engine of the Renault stalled. Thompson swore softly.

The man with the portfolio pushed on the gleaming brass of the revolving door and entered the lobby. He tapped on the marble counter until the desk clerk turned. Placing the wet portfolio on the counter, he grinned and adopted as much of a flat American accent as he could manage. "Excuse me. I need to speak to Mister Meade, please."

The desk clerk shifted to English instantly. "I regret that you have just missed him. May I be of service?"

Tapping the portfolio, he said, "I have some papers for him to sign. I am from his office. Do you know when he will return?"

Looking at a list beside the blotter, he said, "He made dinner reservations for this evening here at the hotel. At eight."

"That will do just fine. Thank you." Stahl smiled, decided to find a bar, and planned to return to the lobby of the Hôtel Ritz at five. He left the hotel just as Thompson turned the bucking Renault from the Place de Vendôme onto what Meade recognized as the Rue des Capucines, even without the sign.

Thompson navigated the unmarked streets of Paris until he was out of the city and in the countryside driving north. The road had been ground into a slurry of mud and stone. Meade braced his hand against the wood door as the Renault jolted over a rough patch and slid toward the stagnant water in the ragged ditch. Thompson regained control. The fields to the right of the road had been harvested in summer, but the winter planting had been abandoned. Patches of opportunistic weeds dotted the fallow fields.

As they drove to the north, fewer and fewer of the whitewashed farmhouses edging on the road appeared occupied. A small winter garden scratched into the earth near the side of a house, or a bicycle leaning by a door were among the few suggestions of human habitation. A clothesline ran between two trees at the edge of a farmhouse. Pale blue shirts waved empty arms and steamed in the crisp air. As they drove past her house, a stocky woman in black tossed a wet sheet over the line with the unconscious grace of a fisherman fanning open a net. She paused and watched the sedan as it jolted past her.

Alone on the road, Thompson pushed the limits of the car. When the front tire dropped into a hole, Meade's head slammed into the oak side post. He took off his fedora and restored the center dent to the crown and pinch to the front before dropping it on the seat. "Is it always this bad?"

Resuming speed, Thompson said, "Although you may find this difficult to believe, it is ever so much better now than it was in the heavy rain last week."

Meade looked at the clouds, which were thin and high. "I don't think we'll see any more rain today, do you?"

"Not if she's pinning up her wash." Thompson slowed where the road bore only a few black shards of its original macadam in a sea of mud. As soon as it smoothed, he accelerated.

"What's the rush?"

"We need to make miles when we are able. If we get behind a supply convoy, it will be slow going."

Meade nodded. "How far?"

"Cumming's cable had Crispin reporting to headquarters at noon. We should be there by then."

The road crested and began the gradual drop into the Somme valley. The tree-lined river took gentle twists and glinted in the silky light, which had assumed a pale yellow cast as it filtered through the haze. A tight line of putty-gray vehicles sped west and others east on the long straight road.

Meade pointed. "Is that the supply convoy? There, through the trees."

"Ambulances. Taking the lads from the field hospital at Albert, near the front, to the larger hospital at Amiens. Glad you noticed them; I'll drive the back way to headquarters."

At 11:20, Thompson turned onto a rutted road and joined a slow procession of horse-drawn wagons and battered trucks carrying crates of produce and stained barrels. Pointing, Meade asked, "Is that your convoy?"

"No. Local farmers. After they deliver to the commissary, they go to the bursar at headquarters for payment. Good thing. Otherwise, we would be the odd man out, not being in uniform."

Twenty minutes later, Thompson stopped the Renault in front of a large pale canvas tent. As a boy, Meade had seen a brightly painted circus tent almost as tall. But this one was as large as a barn. A neatly lettered sign under a tangle of telephone and telegraph wires announced "BEF HQ."

The stench from a latrine hung in the air as Meade got out of the auto and put on his hat. He adjusted the holster at the small of his back and straightened his overcoat as he and Thompson walked toward the tent. They passed a dozen older French men clustered around a soldier with a cash box. Just before they entered the tent, Meade glanced at Thompson. "Know what he looks like?"

Shaking his head, Thompson said, "Thought I'd ask the duty officer for him."

"I've seen his photograph. Let me approach him."

Thompson nodded and returned to the Renault. Meade stepped into the dimly lighted tent. As he glanced at the soldiers, the brim of his hat grazed a small wire birdcage hanging in the doorway. The canary squawked and flapped its wings. Soldiers seated at desks looked up immediately, and those who were standing spun toward the cage.

"What the–" Meade said, ducking away from the swinging cage.

A lean officer turned, reached past Meade, and steadied the cage. But for the mud splattered on his worn wool breeches and caked on his boots, he could have stepped from the latest recruiting poster. Crispin was leaner than the image in his file. He looked barely twenty-one, but his eyes were hard. Meade waited.

Crispin nodded toward the canary. "Sorry, but we need to post our little conscript in the doorway."

Meade tugged his hat into place. "Your mascot?"

"Sentinels. Coal miners have relied on them for years. Even the faintest whiff of mustard gas offs the poor little blighters and gives us time to get our masks in place." Crispin paused. "American, aren't you? You must be looking for the Red Cross tent. It is—"

Meade shook his head. "Crispin?"

Standing straighter, he asked, "Do I know you?"

"No." Meade started walking and gestured toward the Renault. "Let's talk out there, Crispin."

"Is that how Americans address their officers?"

Meade turned with deliberate slowness. "I wouldn't know. I'm not in their army, and they're not in your war."

Crispin glared at him. "As we are well aware."

"You *are* Crispin, aren't you?"

He almost came to attention as he recited, "Second Lieutenant William Crispin, in His Majesty's service, British Expeditionary Forces."

The concussion from an exploding artillery shell rocked the overhead lights and jolted the canary cage. "We can't talk in here." When Crispin did not move, Meade smiled the smile he used in business negotiations and pointed at Thompson. "That man could have some good news for you."

"It's our men who need any good news you might have to spare." Crispin pushed past Meade and marched to the automobile.

Thompson pulled a tan envelope from the interior pocket of his black overcoat as Crispin approached. "Your orders."

"Orders?" Crispin did not take the offered envelope. "And just who might you be?"

Thompson spoke so softly that Crispin had to lean forward to hear him. "I'll thank you to keep your voice down," Thompson said as he pulled a black leather identity folder, just smaller than a passport, from the interior breast pocket of his suit. He opened the case before handing it to Crispin.

After examining the identity card and matching the photograph on it to the face in front of him, Crispin returned the identification and accepted the envelope. Thompson said quietly, "You are being seconded to military intelligence."

Crispin stood next to the car and tore the envelope open. He read the paper twice and muttered. "To intelligence? As a spy?"

Thompson whispered, "We prefer the term 'secret agent' these days."

Crispin smirked as he glared at Meade. "Call it what you may, I am being detached to an American." He leaned against the wood rear panel of the vehicle and crossed his arms, letting the paper dangle from his fingers. "Well, there's a black day."

Meade pointed to the orders. "Read it again. You are not being detached to me. The Army is lending you to your military intelligence. During that assignment, you will report to me, exclusively."

"And just what is this assignment?"

"Let's go and get you packed."

"I'll do nothing of the sort. My regiment is one of the pals units drawn of school chums and lifelong friends. My duty is to—"

Meade pointed to the papers in Crispin's hand. "You have new orders."

"Perhaps I have not made myself understood. I cannot just walk away and—"

Meade lowered his voice. "That is exactly what you are going to do. Disappear completely." He motioned to the car. "Get in. That's an order."

Thompson held a blanket for Crispin. "Lieutenant, would you be good enough to give me directions to your billet as we proceed?" After he nodded, Thompson handed him a blanket.

"No need. I have become accustomed to being in the elements."

"Either wrap up or I shall require that you strip off that filthy uniform. I'm not picking mud and lice out of my upholstery."

Crispin folded the orders carefully, placed them back into the envelope, and shoved the envelope into his jacket pocket before grabbing the blanket from Thompson. He snapped the blanket open and swung it over his shoulders like a cape. He slid onto the bench behind the driver, sat on the blanket, and wrapped it over his legs.

Meade slammed the door, circled the car, and got in. He ignored

Crispin's sulking while Thompson drove to the west, toward the hospital tent and line of ambulances.

As they approached the hospital tent, a smell unlike any Meade had encountered suddenly permeated the Renault's cabin. It was almost that of burning rubber or rotting cabbage. It grew in strength and complexity into a potent blend of Chicago stockyard and slaughterhouse, train depot and refuse dump. Meade started to unfasten the side curtain.

Glancing at him, Thompson said, "I wouldn't do that if I were you, sir."

Meade started to move the handle. "I just want some fresh air."

"There isn't any."

A light wind was coming from the battlefield. Shifting columns of black and gray smoke blurred the edges of the trees in the distance. Meade pulled a handkerchief from his trouser pocket and held the clean linen over his mouth and nose.

Meade knew that sulfuric stench of rotting egg from working the oilfields. He knew the acrid sharpness of gunpowder. He had smelled death before. Goats slaughtered in the Persian open-air marketplace were pleasant compared to this. He had seen drought years and dead cattle balloon up in the prairie heat until their gut rumble stopped and left only a formless stench. He had smelled rot before when a potato crop was ruined. Skins, empty of flesh. 'Pus ball' the foreman called it and swore when he dropped the rotten potato back into the field. But Meade had never smelled anything like this fetid stew. His eyes watered. He wiped his face with the handkerchief.

Thompson glanced at him. "Inhale through your mouth."

Meade coughed twice and pressed the handkerchief even tighter against his face.

The canvas walls of the field hospital tent were painted with large red crosses which looked faded and cracked as they came closer. The stench was joined by the sharp chemical smells of gasoline and turpentine, of carbolic and lye. He saw a soldier empty something dark, almost black, from an enameled pan into the steaming bin behind the tent. Meade had field-dressed deer in the cold and remembered the steam swirling around his knife. He looked away. "How far to the line?"

"Our closest trenches are five or six miles to the east of here. Then they run for about five miles north and over ten to the south."

"And theirs? How far to theirs?"

"Couple hundred yards to a half mile past ours. It all depends on the terrain."

The car slowed as they approached the front of the hospital tent.

Ambulances idled in a long line. Stretcher-bearers pulled litters from the front ambulance as exhaust swirled and fogged around them. They walked a few paces and placed the stretchers on a large canvas tarpaulin in front of the hospital tent and ran back to their ambulance. The empty ambulance ground its gears and bolted forward, making way for the next.

Meade watched a nurse wearing a white apron over her dark wool uniform kneel beside the litter, which held a mud-caked soldier, and search for the linen tag. As soon as she found it, she spoke to two uniformed men who then carried the stretcher into the right door of the tent. As soon as they were gone, other stretcher-bearers replaced them. Two new stretchers were placed on the tarpaulin. She leaned down, read the tags, and pointed to the right door for the first and the left for the second.

Meade could not look away. The forms, which were covered in the slurry of chalky mud and blood, were barely recognizable as human. One man had contorted into a writhing ball. Another was limp and his arm dangled off the edge of the litter. Meade turned and saw a soldier sit up on his litter. Jutting chin, black hair. His forehead bore a large orange letter M. A ripple in the isinglass made the other details blur. Meade turned forward. "His head—"

Thompson glanced quickly. "If it's not blood, it's iodine. The dressing station scribes an "M" if they have administered morphine, a "T" if they gave the serum against tetanus, or both. Takes an age to wear off."

The Renault slowed as an empty ambulance pulled around to the side of the tent. Before it stopped, stretcher-bearers were carrying men cocooned in blankets toward it. The white edges of bandages and ends of splints escaped from under the dark blankets. The rear door of the ambulance opened and four litters were loaded into it. After the doors were latched the last stretcher-bearer slapped his hand twice against the rear door and the ambulance took off to the west.

The sharpness of chloroform and disinfectant filled the interior of the Renault. Meade motioned for Thompson to stop and held his breath as he opened the door. Thompson slammed on the brakes just before he came to the convoy, and the auto slid to a bumpy stop.

Meade stumbled out of the sedan onto the muddy shoulder of the road and vomited. First the coffee, eggs, and bread he ate at the Hôtel Ritz, then bile. He spit twice and sucked in a deep breath. The taste of cordite and ash in the air made him shiver. He staggered back into the car.

Meade wiped his face with his handkerchief and looked at Thompson.

Thompson did not look at Meade. "You stop noticing, after a time."

Thompson dug into his jacket pocket and pulled out several tan candies with a sanded sugar coating. He tossed one in his mouth and held others in his open hand for Meade. "Horehound drop?"

Meade took one. "Do they help?"

Engaging the gear and pulling around the ambulance, Thompson said, "Nothing helps."

After another twenty minutes of following Crispin's terse directions, Thompson stopped the car in front of a stone farmhouse.

Crispin looked at the back of the American's head. "Be a good fellow and tell me what this is all about."

Without turning, Meade said, "When we get to Amiens."

Crispin asked, "Am I being assigned to the evacuation hospital there?"

"No. Go pack your things. If anyone asks, be vague about some reassignment." Meade looked at him, clotted in mud from the knees down, smelling like a cesspool. "And you won't need those filthy boots. You won't be coming back here."

Crispin promptly marched toward the farmhouse, stamping off as much of the mud as he could. Meade got out of the car, leaving the door open and walked to the front bumper. Thompson followed. "He meant no offense, Mister Meade. It's madness out there. Try to remember that."

Thompson went into the farmhouse for a few minutes and returned with a canvas sack, which he put in the rear of the vehicle. The wet earth shook as a booming roar hit them. Meade flinched and ducked instinctively.

Looking behind him Meade yelled, "Where'd it hit?"

"Hasn't yet." Thompson held his closed fist in front of Meade. "Count."

A battery of British artillery answered quickly with three sharp pops. Three gusts of air slammed past Meade, and the hem of his coat fluttered.

"What was–"

"Ours." Thompson made a fist and unrolled his fingers. As the fifth uncurled, the ground shook violently and the thudding boom seemed to come from the earth under them.

"Theirs. That's Big Bertha, one of the Germans' new cannons. You heard it fire over eight or nine miles off. The shell landed about ten miles south of us."

"You're not just a driver, are you?"

"No, sir."

"Is Thompson your name?"

"Usually."

Meade pulled a business card from his pocket and handed it to Thompson. "If you need a job after this is all over, you can reach me through Meade Oil's London office."

Thompson looked at the card and handed it back to Meade. "I'll remember that, sir."

"Does he know what he smells like?" Meade motioned toward the farmhouse.

"I doubt it."

"Is there any hope that you could get him to take a bath before we leave? I think he might take the request better from you."

"There is no time for that now. We will be in range of the new artillery in a few minutes– if we're not already. Anyhow, there are just buckets and basins here. I believe you both will be better served to wait until you get to town, where he can have a proper soak."

Meade forced a smile. "Okay, but roll up the rear curtain for air before he returns?"

Chapter № 6

Friday
October 27, 1916
East of Amiens, France

Crispin stripped off the wet leggings and left them on his filthy boots by the door. He stalked to his room, changed into dry stockings, and pulled his brown riding boots up and over the laced legs of his breeches. He sighed at the familiarity of the custom-made boots and the hope that his new assignment might not require standing in mud for weeks at a time.

He packed his uniforms and toilet kit in his duffel bag, cinched the strap on his small tan leather suitcase, and nodded to the corporal to remove the bags. Crispin shrugged into his heavy greatcoat, tugged the visor on his cap, and marched to the vehicle.

As the corporal loaded the baggage into the rear of the Renault, he turned to Crispin. "Your wet boots, sir. May I fetch them?"

"No. I thought you might make better use of them here."

"Thank you, sir. Best of luck."

Crispin glanced at the American, who was leaning on the front fender and finishing a cigarette. He tugged the blanket over his legs, slouched in the rear seat, and stared at the American.

As Thompson started the automobile, Meade got in and said, "We're going to Number 2 Rue Charles-Dubois."

Thompson turned and asked, "Near the station?"

"Yes. But drive down Boulevard Longueville. I want to show him something."

Crossing his arms, Crispin slid deeper into the rear seat and watched the back of the American's head jerk and bob as the car bounced over the rutted road.

Thompson shifted and slowed as the smaller road approached the highway. He looked for a break in the line of speeding ambulances, found one, and accelerated sharply. Meade braced his foot against the floorboard as the Renault bucked and slid. The acrid air reminded him of bonfires of wet wood. He tipped his head toward the ambulance in front of them. "Can you tell how the fighting is going from this?"

Shaking his head, Thompson said, "Can't gauge a thing by them. The *brancardiers* run like the number ten bus."

"Who?"

"Sorry, the stretcher-bearers. The drivers are called that as well. Bad French, but well intended."

Stones and clots of mud thrown up by the ambulance tires hit the glass windscreen. The flat rear doors of the ambulance ahead of them had scratches and a gaping gash below the handle. A line of bullet holes ran from the upper right to the lower left of the double doors.

Meade turned toward Thompson. "Why move them if there was a hospital in Albert?"

Thompson glanced at Meade and then fixed his attention on the road. "That was just the tent we passed. The medical services increase as you get farther from the battle line. At the front, a lad can walk into the battalion aid station, get a swab of iodine, a quick bandage, and be back in the thick of it in minutes. If it is a bit worse, there is a dressing station about a mile back."

"What if–"

"You were a serious case? Then they would stabilize you, administer morphine or antitetanic serum, tie a linen tag with your particulars on you, and pack you off to the field hospital."

"Where's that?"

Thompson wrestled with the steering wheel. "About five miles be-hind the line, like the one we passed after we picked up your silent friend." Thompson jerked his head toward the rear seat, where Crispin sat with his arms crossed. "They work under canvas. They are as close as they can be without being under direct fire and are ever at the ready to pack and move as the battle line shifts."

"How could they perform surgery under those conditions?"

Thompson gave a small chuckle. "That is not their desire, let me assure you. When required, they tidy up the amputations started by the Hun. But their aim is to keep the chap alive long enough to successfully arrive at the evacuation hospital."

"So really, they just sort out—"

Veering to the right, Thompson evaded a huge crater in the road. "It would be a grievous error to sell them short. I've seen them work a few miracles on chest wounds when the bloke wouldn't have survived the trip to the evacuation hospital."

"And from the evacuation hospital, they go back to the front line?" Meade's shoulder slammed into the side post when the car bucked.

"Some do, but men needing a longer recovery might go to a base hospital here in France or back home."

At a gentle bend in the road, Meade tried to count the ambulances racing ahead of them like frenetic ants and failed. "The ambulances… their speed—"

"They have no choice but to push it. Minutes count. They repair the road most every night for the do-gooders."

"I don't follow—"

"Most of the drivers are volunteers from the Society of Friends. I think you Americans call them Quakers. Their motto is 'to do good.'"

Meade said, "That's a new one on me."

Shaking his head, Thompson said, "It misses the mark by half. They are ministering angels. I've seen them drive at full throttle in the dead of night without running lamps if time were of the essence for their patient."

"English?"

"Yes. Quite a few of your countrymen as well. There is no name for that unbidden heroism of your volunteers. Your aviators, joining the French to fly. And the women. College girls coming from America to serve in our hospitals. Remarkable. I have no praise high enough."

Crispin soon tired of looking at the rear doors of the ambulance in front of him and listening to the American. He twisted and leaned on his elbow to look out the open rear of the Renault. The ambulance driver behind them had a sandy moustache and wore spectacles. Crispin slumped in the seat, adjusted his holster, folded his arms again, and tried unsuccessfully to sleep.

He looked at the back of the driver's head. "Have you a map?"

"Yes, sir. In the box on the floor, by Mister Meade."

Meade handed a map case over the seat. Crispin flipped through the maps and pulled out the one of Picardy region. He searched it and catalogued his finds to amuse himself. Amiens was the seat of government for the province. The region was bounded by Normandy to the southwest and Belgium to the north. Paris was due south. He closed his eyes. What the map failed to depict was how the apple orchards of Normandy had provided the sweetest apples he had ever tasted, or how the trenches had scarred the land and the shelling had splintered the trees.

The Renault jolted against a pothole. Dust, smelling like bricks and plaster, swirled out of the upholstery. Crispin exhaled sharply, held his breath, and tried not to remember that day in late summer. Their mission was to reconnoiter a town and list the serviceable buildings. They had followed the ordinance map impeccably but found that the town had been reduced to a smear of pink powder that the wind swirled into small cones the color of frosting on a birthday cake.

Crispin put his full attention to folding the map precisely on its creases and tried unsuccessfully to ignore the surge of nausea and sudden clamminess that surprised him. He felt a trickle of sweat under his armpits and along his spine, quickly leaned back into the seat, and sucked the cold air deep into his lungs. After a moment, he handed the map packet over the seatback to Meade. "Say, any chance of finding a spot for a lunch on the way? Some of these farmhouses sell a rather good plate for lunch–"

Meade turned. "We'll be there soon enough."

Crispin gazed at the gleaned fields where grain had grown on the thin layer of alluvium that covered cretaceous chalk beds. The road shifted closer to the river, and he discovered birds splashing in the shallow water at the edge of a marsh. He smiled at seeing songbirds again. On the far bank there were some larger birds, with banded wings and raptor beaks that he could not name. He made a mental note to identify them when he found himself in a good library again.

As they approached the outskirts of a city, poplars lined the road and a cathedral's spires soared above the tile rooftops. The yellow haze and acrid sting in the air lessened. Meade cleared his throat. "We are coming up on Amiens now."

The ambulances turned off the road into the courtyard in front of a large school. Thompson drove past the chipped white sign for the school on which a red cross had been freshly painted. Theirs was the only motor vehicle on the road into the town.

The long country lanes of rutted macadam gave way to a web of dark cobblestone streets dating back to before the Crusades. Thompson drove around the slower horse-drawn farm wagons loaded with wood-slatted crates of produce. The metal rims of the wooden wheels clattered against the cobblestones. Old men in the baggy black attire of the local farmers swayed on the wagon seats. Thompson slowed as his tires skidded on the stones. As he turned down a street lined with small homes, he drove under a plume of smoke from wood and coal fires that mixed with the old stench of burned-out buildings. Turning onto a larger street, they passed small shops, half of which were boarded shut.

Crispin saw an old man peddling toward them on a battered bicycle. He balanced two baguettes across the front basket. Several older women in long black dresses were walking toward a bakery. As they passed it, Meade called, "Pull over." He jumped from the car and ran back to the

SHARON O. LIGHTHOLDER

bakery. In a few minutes, he returned with four baguettes under his arm.

Crispin watched in amazement. "Are you planning to eat all of those yourself?"

"Not hardly. I thought we might like some fresh bread for tonight."

The isinglass side curtain next to Meade began to fog from the moisture of the warm loaves. Crispin turned as they drove past the Cathédrale de Notre Dame.

"Take a look, Lieutenant Crispin. It is the largest gothic cathedral in France. You could put the Notre Dame from Paris inside it." Crispin was silent as he stared intently at the detailed carvings in the arches. Meade pointed. "You ought to have seen it before they removed the windows. The most remarkable range of blue, from cobalt to the pale blue of a summer sky. I like the windows here even better than the rose window in Paris."

Crispin continued to look at the cathedral.

Meade twisted and looked over the seatback at him. "It has a labyrinth inside. And there is a reliquary said to contain the head of John the Baptist."

Crispin sighed. "I gather that you have visited here before?"

"Yes. It was the obligatory Europe trip the summer after my junior year. Mother insisted. I would have preferred to be at my grandparents' ranch. Nothing but cathedrals, museums, and battlefields all summer. Maybe someday I'll understand half of what I saw."

Smirking, Crispin asked, "You really think so?"

Meade ignored the jibe. "You should come back after the windows are—"

Crispin stifled a laugh. "When I have the good fortune to return to England, I think it will be a rare moment in which I even contemplate a return to France."

"You're really missing something by not—"

Crispin looked through the ripples in the side curtain. "Let me be quite clear. I do not require your advice about my leisure activities." He folded his arms and turned in his seat as the automobile passed in front of the cathedral. Crosses flanked a huge statue of the angel Gabriel hovering above the double doors of the main entrance. Higher up, more than twenty full figures of saints stood watch over the town. At the crest of the roof, there were gargoyles. He stared at a winged panther with a human face.

Thompson turned down a narrow deserted street that was like a canyon walled by the two-story façade of connected row homes. As they passed in front of them, Crispin saw that most of the homes on his right were hollow shells and some lacked rear walls. He leaned back and sighed.

After Thompson turned onto the larger Boulevard Longueville, Meade pointed at a life-size bronze statue of a stout man in a frock coat as they passed Number 44. The wavy hair and full beard made the man resemble a sea captain of the 1800s. Meade pointed. "There it is. The statue I wanted you to see. Take a look. That's Jules Verne."

Glancing casually at the statue, Crispin asked, "Didn't he write about ballooning around the world and submarines battling a giant octopus?"

"A squid. *Architeuthis dux.*"

Crispin raised his eyebrow. "Well, you do know some Latin, don't you?"

"So you have read him."

"No. A lad at school did. Chattered on about his books incessantly."

Thompson turned the corner onto a larger street crowded with a gray military convoy, which was rumbling toward them. Two of the larger trucks towed small cannons.

At Number 2 Rue Charles-Dubois, Thompson stopped in front of a tall black iron gate, jumped out, pulled Crispin's bags from the rear of the Renault, and dropped them on the stone walkway. Crispin got out of the car, folded the blanket with the muddy side inward, left it on the rear seat, and stared at the home. The three-story brick residence had a large carriage house. A circular tower on the left corner of the house made it one of the most imposing, if not the largest, residence that Crispin had seen in the town. White painted shutters framed the glistening windows on all three floors. An attic might be under the steep black-slate roof, he thought.

The ground floor had a glass sun porch extending into the courtyard. The dark door at its center was more then twice a man's height and had a gleaming brass mail slot.

Between the carriage house and residence, the gravel at the gate gave way to tight brickwork. A bench was at the far side of the courtyard near a flowerbed in need of weeding. Meade opened his briefcase, tore open the small package, and slipped the house key into his jacket pocket. He got out of the vehicle, tossed his coat over his shoulder, put three baguettes under his arm like a shotgun at rest, and opened the tall gate.

Thompson called to Meade as he pulled a bulky canvas sack from the rear of the vehicle. "You forgot a loaf."

"Since you have to go straight back to Paris, I thought you might like it."

"Thanks." Lifting the lumpy sack, he said, "I caged some tinned food from his billet for your stay here. The corporal there was quite obliging. I'll bring your things."

Pointing to a low gate at the side of the entrance, Meade said, "Thanks. The kitchen is around through the garden. I'll open the rear door for you."

Thompson followed Meade into the courtyard. Their boots crunched across the gravel. Thompson took the baguettes from Meade and went through the garden gate. Meade walked up the steps to the front door and opened it with the key from his jacket pocket.

Snatching up his two bags, Crispin followed Meade into the house. The interior was dim. As his eyes adjusted, Crispin noticed that the ceiling was two stories tall. A stairway edged with a banister of carved oak dominated the end of the long hallway. Their heavy boots thudded against the honey oak floor for several paces until they reached the

Persian carpet runner. As they walked down the hall, a large sitting room lay to the left and a formal library with a small fire in the fireplace to the right. The doors to both rooms were open.

Pointing to the staircase, Meade said, "Your room is on the second floor, with an adjoining bath, Lieutenant Crispin. We'll be staying here a few days while we do our work."

"And just what work would that be?"

"I'll brief you after your bath. Take your bags up and I'll send up Madeline to—"

"Isn't there a bath on the ground floor so I don't have to carrying water upstairs?"

Meade snickered. "Mister Verne was quite the inventor. He installed a cistern in the attic to provide running water throughout the house. Pumped full every night by staff down here. But that wasn't enough for Verne. Next he installed a gas burner and water reservoir to heat the bath water upstairs. As I was starting to say, she'll show you how to use it. Quite clever. One of the first with indoor plumbing in the town."

"Who else is living here? Besides staff."

"Just her. And us."

Crispin looked resigned. "Grand."

"Your room is at the top of the stairs, first right. I'll wait for you in the library."

Meade ducked into a small door past the stairway that Crispin assumed to be the kitchen or butler's pantry. By the time Crispin had dropped his bags, he heard light footsteps approaching his room. A petite white-haired woman tapped on the open door. She was dressed in a floor-length black dress covered with a white apron and looked almost seventy. She held three Turkish cotton towels and smiled. Crispin greeted her in French and followed her into the bathroom, which was larger than his room at college.

He glanced at the huge white claw-footed tub. Next to it was a porcelain toilet with a polished brass pipe leading to the tank above it. He tried to ignore the bidet beside it. On the facing wall was a large porcelain sink resting in the top of a carved walnut dresser, which had been modified to accommodate the modern plumbing. After placing the towels beside the sink, she quickly explained how to light the burner and manage the spigots to the tub. She seemed relieved that he spoke fluent French.

Once she left, Crispin filled the tub and stripped, folding his soiled clothing into a tight pile on the bare oak floor. The water steamed in the chill of the large room. Carefully lowering himself into the large tub, he let himself slide under water. After an instant, he scrambled to a sitting position, gasping for air, trying not to think of the shell hole and death. After wiping the water from his eyes, he was shocked to see that the bathwater had turned chalky and muddy grit lined the bottom of the tub. He stood, soaped and rinsed before letting out the water and starting over. After his second bath, he felt almost clean. He wrapped the thick Turkish cotton towel around his waist and returned to his room to dress. He buffed the leather of his boots and belt with the damp towel and brought back a gloss.

When dressed in his clean uniform with dry boots, he returned the towel to the bathroom, cleaned the soiled tub, and left the wet towel on his filthy uniform. After he combed his wet hair, he retraced his steps. Meade's briefcase and Gladstone bag had been brought to the foot of the stairs by Thompson.

As he walked to the library, he paused to examine each of the eight ornately framed oil paintings of sea battles and maritime themes that flanked the long hallway. Most of the paintings were over six feet wide. Cutters and clipper ships were under full sail. Sea battles that he could only guess as being between the Dutch and French were captured in dark tones which emphasized the orange and red of the cannon fire and flaming sails.

He stopped to read the brass plaque on a painting and smiled when he saw that it was in English, 'The Battle of the Gabbard, First

Anglo-Dutch War.' Crispin shook his head as he stared at the scene of drowning men. Soldiers drowned every day in the rain-filled shell holes at the front, miles from the sea. At least the sailors didn't have to contend with the bottle flies buzzing on their wounded.

Although without a plaque, the painting closest to the library door was clearly the Battle of Trafalgar. Crispin brushed his hand over the back of his neck, which was still damp, and turned quickly when he heard Meade coming toward him.

Balancing a teacup with care, Meade passed Crispin and went into the library. "Rounded up a cup of tea for you. Had Madeline make it while I pumped the cistern full again."

Crispin followed him and found something familiar in the massive room. Glass-fronted bookcases covered the two longer walls. At the far end of the room, there was a rectangular oak cabinet, eight feet across and five high. Brass pulls studded its many drawers. Above the cabinet was an oil painting of a luxury yacht under sail. Heavily curtained windows flanked the painting. The large fireplace dominated the wall near the door. The bookcases climbed thirty feet to a cream-colored plastered wall which extended another fifteen feet. Wheeled oak and brass ladders attached to a top rail allowed access to the upper shelves.

Hand-hewn dark oak beams started along each of the plastered walls and soared until they joined in the arched ceiling. Crispin nodded as he placed the style of the room. It was similar to the library at Lambeth Palace, where he had examined medieval documents. Yet the Lambeth library lacked the huge Persian carpet covering this floor, leaded doors to protect the leather-bound volumes which filled the cases, or the invitation to linger that was implicit in the small table and two claret-colored leather wingback chairs that faced the fireplace.

The firebox was tall enough for a man to walk into carrying logs of five to six feet, yet it held only a few embers. Beside it was a basket of split logs and a stand holding a set of tongs and an ash shovel. The mantel was almost out of reach and held polished silver trophies and engraved platters that looked like awards. Both chairs were illuminated perfectly for reading by the chandeliers in spite of the heavy curtains which blocked out the sunlight.

Crispin started reading titles through the glass. "Impressive collection," he said.

Placing the cup on the large reading table in the center of the room, Meade walked toward the cabinet with long strides. "We're not here for the books." As Crispin took a sip of tea, Meade slapped the shoulder-high top of the cabinet. "This is why we're here."

Meade opened the upper of the dozen drawers, which ran the full five-foot width of the cabinet. Crispin quickly joined Meade and stared into the drawer. "Maps?" He stepped back and stared at Meade as though waiting for his regimental photograph to be taken in his clean green wool uniform. Jaw jutting and feet apart. His officer's leathers were shining, from the riding boots to the holster on the wide leather belt and the narrow strap across his chest. The lighter colored lanyard around his neck swept perfectly to the brass button at the base of his holstered pistol. He was perfectly motionless, challenging Meade for an explanation.

Meade shut the drawer and leaned his elbow on the cabinet. "Jules Verne's collection is critical to our work. His son, Michel, has offered it to us. They are closing the house. No one lives here now."

Holding up a finger to correct him, Crispin said, "Except the housekeeper."

"Right. Michel should be by later today."

Crispin raised an eyebrow. "What has he to do with our mission?"

"Nothing. Doesn't have a clue about it, and we need to keep it that way."

Chuckling, Crispin muttered, "What could I possibly tell him?"

"He's an okay guy. Not a bad shot. He manages his father's literary estate. Smokes a pipe like you do so there should be a supply of pipe tobacco for you."

Crispin cocked his head as he asked, "How do you know I smoke a pipe?"

"I read your file. I know that your middle name is German and your surname is English. Probably got teased for that in school when your class read *Henry V* and it came to that speech before the Battle of Agincourt on Saint Crispin's Day. I know your preference for Darjeeling over Earl Grey tea, that you prefer a pint of Bass or Guinness over... what do you English call hard liquor? 'Spirits'?"

Stalking back to his abandoned teacup, Crispin said, "Bloody hell. What else?"

Meade leaned on the table. "That you invented languages and wrote imaginary dictionaries."

The veins in his neck stood out as he said, "How dare you spy on me!"

"It's not me, buddy. Your country's military intelligence did a lot of looking to find the right guy for their communications officer. That's a key security post. All I did was find you through a friend of mine, a writer I know in Geneva named Maugham."

"What else do you know about me? Favorite treat after dinner? Nicknames from school?"

Meade smiled. "What was your nickname? I'll see if they got it right."

"I think not. Honestly, I cannot fathom what my personal life has to do with—"

Meade suppressed a smile, turned, and sat facing Crispin. "Listen. I have something that I need translated. It has stumped everyone who has seen it so far." He glanced at Crispin's puzzled look. "Well, the fact is I don't need just a translator. I need a scholar...a thinker who can get past what the words say to what they mean. Your file had quite a lot on your language skills. Said you took to Latin and Greek like a duck to water. But when your schoolmaster gave you a copy of *Beowulf* in Old English and an Old English Primer, it was like you had rediscovered your own language." Meade frowned as he tried to recall precisely what had been in the file.

"Headmaster Wood's notes in your school file said that you had a natural affinity for languages unlike any he had seen before. Did you know that?"

Staring into his cup, Crispin muttered, "He never told me that. How kind of him to have thought so."

"I know that you did your own translation of *Beowulf*. Maugham said you were even able to distinguish the handwriting of the different scribes who wrote the copy. You studied other dead languages. Gothic, if I remember your file, and you invented words to add to your Gothic dictionary–"

"Primer, not dictionary. I wanted to speculate as to the precursors of certain words, so I invented some antecedent words. Just word games, like crossword puzzles and anagrams." Crispin looked into his cup as though he were reviewing each of the puzzles.

"In college, you mastered Old Norse, Welsh, Finnish. You speak modern Swedish and have read about every folk tale there is."

He said softly, "I would never claim to have mastered Welsh–"

"And you tutored others in French and German and were awarded a pure alpha for your term essay that proposed that myth is an invention about truth, and that England needs a national myth."

Setting the cup on the saucer with a clatter, he asked, "You read my paper?"

"Yes. Maybe something to do with your security clearance, but they had a copy of it in your file. Look. I need an expert in language with the mental agility to read words of a dead language and then read between the lines. I need a guy who can think like people did over a thousand years ago so we can find the meaning that has escaped others."

"What sort of–"

"I know you're a really smart guy. Your file shows that. People admire you. But what I don't know is if you are up to it. It's going to be grueling work. And we are against the clock. Document review, research–"

"I excel at that sort of challenge. Would you be kind enough to tell me what needs translation and what this mission is?"

Meade paused for an instant trying to reconcile Crispin's youth with his many accomplishments and bearing of a much older man. Pointing to the map cabinet, Meade said, "We're going on a treasure hunt. Those maps might help on one a part of the puzzle. But your translation is key."

Chapter № 7

Friday
October 27, 1916
Amiens, France

The teacup bounced in the saucer as Crispin slapped his hand on the table. "A treasure hunt?"

Meade closed the library door and turned the key in the gleaming brass lock. He pulled off his sweater and dropped it on a chair by the fireplace as he paced back to Crispin. A leather pouch hung on a thin cord over his shirt. Meade pulled the pouch's cord over his head.

Crispin looked at the pouch dangling from Meade's hand. "Just whose treasure hunt is it?"

"Your government's."

Smirking, Crispin said, "You can't be serious."

"I am deadly serious. The map inside the pouch is a *portolano*."

"By definition, a mariner's map."

Meade placed it on the table in front of Crispin. "Yeah. But this one is older than any I've ever seen outside a museum. Go ahead. Have a look."

Crispin put the cup on the floor and reached for the pouch. He unbuttoned the flap, wiped his hand on his breeches. Using only his thumb and index finger, he gently slid the stiff hide onto the table. The thin layer of cotton batting over one corner snagged on the pouch. He peeled back the padding and discovered a thin ribbon of leather holding a cracked wax seal.

The hide was slightly warped and sat unevenly on the polished table. "It's not on just a hide. This is a fine–" As he turned it, sideways to read the text, the portolano scratched on the tabletop like a dry leaf

His eye darted over it. Ink, in shades from coal to rust, marked the pale hide. Unfinished edges. A few rends and rips. A remarkable state of preservation. A coastline was drawn along the right side. Above and below the coast were letters in uppercase. In the lower-right corner of the map was a straight line with a dot of ink at each end.

Seven lines of text in early Anglo-Saxon were centered on the hide. Crispin read them and took a deep breath. He leaned back in his chair and looked at the ceiling.

Meade stood at the table. "Well?"

"Give us a moment, if you please."

Meade paced to the far end of the room. Crispin watched him and noticed a holstered gun on his belt at the small of his back. After Meade turned and leaned on the map cabinet, Crispin took another deep breath. He blinked, sat straight as a first-term student, rubbed his eyes, and leaned over the portolano.

The hide was smaller than a sheet of modern writing paper. It was mottled with hues ranging from mid-amber at the darkest to the shade of milk in tea. The edges were uneven and worn. A small ragged void the size of a cherry was on the bottom edge. There were small holes, the size of a thick pencil lead, at the top and center of the right edge. At the left edge were two holes which were close together and appeared to have been made intentionally.

Crispin ran his thumbnail over an uneven stain on the right edge. He tipped his head sideways for a closer look.

Meade called from the far end of the room. "Need a hand lens?"

"Yes, please. If you have one."

Crispin stood and stretched. Meade walked back to the table and pulled a small folding hand lens the size of a silver dollar from his pocket, rotated the magnifying glass from between the metal covers, and handed it to Crispin. "Well?"

"Interesting. Do old maps normally have this much text?"

Meade rubbed his chin. "Never seen anything like it."

"What do you know about this hide?"

Meade looked confused. "Besides being parchment?"

Shaking his head, Crispin said, "No. By definition, parchment is the skin of a sheep or goat prepared for writing. In fact, it required an entire flock of sheep to make one Bible. This is a much finer hide than that. Technically it is a *vellum*."

"How do you figure?"

"First, from the hair patterns. See these dots? Hair follicles. I will venture that this is the upper part of a lambskin. The neck was to the left, see the slimming–"

"What's that got to do with–"

Holding the hide to the light, Crispin said, "It is very thin. It is almost translucent. This is quite similar to the vellum used in Queen Christina's Gothic Bible. Vellum is much too frail and rare to be prepared for use as an ordinary map."

"But it was."

"I agree. And it was not trimmed for binding." Crispin pointed to the small holes on the right and left edges of the map. "Are these customary in maps?"

"Yes. The ones on the right of the parchment were used to tie it to a rod. Like a flag to a pole."

Crispin sighed when Meade failed to distinguish vellum from parchment after his clear definition. Deciding it was pointless to correct him again, Crispin asked, "And the two holes on the left?"

"They'd run a leather thong through them. After they wrapped the map around the rod, they'd tie it for storage."

"Rather like tying up a scroll?"

Meade shrugged. "Yeah. I guess."

Crispin opened the hand lens and put it to his eye. He leaned over the right edge of the portolano. The map of the coast began as a slim line starting in the upper right quadrant. It slid evenly for an inch before it began a slow serpentine crawl shooting far to the left and then back to the right, outlining the bony fingers of three rivers. The ink cartography was crisp and clean. There were no overwrites, erasures, or edits. No smudges or odd fading.

A rumble like thunder rattled the windows. Not as loud as at the front, but it was cannon fire, nonetheless. Meade flinched. Crispin sat back and placed the lens beside the map. After a deep breath, he resumed his survey.

There were oddities he had not seen before on any of the literary parchments he had studied. Above the coastline were the capital letters "**PQTXLM**." At the tip of the lowest river, almost at the bottom edge of the parchment, were the capital letters "**QTSH**" abutting the small hole.

A straight-inked line cut across the lower-right corner of the parchment. There was a small ragged circle of ink at each end. Putting the lens to his eye, Crispin concluded that it was not the simple drop of ink that it first appeared to be, but more intentional, almost like an asterisk.

There were three symbols on the map that seemed to be astronomical or perhaps astrological. A sun or full moon floated above the block of text. A star sat under the text, near the letter "Q." A crescent moon hung above the inked coastline, in front of the letter "P."

The block of centered text was in Old English, early Anglo-Saxon, upper- and lowercase in a precursor to the English square minuscule style of lettering. They had the sharp quadrangle shape of letters used in the first millennium, before time melted the letters into the more familiar rounded shapes.

There were no errors or corrections in the text. The scribe must have copied it. No one could center one line under another so precisely without knowing exactly how many letters were going to be in the line and the width of the letters themselves.

Crispin read the Old English and mumbled the words.

Dryhet oðberan dēormōd cyning ond hord
Randhæbbend tō metod ond ēadnes
Ymbfæstnung under flōc
Hafela twā Michael ofer
Twā micel ceaster betwuh
Ēaststæð æt rēfmæd
Ne yðwōrigende on bēam

He folded his arms and exhaled.

Meade pointed at the map. "What do you make of it?"

"At first glance, it appears to be a set of directions to a location midway between two great cities. Above the two Michaels. Below the fish."

"Yeah. I know that. But what does it mean?"

Shrugging, Crispin said, "I haven't the foggiest notion. The phrase 'below the fish', or flounder more properly, is not a standard kenning or poetic reference. But it may refer to a sea burial, with the fish…but then the preposition is clear that it is *below* the fish, not *with* the fish."

"You are here to tell me what it means, so that the map makes sense."

Crispin chuckled. "This fragment lacks any context. It is as though they wanted to hold a secret back. Look. Letters that are not words. These symbols, which may be astrological or even pictographs."

"Maps have always had secrets. In ancient Rome, it was a crime even to own one. Most of the early portolanos left out details or added false ones to conceal trade routes for merchants or monarchs."

"Listen, my good fellow, this is oblique language and one which appears to be riddled on the map. Nothing like directions to the local pub, if that's what you wanted."

"If it were that easy, we wouldn't be here, pal. Think it's real?"

"The document? Yes. The hide and the manner of the lettering are from five or six hundred years after the birth of Christ. Seven hundred, possibly, the millennium at the very latest. I cannot attest to the validity of the content."

"What do you make of the words?"

"Pure nonsense. Not in a poetic form or standard structure. Almost slap-dash construction. Yet, the manner in which it was scribed suggests a thoughtful approach. Centered. No errors." Crispin paused and looked at him suspiciously. "You do read Old English, don't you?"

"Not a word."

Crispin pulled a small tan leather-bound journal from the front pocket of his uniform jacket. "Oh, my. Let me make a few notes and then translate it for you." He took a small silver mechanical pencil from the loop inside the back cover and twisted the lead into place.

He placed his journal to the right of the portolano and pulled it open by the thin black ribbon attached to the spine. Crispin copied the Old English block of text on every other line. He made a few notes next to three words and paused to consider alternative meanings.

He scratched through his notes, and then wrote his translation under each line. No place now for reckless supposition. He held his book with trembling hands like a hymnal and recited, first the old then the modern words in a strong voice.

Dryhet oðberan dēormōd cyning ond hord
Retainers bear bold king and treasure
Randhæbbend tō metod ond ēadnes
Warrior to God and peace
Ymbfæstnung under flōc
Monument under flounder
Hafela twā Michael ofer
Head two Michael over
Twā micel ceaster betwuh
Two great cities between
Ēaststæd æt rēfmæd
East bank of stream at reeve's meadow
Ne yðwōrigende on bēam
Not wandering the waves in wooden ship

Meade almost pleaded, "But what does it mean?"

"I can't say, yet. This is a literal word-for-word translation, so there may be a nuance or two that could come from added study and reflection, but my impression is that this relates to a king's burial... and there is a treasure involved."

Widening his eyes in frustration, Meade asked, "That's it? That's all you can make of it? That's no help at–"

"It is a riddle. Look at the first two lines and the last. Whether it means that they were directed to conduct the burial or they pillaged the treasures from the king or the king's ship is simply not clear."

"Swell."

"But the other four lines appear to offer directions to a location between two great cities, on the east bank of a stream. Plain enough. All we need to do is find the cities and that should point us to a coastline that matches the portolano. And from there, the stream."

"But what do you think the other lines mean? Two Michaels head and fish?"

Slightly raising his voice, Crispin said, "I have already said all I know on that matter."

"I don't want your off-the-cuff impression. I need your analysis. I told you that I had the words translated already by a guy in Geneva."

Crispin pointed to the letters above and below the serpentine line. "And these?"

"Those two words? No. He couldn't translate them."

Chuckling, Crispin said, "No wonder. Those two words, as you call them, are not words at all. They are as devoid of meaning as bookends."

"Not words?"

"Honestly! They used vowels back then, you know. Do you see any vowels among those letters?"

"No. Now that you mention it."

Waving his hand to dismiss Meade, Crispin said, "Your notion of the ease of translation of an ancient text is, well, optimistic."

"Maybe. What's your take on it?"

"Although I do not recognize the specific hand of the scribe who wrote this, I do deem it authentic as to time. Linguistically, I do believe you are correct as to the era."

"I thought you'd have an idea to solve the mystery."

"Why bother me with a chore that any bright student or instructor could complete?"

"Because they can't. I told you, I need a solution, not just the translation of seven lines of old text. I need your imagination."

"You flatter me."

Meade frowned. "There isn't anyone else. It's up to you."

Chapter № 8

Friday
October 27, 1916
Amiens, France

Crispin straightened his tie and looked at the portolano and not at Meade, who was standing beside him and leaning on the library table. "The language was in its formative state then. Old English was principally a spoken language. Spelling was not uniform. Few knew how to write. Fewer still had the materials to do so."

Putting his hands on his hips, Meade said, "Great!"

"I believe that the language placed a heavy reliance on intonation, the stress of one syllable over another rather than inflection."

"What's that mean?"

"You garner tense, number, and gender from the modern inflected languages. 'Las Damas', the ladies, feminine and plural. Our pure language became muddled as we shifted to Middle English after the Norman Conquest and added words from the French."

Meade shrugged. "Why should I care about that?"

"The intonation could make a substantial difference in the translated meaning."

"I just need to go where the map tells us to go. This is not just translating a couple of words for a term paper, or whatever you call them in England. Get it?"

"Certainly." Crispin thought a moment. "Has anyone, other than your friend in Geneva, examined the complete parchment?"

"No. I showed a tracing of just the coastline to geographers from the National Geographic Society in Washington D.C. who had been at the auction and to your Royal Geographic Society. But without any starting point or orientation, they were as stumped as I am."

"I would like to complete a more extensive examination of the entire document."

Crispin took a white linen handkerchief from his trouser pocket, patted his forehead, and wiped his hands before reaching for the portolano. He rotated it slowly until he was looking across the face of the parchment. His lips moved to sound the Old English words, round and rhythmic. Then he whispered the first of the lines again, but with a shift in emphasis, "We take our King and his treasure—"

"Crispin, listen to me for a second. I think this leads to a buried treasure—"

Glancing at him, Crispin smirked. "Yes, yes. It's usually about the money—"

"It's more than that. What if this map gives England its myth?"

Crispin jolted back in his chair as if pushed. He stared at Meade. "You actually read my thesis?"

Meade nodded. "You wrote that England had no myth, and that a myth is necessary for a country and its language to endure over the ages. A myth is what binds a society together."

"Well, that's not it exactly, but close enough to my point. Proceed."

"England's myth is waiting to be discovered."

Crispin scowled. "And why are you, an American, so interested in England's myth? It is your portolano, why not just toddle off and find the treasure?"

"I can't find it alone. And I don't want the Germans to get it."

Frowning, Crispin asked, "Why would they want it?"

"If the Germans get it first, they get their myth *and* they can pay for another couple years of this war. That would certainly draw the United States into it. I don't want that."

"By what grand delusion would you possibly believe that anyone other than you could be interested in this, or even know about it?"

"I'll tell you later."

Crispin put the hand lens to his eye and leaned over the hide again. "I want a second look at it. I must be absolutely certain that this is the genuine article; although, I admit that I am confounded as to why they would have used such a fine piece of vellum, or parchment as you insist on calling it, for a map."

"Did they just erase an used hide?"

Crispin laughed and looked up to see if Meade was joking. "You mean make a palimpsest? I suppose one could scrape and bleach it. But even then, this ink leaves a trail. It physically bonds to the hide. Quite waterproof."

Meade said, more to himself than Crispin, "Ideal for a mariner's map."

"Indeed. Think for a moment of our word 'ink.' It is from the Latin *encaustum*, to burn in, as in the word 'caustic.' That's what happens, the ink oxidizes and burns into the hide."

"How fast?"

"Fast! The iron gall nut ink they used chemically fuses with the hide and actually becomes part of it. A scribe could use his metal scraper to remove the wet ink immediately, but once it dried, you would be required to physically scrape off the inked hide, which would leave it noticeably thinner."

"Is it thinner in places?"

Crispin looked at the parchment at an angle and then held it up to the light of the chandelier. "Not that I see."

"But the ink is not all the same color."

"You must understand that the ink had iron in it. As the iron oxidizes, it is transformed from a muddy gray to obsidian black within minutes. But then, over the ages, the iron in the ink continues to oxidize." Crispin pointed to the edge of a letter that had faded. "See, here. This rusty halo. The writing is very, very old."

Meade took the hand lens from Crispin and examined the letters. "How do you know this stuff?"

Sitting back and folding his arms, Crispin said, "If you want to understand the language, you need to understand how it is made and preserved. How it was written at the early moments of our language interests me. I have made my own ink, boiled gall nuts—"

"Gall nuts? Never heard of them. What are they called in America?"

Crispin glanced at Meade. " 'Gall nuts,' I presume. It's a blight on an oak tree. A growth which remains on the bark after a wasp has made a cocoon there. Grind up a few, add green copperis, that's an iron compound, and some water, and you have ink."

"That sounds simple enough."

"Well, it is not. I've made ink. I can assure you it is quite complex. The later inks also added some gum Arabic to thicken it. That was important, as they wrote on a slanted board. That is the ink that was used for the first seven hundred years of our language. Perfect for a quill pen. But ill suited to a modern metal nib."

"I suppose you cut your own quill pens as well."

Crispin stood and paced. "Of course. How else could I really understand the challenges of early writing? Look at the letters again. You can see the ink is thicker at the bottom of a letter than at the top. It all makes sense if you understand the mechanics of writing at that time. But look, the line which you contend is a coastline appears to be of the same tone and density top to bottom."

"Meaning?"

Crispin held his finger above the coastline. "I speculate that it was drafted by a mapmaker, or at least someone writing on a flat surface, as we write on a desk today."

Searching his face, Meade asked, "The mapmaker and the writer? Could they be two authors? Or one?"

"That is not clear. The paleographical evidence suggests the handwriting is consistent with the few other samples between 500 to 700 A.D."

Meade squinted slightly as he watched Crispin. "That's a plus. Isn't it?"

Nodding, Crispin continued. "However, the codicological and orthographical evidence is insufficient. You have too small a sample of text to perform the analysis of the construction of the manuscript. Tell me, did your friend examine the reverse of the document?"

Meade nodded. "Just to translate the list of items." He flinched as the cup rattled in the saucer on the floor. The table shook and kept shaking.

Crispin smiled. "Relax. That's not artillery."

"Then what is it?"

"Feels like tanks on a road…about a mile off. Possibly unloading at the train station we passed."

Meade pointed to the portolano. "You might want to take a look at the back as well."

Crispin stared at the Old English list of words in the same bold hand. "As you no doubt have been told, *helm ond byrnan* means 'helmet and mail shirt.' The next line, *mære sweord* means 'impressive or best sword.' *Earm-reade twa* is 'two arm bands.' These were the rings that kings awarded to the most courageous of their knights. *Hrings glyden twa* is 'two golden finger rings.' *Purs* is 'purse,' what you might call a coin purse rather than a woman's handbag. *Byden ealoð* is a 'barrel of ale' and *drynet-fæt* means 'cups.' The last word is *Rod*. Could mean 'cross' or 'gallows' or it might refer to a land measurement. Context is needed to clarify that."

"What do you think?"

"All are personal possessions. Assuming *rod* translates as a cross and not gallows or a parcel of land."

The rumbling grew louder and a silver-framed family portrait on the mantel jolted and tipped against a vase. Meade watched the chandelier sway. "Okay. Why the list?"

"I haven't any idea. It could be a spelling lesson or a royal shopping list. These are simply guesses and somewhat improbable; parchment was too valuable for such trivial uses."

Crispin thought he saw a thin line starting at the left margin, near the bottom of the parchment. He tilted the parchment and looked again.

Without looking up, he patted the table until he found the hand lens.

The pale tan line that almost looked like a wrinkle in the hide began at the torn edge. Under the lens, it became a line of faint brown ink forming the letters: "s A XV."

Crispin sat back and looked at the ceiling as though an answer were lingering there, just out of sight. He was breathing quickly.

"What is it? Are the tanks German?"

Laughing, Crispin said, "No. They would have fired on us by now if they had been. Listen carefully, they have turned to the east, away from us." Crispin drew a deep breath and pointed to the small faint lettering. "Had you seen this writing?"

Meade took the hand lens from Crispin and strained to see the letters. "No. I hadn't. Is that a word?"

"Much more than that, if you know how to read it. It is a shelf-mark of a book. It means that this document is priceless." Crispin quickly twisted the lead back into his pencil and used the tip as a pointer. "Do you see the lowercase letter 's'?"

Meade put the hand lens to his eye and squinted at the faint characters. "Just at the edge."

"Uppercase letter 'A.' Then a space, not large, I grant you. Then the uppercase 'X' and uppercase 'V'–"

"Another Old English word?"

"No. Latin. The 'X' and 'V' are not letters, but Roman numerals. The number fifteen."

Meade looked at Crispin and put the hand lens on the table. "How do you figure?"

Crispin paused before speaking. "I know this shelf-mark. There is only one like it in the world."

"You got all that just from a couple letters and numbers?"

Crispin said softly and very clearly, "The complete shelf-mark of the *Codex* is 'Cotton MS Vitellius A. XV.' It is a collection of the most valuable parchments in the world bound together as a book."

"How'd you know that?"

Crispin sighed. "I have written it scores, possibly hundreds of times. When I go to study the *Codex*, I need to complete a pull-slip for it. It is filed reflecting the manner of the initial collection and the donor. That is how manuscripts are filed. Modern books use other shelf-marking systems, like the Dewey Decimal System in the United States—"

Meade looked confused. "So? I still don't—"

"Look here." Crispin sighed, opened his journal, and scrawled "Cotton MS Vitellius A. XV." He turned the page to face Meade. "This is the shelf-mark, the title of the *Codex*."

"Yeah. I heard you. So what?"

"Can't you see it? Here, look at my paper again." Crispin made a dark pencil line severing the "s" from "Vitellius." "Look at what remains if you break the manuscript's name at this point. All of the word 'Cotton' is missing. That designates Sir Robert Cotton, who collected this parchment and put it into his personal library. 'MS' means manuscript. Hand written, not machine printed."

"Okay, but the other word?"

"'Vitellius'? Atop each of his bookcases, Sir Robert had a bust of a different Roman emperor. The Emperor Vitellius topped the case where he filed this *Codex*. All but the 's' of 'Vitellius' is missing. Then a capital 'A.' That was the shelf designation where Cotton stored this parchment, top shelf. The Roman numeral XV was the designation of the fifteenth position on that shelf. There is your provenance."

"My what?"

"Proof of origin, of authenticity. This map was once a portion of Sir Robert Cotton's *Codex*. The notation is a binder's mark."

Meade leaned on the table. Crispin looked at him. "The page number would have proceeded the shelf-mark, but that part of your parchment is missing."

"And you've really seen the rest of this *Codex*?"

Crispin picked his cup from the floor and balanced the saucer on his knee. "Yes. The folio is about twenty centimeters by thirteen centimeters. Most of the pages are nested in paper frames to protect their fragile edges from crumbling." Crispin shut his eyes. He smiled as he opened them. "It is bound in brown calfskin, a medium brown. I've used it numerous times for my research."

"What's it about?"

"About? It is a collection of writings. Poems. Letters."

"By one person?"

Crispin took a sip and choked as he laughed. "Not at all. It holds parchments containing religious texts, a letter from Alexander the Great, a fragment of a work on the life of Saint Christopher, the poem *Judith*, and the poem we know as *Beowulf*."

"*Beowulf*?"

"You know it?"

Meade shivered and paced to the fireplace, where he placed a log on the small blaze. "Had to read it in school."

"In translation, I presume. Then you know that it is the oldest poem in our language. That is why I have used the *Codex*, to study the original *Beowulf* text. And as much as I would like for your map to be a part of that poem, it is not."

"Why not? It was in the book. The *Codex*."

"The poem ends clearly and logically. Thus, this portolano could not relate in any way to that poem."

Meade spoke quickly. "Could it have been an illustration?"

"My dear fellow, *Beowulf* was not a picture book for tots." Meade suppressed a smile at Crispin's superior tone as he continued, "The *only* similarity between your portolano and *Beowulf* is in the use of Old English." Crispin put down the empty cup and examined the edges of the portolano with the hand lens.

Meade asked, "What are you looking for now?"

"Scorching. You see, the outer margins of the *Beowulf* poem and the other pieces in the *Codex* were damaged in a fire in 1731, long after Sir

Robert had given it to the British people. Your shelf-mark must have been made by the original binder to note the order of each page. There was a second set of binder marks made during the repair work after the fire."

Meade pointed to the thin line. "So this was part of the page-numbering system as well as the filing name?"

"Correct. Pages, whether for the original binding or rebinding when they put each charred page into a sturdy paper holder to protect it, required some markings to allow them to be ordered properly. But—" Crispin stopped and cocked his head.

"What is it?"

"It just occurred to me that there is no mention of this portolano in the copy that Thorkelin commissioned or his translation. They would have seen it."

Meade scowled. "Who would have seen it?"

"Thorkelin. He was a Professor of Antiquities at Copenhagen University, one of the first scholars in Germanic and Nordic studies. He came to London in pursuit of what was thought to be an old Germanic text, saw the *Beowulf* parchment, and hired a clerk to copy it in Old English, stroke by stroke. Then he translated the copy into Latin and published his translation in 1815. His was the first full translation of *Beowulf*. It was chock-full of errors. In fact, some scholars are so critical of it that they contend you can't go five lines without finding some error—"

"Okay, but that was after the fire. If the portolano had been stolen or sold before the fire, it wouldn't be in his copy. And it wouldn't have been burned. But it would have the first binder's mark. Right?"

Crispin tipped his head as he stared at Meade. "Interesting idea. I wonder if his copyist would have noticed a gap in the pagination?"

"Does the writing on the portolano look like the writing in *Beowulf*?"

"There *is* a similarity between the lettering. But there were only so many styles of writing Old English. To an untrained eye, they all look the same. If I were to show *you* samples of Arabic writings in Farsi, Urdu, and other languages in regional writing styles, they all would appear similar to your eye."

Pointing to the map, Meade asked, "Why are you so sure that it's not a part of the *Beowulf* poem if it was part of Cotton's book?"

"Even you can see that the caesura is missing."

Sighing, Meade asked, "What's that?"

"The poem is composed of two half-lines on a line, with a pause…a space, if you will, between them. The pause is called a 'caesura,' thus the name of the poetic form."

Meade stared at the block of centered text. "No extra space."

"Correct. The use of alliteration is also absent. I won't burden you with the other reasons. Sorry. It is simply a list of words on the back and rambling on the front."

"But the Roman numerals—"

"That is your link to the *Codex* prior to the fire. Ah. That could explain the glue on it."

"What glue?"

Crispin pointed to the stain on the edge. "They must have glued it to something to bind it, rather than trimming it straight."

"Maybe to protect the seal?"

Crispin brushed his hand above the seal dismissively. "Balderdash! You buy a map with a wax seal on it and suddenly think it is imbued with some grand history. If I had a shilling for every sealed document passed off as—"

"Have you looked at it?"

"Merely to note that it is old and cracked. Left half is almost all gone. Not at all uncommon for collectors to affix their seal as a indicia of ownership."

Meade pointed to the dark seal. Crispin leaned over it and began his examination. Standard look to the dark red wax. Old. Brittle. Resinous. He used the hand lens to examine the center and discovered a seated man, crowned, and holding an orb. On the rim, there was a cross. He turned the seal and tipped it slightly. The shadowing helped him read.

"'BALDVINVS DEI GRAT.' That last is not a full word. It should be. 'Gratia.'" Crispin spoke in a whisper. "It translates as 'Baldwin by the Grace of God.' This is the seal of King Baldwin. The King of Jerusalem." He looked up from the magnifying glass. "Well, well, well. This does cast a new light on your portolano.

Meade nodded. "Well, Crispin? Are you in the game or not?"

Crispin said, "I don't believe we were properly introduced, were we?"

Extending his hand, Meade said, "It's Jack Meade. Call me Jack."

Crispin extended his hand. "It is a pleasure to meet you, Mister Meade."

Chapter № 9

Friday
October 27, 1916
Amiens, France

Closing his journal, Crispin watched Meade return the portolano to the pouch. After it was hidden under his sweater, Meade unlocked the door. "Wanna rip out those pages and toss them in the fire?"

"I will do no such thing. This was a gift from my school don. I intend it to remain intact. It is my *vade mecum*."

Meade frowned. "Your what?"

"*Vade mecum*. Literally, 'go with me.' Something I carry everywhere, not unlike your portolano. It won't go missing, I assure you."

Meade extended his hand. "Can I see it?"

Standing, squaring his shoulders, Crispin said, "Mister Meade, I am very aware of security. What I have written is only what anyone could deduce from the most basic reading of your portolano. I have used a pinched and somewhat obscured hand in making my notes, which further protects the information. I believe it would be of assistance if I were able to retain the page of the text for reflection." He handed the book to Meade with a formality that demanded its return. Crispin glared when Meade flipped through the pages and glanced at his notes on the birds of the Somme, word lists, and unreadable drafts of what Meade suspected were poems that had been scratched over and wildly interlineated.

Meade returned the book. "You're right, no one could read it. What are those lists?"

"I am compiling a glossary of words emerging from this war, both military and vulgar use." Seeing Meade's surprise, he continued. "That means 'common' not 'obscene' in English."

"Okay. As long as it stays with you."

Crispin nodded. "You have my word on that."

"Keep it out of sight."

Crispin returned the book to his jacket pocket and buttoned the flap. "Certainly."

Walking toward the map cabinet at the end of the library, Meade called, "Give me a hand over here."

The rumble in the distance made the vase dance on the mantel.

Crispin stopped halfway across the room. "Boche artillery. Expect us to answer it in just a moment." A summer's worth of thunder compressed into a minute of cannons firing almost in unison. The thick windows shook in their frames. The chandelier swayed. Meade flinched as he opened the top drawer of the large map case and began tossing maps on the Persian carpet. When the barrage had subsided, Crispin stared at Meade. "Didn't you say that these maps are historic documents? What are you doing?"

"Trying to save them. Verne was a map collector. But he never catalogued them. I've arranged with his son to let us inspect his maps in exchange for sending some to England for safekeeping during the war. I want to get the important maps done first."

"Why? How does this assist in your 'treasure hunt,' as you so quaintly put it?"

Meade sorted the maps into two stacks. "I need an old map to tell me what the ocean's height was when my portolano was drawn. That's the only way we're going to find the matching coastline and the treasure." He returned one stack to the drawer and took the other to the table. "Can you organize these by size so they pack better? I'll get some boxes in a minute."

Crispin gently moved the larger of the maps to the side of the table and created an orderly pile. "Now what?"

"I'll keep sorting. You write the inventory as a receipt for Verne and then–"

"If there is clerical work to be done, we should have brought my batman or a clerk from the regiment."

Meade stopped and looked at him. "Your batman?"

"Officers have an assistant. Keeps uniforms in order, posts our correspondence, and generally facilitates routine matters."

"This is a secret–"

"I am acutely aware of that but I see no reason for–" Crispin turned away from Meade and faced the fireplace.

Meade stood. "Look, what's the problem?"

Crispin turned quickly. His face was flushed. "You. You are the problem. It's simply not proper to press-gang another–"

Meade crossed his arms. "How's that again?"

"Mister Meade, you and I are as different as chalk and cheese. I really do not believe that we are suited to work together. And the hard part is that you don't even understand that."

"Sure I do. Chalk and cheese? You write with chalk and–"

Crispin sighed. "My point precisely. For your future information, 'chalk,' by definition, in this context, is young cheese, immature cheese, not what one uses to write upon a slate board."

"Big deal. You have some odd manners of speech. I can deal with that. So what's your real beef?"

"Gentlemen do not behave in this manner."

Glancing at him, Meade asked, "In what manner?"

Crispin's face flushed deeper. "How dare you solicit private information about me, intrude into my life!"

"Intrude?" Meade pointed back toward the trenches. "I got you out of that hell-hole–"

Crispin took a step closer to Meade and struggled to hold a level tone. "I did not ask you to–"

"Knock it off. I just want you to do your job. Think of this as a partnership like Gilbert and Sullivan. You do the words and I'll—"

"Bloody hell, how can you make light of this situation? This is not a singsong at school. You can't just pluck me out of a battle to sit in a library or do the work of some desk clerk. My duty is—"

Meade interrupted him. "Is to follow your new orders!"

Crispin's jaw clenched as Meade stalked out of the library. He returned a few moments later with two well-finished wooden chests, about two feet square and a foot high. Each had a lid with brass hinges and a small hasp. After putting the chests on the table next to Crispin, he closed the library door and left it unlocked. He walked back and stood too close to Crispin. Almost in a whisper, Meade said, "Listen. It's all arranged. Prime Minister Asquith thinks this is as important as I do, so pipe down. No one else here knows about my map."

Crispin took a deep breath and asked, "What do I tell my friends? That I was at the front for a time and then vanished? I correspond regularly with one of my professors."

"No. Your record will be fine. It will show that you did your service at the front, under fire. Honorably. You were a good soldier and fine leader. You just got sick."

"With what, if I may inquire?"

"Trench fever. Common enough. We'll go to England, find the treasure, and you get to go to an assignment there, after a brief hospital stay."

Crispin lowered his voice. "May I drop my professor a line letting him know that I shall be out of pocket for a time? I do not want to cause undue worry, you know."

"Secret means secret."

Crispin stretched his neck, as though his collar were suddenly too tight. "Well then, after I bundle up these maps, what other chores shall I expect to expedite this undertaking?"

"You'll do your translation for me in England while you are recuperating from your imaginary trench fever. You'll have nothing to be ashamed of."

"In addition to you and the Prime Minister, who else knows of this?"

"A guy named Smith-Cumming. Goes by just 'Cumming.'"

Crispin sniffed. "Never heard of him."

"He signed your orders." Meade looked toward the windows as a low rumble began. "He's the head of the Foreign Section of Military Intelligence."

The rumble grew into a loud hum in the room.

Crispin put his fingertips on the table and evaluated the vibration. "Steady, Mister Meade. It is only a truck convoy. It's not artillery. If all you require of me is translation, shouldn't we just pack it in and leave now?"

"We can't. We need Jules Verne's map collection."

Crispin raised his voice over the din of the passing vehicles. "Honestly, Meade, there are museums that have maps in them—"

"I know. I have visited most of the better collections. I can't get to those in Germany or Vienna now without arousing an unhealthy interest."

"Spain is neutral. They were a seafaring nation."

"Madrid doesn't have what I need. Those in Paris are locked away, after the bombing. Look, less than a hundred portolanos made before 1500 even exist today. I know what's in museums. But I don't know what might be in this collection."

Crispin lowered his voice after the last of the trucks passed. "I have not seen anything on parchment—"

"You won't. That's not what I am looking for here. I just want to see the early paper maps that were copied from older portolanos. So, are you going to help or not?"

Crispin straightened his shoulders. "Best we get on with it, wouldn't you think?"

"Sure."

"Shouldn't we make a duplicate inventory to pack with the maps?"

Meade nodded. "Good thinking. One more thing. We need to keep the curtains shut and the outside doors locked."

"Certainly."

After Crispin listed a map on his inventory sheet, Meade wrapped it in several sheets of tissue paper and crated it.

"Mister Meade? How shall I list this one? I do not see a title on it."

Meade picked up the map, barely a foot by a foot and a half. "An Ortelius. I swear it is. Not signed, though. Or dated. Put 'Ortelius' and a question mark after his name."

"Certainly. These of the New World are astounding. A Dutch map. *Die Neuwen Inseln, zo hinder Hispanien.* Looks as though the continents had melted at the edges. This one of Chile. *Chili Provincia Amplissima* from 1597."

"You see what I mean. He had a great collection for an amateur."

Meade was interrupted by a light tapping and the opening of the door. Madeline curtsied slightly. "May I bring a service of tea?" The light from the library illuminated her breath as small puffs of cotton in the hallway.

Meade nodded. "Yes. Thank you, Madeline."

"Very good, sir." The hem of her long black dress swished against the carpet as she turned and walked toward the kitchen.

Crispin frowned. "And just how do you know her name?"

"I had seen Michel Verne at auctions on and off for years. He invited me here for a party once. Maybe eight years ago."

Crispin watched Meade shrug his shoulders and return to the map sorting. Crispin sat properly at the library table and carefully wrote the names of the maps as Meade dictated them. After a few minutes, Meade said, "You might as well get comfortable; we're gonna be at this for a while."

Crispin stepped away from the library table, loosened the waist of his Sam Browne belt by one notch, and tested the flap on his holster before resuming his seat.

Meade looked up. "Want me to see if there are warmer clothes for you?"

"No…thank you. I am quite accustomed to the chill, and I must remain in uniform. Rules, you know."

Meade threw one of the split logs from the basket by the hearth into the fireplace. A small cyclone of sparks swirled up the chimney.

As each chest was filled, Crispin handed a neatly printed page to Meade to enclose in the chest and placed a copy on the table. Soon there was a small neat stack of inventory pages. Five latched map chests sat against the wall. A pile of oversized maps nested at the end of the table.

Madeline arrived with the tea tray, placed it on a small table near the fireplace, poured two cups, and retreated. The men suspended their work and walked toward the fireplace. Meade took one of the stale wheat crackers from the small plate and popped it into his mouth before he picked up his cup. He held the fragile cup in the palm of his hand and watched Crispin balance two of the small crackers on the edge of his saucer before coming closer to the warmth of the fire.

Crispin examined the fragile Limoges cup. "How on earth did you get interested in maps, of all the antiquities?"

"I watched the surveyors and engineers working for the railroad in the Dakotas, where I grew up, and discovered mapping and geography. Ended up working as a surveyor for the Northern Pacific for a while, then knew I needed to go back to college."

"And you are a surveyor now?"

Shaking his head and smiling slightly, Meade said, "No. I'm a wild-catter." Seeing Crispin's confusion, he continued. "A prospector for oil. I have a couple of geologists and a surveyor that do most of the fieldwork now. When they find a place that might have oil, I buy the land, sometimes just the mineral rights. I sell the oil or drilling rights."

Crispin looked skeptical. "And you can make a living doing that?"

Meade chuckled. "Yeah."

"Really? I would not have thought that possible." Crispin finished his crackers and tea and returned to the library table.

Meade followed him. "Oil's going to run the world's machines some-day– and its economy."

"Why would you think that?"

"Your navy just converted all of its coal-fired boilers to oil. Besides, coal can't run an automobile. My business is to meet that new demand."

"But others were running your business while you were spending your time collecting—"

Meade pointed to the map case and the inventory sheets. "Right. Sometimes collections like this come up for auction. They are usually a mess."

"Well then, why would you bid on such a thing?"

"Because nobody's sorted through them to see what's what, and with the war, a lot of folks are selling stuff without knowing its value."

"Ah, blind chance."

Meade stretched his back. "More like an educated guess...like my exploration for oil. Thought there might be something interesting in the collection, a wall-hanger for one of my offices at least. I never expected my bid to win."

"So the portolano was a part of the collection you bought?"

"That's what I thought at first. But now, I think it might have been packed with my lot as a way to smuggle it out of England, probably to Germany."

"Germany?"

"Yes. It's a center of the black market in antiquities. Nobody would have just overlooked a portolano on parchment in a collection of paper maps."

"Oh, be serious. Smuggling? Black market?"

"It is even more active now. Looting and all. I thought I was nuts even thinking something like that until my apartment was broken into. Ransacked the box of maps. But nothing important was taken."

"Why didn't they find the parchment?"

"Had it with me. Every serious collector has heard rumors about a map to some lost gold mine in Mexico or a king's ransom in Africa. The Baldwin Portolano is the stuff of dreams."

Meade pulled a tattered paper map from the cabinet and handed it to Crispin.

"Here. This is a print of a typical portolano."

Crispin tipped it as he examined it. "Simple line drawing of a coast, almost childlike. Not unlike yours. The word, 'port' to *porto* and *portalan*."

Meade held up his hand. "Actually, it is from the word *portolani*. Italian for 'pilot' or 'rutter.' The navigator, the port's pilot, not the port itself or the directional device on a ship."

"Oh, really? I'll have to research that."

"See how simple it is? They were personal maps, just for the ship's captain. Some had gaps or false lines to protect secret trade routes. About the year 1200, accurate portolanos with city names started being drawn for the routes in the Mediterranean. But held close by—"

Crispin tapped an ornate arrow at the corner of the printed map. "You know, I do not recall seeing a north arrow on your portolano."

"Didn't need one since it was personal."

Crispin refilled his cup and sipped the last of the tea. He stood with his back to the fire. "Mister Meade, would you mind if I asked you something?"

"Not at all."

"If you think this portolano came to you as a part of an illicit transaction, that the auction was somehow contrived, is there another contact in that trade in antiquities who could lead you to the map you need?"

"You mean another crook?"

Looking slightly shocked, Crispin said, "I suppose I do."

"I'm way ahead of you. I was in Constantinople, the black market there—"

Crispin brightened. "Ah yes, Byzantium. Where Asia meets Europe. Where Marco Polo bought—"

"Where you can still get just about anything, for a price. I tried to buy a map by some Ottoman mapmaker that was supposed to show ports in Italy and Greece in detail at about 800 A.D. That would have given me the rock-bound port reference I need."

"I gather that it did not."

"The deal never came together. I saw a scrap of thin hide, like deer-skin with some interesting marks, but never a whole map. Before I got to the final part of the deal, it got…interrupted."

"When were you there?"

Madeline pushed a small serving cart to the door, removed the tray from the library, and replaced it with a fresh tray holding new cups, a steaming pot of tea, and a platter of sliced baguette and cheese. After Meade took the heavy tray from her, he nodded. "Madeline, there are some tins of meat. Did you see them in the kitchen?"

"*Merci beaucoup*. Tomorrow, I make a beef bourguignon, how to say…a beef stew for dinner with them. But tonight is soup." Madeline left quickly, closing the door behind her.

After she was well down the hallway, Crispin turned to Meade. "Heaven help us, French cooking is so, so… saucy."

"We're lucky to have dinner at all."

"Indeed, I was just thinking that potted meat might just be in need of a sauce to overcome its basic unpleasantness. Again, let me ask, when were you there?"

Meade poured tea for both of them. "Last week."

"Good God! After the Dardanelles Campaign, I wouldn't imagine much remained. How could you even get in there?"

"I've traveled a lot in that area. Negotiated several of the railroad concessions with the Ottomans. I had a few contacts left. Getting in was a lot easier than getting out. Some of the soldiers thought I was a Brit. Took me under guard for a time."

Crispin looked away.

Meade saw a sadness that made him seem old. "Horrible thing, Gallipoli. What'd you lose? Over a hundred thousand men?"

Crispin turned toward the crates of maps. His voice was unsteady for a moment. "Mister Meade. I really don't understand why you need more maps, if your parchment shows the location. Why can't you just go to an atlas, open it up, and put your finger on the matching shoreline?"

"Modern maps show modern conditions. We're looking for a needle in an older haystack. That's why I'm sorting the maps by age."

After sipping his steaming tea, Crispin asked, "Can the shoreline really change that much?"

"Sure. The sea can eat into land in one area while a marsh may silt up and extend that land into the sea somewhere else. And storms, massive storms, can change the shore and even the course of rivers. But these are minor. The actual height of the ocean varies."

"Of course, any child knows about tides."

"No, not tides. Tides are the high and low for a day. Sea level is the average of those highs and lows over a longer time. And that can change as the amount of ice in glaciers increases or decreases." Meade put his empty cup on the table and scooped up a bit of bread and cheese. "Here's the problem. There was a huge ice age about ten thousand years ago. Scientists think the sea dropped by almost a hundred seventy five feet. But there are smaller cold spells. We know that Europe had a couple years essentially without a summer that are well documented. In particular, 1693 and then again in 1816. I need to know what was happening when the Baldwin portolano was made, to see if the sea level was higher...or lower, because it doesn't match any modern English coastline."

"So then you are seeking a map illustrating this inlet, or another from the same era, with enough other information to let you adjust a modern map."

Meade smiled like a proud parent. "Give that man a prize."

Crispin finished his tea and poured a second cup. "Rather thin teacups. Barely hold the heat. Well, back to it."

Gravel crunched outside. Meade spun and went to the window. He carefully slipped behind the heavy curtain and peered down into the courtyard.

Chapter № 10

Friday
October 27, 1916
Amiens, France

Crispin slapped his hand on his holster and started for the window. "What is it, Mister Meade?"

"Someone just came through the gate. Just got a glimpse of him."

"Intruder?" There was a heavy thud of the brass knocker followed by an insistent rapping on the front door.

Meade shrugged and drew his blued pistol. "Wait here."

Madeline scurried past Meade to the front door. Crispin paused just inside the library. The diamond pattern of the Webley's grip dug into his palm as he watched Meade press into the wall behind the opening door. Crispin pulled back into the library and listened to Madeline's crisp directions to the man. Her heavy keys clanked as she pulled them from her pocket. When the front door slammed shut, Crispin took a step into the hallway. Meade's pistol was pointed to the ceiling as he stood by the wall.

Crispin motioned for Meade to return to the library. "No harm there. She told him to carry some wooden crates to the carriage house."

"Nobody was supposed to be here now except Madeline and Michel, whenever he shows up."

Crispin looked calm. "It appeared that she expected the delivery. It was just a bit early."

"I guess Michel is finally having the oil paintings and a few other things crated to ship to a warehouse near his home. I told him the house was a target for looters if the battle line shifts."

Crispin squared his shoulders. "Shall we get back in harness?"

Meade silently resumed his review and sorting of maps. A few minutes later, Crispin cleared his throat. "Am I correct that what you seek is a map contemporaneous with the writing of *Beowulf*? That is, of course, based solely on the similarity of the hand, not the inclusion in the *Codex*."

Meade looked up from the pile of maps and smiled at Crispin. "Yeah. I guess I am."

"What part of *Beowulf*?"

The smile left Meade's face. "What do you mean 'what part'?"

Crispin sighed. "You may recall, Mister Meade, that the poem *Beowulf* is a multigenerational saga of the royal houses of the Northern clans, Danes and Swedes, covering about 400 to 600 A.D. Think of it as the prelude to the fictitious King Arthur stories. Full of chivalry, law, morals, battles, love, death, honor. It's all there. How to live as an honorable warrior. How to do your duty."

"Sort of a guide book."

"Not a book at the start. It was orally transmitted, probably sung or chanted on formal occasions. It has life lessons in it. Things a father would teach his son, I'd imagine. About charity, honor and the like. The need to be generous in peacetime to have allies in time of war. When it was finally written down, probably by monks, as few others had either the skill or materials to write—"

"Which was when? When did they first write it down?"

"I don't believe that anyone knows that with any certainty."

"Guess!"

Without pausing, Crispin said, "Most scholars put its drafting at about, well, at the turn of the millennium. The year one thousand. However, I will venture my opinion that it was transcribed about 800 A.D., although the described events took place several hundred years earlier."

"Great, you've given me a range of 800 to 1000 A.D."

"That's for *Beowulf*. Your portolano could be as early as 500 or 600 A.D."

Meade grimaced and sank back in his chair.

"You don't seem pleased by my estimate."

Meade clasped his hands behind his neck. "I'm not. Your estimate falls in the middle of the worst time possible. There was a dark age of western mapmaking from about 450 to 1000."

Frowning, Crispin asked, "Why?"

"For a lot of reasons. Just when mapmaking is starting to get good in Europe, the church starts dictating the way the maps could look—"

"The look?"

"Lactantius literally applied the Bible's statement that the earth is God's tabernacle to his maps. He drew flat maps, like a carpet on the floor of a church."

"A flat earth was the common understanding, until Columbus, wasn't it?"

"Just in Europe. But in Arabic countries and in the Orient, there was really accurate mapping of their territory and for trade."

"Why can't we look at one of those?"

Meade shrugged. "That's another problem. The Crusaders destroyed almost all of the Roman and Greek maps of the ancient world as well as the newer Arabic and Oriental maps."

"Why would they do such a thing?"

"It didn't fit their view of the world. So they replaced the accurate maps with their own primitive maps. Some just had three big landmasses called Europe, Asia, and Africa. Other maps just labeled Europe as 'Upper Earth,' identified the Mediterranean area as 'Middle Earth,' and called Africa 'Lower Earth.'"

Crispin cocked his head. "Never really thought of the word 'Mediterranean' as 'Middle Earth.' But, by definition, that is just what the name says...*median, medial, midi,* 'center or middle,' and then *terre* becomes 'terrain.'" He pulled out his journal and jotted a few short sentences. "Old English *middanearde,* Middle English it's ... *middelerthe.*"

Meade shook his head. "And all of the Americas were simply unknown and unimagined."

Madeline tapped on the door before she entered with a dinner tray. Vegetable soup and bread. A glass each of white wine. Crispin and Meade sat facing the fireplace and ate quickly. About halfway through his soup, Crispin looked at Meade. "When did maps begin to resemble what we know today as a map?"

"Early 1300s. One map drawn in 1375 is my benchmark. The King of Spain commissioned the *Catalan Atlas*. It was a world map, but it also had tide tables and other data that might help their fleet...and us. It is a huge work."

"Drawn by Catalan?"

Meade stretched his hands toward the fire. "Good guess. But that's what they call the school of mapmakers from Catalonia. Like the La Carte Pisane, it's an old map from Pisa."

"I see, a regional designation, not authorship."

"More like a school of cartographers. The king's Jewish mapmaker, Abraham Cresques, drew it."

Crispin frowned and looked up from his soup. "Why do you remark on his faith?"

"Remember, Christian maps at that time ignored physical reality. Some even added Paradise as an actual location. He brought us back to reality. His was the map that Columbus used."

"Does Verne have that one too?"

Meade choked on his last spoonful of soup. "It's in some museum."

At precisely nine, Madeline tapped on the door. Crispin jumped at the sound and had his pistol drawn when she opened the door. "A soldier, Monsieur Meade." She nodded toward Crispin. "Like him."

Meade followed her to the kitchen door where a tall muscular British soldier waited. "Mister Meade?"

"Yes."

At Meade's smile, Madeline left the kitchen.

Meade stepped closer to the soldier. "Who sent you?"

"RLS, sir."

"Thanks." Meade pointed to the five small chests. "Same again tomorrow night, I expect. Maybe one more crate that is a little larger."

"That's the lot of it? Won't be needing the larger lorry tomorrow, now will I?"

Meade grabbed two chests and the soldier carried the others, from the kitchen, along the side of the house, to the small truck in the courtyard. Meade watched him tie down the load in the open bed of a truck and cover the cases securely with a canvas before driving away.

Pausing at the door to the carriage house, Meade went in and looked through a pile of rough lumber crates. When he found one about three feet by three feet and two feet high, he brought it into the library.

Crispin looked startled as Meade dropped the open crate near the map cabinet and leaned the lid against the wall. "Isn't that a bit rustic for these maps?"

"See if you can find a blanket or something to pad them."

Crispin stood. "Certainly. Are there more of the finished chests?"

"Yeah. In the cellar."

Crispin brought back two torn blankets and lined the large rough wood crate with one. He left the other by the lid. Meade returned with a new bottle of white wine in one hand and a small map chest in the other. He poured a glass for each of them without asking.

Meade and Crispin worked steadily until almost ten.

When he completed the list, Crispin stood and stretched. He handed it to Meade to include in the chest. "When do you think we will get the definition on the coastline that you need?" Meade was shocked to see precise even lettering, almost that of a draftsman or architect, which was in sharp contrast to his personal scribbles in his little book.

"Soon, I hope, although the maps have no order to them. I did get a few ideas tonight, but not the polestar I wanted."

Crispin sipped his wine. "Let me see if I understand your plan. The maps for the time of your portolano were mostly destroyed by age or invaders, or they were private and full of secrets."

Meade poured more wine for each of them. "Right."

"And the sea level changed from the time on your portolano to the printed maps that we are boxing now."

"I think so."

"Still, you keep examining them with your hand lens. That is what puzzles me. If they are from the later time, how could these be of any assistance at all to you?"

"I'm playing a long shot. Lots of mapmakers just copied earlier maps."

Crispin put down his glass. "Why would they plagiarize another's work?"

"Mapmaking expeditions were expensive. So, if I can find one of the maps from the 1300s or 1400s that simply lifted earlier information, I have a chance of finding the reference point I need to adjust the coastline."

"That's only half the puzzle. When first I read the text on your portolano, I had the impression that I was reading the babbling of a madman. But now, I believe it to be a well-crafted set of directions."

"Good. If I can find the matching coast and you can read it—"

"And if we can't, Mister Meade?"

"Then…the treasure evades us, and England has no myth."

Crispin narrowed his eyes. "We need to be equally certain that it is denied Germany."

Meade looked at the open drawers of maps and shook his head. "No more for tonight."

Crispin stood and tugged down the sides of his uniform jacket. "A short rest, then the same again tomorrow? Say we start again at five?"

"Fine. I'd like you to start working on any alternate translation as soon as you're up. I'll start on the maps again."

"But what if we still have no idea where this place is located?"

Meade looked over at Crispin, who had crossed his arms. "Then you can translate it again and give me more alternative meanings, not just the obvious. Look for puns, wordplay, poetic meaning, and metaphors– that sort of stuff. Massage the language until it gives up its secret. Squeeze meaning out of it."

"Any broad concept of where it could be?"

"I think we can safely limit our search to England."

"Why? Just because of the text being written in Old English?"

Meade answered slowly. "In part."

"And?"

"What if they were looking for a ship that was set adrift, like the start of your poem?"

Crispin cleared his throat. "At the start of *Beowulf*? 'And so, after piling on the many treasures as befit such a good king, they set the boat into the flood, they launched him alone out over the waves and let him drift to wind and tide.' Is that the section on which you are basing your idea?"

"Exactly. I wondered where a boat would drift. Come here." Meade pointed to a modern map in the open drawer and traced a pathway above it as he spoke. "The warm Atlantic current from the Gulf of Mexico to Stockholm is constant. After the current flows up into the sea between Sweden and Finland, it turns and goes south, then west around Denmark and south again into the English Channel. If a low-profile boat, heavy with cargo, were set adrift off eastern Sweden or western Norway, the Atlantic current would finally push it into the North Sea and then to the English Channel."

Crispin smirked as he looked up from the map. "That's your idea?"

Meade shut the drawer to the map cabinet. "Until you get a better one."

Crispin looked at the last embers in the fireplace. "Tomorrow it is, then."

"Okay. I figured we'd be reviewing the maps for a couple weeks at least. It's going faster than I thought."

Turning to look at Meade, Crispin asked, "You mean we could be at this for days?"

"Yeah. His map collection is a mess." Meade poured the last of the wine.

Crispin took his glass and walked to the shelves. "Well, at least the library is in perfect order."

Meade followed him. "He used maps to prime his imagination for his writing, did you know that?"

"No. Sorry, I know almost nothing of the man's work. Good references, though. Do you think he might have a book on the local birds?"

"He might. He wrote great travel adventures about unexplored regions like the Amazon and Orinoco rivers in South America. Actually, he took over some other guy's project of writing the geography of France, province by province, when the fellow got sick. Haven't you read any of his novels?"

Crispin continued to read titles as he walked along the bookcases. "Can't say I have. I prefer history and fact to speculation, Mister Meade."

"Call me 'Jack.' Should I call you 'Lieutenant Crispin' or 'William'?"

"Odd. No one has ever asked me what they should call me. One always just knew. I suppose 'Crispin' would suffice. That whole naming thing at university is very interesting, based on shared experiences and class, I suppose. So often one does not see what is so obvious to others, for example–"

"Fine, Professor."

"I'm not a professor, not yet."

"Yeah, but you already act like one. You footnote everything. You know, if I asked you for the time, you'd give me a history of time, starting with sundials or druids shoving sticks in the ground on May Day."

"Did they really do that?"

Meade took the small shovel from the stand. "I just made it up. Look. It's late. Let's call it a night. Maybe we'll find the answer tomorrow." It scuffed against the stone as he scooped it under the ashes and scattered the embers against the rear of the firebox.

"Oh, Meade. If you do solve it tomorrow, I'll stand you a pint of Watneys at my favorite pub." Crispin left his glass on the tray.

"Is it still the King's Arms, in Oxford?"

"Damn dossier. Well, is it a wager?"

"You got a bet."

Meade followed Crispin. Meade picked up his bags and went up the wide stairway. At the top of the landing, Crispin went to the bedroom to the left. Meade went into the bedroom across the hallway.

"Good night, Professor."

"Oh, Meade. You might consider sleeping in your clothes. If the line shifts...."

Chapter № 11

Saturday
October 28, 1916
Amiens, France

Crispin felt the mud clogging his mouth and choked. The sound of his own gasping woke him. Sweat soaked and shivering, he turned, fought against the tangle of smooth sheets and thick blankets to check his wristwatch. Just after four. The dream, again. The only thing that changed was the hour in which the dream presented itself. Today, it let him sleep until four.

He had invented a ritual. If he could tell the time, he knew he was still alive. Looking at his watch became the first thing he did when the dream roused him. Even in the dead dark of the trench at night, he would stare at the glowing radium dots as though they were a miniature celestial system.

He fell back onto his down pillow and gasped as he realized that he was a guest in a fine home. He suddenly felt unworthy of the comfort in which he had slept while his men were bedded in wet trenches and drafty farmhouses. Shutting his eyes did not make his guilt diminish. It merely forced him to feel the heat of his unexpected tears.

Crispin balanced his watch on the basin, shaved, and dressed. On his way to the library, he stopped to insure that he had made enough noise to awaken Meade.

When Meade entered the library, turning up the cuffs of his sweater, he glanced at Crispin. "Sleep well, Professor?"

Crispin shrugged. "What can I do to assist on your map sorting today?"

"I thought you were going to work on the translation."

"I am. Thinking is the most difficult part of it, you know. No one sees you doing anything. Not like digging a trench at all, is it?"

"So, you can do that? Translate something while writing the inventory?"

"Certainly."

After they had worked for just under an hour, Madeline arrived with tea and the remains of the stale baguette from the prior day. Meade opened the blackout curtains and turned off the lamps. "Why Old English?"

Crispin poured a cup of tea. "I beg your pardon?"

"Why study Old English? Why not French or something obscure like Icelandic?"

Crispin sipped the steaming tea. "First, I already know those modern languages. Principally, it is the challenge. Not all the words we have discovered are even fully defined. It is possible to read all that is written in that age, and to visit it again in a few years as we learn more of this lost language and understand even more. That is a feat which is utterly impossible for a modern literature professor."

"Oh, I see. You study it because it has a limited range." Meade cracked a bit of bread from the stale heel and softened it in his tea. Just before it disintegrated, he popped it into his mouth.

"Limited? Not in the least. What is lacking in breadth is more than made up for in the depth and complexity. Did you know that we are still working to garner a complete lexicon?"

Meade swallowed hard and suppressed a smile. "I had no idea."

"Occasionally, one will come upon a previously undiscovered artifact that uses a word in a new manner or even contains a new word. The fragments of that old language can fall away from us like time itself. It is like trying to pick up mercury from a broken thermometer."

Meade poured more tea. "How can a language vanish?"

Looking over Meade's head, as though listening to a former instructor, Crispin said, "Language is a living thing. They are born and can die.

Old English was once a pure language. Just look at the muddle we have now. The 'F' sound as in 'fish' is so clear in Old English. But now we are muddled with the 'ph' as in 'physics' from the Latin, let alone the French influence."

"Can there really be a new language, or is there just a change in an old one?"

"Of course there are new languages. Look at Afrikaans. During the past two hundred years, the blending of Dutch, French, German, and tribal languages has created something very distinct and new."

"That's right. You lived in Africa briefly. Do you remember any of that language?"

"A few words. Odd thing, I can remember thorn trees from South Africa, which I left as a tot, with greater clarity than the English roses at my last boarding home before university." Crispin paused. "Does your memory ever play games with you like that, Meade? Something in the past can seem as though you saw it just this morning."

"Sure. Everyone has memories they live with. Good or bad."

They continued their work inspecting, inventorying, and packing maps. Distant cannon fire popped intermittently. In the afternoon, they heard airplanes.

At seven, Madeline silently delivered a tray with two large bowls of steaming boeuf Bourguignon, short wine glasses, and an opened bottle of vintage Châteauneuf-du-Pape. Before taking a tentative taste Crispin held the bowl and let it warm his fingers. They ate quickly and returned to work.

Just after nine that evening, Crispin was removing maps from the cabinet when he leaned back from the middle drawer and remained motionless. Meade looked at him from the table. "What is it?"

"This map is huge. Must be five feet across."

"Which one?"

"*Carte de l'Afrique divisee en ses principaux Etats. Dressée sur les Observations Astronomiques.*"

Meade walked over to Crispin, who was kneeling in front of the drawer. "Africa. But which edition? Can you see the legend on the lower edge?"

"I think it says 1776. Bit of a wormhole there. Might be an eight."

Waving his hand dismissively, Meade said, "Leave it. It's a common enough wall map."

"How about these smaller ones under it?"

Meade looked down into the drawer. "They need to go. Be very careful."

Crispin gently slid his hand under an untitled map printed on coarse paper and put it on the table. "I can't find a name or date on this one."

"*Mappæ mundi.* It's a woodcut before 1500."

Crispin placed it with care on the table and chuckled. "Did you just use Latin?"

"Means 'world map', right?"

"By definition, *mappae* means 'napkin' or 'towel' which is derived from the notion of a flat surface upon which–" Crispin froze at the sound of an automobile stopping in front of the house. Meade dropped the map he was packing, slipped behind the blackout curtain, and looked out into the courtyard.

Crispin whispered, "What is it?"

"Relax. Someone just drove our host home."

"Well, it is time that I pay my regards to Mister Verne, even at this late hour." Crispin tugged the cuff on his uniform and straightened the leather strap of the Sam Browne belt that ran across his chest.

"You'll meet him soon enough. We need to keep working."

The massive front door of the Verne home shut with a slam that echoed in the library. Shortly thereafter, Madeline collected the tray that held the empty bowls, glasses, and wine bottle. The library remained perfumed with the richness of the simmered stew and the wine.

Almost an hour passed before Madeline tapped on the door of the library. Crispin and Meade stood quickly. She looked weary as she placed two small logs on the fire. "Gentlemen, if you please, Monsieur Verne will join you in a moment."

Crispin squared his shoulders and stood by the fireplace, hand resting on his holster. Meade closed the cabinet drawers and was almost to the fireplace when the door opened and hit the paneled wall with a crack.

Michel Jean Pierre Verne, the only son of Jules Verne, had exchanged his shoes for velvet slippers with a gold fleur-de-lis embroidered on each toe. He walked to the large leather chair closest to the library door and steadied himself by placing his hand on the back of the chair. Crispin stood at attention and inspected Michel Verne. The well-tailored blue suit could not disguise a body that was slack and unaccustomed to exercise. Extravagances were core to Verne's expectations. A life of good food, abundant wine, privilege, and comfort had taken a certain toll. Although in his mid-fifties, his light brown hair thinned at the temples and his small watery-blue eyes were almost lost in the puffiness of his face. Crispin waited to be introduced. When Meade was late in doing so, Crispin gave him a look of reproach and cleared his throat.

"Michel, let me introduce Lieutenant Crispin, who is assisting me in preserving your maps."

Crispin squared his shoulders and nodded formally. "It is a pleasure to meet you, sir. Thank you for your hospitality."

"Enchanted." Michel Verne extended his hand to be shaken. The sharpness of his cologne was muted by a swirl of aromas from a rich dinner, wine, and cigar smoke. Crispin tried to distinguish one scent from another and surrendered when he could not.

Verne released his hold on the back of the chair and leaned in the direction of the library door. He steadied himself by letting his fingertips brush against the wall. Verne tugged twice on a bell cord beside the door, returned to the front of his chair, leaned back, and let it catch him. Meade stood at the edge of the fireplace and examined the mementos on the mantel.

Crispin sat stiffly in the other chair and smiled. "Mister Verne. Let me thank you for the opportunity to stay in your charming family home."

"With pleasure. Any friend of Mister Meade is most welcome."

"I would consider houseguests an awful nuisance during a war."

"Not at all. Mister Meade's offer to remove the dearer of the maps to England is a great comfort to me. Is our Madeline treating you well? You dined this night?"

Crispin nodded quickly. "She prepared an excellent beef stew. Quite flavorsome. Even gave us a very pleasant red wine to have with it while we worked."

"Been with the family forever, it seems. I ask her to leave the house and come to my home far from all this, but no, she says. Wait and see what she is going to bring us in a moment. You must join me in my celebration."

Meade looked at their host. "Of what?"

Verne laughed. "Patience, my American friend. Patience."

"Not my strength." Meade pointed to the map cabinet. "But it certainly was your father's. It must have taken years to build this collection. The 1525 Waldseemuller map of Scandinavia, the 1486 Germanus of the Nile, and—"

Verne held up his hand and stopped Meade. "I know nothing of his maps. I will agree entirely with your selections."

"Were there any maps that your father was particularly fond of? I want to be sure I take your family favorites as well as those I think have value."

"There is an atlas."

Meade leaned back into the wall and asked, "Where?"

Verne turned in his chair and pointed to a tall, leather-bound book on a shelf. "Up there. The fat one." The gold lettering on the book spine glinted in the light. Crispin saw it immediately, walked to the case, and picked up the three-inch-thick volume so that the bottom binding did not rub against the shelf. "Meade. Look here. *Atlas Maritimus, Or The Sea-Atlas; Being A Book of Maritime Charts. Describing The Sea-Coasts,*

Capes Headlands, Sands, Shoals.… Oh, Meade the title goes on and on." Crispin opened it slowly and stopped when the spine of the book creaked. He looked at the title page. "Drawn and compiled by John Seller, Hydrographer to the King. *Cum Privilegio Regis.* It is an authorized edition. Must be dozens of coastal maps in here."

Verne chuckled. "Now, tell him the date."

Gently turning the front pages, Crispin said, "Printed in London, 1677. It has the rough paper and heavy binding of the era."

Meade whistled. "We'll pack that one tonight. Make sure it stays safe." Crispin placed it on the table, sat, and continued to leaf through it.

Verne nodded. "Thank you. Now, Mister Meade, tell me. How was the auction? I wanted to go, but–"

Meade stood in front of the fire. "Prices were down. I never thought I'd see a 1538 Mercator on the block."

"Did you bid on it? You being American and all." Verne laughed at his own remark until he coughed and fell back in his chair.

Crispin looked up from the atlas. "Sorry?"

Meade tried not to smile. "Michel knows more about maps than he lets on. Mercator published a map that was intended to be cut and pasted on a globe, like gluing a peel back on an orange. Remarkable feat that, making the earth round, not flat."

Crispin raised an eyebrow. "I still don't–"

"The joke is that he stole, or borrowed generously, from the 1507 map of Vespucci's explorations of Brazil's coast. Vespucci printed his map in an obscure shop in Saint Dié and named his discovery for himself."

Crispin frowned. "Never heard of it."

"He used his first name, 'Amerigo.' Then Mercator Latinized it on his map to the feminine 'America' and assigned it to both continents. The Americas."

Crispin laughed before returning to the atlas.

Verne turned to Meade. "Do you have one in your collection?"

"Not yet."

Verne pitched forward and lifted himself out of the chair. He lumbered across the room. "Come look at the one my father found at a gallery in Paris. Not the oldest, but–"

"A Mercator!"

"It was badly framed. The proprietor presumed it to be a copy. Open the lowest drawer."

Meade opened the bottom drawer and stood with his hands on his hips staring at Mercator's map of North and South America surrounded by a thick border of gold leaf. Ornate gold flourishes in an acanthus leaf pattern embellished each corner. Meade sounded out the Latin. "The Americas and *India Nova.*"

Meade carried it with care to the large table. Crispin craned his neck to see the lettering. Meade held his finger just above the cluster of islands. "The New India. What we call the West Indies now. Remarkable detail of the isthmus there, that narrowing between the two continents. Strange to see a map that old which seems familiar."

Verne looked at Meade. "And what did you get at the auction?"

"A couple wall-hangers. Prints. Nothing special."

Crispin gestured toward the shelves. "Did your father write in this magnificent library or in the impressive tower?"

"Neither. He was a practical man. He wrote in the small study upstairs from six in the morning to eleven without any interruptions. Then luncheon with the family. Afternoons, he read. Here or at the library at the Societé Industrialle, keeping current on engineering matters. This room was for the formal greeting of visitors."

"Oh, a receiving room."

"Yes. Your friend, Meade is not the first American to visit. Oh, no. There have been others. Nellie Bly, the American journalist, visited my father when she went around the world, in less days than the eighty days of my father's book. You must know of her, she even wrote her own book about her trip and mentioned her meeting with my parents." Verne nodded toward the mantel. "Her photograph with my father is there."

Crispin glanced at the mementos. "Mister Meade has been telling me that many of the inventions in your father's books came to pass."

"He never thought he invented, just extended…how do you say, projected the ultimate logical outcome of science. He made a good life for us with his diligence and imagination."

Meade turned at the sound of Madeline's light footfall on the Persian carpet. She had tied a long white apron over her dark dress, the hems of both ended just above her well-polished black shoes. She entered the library carrying a large silver tray with a bottle of Champagne, glasses, and caviar.

She placed the tray on the table next to Verne. Beads of moisture clung to the bottle of Veuve Clicquot Ponsardin Champagne. Three slender crystal Champagne flutes, a plate of toasted baguette rounds, and a large scallop shell holding a mound of dark shiny caviar and three small mother-of-pearl spoons were on the tray as well. Madeline gave a nod to Verne.

Verne stood and picked up the bottle. "*Merci*, Madeline."

She backed two steps before turning, leaving the library, and closing the door. Crispin watched as Verne twisted the base of the cage over the cork free, tossed the wire into the fireplace, and rested his hand over the cork. Verne simply tipped the bottle slightly, held the cork, twisted the bottle, and eased the cork into his hand as the pressure of the Champagne expelled it. He splashed Champagne into the three glasses and left them on the tray for each to take. The men stood by the fireplace.

Meade looked at the small bubbles, like a string of pearls, in the wine. "What's the occasion?"

"My birthday, belatedly."

Meade was the first to raise his glass. "Happy birthday."

Raising his glass, Crispin said, "Yes. All the best."

"*Merci.* Thank you." Verne pointed to the painting above the map cabinet and smiled. "You know. I never knew if my father named me after his sailboats or his boats after me." Crispin glanced at the large brass plaque on the bottom of the golden frame, which said "Saint-Michel III" as Verne dipped his spoon into the caviar. "I think he gave me Beluga. The Sevruga is a smaller fish egg but how you say, more like cream or butter. What do you think Mister Meade?"

Meade looked carefully at the caviar and took some on his spoon. "Definitely Beluga."

Verne took a taste from his spoon. "A friend just back from Russia brought it."

Crispin put a bit on toast and tasted it carefully. "Russian, is it?"

Meade took a second taste of the caviar from the mother-of-pearl spoon, which he continued to hold. "Michel, you do have remarkable friends, getting this past the Bolsheviks."

"I am sorry we do not have crème fraîche to put on it for you, but we all have sacrifices."

Crispin stared at Verne's reddened eyes as he blinked and turned to Meade.

"Mister Meade. I just thought of another American that you might know. Medora Vallombrosa, the Marquise de Mores. She once lived in your Dakotas."

Meade leaned back into the wall. "We've met."

"I knew it. She said that her husband had a hunting lodge in the Dakota wilderness–"

"The Chateau. That's what the locals called it. Fancy place in the middle of nowhere."

"She spoke often of her hunting buffalo, antelope, and pheasant. Her father was a banker, wasn't he?"

Meade pushed off the wall and came closer to Verne. "Yeah, von Hoffman was a New York banker. When was Medora here?"

Crispin was startled by the firmness of Meade's tone and watched for Verne's reaction.

Verne smiled, taunting Meade. "Just before the war, she came up for the partridge hunt. My father knew her late husband when the Marquis de Mores was quite young and working as a stock trader at the Bourse. When the bubble burst, the Marquis lost much of his wealth. But then… he married well and went to America to start his cattle-shipping business. Pity it did not prosper."

"Is she in New York?"

Verne took a slow sip. "No. She stayed at the estate in Cannes."

"Her children?"

Verne laughed. "Athenais married the Baron Pichon, who is an Ambassador for France. She is now in Switzerland."

"Louis? Where is he?"

"Enlisted. Against his mother's wishes. Cavalry."

Meade nodded slowly. "He rode very well. He was a good wing shot, like his mother."

Verne said, "I do not know the word 'wing shot.' It means what?"

"An excellent marksman. Easily took game birds in flight. Still a good shot?"

"She did not hunt with us. She went to the cathedral. She said she wanted to see the labyrinth. Someone told her it was the most perfect of all the cathedrals." He shrugged. "Which of course it is."

Meade looked into the fireplace. "She was well?"

"Quite. You know she converted her chateau in Cannes to a hospital for the wounded. Beautiful woman."

Meade's words were slow in coming. "Yes. She was."

"Every time I see her, she is more beautiful. My wife even says so. There is a perfect moment for a wine, a pear, a cheese, and a person. I don't know the word in English. In French, cheese makers have a word. *Affinage*, that is, the summit of taste and texture. But her…every moment seemed to be better than the one before."

Meade took a sip, turned to the fireplace, and exhaled loudly.

Verne gestured to Crispin with his glass. "Tell me, Lieutenant, other than the war, how do you find France?"

Crispin took a dot of caviar on another small piece of toast. "Quite beautiful, what of it has been spared." He paused. "And the birds, I saw one earlier that I could not identify."

Verne lunged out of his chair and lumbered toward the bookshelf near the fireplace. He shifted his glass to his left hand. "I gave my father a book on birds for his seventy-year birthday. He would put a tick mark by each that he saw." He grabbed for the book. "*Atlas de Poche Des Oiseau De France Suisse*–" As he pulled it from the case, a smaller volume next to it fell to the floor.

As Crispin retrieved it, he replaced a small map that had slipped out of the book. When he stood, Verne handed the larger bird book to Crispin and returned to his chair by the fire.

Crispin placed both books on the table. "Thank you. I shall enjoy researching the identity of the mystery bird tomorrow."

Meade walked over to the table and picked up the small book. "What's this?"

Verne waved his Champagne flute toward the shelf. "One of the journals of my father's ship voyages. The small one was when he was on a collier–" Meade looked puzzled and Verne continued. "A ship that delivers coal. Sailed along Norway's outer shores and islands with his friend Aristide Hignard. I heard a lot about that trip. My mother would tease him about that journey."

Meade asked, "Why was that?"

"You see, he departed just as I was about to be born. Research for a book he was considering. He returned the day of my birth." Verne pointed to the bound journals on the shelf. "But there are more interesting voyages. There you see, in 1867 he sailed on the *Great Eastern* to New York for his one visit to America. That was the largest ocean liner then."

Crispin walked to the bookcase and looked at the titles of a dozen thin books identically bound in fine-grained maroon leather. Each had a gold-stamped title on the spine. They were in chronological order from 1861 to 1884 with destinations including Norway and Denmark; the Baltic and North Sea; London and Woolrich; Jersey, Sark and Guernsey;

Tangiers, Lisbon, and Algiers; England, Scotland, Yarmouth, Dover, Edinburgh, and the Hebrides; as well as Algeria and Malta.

Verne looked up from pouring more Champagne into his glass and saw Meade leafing through the journal. "Please. Take it with you, Mister Meade. A remembrance. Return it if you tire of it."

Meade slipped it into his jacket pocket. "Thanks."

Verne cleared his throat. "Lieutenant, what to you do for amusement in England?"

"I study languages."

"No! So did my father. He invented word games. Anagrams, logographs—"

Frowning, Crispin asked, "Logographs? Do you mean word squares? Those puzzles offering a clue to a word across and another word down?"

Verne grinned. "Precisely. He had to be able to read our words, properly spelled, both across and down, before he would award us a prize. He liked ciphers."

Crispin smiled. "Did he?"

"Yes, he used ciphers in *Voyage to the Center of the Earth*. Challenging."

Crispin brightened. "Ah, I know it is, all too well. I am inventing a language."

"You are making your own language?"

Crispin stood a bit straighter. "Yes, I am."

Michel Verne started to pour more Champagne for Crispin, then, seeing that there were just a few ounces left in the bottle, he put the bottle back on the tray. "Who could you talk to?" Without waiting for a reply, Verne pointed toward the door. "Tug the bell cord, will you? I'll have Madeline bring more from the cellar."

Crispin turned, walked to the door, and pulled the cord. By the time he had returned to the fireplace, Verne had slumped deeper into his chair and was making the soft snuffing sounds of an old dog, dreaming of other days. Madeline promptly responded to the bell, saw Verne asleep, placed the lap robe from the small table over his legs, and removed the tray. Crispin closed the door behind her and walked quietly toward the map cabinet.

Meade stared at Crispin. "I thought you wanted more wine."

Crispin opened the top drawer and leafed through the maps they had reviewed and replaced. "Not really."

Meade joined him after Crispin had pulled several maps from the drawer. "What are you doing?"

"That map that fell out of the journal. There was another like it, with many more blue pencil marks. Here." Crispin handed a modern map to Meade.

"Good eye, Professor. This is not a rare enough specimen to transport to England, but still a collectable if he had not made the notations on it."

"What do you think they mean?"

Meade took it over to the table and motioned Crispin to join him.

Chapter № 12

Saturday
October 28, 1916
Amiens, France

After Crispin joined Meade at the library table, Meade stared at the large map, shook his head, and whispered, "I can't believe that he'd write on this map."

Crispin read the map's title to himself. *Svecia, Daniae, et Norvegiae Regna.* "What is this?"

"It's a 1776 Homann Heirs of Scandinavia."

"No need to whisper, Mister Meade. Our host seems to be a bit the worse for the wine and the late hour." Looking at the map, he said, "But it's almost a thousand years after the era you are seeking."

Meade pulled his small hand lens from his pocket, rotated the glass out from under its steel cover, and put the glass up to his eye. He leaned over the map and studied it. "You're right. But look at the blue pencil marks here and here. Those are not a part of the hand tinting of the original map."

"Could it be his travel itinerary?"

"Possibly." Meade groaned as he got up from the table. "I'll get that journal. We can see if this matches their coal delivery schedule."

Meade opened the book. They compared the first three ports to the map's markings. Crispin took his finger off the third port mentioned in the journal. "They do not coincide. Was he charting the current?"

"Maybe. Didn't he say his father traveled to research ideas for his books?"

Nodding, Crispin said, "Best we take it for further study."

"Good idea. And I want to have a look at the *Seller Atlas* before you pack it."

Crispin carefully handed the thick book across the table to Meade. "Certainly, let me ring for Madeline. I could use a pot of tea. This could go on well into the small hours." As Crispin was about to tug on the bell pull, he heard muffled arguing down the hallway. He opened the library door quickly and reached for his holster. Meade jumped to his feet. A small crash of something ceramic shattering against tile echoed through the long hallway.

Opening the flap on his holster, Crispin said, "I will require five seconds to go through the courtyard to the back door. Go to the interior door."

Without waiting for Meade's reply, Crispin drew his revolver and sprinted out the front door. He cocked his gun as he ran through the garden. He stopped at the open kitchen door. He listened and only heard his pulse pounding.

He looked into the kitchen, which seemed abandoned. The room's white tile floor, white painted cupboards, and light gray granite counters maximized the light from the gas lamps. On the wall opposite the garden door were the icebox, gas stove, and an open door leading to a large pantry. As he shifted, he saw the back of the intruder at the edge of the pantry. He wore the beret, loose black pants, and square jacket of a local farmer. His right forearm was pressing hard against Madeline's throat. She was struggling. There was a glint from the knife blade over her left shoulder.

Crispin holstered his gun, ran through the door, and grabbed the man's wrist from behind. Crispin wrapped his other arm around the intruder's chest and held on like a bear.

The intruder was taller than Crispin, lean and well-muscled. Crispin tugged the knife blade away from Madeline's throat. She fell to the floor and began screaming.

Meade kicked open the swinging door from the hallway and saw

Crispin maneuvering the man to the center of the kitchen. Meade could not find a shot. The man twisted. His sharp features and high cheekbones bore no resemblance to the stout farmers of the area. The man's face was not tanned but ruddy and contorted by exertion. The knife came closer to Crispin's wrist.

Madeline was on the floor and tangled in her long dress. When she saw Meade she screamed, "*M'aidez!*" She extended her arm.

Crispin shouted, "Out! Get her out!" The intruder's booted feet mule-kicked at Crispin's shins.

Meade grabbed Madeline's arm and pulled her across the slick tile as though she were a sack of flour.

Crispin tried to wedge the intruder's arm behind his back, but met equal resistance. Each strained until their arms quivered. Deadlocked. Frozen in place, the two men panted in the same primal rhythm, pushed their limits in a battle of pure strength and will. Sweat covered their faces. Spittle flew from the man's mouth as he snapped his head back trying to hit Crispin's face. Crispin anticipated the move and dodged it.

When Madeline was out the door, she started screaming and ran toward the library.

The man's coat flew open as he flailed.

Meade lunged at him. "He's got a gun."

Crispin rocked back and lifted the taller man off the floor. "Get it!"

Meade grabbed for the gun. The intruder kicked him in the chest. Meade skidded across the floor. His leather soles slipped on the tile as he scrambled to get up.

The man kicked backwards. His heel slid off Crispin's boot. The second strike connected squarely, just below the left kneecap.

The grinding sound radiated from his knee as the searing pain shot through him. Spots of light dotted his vision. Then the sounds in the room became muffled, like the time he was head-butted on the rugby field. The fabric of the man's rough wool coat began to slide between Crispin's fingers.

His leg crumpled under him, but he tightened his grip as he fell. He slammed his forehead into the base of the man's skull just before they crashed to the floor. The pistol broke free from the intruder's belt and spun away on the tile. Meade grabbed it by the barrel.

Crispin stayed with the man, and jerked his wrist past the crest of the shoulder blade. There was a small sucking sound followed by a loud pop as the top of his arm slid in front of his right collarbone. The man screamed, shuddered, and went limp. Crispin continued holding the man's wrist.

Meade held the pistol. "It's a Luger."

Suddenly, the intruder rolled behind him and snagged the lanyard around Crispin's neck. Crispin spun like a dog on a leash, and his revolver flew out of the holster. The man lunged for it.

Crispin rolled over, snatched the Luger's grip from Meade, and slammed the thin barrel toward the intruder's temple. He had turned into the blow and the barrel split open his eyebrow and crushed the bone under it. He fell back and was motionless. Crispin retrieved his Webley.

Meade gasped. "Nice work, Professor."

Crispin propped himself up on one elbow and aimed his Webley at the intruder's head. "I'll guard him." He panted and said slowly, "Go secure the remainder of the house. I want to be certain he was alone."

Meade pulled his revolver, went to the kitchen door, and looked into the garden. "No one in back." He locked the door and ran out of the room.

When Meade returned, he was breathless. He nodded to Crispin, took the Luger that he held out for him, and slipped it into his waistband. Meade kneeled over the man and peeled back the farmer's coat. "Why didn't you just shoot him?"

"Honestly, Meade! One cannot interrogate a dead man." Crispin paused to catch his breath. "He is obviously a German agent."

"Just from the Luger?"

"That model is only issued to German officers. A 9 millimeter Luger. The engraving on the barrel says German Secret Service."

Meade searched the back pockets of the unconscious man's trousers. "Some secret!"

"I doubt if it were intended to be a secret."

"What–" Meade turned him over. Blood had pooled on the white tile. The gash through the intruder's eyebrow was narrow but continued to trickle. Meade ran his hands over the patch pockets on the coat.

"Rules of engagement." Crispin swallowed hard and sucked in air. "He is my prisoner, and under my protection, if he has identification."

Meade let his hand stay on the wallet he had discovered in the interior pocket. "If not?"

Crispin struggled to sit up and then leaned against the cupboard door. "I could dispatch him, without question. But he is clearly–"

The sound of shouting in French and a clatter made them turn toward the hallway door. Madeline ran into the kitchen holding a single-barrel shotgun. Verne was a step behind her.

Crispin gestured for her to stop. "No! No. Madeline. It is all over." Meade scrambled to grab her gun.

She relinquished it after seeing the intruder sprawled on the floor. Meade carefully released the tension on the hammer and leaned the bird gun against the wall.

Verne leaned into the doorjamb, gasping.

Meade turned to Madeline. "Do you have any rope?"

"*Corde.*" Crispin gasped. "The word is *corde.*"

Madeline went to the cellar. Meade handed the intruder's identity card and wallet to Crispin. She returned with a ten-foot length of heavy rope, which she handed to Meade.

Crispin watched carefully as Meade dragged the unconscious man into the large pantry and leaned him against sturdy wooden shelving. Meade started to pull on the man's arm.

Crispin shouted. "Meade, stop that! What–"

"He's got a dislocated shoulder. It's better to get it back in its socket while he's feeling no pain."

"Very well, proceed."

Meade tugged on the man's arm and turned it until he heard the shoulder snap back into place. Not a grimace or a whimper. Meade tied him to a sturdy timber of a shelf. His head flopped to the side and his breathing was shallow.

Meade closed the pantry door and looked at Crispin, who was reading the identity card. "What's it say, Professor?"

"The name on this identity card is Stahl. German for 'steel.' They've got to miss him, eventually." He looked at Verne. "You and Madeline must leave at once." He shifted his weight as though to get up, but then winced.

Verne pointed to the old woman. "I send Madeline for the police? No?"

Crispin snapped. "No. He is my responsibility." He pointed to the pantry door. "Is there a key to that door?"

Madeline pulled a skeleton key from her dress pocket and handed it to Meade.

Crispin reached up to the counter and started to get up from the floor. Meade locked the door and turned to hand the key to Crispin. "Are you okay?"

"In actual fact, I may have strained something. How about a hand, Meade?"

Meade reached down for Crispin, who stood very slowly. When Crispin tested his left leg, it folded. He leaned on the counter.

Verne lurched toward Crispin. "Madeline, fetch a walking stick." Then he said quite softly to Crispin, "I have many walking sticks in the house. My father needed them after Gaston shot him; he was mad of course, and it was a blessing that he was a poor marksman. But the foot never was right after that."

Madeline returned promptly with a walking stick, slightly knobby along the shaft but with a stout rounded handle. She presented it to Crispin.

"Well, if you insist." Crispin stood, leaning on the cane. "Thank you, I'll return this–"

"A gift. God's speed to you both. Madeline, get your things. I'll send others back for the paintings."

After Madeline and Verne had left the room, Crispin turned to Meade. "We are in no position to deal with several of his associates at once. I believe you should telephone your emergency contact in Paris for assistance."

"Sure." Meade reached for the earpiece of the wall phone in the kitchen and turned the crank on the side of the box twice. He slammed the earpiece back on its brass hook. "Dead."

"Dead?"

"As a doornail. I guess that's why he was going to send her for the cops. Let's get the maps packed and get out of here."

"Let me have a try at it." Crispin cranked the telephone six times and jiggled the wires entering the wooden case on the wall. He smiled. "It was merely a loose wire. I have a connection now. What exchange shall I request?"

Meade whispered it to Crispin, who shielded his mouth as he spoke to the operator. In a moment, Crispin handed the earpiece to Meade.

"Meade here." He listened. "Yes. It has gone badly. We had an intruder. Crispin's guarding him. Yes. We will. Of course, I'll put him on."

Crispin took the earpiece and leaned against the kitchen wall as he listened. He hung the earpiece on its hook and looked at Meade. "They will send your Mister Thompson for us. He remained in Amiens, but it may take some time to locate him. Some business at the hospital."

"Okay. I'll get our gear from upstairs."

"As he is restrained and under lock, I'll finish up in the library."

Meade ran up the stairs, shoved their belongings into their bags, and

SHARON O. LIGHTHOLDER

returned with them to the library. Meade shook his head when he saw Crispin seated at the table sorting maps. "Now I've seen everything."

"Did you collect my soiled uniform?"

"No. Where is it?"

Crispin shrugged. "How should I know? I can't leave it behind. The Germans can't–"

Meade stood over Crispin. "What are you doing?"

"Removing the modern maps to speed your review. *Tempus fugit.*"

"I know that one. 'Time flies.'"

Crispin fanned several maps out on the table. "Mister Meade? These seem almost identical. Should I pack all of them?"

Without looking up from his sorting, Meade asked, "What are they?"

"*Svffolcia Vernacule Svffolck,* by Blaeu 1645. The same area mapped by Christopher Saxon in 1607, and a Dutch one from 1617. All are of the west coast of England. And these two show the German coast and shoals."

"Area is less important than time. Anything before 1700 should go with us. We can sort them in England."

Verne lurched down the hallway and glanced into the library. "We're departing now. There is an old truck in the carriage house; I can run it. My thanks to you both."

A few moments later, there was a cough and sputter of the engine catching. Madeline ran into the library and handed Meade the heavy key to the front door.

"For you. Please push it through the mail slot after…."

She looked at the painting of Jules Verne's last yacht and began to cry. She tried to remove the large painting of the Saint-Michel III, but it was too heavy. Meade lifted it down for her, wrapped it in the lap robe by the fireplace, and carried the painting to the courtyard. He put it in the rear of the truck.

Meade helped Madeline into the cab and slammed the tinny door. "Madeline. Thank you. Be safe." Reaching past her, Meade shook

Verne's hand. "Take care of yourself. Oh, Madeline? Where is his uniform?"

"Outside the kitchen." Madeline smiled. "You both will be in my prayers."

Meade slapped the door and turned to go.

"*Attendez ici.* Wait." Madeline dug into the large cloth bag at her feet. "Sausage and a Calvados, especially for you, Monsieur Meade. Brandy from the apples of Normandy. Older than a century. Celebrate when this is ended. Bon voyage." Verne shifted into gear and gravel splattered as they left the courtyard.

Meade held the sausage wrapped in white paper and put the clear glass bottle with its amber contents and red wax seal under his arm. He shut the gate, went into the carriage house where he found nails and a hammer, and ran back to the house.

Putting the brandy and sausage into his briefcase, Meade reviewed all of the maps in the remaining two drawers. He and Crispin boxed them quickly in the map chests and crate that Meade padded and nailed shut. Meade retrieved Crispin's filthy uniform, packed it in a pillowslip, and shoved it into the duffel bag.

Just before dawn, a Renault pulled up to the gate. Thompson and Meade loaded the luggage, map chests, and the crate into the rear deck of the vehicle while Crispin unlocked the pantry door and guarded Stahl.

Crispin turned as Thompson entered the kitchen. "Did they send the ambulance I requested for Stahl?"

"Sorry, I'm all you've got. We'll have a doc at the train station take a look at him."

Meade unlocked the pantry door. Stahl's head was cocked back at an angle and his jaw was slack. Thompson rushed to Stahl and put his fingertips against the man's neck. "Good. For a minute, I thought he was dead. Looks like we're going to have to carry him."

Crispin grimaced. "I fear that I tapped him a bit harder than I intended."

Meade and Thompson propped Stahl into the corner of the rear seat. Crispin sat in the rear with his revolver pointed at his prisoner's chest throughout the brief drive to the train station.

Thompson stopped the car near a sentry at the dark edge of the platform. The soldier brought his rifle to the ready and trained it on Thompson as he got out of the automobile. Crispin continued to guard Stahl while Thompson presented his identification to the guard, went into the stationhouse, and returned with two soldiers who took custody of Stahl.

Meade got out of the automobile and helped Crispin up the steps onto the platform.

Chapter № 13

Sunday
October 29, 1916
Amiens, France

The clock on the platform showed 5:45. Crispin checked his wristwatch. A small stain of yellow light spread from the stationmaster's office across the center of the platform. At the edge of the darkness, Crispin noticed that the sentries at the train doors were holding their rifles at the ready, not over their shoulders.

While Crispin presented his letters of transit to the officer in charge, Meade returned to the Renault and unloaded their bags. Thompson shook his hand and then sped into the night with the last of the Verne maps.

When Meade returned to the stationhouse, Crispin was seated on a bench and handed Meade one of the letters of transit, which he slipped into his jacket pocket. "Meade, you know, this train isn't scheduled to depart for an hour or so. We have time for a shave before the station becomes overrun."

Meade put Crispin's duffle bag on the bench next to him and opened his own bag. "Let's get to it." They left their hats, coats, and jackets on their bags and slipped into the lavatory.

The door moved so easily on its hinges that Crispin's vigorous push sent it into the plaster wall with a sharp crack that echoed off the room's high ceiling. Crispin walked to the last of the line of five sinks nested in dark granite. He leaned into the wall, set his cane on the counter, and arranged the contents of his shaving kit on a small towel. He unbuttoned his shirt to the waist and tucked his collar inside the shirt. He pulled the cord holding his identity disk away from his neck.

Meade stripped off his sweater, placed the pouch on it, and dropped his shirt over the pouch. He soaped his hands on a bar of Lifebuoy and rubbed his face vigorously before opening his straight-edge razor, stropping the edge on the smooth leather of his boot top and shaving. Crispin was still stirring his badger shaving brush over the cake of shaving soap and building lather when Meade finished.

Crispin faced the mirror and brushed lather carefully over his pale stubble, "What's the day?"

Meade splashed the cold water against his face and neck and reached for his small towel. "October 29."

"No, not the date. The day."

"Sunday."

"You know, Meade, this will be the first Sunday since coming to France that I'll not be attending Mass. My priest at Oxford says you can set your clock by me. First pew. First service."

Crispin stopped lathering his face and looked at Meade in the mirror. "We passed the cathedral on the way into town. If I recall Thompson's map correctly, it should be quite nearby. Is it?"

"A couple of blocks."

Crispin picked up his safety razor. "My leg's up to it." He took a measured pull against his cheek.

Buttoning his shirt, Meade asked, "Up to what?"

Crispin shook the lather from his razor into the sink. "Up to the walk to the cathedral. Even if there is no service, I would like to—"

"Oh, no you don't. It's dark out there."

Crispin stretched his chin upward and shaved his neck. Then he turned to Meade, who was slipping his sweater over the pouch. "In actual fact, the moon is a waxing crescent. A sliver I grant you, but—"

"Who knows what sniper, or deserter might be out there."

"Oh, be serious."

"I am. Even if there isn't anyone associated with Stahl, we're as likely as not to get shot by some old lady wondering who is walking by her window in the dark."

"Then we'll just have to walk softly."

Meade glared at him. "With your cane tapping out a drumbeat? You look like the Dodo bird from *Alice's Adventures*."

"Is that what you Americans call *Alice's Adventures in Wonderland?*"

"I guess. I was just trying to point out that you could become as extinct as the Dodo bird if you went out there."

"I'll get crutches. They were stacked at the edge of the platform. Didn't you see them?"

"No."

"How could you not see them—"

Louder than before, Meade said, "No! You're not going. I can't lose you."

After pulling his razor over the last of the lather, Crispin said, "I don't intend to become lost. I intend to walk the Road to Jerusalem." Crispin carefully rinsed the safety razor under the running water and shook it dry before returning it to its leather case. He combed his tidy moustache, trimmed it with small scissors, and combed it again while Meade stared at him.

"The labyrinth? Is that what you mean?"

Crispin closed his case and turned to Meade. "I believe I was clear. Since the Middle Ages, it has been an alternative to an actual pilgrimage to Jerusalem."

"No. You can't go. I'm sorry, but that's an order."

Crispin clenched his jaw and hobbled to his bag on the bench. He packed his kit, put on his jacket, and cinched his coat's belt.

Meade latched his Gladstone bag. "Go on. I'll get the bags."

Crispin marched from the stationhouse and reviewed the jumble of crutches near the door, which looked like the jackstraws he had played with the other young boarders. He rooted through a stack of crutches on the platform. Some were just a shaft of peeled wood with a crossbar at the top resembling old woodcuts of Tiny Tim.

Finding a matching pair of the new split crutches, Crispin slipped the cane into his coat's belt and tested them. He found a rhythm, walked the length of the platform, past a sentry, and turned toward Meade as the headlamps of an ambulance fanned against the stationhouse wall.

A British soldier with a clipboard jumped from the front of the ambulance and took a post on the station platform under a lamp as other ambulances arrived. As each stretcher was removed from an ambulance, he looked at the man's tag, wished him well or patted his shoulder, and called out a car and bunk number, filling the train car behind the engine first. As the first ambulances pulled away, others replaced them.

Crispin walked to the soldier and after a brief exchange, returned to Meade.

He tipped his head toward the train of a dozen cars. "We're assigned to the first car." Meade stared at the clouds without moving. The morning light was tinting the high spotty clouds a brilliant red. The entire sky was soon splashed with crimson.

Crispin asked, "What is it, Meade?"

"The weather's shifting."

"For the better, I hope. It's ruddy cold now and the Channel crossing—"

"Red in the morning, sailors take warning. Red at night, sailor's delight."

"*Matthew 16*, isn't it?"

"Huh?"

"Aren't you paraphrasing the response that Jesus made to the Pharisees when asked for a sign?" Crispin waited for a reply. "Oh, I see now. Is that a part of your Yankee ingenuity to teach children weather forecasting by rhymes?"

"Thought it might have been an English rhyme."

"Not that I know. But if it holds true, the weather is going to go bad on us."

"Shouldn't rain before late afternoon. We ought to be on the ship by then, nice and dry."

More ambulances parked by the platform. Stretcher-bearers marched toward the train with a slow precision. With the daylight, the neglect of the dozen maroon railroad cars became evident. The gold paint was chipped and a layer of dried mud and dust covered the lower half.

A few of the soldiers on the litters had gauze wrapped around their heads covering their eyes. Most had lumps of bandage at the place where a leg or arm should have continued. A stretcher-bearer hurried past them to the rear of the first car. Crispin stepped aside. Another passed him and then a third, whom they followed into the dim coach.

Crispin stumbled on a rip in the worn carpet. He grabbed the rough lumber that had been used to make bunks. He adjusted the crutches and walked past the bunks, which were four high on both sides.

The burly men lifted stretchers to shoulder height and gently maneuvered the bandaged men into bunks. Once their patients were settled, the men sprinted down the corridor, past two glass-enclosed seating compartments at the front of the car, and jumped down the stairs. Two of the bandaged men moaned as Crispin hurried past them. Every three paces there was a new set of bunks to fill. When eighty to a hundred men on litters had filled a car, the door was shut and another man with a clipboard pointed the stretcher-bearers to the next.

Crispin opened the smudged glass door to the compartment overlooking the platform. The thick glass was beveled at the edges and framed in a chipped walnut. He toppled into the seat next to the window and a plume of dust surrounded him. Meade tossed their bags up onto the ornate silvered rack above the seats and sat facing Crispin. The bench seats were well padded and covered with velvet that once was ruby-colored.

By 6:20, the steam engine was huffing, and the interior lights were glowing in the train compartment. Crispin cleared his throat. "Meade, I know we both are tired, but I think that we need to stand a formal watch, given the, uh, parcel you have. Safer that way."

Meade slammed the compartment door shut. "Agreed. I'll take the first watch." He opened the 1861 journal. "I wonder what old Jules found interesting on his trip. Grab some sleep."

"If you insist." Crispin slumped, crossed his arms over his chest, and mumbled something.

"What'd you say?"

Without opening his eyes, Crispin said, "Just thinking of the Finn saga from the poem. It's the story told by the court poet. A story inside the story. About how Finn saves the kingdom. The line translates as "saved by a mindful God and one man's daring." He muttered as he fell into a soundless sleep.

Meade forced himself to look away from the activity on the platform and read. He found the journal simplistic. The scrawled handwriting in French followed a pattern of listing the port, its weather, and occasionally a reference to food or wine. Even his marginal French was up to this task. Page after page, ports listed in the journal matched up against the blue checkmarks on the small map that had been stored inside its front cover.

Meade read for a while and then was unable to concentrate. He looked up from the journal to the platform for some sign of departure. Almost twenty soldiers on crutches came from two large trucks and struggled past their window to the last rail car.

A corporal with a limp, his right arm in a sling, stopped at the window and tapped on it. Crispin awoke with a scowl and then smiled. He looked down as he stood and said quietly to Meade, "It's someone I know. Turn away. Don't let him see we are travelling together."

As Crispin opened the window, the corporal grinned until the corners of his eyes were deeply lined. "Lieutenant Crispin!"

Crispin smiled. "Corporal! How is your arm healing?"

He shrugged and chuckled. "No more rugby for me. Fancy they'll find some assignment for me in signals back home." He squeezed back tears. "Thanks to you." He backed away from the window.

"Best to you, Corporal …."

"It's Blair, sir." He braced to attention, snapped off a salute with his left hand, and turned with parade-ground precision. After a few steps, he called over his shoulder, "Me folks have a chips shop at Bournemouth. On the promenade. If ever you are on holiday, come by."

Crispin nodded and closed the window as the corporal hurried to catch up with the others on their way to the last car.

By the time the soldier at the far end of the platform made a note on his clipboard, turned, and walked into the stationhouse, Crispin was asleep. When the glass door in the compartment opposite theirs opened with a bang, Crispin jerked and glanced through the smudged glass to see several Red Cross stretcher-bearers in gray uniforms filing into the compartment. Armbands that were once white now looked as though they had been soaked in tea for a week, and the crosses had faded from crimson to a scabby shade of brown. Nurses in long dresses with aprons under open coats walked past them toward the injured soldiers with a weary resignation. He shut his eyes again.

The sentries slammed the doors of the rail cars. Crispin shifted deeper into his overcoat at the sharp sound of iron latches catching.

Meade turned a page to a journal entry titled "Paris" dated in September; a month after Michel was born. He read the two paragraphs under the heading with care before he shook Crispin and shoved the opened journal at him.

"Translate this, quick."

Crispin pawed the air in front of him. "Surely it can wait, I'm just now asleep."

"Read it now!"

Crispin pulled the book from Meade and squinted at the spidery penmanship.

"Paris–"

"I can read that and the date, read under that."

"*Le plus ancien portulan occidental–*"

"What's that in English?"

"Seems he went to Paris and saw three old maps. Literally translated…the most old western map, called the Pisane map of 1209, the portolano by Angelino Dulcert 1339, and the map, then he corrected it to say *Atlas of Catalan of King Charles V.*"

The train whistle hooted twice as Meade pointed to the page. "And the next part? What does that last paragraph say?"

"And the map in the BnF in Paris shows the sea height at the *Île de Røst* in French, perhaps Røst Island in English. Whatever that means."

"It's the perfect place for finding sea level. Does it say which map has it?"

Crispin sat forward and whispered, "No. But the dates are good for you, aren't they?"

"Yes. I didn't trust my reading of it. I need to go to Paris."

Crispin shouted over the next blast of the whistle. "Paris? Are you mad? We are departing for England!"

Meade pointed to the strutting stationmaster and tugged open the window of the carriage. "Ask him if there is a train for Paris. Hurry!"

Crispin leaned out of the window and hailed the stationmaster who marched smartly to him. Coal smoke blew around them as they spoke and filled the compartment. Crispin shrugged as he slid into his seat. "Nothing scheduled."

Meade closed the window, pulled his Gladstone bag from the overhead rack, and put his briefcase over his shoulder.

Crispin stared at him. "What are you doing?"

"I'm going to see the maps at the BnF."

"Do you even know what the BnF is or how to get there?"

Meade tugged the handle to the compartment. "I'll find out."

Crispin laughed and leaned forward, hands on his knees. "Your French is terrible. It's a library! *Bibliothèque national de France.*"

"So now I know. You've got your papers. Go to England." The

stationmaster blew his whistle and the engine's noise shifted from a wheezing to a deep huffing.

"I believe my orders are to assist you. Which is precisely what I intend to do."

"You have." Meade patted the letter of transit in his coat pocket. "I'll catch up with you in England!"

There was a groaning and then a lurch as the rail cars started to move. Meade jumped down to the platform just as the car jolted forward.

He walked to the edge of the platform and turned to watch the train. When the swirling coal smoke cleared, Meade saw Crispin leaning on his crutches next to his overturned bags.

Chapter № 14

Sunday
October 29, 1916
Amiens, France

Crispin watched Meade walk toward him. Meade was grinning and wagging his head. The train clatter faded and the sentries had returned to their posts before Crispin spoke. "Be a good chap and carry my bags into the stationhouse, will you?"

"Sure. Then what?"

"I'll telegraph headquarters in Paris and have a car and driver sent for us now that Thompson has departed. Meade, when we go in there, pay strict attention, and play along."

"Fine."

Crispin adjusted the crutches under his arms. "Where do you want them to collect us in Paris?"

"What do you mean 'collect us'?"

"Meet us. Standard procedure is to establish a contact point. They verify the security and arrange drop points. I learned that much in my signal briefings. You certainly did not expect to walk into the BnF, did you?"

Meade shrugged and smiled.

"Honestly, Meade! Can you recall any place in Paris which we could find easily? A restaurant or out-of-the-way hotel?"

"There's a café I know. Café de Flore on Boulevard Saint-Germain."

"Splendid."

Within moments of marching into the stationhouse and greeting the officer in charge again, Crispin had commandeered the telegraph key from the operator. He motioned for Meade to sit by him and used Morse code to cable Paris. He listened for the answer and wrote the response, letter by letter, on yellow paper with a stub of a pencil. What sounded like random electrical snapping to Meade was intelligible to Crispin. At the end of the message, Crispin frowned at the paper. "Meade, have you ever ridden a motorcycle?"

"Sure."

Crispin tapped the telegraph key again. Under Crispin's touch, the black pad on the brass telegraph key snapped out the long and short electrical buzzes that became letters and then words. Crispin waited for the response.

"Good show. They are sending a motorcycle for us to use. No cars were available."

"Okay. Guess that'll have to do."

Crispin pushed a yellow paper across the desk to Meade. "Would you write the name of the café for me? I need to be clear with Military Intelligence in Paris."

"Why? I told you what—"

"I must spell it properly when I am on the key. Your pronunciation is, well…so variable."

Meade printed the name and pushed the paper back to Crispin. When he read it, Crispin said, "Oh, is that what you meant?"

After a series of exchanges between Crispin and Paris, the contact was confirmed.

Meade watched Crispin make a note on his paper. "How'd you learn all this, Professor?"

"This is what a signals officer does. Telephone, telegraph, flag, lights, and semaphore. Plain and encrypted messaging. I have even used the homing pigeons that the bird fanciers raced before the war to send messages. I memorized all of the intelligence and divisional call signs."

"You memorized all that?"

Crispin laughed. "One can't very well go writing down the secrets, now could one? Never thought for an instant I'd ever have occasion to use it." He held up his hand as a new series of code buzzed on his set. "They'll send over a motorcycle, dusters, and goggles."

"From Paris?"

"No. Somewhere closer. We may expect it to arrive in about half an hour."

"Get a map, too. Almost all the street signs are down."

"I'll key that request now. Would you be kind enough to put our bags over by that desk? The officer in charge has agreed to mind them here until our return."

Meade stood but hesitated. "What if we get back late?"

"This war is not run as a sweets shop. I assure you that they shall be fully staffed when we return."

Meade carried their bags where Crispin had pointed. He put the Calvados into his Gladstone bag, leaving the writing paper, pencils, and sausage in the briefcase. He slipped the long strap of the briefcase over his shoulder.

Crispin and Meade walked outside to a bench at the edge of the platform. While they waited, they watched an open truck arrive and soldiers load the crutches and stretchers. The truck departed and a swirl of dust blew over the platform.

Crispin took out his briar pipe and filled it with tobacco, which he tamped and lighted. The booming seemed more distant than usual, and the sun was warming as they waited.

After a brief wait, a 1914 Triumph motorcycle with a sidecar sped toward the platform. Leather coats had been tied to the rack above the rear fender and flapped like a wounded bird. Crispin held the pipe by the short straight amber stem, tapped out the small ember, and stared at the motorcycle with apprehension. The frame was painted a deep green. The wide knobby tires appeared to be in good shape. However, the gas tank was an unpainted dull metal cylinder strapped to a bar running between the handlebars and the tan seat. The two-stroke engine under the tank had a chain drive to the back wheel. The fenders were dented. The side-car seemed to be a slightly modified oil drum on wheels.

Crispin and Meade watched the driver dismount, pull a block from the sidecar, and wedge it under the front tire. Meade ground out his cigarette on the platform.

"Well, Professor, it doesn't look much better than the bicycle I had as a kid. That gas tank looks like an afterthought."

"Steady, Meade. Paris is only a couple hours away."

"It is probably three or more on that thing. Any faster, and we'll jolt to death."

"Your point is exactly what?"

Meade put his hands on his hips and stared at the machine. "That sidecar looks mighty uncomfortable to sit in for three hours."

"I'll manage it."

Meade stared wide-eyed at Crispin. "You? I thought you were gonna drive it!"

"I asked you if you had ridden motorcycles—"

"Yeah! On the back of one. Never drove it."

Throwing up his hands, Crispin said, "Bloody swell. I can't possibly manage it with this leg."

Before Meade had an opportunity to respond, the private who had delivered the motorcycle walked up and saluted Crispin. He placed both coats and goggles on the bench next to Meade, who then stood.

Crispin remained seated and returned his salute. "The map?"

"It is in the pocket of the uppermost coat, sir. Gloves too."

"Thank you, private."

"Oh, Meade." Crispin said, fishing out the map, opening it, and searching Paris proper. "I had them check. The café is at number 172 on the Boulevard Saint-Germain. Here it is on the map. I'll navigate."

Meade turned to the driver. "Where's the key?"

"No key, sir."

"We'll be in Paris. How do I keep from having it stolen?"

Pointing at the small engine, the private said, "Just pull off the spark-er plug and keep it in your kit."

"How do you do that?"

The private cast a glance that would have been insubordinate had Meade been an officer. He pulled a small spanner from the leather bag under the seat, tugged off the wire, and unscrewed the spark plug. He handed it to Meade to replace, which he did slowly.

"Sir, mind you, don't strip those threads or she'll not have the com-pression to fire. Anything else?"

"Can you show me how to drive it?"

The soldier looked sideways at Meade. "You *are* having a laugh on me, aren't you, sir?"

"Wish I was."

"Right you are, then. Shall I just take you for a ride? You can watch me run the gears and brake."

"Fine." Meade tossed his briefcase, overcoat, and hat on the platform next to Crispin and put on the goggles and leather coat. He tugged on his hat and stood to the side of the machine and watched with crossed arms while the private demonstrated the controls. After Meade struggled into the sidecar, they roared away, spewing gravel behind them. Meade's hat flew off, and they circled back. Meade reached down from the sidecar and retrieved it.

Crispin went back into the station and was seated on the edge of the platform by the time they returned. This time, Meade drove. The private slouched deep into the sidecar and gripped the edge. The stop was abrupt, and the bike started to slide sideways. When it stopped, the private got out and kicked the wood wedge under the front tire.

"Thanks," Meade said as the private walked away and shook his head. He joined the other soldiers, leaving in a truck with the sentries. Meade walked up to Crispin and eyed the machine with caution.

Meade took off the leather coat, put on his overcoat, and then topped it with the leather duster. "You'll want to wear both coats. How about I first take it for a spin alone?"

"That is a splendid idea."

The motorcycle engine spit and popped with Meade's first kick on the starter pedal and then sputtered to life. He engaged the gear smoothly and let the chain catch the rear wheel gradually. He looked over at Crispin when the motorcycle did not move.

Crispin scowled and pointed to the wedge. Meade dismounted, kicked it aside, threw it into the sidecar, and remounted. As he let out the clutch, gravel sprayed behind him. Weaving down the road, he barely managed to hold on to the handlebars. He shifted through the gears, tested the brakes, and stopped. He turned and drove back with a moderate level of control. By the time he had stopped the machine, Crispin had buttoned the leather coat over his wool coat. The goggles were around his neck.

Meade held Crispin's crutches as he slipped into the sidecar. "Meade, although the front is well to the east of us, you do know that we could encounter deserters wanting the motorbike." Crispin took the crutches from Meade and wedged them beside him.

"I'll worry about the holes in the road and you keep an eye out for problems and keep your pistol available. Okay?"

Crispin put the goggles in place and slid down slightly. He tugged the visor of his uniform cap down. "Hand me your case, if you will."

Crispin extracted his pistol from under his coats and slipped it into the briefcase with the map. He clutched the briefcase on his lap as Meade started south. By the time they reached the outskirts of town, they had developed some stability and picked up speed. Meade slowed as they approached the high black iron gate of La Madeleine Cimetiere.

Crispin looked up at Meade. "Is there a problem?"

"No. That's where Jules Verne is buried. I'd like to pay my respects. Michel told me where to find the grave."

"Quickly then, if you must."

Meade drove through the open gate. Much of the cemetery was

shaded by old evergreens. Meade stopped the motorcycle just a few steps away from Jules Verne's grave. Gold leaf covered the incised letters on the pale marble headstone. A marble sculpture of the upper torso of a wizened older man sprang from the marble slab covering the grave. The sculpted torso extended his right hand to the sky. Meade walked to the side of the grave.

Crispin slouched in the sidecar and looked around. New graves with fresh earth spotted the cemetery. He read a new marker for a French soldier who was his age-21. Crispin looked past the fresh graves. He watched Meade pick up a small dried branch that was leaning against the sculpture and toss it aside. By the time he returned to the motorcycle, Crispin was studying the roadmap.

"Ready, Professor?"

Crispin looked at his watch. "What do you anticipate our speed to be?"

"The roads are pretty chewed up. Maybe thirty miles an hour. Tops."

Crispin folded the map to show their planned route and slipped it into the briefcase. "At that rate, we'll make Paris in about three hours. Why not plan a break in about an hour or so. Somewhere with cover. I suspect it will be raining by then."

"Those are fast-moving clouds. Might just miss us."

They rode south in silence, passing an occasional horse-drawn farm wagon loaded with pale straw. After a few minutes, Meade found a speed that got them around the potholes without jarring their teeth. He called down to Crispin, "Thirty-five."

Crispin looked at his watch and recalculated the journey's duration.

They passed a few women riding bicycles with the greens of carrots or turnips spilling out of wicker baskets.

After an hour of jolting over the damaged road, Crispin looked at the tightly folded map and motioned to his watch. Meade slowed and searched for a safe place to stop. Treeless. Barren. Finally, he saw a side road that led down a small hill. He shifted, turned onto the side road, and stopped at the foot of the small grassy embankment.

Crispin handed the briefcase to Meade and squirmed out of the sidecar. He hobbled to the hill, dropped the crutches on the long brown grass, sat, and stretched his cramped muscles. The day had become colder. The clouds had blown past them to the south.

Tapping the map, Crispin said, "I make us here, near Beauvais. That's the next big town."

Meade pulled the sausage from the briefcase and tossed it to him. "Got a knife?"

"Just the one on my pipe tool. I fear that its limit is sharpening pencils."

Meade pulled a slim three-inch folding knife from his pocket and handed it to Crispin, who opened the longer of the two blades, cut several thin slices, and handed them to Meade before tossing a piece into his own mouth. The spiced meat was welcome in the cold air.

Meade finished chewing, then asked, "You doing okay?"

Crispin nodded.

Meade said, "Hope it's worth the trip. I sort of envy Stahl, he's almost to the ship by now."

Crispin looked at his hands. "I asked after him while you were out driving the bike. They removed him to the hospital."

"Why?"

"He had a seizure and then fell into a coma. Bit dicey."

Meade shrugged. "Wasn't your fault." Crispin did not look at Meade, who continued. "Do you still think I'm on a wild goose chase?"

"To paraphrase Goethe, having a hypothesis, even an incorrect hypothesis is better than having none."

Meade stood and started for the motorcycle. "Want any more, Professor?"

"Thank you, no." Crispin wiped the knife clean on his handkerchief, closed it, and held it for Meade, who slid it into his pocket.

Crispin used the crutches to stand. As he walked to the motor-cycle, he was unable to bend his knee. Meade helped him slide into the sidecar, mounted the motorcycle, and tested the controls. It started on the first kick.

Chapter № 15

Sunday
October 29, 1916
Paris, France

J ust after noon, Crispin motioned for Meade to stop the motorcycle at the northern outskirts of Paris. There were no cars in sight and only a wet horse, pulling a wagon loaded with crates of potatoes and carrots, plodded ahead of them.

"What is it, Professor?"

"Map. Need to take a squint at it before we get in the city."

After Meade stopped the motorcycle, Crispin opened the map on the top of the sidecar, and looked at the detail. "The city is nothing but angles and streets ending in roundabouts and monuments. I just wanted a moment to memorize the number of streets before each of our turns."

"You're sure we can find it with the signs down?"

"I propose we navigate by landmarks." Crispin pointed at the map. Meade watched the route as he drew it. "First, we get to the Eiffel Tower. Easy enough to spot. Then follow the river to the east about a kilometer and a half. Past this large bridge, Quai d'Orsay, past the next one, the Pont Alexander III, and here…we veer right, go away from the river for a few blocks. I shall count the streets once we get to this area."

"Fine. Just point which way I should turn."

"Certainly."

Crispin slid the map into his coat pocket. Meade gunned the throttle.

The heavy clouds that had blown over them earlier had released rain on Paris. Now the city glistened. When the shafts of sunlight cut through the clouds, slate roofs became silver and shimmered. Crispin tightened his grip on the sidecar as they jolted over the slick cobblestones near the Eiffel Tower. They joined the bicycles, horse carts, and trucks moving slowly along the Seine, past bridges, into the heart of the city.

Meade turned to Crispin and saw that his arms were shaking. "Cold?"

"It is a bit bracing."

Crispin reached forward and pointed to the right. Meade veered to the right, away from the river, and drove deeper into the city. Crispin counted intersections silently. He thought he heard Meade laugh just before the motorcycle skidded to a stop.

Meade jumped off and ran a few steps to a street vendor huddled under the awning of a building. Raindrops still balanced on the man's beret and black wool coat as he slouched in front of a wheeled metal cart. Its top consisted of a flat tin plate with rolled edges on which chestnuts danced from the heat of the sputtering alcohol stove below it. The man rolled a sheet of newspaper into a small cone and filled it with steaming nuts. Meade pressed bills into the man's hand.

Meade grinned like a truant schoolboy as he ran back to the sidecar and poured some of the hot chestnuts into Crispin's opened hands. "*Marrons.* Warm you right up." Meade put the folded cone in Crispin's coat pocket and started the motorcycle.

Crispin held the hot chestnuts in his gloved hands and sighed. He counted the streets and matched angles of intersections. After several blocks, they drove past the lettered awning of the Café de Flore and started a series of random right turns.

Once certain that they were not being followed, Crispin guided Meade to the alley behind the café. Meade stopped in a small bricked courtyard. They walked down the alley to the wet sidewalk, past the outdoor tables and chairs stacked against the wall of the café, and entered through the front door.

Crispin searched for anything appealing in the café. It lacked the dim lighting, intimate scale, familiar ale scent or haze of a pub. At the doorway, he took an instant dislike to the bright and open café. It, as Gaul, was divided into three parts. The outdoor tables, indoor dining at the banquettes or marble-topped tables near the door, and finally the bar with smaller tables and a respectable dark wood bar where a man could buy a drink. Meade walked slowly toward the bar, waiting for Crispin to manage the crutches on the damp floor.

The café had some primal undertones of wet wool, old cigarette smoke, and yeast from bread and beer mixed with the treble crispness of new wine and sharp colognes. Then there was the overlay of that almost-burnt smell of coffee laced with chicory accompanying the French confusion of dispensing spirits and coffee at the same establishment, failing utterly in the most basic civility of separating tearooms from pubs.

Crispin glanced around the café. It lacked any welcoming sense. The ceiling was too high and covered with fussy pressed-copper plates. The lighting was too bright with both overhead brass lights and the great plate glass windows, with ruffled half-curtains. Gaudy. Lavish in size. Probably could hold a hundred patrons. And the oil paintings were of landscapes, not the fox-and-hound prints that gave a place real character.

Students infested the banquette tables next to the window, waiting out the war. They had adopted the current uniform of unconventionality: dark leather jackets with long scarves dangling untied at the neck. They dawdled over coffee and occasionally tugged back the half curtain to look at others passing on the sidewalk and tap on the glass. In a darkened corner of the dining area, three young men seemed to have taken up residence, flaunting their school scarves and youth. Their wet jackets and sweaters were piled on an empty chair and dripped on the tile floor. Cups were stacked three high in a basket that once held bread. They were in some esoteric debate, occasionally shaking a pencil-clutching fist in the air. Crispin had seen this type before, in England. Students who were mad with passion, or simply mad.

He listened, chuckled to himself, and envied the luxury of arguing over whether Victor Hugo, Baudelaire or Rimbaud best reflected the symbolist poet of the previous generation.

A stocky man with a shaved head and stubble of a goatee and moustache bumped into Crispin and stumbled toward the loud students. Crispin kept his balance and watched the man drag a chair from an empty table. The man's uniform tunic was half-unbuttoned. He turned his head as he motioned to a waiter. The ragged red net of fresh scars spread from the corner of his eye into his hairline. Crispin hurried to the bar and looked back at the students composing a paper for the university, a poem, or some radical polemic text.

Cigarette smoke spiraled into a shaft of sunlight, which sliced across the room and lit the floor in front of the bar, which was almost fifty feet from the door. Blue-smocked laborers leaned on the bar and argued over wages for war-work while downing a fast cup of coffee or short glass of white wine with a hardboiled egg and chunk of bread for lunch.

Crispin nodded to Meade and ordered two coffees, bread, and two hardboiled eggs from the wire rack on the bar.

Before they were served, Crispin whispered, "Lean over your food and linger as long as possible." Meade nodded.

Crispin put a few of the chestnuts on the bar between them. "I do appreciate your stopping for these. Thank you."

Nodding, Meade peeled a chestnut and popped it into his mouth as the bartender slid cups of coffee in front of them.

Each time the door opened, Crispin glanced surreptitiously at the mirrored wall behind the bar. Just as Crispin finished his coffee, he saw the reflection of a tall French officer in the mirror. He was wearing the blue winter uniform under a midnight blue overcoat. He tugged on the black brim of his pillbox cap as he entered the café. Something in his manner struck Crispin as being that of a solicitous bellboy at a pricey hotel rather than a French military officer. Crispin started to turn as the officer called to another man across the room and joined him.

A few moments later, a man of Meade's height entered the café and stood just inside the doorway. He removed his derby hat and shook the rain off it before walking over to the bar next to Crispin. As he approached them, he used the mirror to look at Meade and Crispin. He slid between them and waved away the approaching bartender. He turned to Meade. "I believe we have a mutual friend."

"Who sent you?" Meade held his breath as he waited for the response to the recognition code.

The man looked down and quietly said, "RLS."

Extending his hand, Meade said, "Good to see you, I'm–"

Crispin interrupted him. "Not now."

The man pulled several folded bills from his pocket as he looked at the coffee cups. "Did you have anything to eat?"

Crispin answered softly. "Enough. Bread and an egg, each."

He waved the bills at the bartender and let them fall to the bar. "Follow me." Crispin noticed an indistinct scar on the back of his hand, almost like a star.

The man walked down a narrow flight of stairs at the end of the bar, past a lavatory, through the storage cellar and up stairs of unpainted wood. Crispin struggled to climb them. When the door opened, they were in the cold wet courtyard where Meade had left the motorcycle. A cloud of exhaust drifted behind a boxy black sedan.

Suddenly the man was affable and turned to shake Crispin's hand. "I'm Fowler. HQ got your cable, Lieutenant. The driver will take you–"

Crispin asked, "To the BnF?"

"No. Closed. Locked tight as a drum."

"But how could that be? I was quite clear that–"

Fowler opened the door of the sedan for Meade and Crispin to enter. "It's the war, sir. Everything is in the vaults or moved out of the country. Don't worry. We were able to secure two of the maps you requested. We've moved them to a safe place for you to inspect. But you need to be quick about it– the guard changes in just under an hour. They need to be back in the vault before then."

After Crispin had climbed into the rear of the sedan, Meade handed in the crutches and pulled the door shut. Fowler put his hat on, snapped down the brim, and tapped his fingers to it as an informal salute to Crispin.

Crispin searched his profile, wanting to memorize him. No beard or moustache, no facial scars. His features could have been at home almost anywhere. He could have been the most ordinary man he had ever seen.

The stocky driver never looked at Crispin or Meade in the rear seat. He ground the gears, drove over a large bridge, and sped past Notre Dame. Crispin rubbed the fog from the car window and looked at the cathedral. The rain darkened the stone. He looked up to the spires and then at the gargoyles that lurked at corners. Then he noticed others hidden in the carvings above the arches. Goat-bearded men with the legs of lions. Winged panthers resembling serpents or dragons. Pensive, winged monkeys; alert griffins, an eagle-beaked dragon with the chest of a man. Ravens. Menacing mutants with cloven hooves.

Elfin men with animal parts posed with animals having human parts in the hallucinatory sculptures. Dwarfed and distorted, these stone creatures were like those that were starting to inhabit his increasingly frequent nightmares, romping with fragmented humans.

Crispin slipped the map from his pocket and glanced at it. They were heading away from the center of the city.

The driver increased the car's speed as the traffic thinned. He snaked through the back streets past the ancient governmental edifices, churches, monuments, and highly ornamented apartments until the buildings became stark and unadorned. Small storefronts offering produce or shoe repair dotted the street. The smell of boiled turnips and cabbage found its way through the closed windows into the car. The shops became less numerous, and were replaced by small apartments nesting in the simple brick buildings that lined the street.

The driver braked hard, skidded, and turned through an archway. He drove past a web of empty laundry lines hovering above a small patch of browned grass. The car stopped on a small bricked section by a rack of bicycles. Crispin looked out the back window and saw a slim coatless woman in a dark brown dress running toward the car. The driver jumped out, tossed her the keys, took one of the bicycles from the rack, and peddled away.

She opened the car door next to Meade. "Come with me. I walk you to my father." Her dark brown hair was cut to collar length and the front was in wispy bangs. The gaze from her light brown eyes was steady. Crispin guessed her age as close to his.

Meade looked over at Crispin, who nodded. They followed her up a short flight of stairs into a small apartment. The sitting room had a walnut-framed settee with matching chairs. The maroon and cream striped silk on the set echoed the colors in the thick wool rug that imitated a Persian design. The wood floors in the remainder of the apartment were a deep honey color and immaculate. There were a few small oil paintings on the walls and spaces where others had been, judging by the odd placement of those remaining. What warmth there was seemed to be coming from the wood cook stove in the kitchen.

An old man shuffled into the sitting room. He was short and thin with sharp cheekbones. His full moustache and wavy black hair were neatly trimmed. His black summer suit had an unmistakable shine at the elbows that even a careful brushing could not hide.

Crispin waited for an introduction and saw that the man preferred not to offer one. Instead, he leaned over and whispered to the woman, "Merci, Marie-Claire." She nodded and returned through an open archway to the kitchen, where bedsheets were drying on wooden racks wedged against the far wall. The small kitchen table had heavy towels over it. Crispin paused long enough to see her unfurl a sheet over the table and take a hot flatiron from the top of the stove and start ironing with it. The last of the moisture sizzled away under the hot iron and the sharp smell just before scorching mingled with the wood smoke.

They followed the old man to his study next to the sitting room. A small workshop with a book press and rolls of leather faced it. The corner of a four-poster bed was just visible at the end of the hallway. He listened and heard nothing in the apartment over the rhythmic thumping of the woman ironing.

The chilly study had a bookcase on one wall which overflowed with leather-bound books. A rosewood desk and matching chair, deeply carved in the Chinese manner, dominated the center of the room. Two scuffed bentwood chairs had been pulled up to the front of the desk. The old man motioned for them to sit and then left the room.

He returned carrying two large black leather portfolios by their metal handles. Each case was almost a meter high and just over a meter in length. He leaned one against the desk, placed the other flat on the empty desktop, and untied the black ribbons on three of its sides.

"Here, for your observation, but you may not touch, please. I will move them for you as you request."

Meade nodded and slid his chair closer to the desk. Crispin sat still and watched as the old man folded back the portfolio like a lover sliding a negligee from a shoulder. The map was facedown. He pulled light cotton gloves from his coat pocket and slipped them on before he reached for the map.

"This is the Pisane map of 1290."

From the first glance at the back of the map as the man turned it over with a slow and careful fluidity, Crispin saw that it was made of fine vellum from the hide of a baby goat. The outline of the small animal was revealed in the narrow neck on the one edge that had not been trimmed.

Meade pulled his small hand lens from his pocket and rotated the glass out of its metal cover with the slow motions of a sleepwalker as his gaze remained locked on the map. Crispin shifted forward to look over his shoulder and saw that this was an elegant mariner's map which detailed ports and coastal areas. Inlets, bays, and navigable rivers were marked only where they joined the sea, while inland was a vast void. There were straight rhumb lines drawn on the map showing the direction of the prevailing winds.

Having heard Meade blather on about maps, Crispin understood how to read this one. The lettering was the same throughout, meaning one mapmaker, not several. The same hand had written the port names, but in several languages. Copying from the maps of others. Names and locations collided. Crispin let his eye take in the scattered data and then tried to bring this knowledge into his world. The spellings may not be in modern English, but he clearly understood that the red-lettered ports were Venice and Genoa. Marseilles and Le Havre. London. Lisbon. Amsterdam.

There were names in black ink, lesser cities he did not know. Vlissingen. Norvik. Esberg. There were patterns and designs he recognized. Crispin looked past the lace of the fjords of Norway where water and land collide and tangle westward to the open sea. No islands of note were there. The bold solid line tracing the Mediterranean coast was crisp, and port names spiked off the shore.

Meade leaned over it, putting the magnifying glass to his eye. He silently followed the lines, moved his body, shifted in his chair, and then stood over the map. He nodded after five minutes of inspection. The thudding of ironing had stopped and the apartment was silent.

The old man shut the first portfolio and opened the second. "Next is the portolano by Dulcert, with a date 1339."

The map was also drawn on vellum, but trimmed square so that it almost resembled a modern map or chart. Crispin wanted to tell Meade that "chart" was from the Latin *carta* for the shape of a napkin or tablecloth, but refrained. It was illustrated with a seated queen, a striding king, a turbaned emperor, a man leading a camel on a tether, and an elephant with a castle on its back. Crispin estimated the dimension at thirty by forty inches. He looked at the names of cities, all in Latin, and wondered if Meade had found the reference point that would allow him to make the needed calculation, but hesitated to look at him.

Crispin recognized the lettering *Mare Germanicvm*, the German Sea, for what he knew as the North Sea. The shading off the western coast of Germany and of the eastern coast of England was more pronounced than on the maps he had packed for Meade.

Crispin stared at the crosshatching and darker shading for the shallow waters to warn merchant ships of shoals and shifting sand bars, and invite fisherman to its bounty. Like sand dunes in the desert, the general margins of the miles of sand could be defined, but the specific shape of each shifting dune or shoal could not. He watched Meade pull the glass closer to his eye and follow the ancient coastlines. Crispin did not see anything labeled Røst Island and wondered if Meade had found it under another name.

The old man tied the ribbons on the portfolio. "I know you desire to see the *Catalan Atlas*." He looked up and shrugged. "But its size. We could not move it or find a way for you to visit the vault."

"Thanks anyway," Meade said softly.

The young woman rushed into the room, holding a large wicker laundry basket filled with rolled bandages. "Now, Maurice. It is time. We must go now."

The old man tied the last ribbon and did not look at them as he left with both cases. "Wait for her in the car."

Crispin tipped his head toward Meade's briefcase and mouthed the word "sausage". Meade nodded and placed the wrapped sausage on the desk as they left.

Chapter № 16

Sunday
October 29, 1916
Paris, France

Crispin crossed the courtyard slowly, crawled into the rear seat of the auto, rubbed the mist from the window, and waited for Meade to hand in his crutches. When Meade had latched the door, Crispin looked at him. "The island wasn't there, was it?"

"No. Did my disappointment show?"

Crispin stared at the door to the building. "Not in the least. It surprises me to admit that I have learned quite a bit about cartography from you."

"I was hoping to see Røst Island."

"Why? Just because it was in that journal?"

"No. That brought my attention on another way to find the sea level." When Crispin frowned, Meade continued. "It's one of the Lofoten Islands off Norway. Even though it is north of the Arctic Circle, it doesn't freeze in the winter."

Crispin rubbed the window again. "Impossible! Even Oxford freezes solid. Is that a myth?"

"No. The current from the Gulf of Mexico warms it. It also has this unusual tidal flow that both Poe and Verne used in their writing."

Crispin rubbed his leg and flexed his ankle. "Is that the same as a tide?"

"Yeah, but this is a twenty-foot difference, twice a day. Since it is such a hazard to navigation, I expected the average sea level to be marked on one of the maps."

"Why do you think it interested him?"

"I don't know, but he used it in *Twenty Thousand Leagues Under the Sea*. Made it a whirlpool that pulled ships under the water."

Crispin tugged his coat tighter over his leg. "Or perhaps he simply appropriated the Old Norse folk tale of Fróthi."

Meade looked toward the door to the apartment building. "I don't know it."

"The tale was first reported in the *Saxon Grammaticus* about 1200. King Fróthi was a contemporary of Christ. During his reign, there were no murders and gold rings left in the open were not stolen. This is called 'the peace of Fróthi', *Fróthi-firth*."

"It sounds like we could use him now. But what's he got to do with the whirlpool?"

As Crispin gestured, his crutches slid off the seat and banged into Meade. "Sorry. You see, Fróthi had two giantesses, who milled gold and prosperity. These giantesses worked so hard that they became tired and ground out an army to kill Fróthi so they could rest. But rest was not to come."

Meade glanced at Crispin. "Why not?"

"Vikings stole the women and set them to grinding salt on their boat during their voyage to the north. Salt being as valuable as gold. But they were too industrious, and the weight of the salt sank the boat. Their grinding is what makes the whirlpool today and why the sea is salty."

Meade laughed. Crispin said, "Hush. Here she comes."

The young woman, now in a thin coat, hurried to the car, slid the wicker basket across the seat, got in, and pressed the starter. Crispin watched her eyes in the mirror. Watchful. Darting. She drove easily and smoothly to an alleyway just past the café. After stopping for the men to alight, she drove into the darkness.

As they entered the courtyard looking for their motorcycle, Crispin nudged Meade's arm and nodded toward a man leaning against the mossy brick wall smoking a cigarette. Rain dripped from the awning and splashed on his shoes.

Crispin thanked her and shut the door as Meade approached the man. "You're a pleasant surprise, Fowler."

He flipped his cigarette into a puddle. "Not entirely. We need to get you two out of Paris. One of my contacts told me that the Germans know you are here."

Crispin stood taller. "How could they possibly know that?"

"It is the nature of the business. You know people who know things. I am afraid that your face is known to many, Mister Meade. Some less desirable than others."

Crispin's eyebrow arched. "I see. Do they know *why* we are here?"

Shaking his head, Fowler said, "Not entirely. Meade's presence makes some think that your inquiries are about oil."

Meade started to say something but caught Crispin's glare and remained quiet.

Fowler looked at them and said, "Well, chaps, the brass wants me to pass you over to the lads at Le Bourget for transit. May I have the key for the motorbike?"

Meade took the spark plug from his trouser pocket. "That's all they gave me."

Fowler stared at it without reaching for it. Meade twisted it into the small engine and snapped the wire to it. He looked up at Fowler and asked, "Where is this Le Bourget?"

"Just north of Paris."

Crispin said, "Awfully good of you to take us—"

Fowler shook his head. "You can't be seen with me."

Crispin pulled the map from his pocket. "Then show me where—"

Fowler lowered his voice. "I set up a hand-off. We have to be there soon, before the crowd." Crispin frowned but Fowler continued. "Walk behind me, it's just at the next corner. When I stop to tie my shoe, go into the bakery just across the street. If I don't stop, keep following me. I'll go to a place where we can talk."

Crispin leaned toward Fowler. "What do we do in the bakery?"

"The baker will ask if you are there to inspect the ovens. Don't speak. Simply nod and follow him into the back. He won't ask unless it is safe. From there, a guide will take you out of the city."

Crispin clenched his jaw and then asked, "And if he does not inquire? If it goes wrong?"

"Come back to the café at six."

Crispin shook Fowler's hand. "We do appreciate your help."

"By the way Crispin, keep up the limp. It is quite convincing. Explains why you are not in the thick of it."

Crispin paused before answering. "I'm not acting."

"Sorry to hear that."

"Thanks."

"Best of luck, chaps." Fowler walked into the street as though he were alone.

Crispin and Meade followed silently. The rain was heavier now, and the wind snapped the tails of their leather dusters. Rain was sheeting from awnings and splashing in the gutter.

The few people on the sidewalk were scurrying, chins tucked in and eyes cast down to avoid the now-slick dog droppings and leaves. Crispin's leg was cramping, and he was grateful when Fowler stopped to tie his shoe where the Rue du Dragon crossed the Boulevard Saint-Germain. Crispin looked for the red awning that Fowler had described. He did not see anything he would call red on either side of the street. Crispin looked down Rue du Dragon again and saw a soaked awning that was almost maroon. He walked slowly in that direction.

When they were directly across from it, Crispin stopped. Bold blocks of gold lettering on the door's glass proclaimed *Boulangerie et Pâtisserie*. In the corner of the front window nearest the door handle leaned a small paper sign with neat lettering announcing *Pains Chaud á 16 heures*. Hot bread at 4 p.m.

Crispin squinted at the glaze of moisture on the large glass windows. "It is difficult to see clearly."

"Stay here. I'll take a look." Meade sprinted up the sidewalk, ran across the road and casually walked past the bright bakery. Crispin shuffled back against the wall. The rainwater from the roof splattered against his legs as he watched Meade complete his reconnaissance. Meade stopped after he had passed the bakery and motioned.

Crispin walked through the high water in the gutter and made straight for Meade, who stood just past the window.

"There's just a couple of customers. An old man and a lady with a kid. Baker behind the counter. That's it."

"Good. We've beaten the queue for baguettes."

Crispin and Meade walked to the door. Crispin paused as he put his gloved hand on the bar to open it. A small child was drawing a round cat's face with broad whiskers in the mist on the glass. A slight woman in a brown wool coat and cloche hat bought a round *boule* of bread. After the last whisker was drawn, the boy skipped back to his mother. She put the *boule* into her cloth satchel, took his hand, and turned to go.

As Crispin opened the door for them, a small bell gave a sharp ring and the baker looked at him. Crispin waited beside the door while a frail older man in a black wool coat held two baguettes in the crook of his arm. He drew a handful of coins from his pocket and transferred them, one by one, from his boney palm to the worn oak counter.

Looking at the pastry case, Crispin saw that the upper shelf held only dusty paper flowers. The wicker trays that once held the rustic loaves of *pain de campagne,* the sweet *pain viennoise,* and the rectangular *fougasse* were stored on the lower shelf. Only a few stale baguettes stood upright in the wicker baskets by the counter, and the baker's cooling racks were empty.

The stocky baker swept the coins from the counter before the old man had finished. "*Merci, Monsieur.*" The old man bowed slightly and gathered up his bread.

The baker had the rosy cheeks Crispin usually associated with small children playing in the snow. He looked at Crispin and Meade without speaking. Meade opened the door for the old man, who then put his coat around the bread and walked slowly into the rain. After the door was shut and the brass bell was silent, the baker shrugged and addressed Crispin in French. "I suppose you are here to look at the ovens?"

Crispin nodded, the baker turned, and cocked his head for Crispin and Meade to follow him. He ducked through the narrow archway into a large room fogged with flour. He walked slowly. One leg was substantially shorter than the other, which gave his gait the rolling motion of a sailor in a storm. To their right was a wall of red brick studded with five large iron doors. The heat from the ovens made the room tropical.

Two gaunt old men with pushed-up sleeves were transferring the snakes of proofed baguettes from the large wooden worktable to large pans that they slid toward a young woman wearing a pink smock. She stopped cutting slashes in the dough and watched Crispin and Meade followed the baker to the stairway.

Crispin squinted when he arrived in the whitewashed cellar. The bare bulb was glaringly bright. Huge white cotton sacks of flour and smaller ones of sugar were stacked against the side walls. Shelving covered the rear wall, holding metal bowls, huge whisks, assorted tools, and tins of yeast.

Looking for a door, Crispin asked, "Just where exactly—"

The baker gripped an upright timber near the middle of the shelving and tugged hard. "Silence. You have but a few minutes to connect with your transit." A five-foot section of the shelf pivoted away from the wall on a hidden hinge and exposed a small rusted iron door. The baker tapped twice on it and stood back as it creaked open into a narrow passageway.

Crispin leaned down and looked into the dark. The rush of cold moist air blew past him. A man of unusually short stature stepped to the edge of the light and squinted at him. The brown-bearded man was dressed in black, from his beret to his high-topped rubber boots. His thick knee-length wool coat would have been a jacket on Crispin or

Meade. His black wool muffler was wrapped around his neck twice and the ends hung over his back like reins.

"I leave you now," whispered the baker. "This is Henrí. *Bonne chance.*"

Henrí waited at the edge of the darkness. Crispin stood aside to let Meade stoop down and enter the tunnel. Henrí snapped on his battery torch and stared at Crispin's crutches and shook his head. He handed a small light to Meade. "*Gaz.*" He turned and started down the tunnel.

Crispin entered the tunnel and sniffed the air. " 'Methane', I believe, is the most fitting translation of *gaz*. Although I do not smell any now, you should be aware that there is a risk of explosion should we light a match or have a spark."

Meade carefully slid the switch on his light and fanned the beam over the walls. Crispin's eyes acclimated quickly and he saw that the tunnel was narrow and lined with broken river rock in a matrix of flaking cement.

Crispin crabbed after Meade toward the pool of light cast from the hand torch, counting his steps should they need to beat a retreat. Irregular walls and amateurish masonry almost suggested a mine from another age. Moss dangled from a gap in the ceiling and brushed Crispin's cheek. As he ducked away from it, he tripped on a pile of rocks, which had fallen from the wall, and pitched forward. He wedged his hand into the wet wall to catch himself.

The baker slammed the door. The echo of iron crashing into rock stung Crispin's ears. It was almost the sound of the 75s near the trench. He stumbled and hit his shoulder against the wall of the tunnel. The crutch tip slid sideways. He steadied himself.

At fifty paces, Crispin was breathing as rapidly as a child in a dark boardinghouse, forbidden a candle or lamp. Crispin brushed sweat from his forehead.

After a hundred paces, Henrí's light illuminated another rusted door. He sprinted ahead to open it. Crispin leaned forward on his crutches, trying to catch his breath.

Henrí pushed at the door with his shoulder. Crispin braced for the grinding sound. The high squeals of rusted hinges and surprised rats blended into a single shriek. Cold air carried the scent of wet stone and mold.

Henrí stomped through the door into the ankle-deep water as though it were a small stream. Meade followed into the wider tunnel that pitched down to the left. He turned to shine the light for Crispin, skidded, and barely regained his balance. He turned back to Crispin and said, "Watch your step. The footing's even worse here."

Crispin walked three paces into the water and stopped. The ceiling arched high above them. Walls were of well-cut stone. He looked toward the gurgling source of the water and saw a hint of light at the upper end of the tunnel and the grated opening at the gutter. He looked down. The floor of the tunnel was a solid sheet of water glistening under the beam of Meade's light.

Henrí motioned for him to go down the channel. "*Les egouts.*"

Crispin turned to Meade. "The sewer! He is taking us into the sewer." Meade stopped, unlaced his high hunting boots, stuffed his cuffs into his boots, and retied the laces.

Crispin watched Henrí wrestle the door shut. Then it seemed to vanish. He blinked and watched carefully as Henrí's light passed along the wall without disclosing a hint of the door. As he ran his hand over the door, which had been painted to resemble the stone wall, he muttered, "*Trompe l'œil.*"

Henrí splashed past them down the grade and waited fifty yards ahead. He flashed his light back occasionally to check on them. As they walked over the mossy stones and approached Henrí, the sound changed from the low rumble to a churning hiss where the small rain-fed stream joined a larger channel of wastewater and sewage. When they arrived, Henrí ran up a dozen stone steps onto the wide walkway. Crispin and Meade followed him.

The banks of the larger channel were stone lined and dropped off at a right angle from the walkway. The grinding rush of water blotted out most of the shrieks of the rats that were scurrying ahead of Henrí.

On the wide stone-paved surface, Crispin picked up speed. Meade was able to walk beside him and shine the light for both of them. After a hundred yards, Meade found himself a few steps ahead of him before noticing that Crispin had slowed. In the dark, the tip of Crispin's crutch snagged on a broken stone. The crutch bow flew from under his armpit into the wall and caromed across the walkway. Meade stomped his foot at the crutch and missed it. He swore as the crutch disappeared into the churning flow and sewage, and Crispin leaned against the mossy wall.

Meade spun and grabbed the remaining crutch from Crispin. "You can't use just one down here." He leaned the crutch against the wall and handed Crispin the light. Meade turned his back to Crispin. "Get on."

"I shall not."

"Ever play pony ride as a kid, Professor?"

"I beg your pardon?"

"Never mind. Hop on." Meade pointed to the river of sewage. "Or you'll end up in there."

Crispin put his hands on Meade's shoulders. Meade scooped one leg, then the other into the crook of his arms. Crispin grabbed the crutch that Meade had leaned into the wall as Meade staggered after Henrí and then found a lumbering pace. Crispin's eyes watered. Meade gagged and coughed. Even the din of the sewage flow could not hide the increasingly shrill chattering and scratching as the rats scurried away from the light.

Meade was huffing. Crispin leaned forward. "Don't mean to be a burden, old man."

Meade panted as he asked, "What's the Old English for 'stench'?"

"*Stincan.* By definition, to exude a smell. *Odour* in Middle English plus *mal* for bad becomes 'malodorous' in modern English."

The carefully crafted stone arches of the chamber were now even higher, and the width of the channel had grown to about fifty feet. After ten minutes, Meade felt his legs going rubbery. A quarter of an hour later, their sewer channel joined an even larger one. At the junction, Meade put Crispin down and wiped sweat from his face with his coat sleeve.

Crispin asked how much longer in French. Without looking up, Henrí shrugged. "*Un peu.*" Crispin did not bother to translate for Meade. Henrí stood and pointed to his wrist. Crispin shoved up his cuff and turned the dial for Henrí to see. He fanned his light over the watch quickly and muttered under his breath. He pointed to the stone floor. "*Attendez ici. Dix minutes.*"

Crispin responded quickly in French and after a short exchange, Henrí fanned his light high on the wall illuminating a blue-and-white enameled street sign before he ran down the tunnel.

Meade called after him. "What the—"

"Easy, Meade. We're running late. He's got to have the driver wait for us. If he has not returned in ten minutes, we can use our street map to navigate out."

After Henrí turned the corner, the dim glow of his flashlight faded. The grinding water hid the sound of his heavy rubber boots thudding on the stone. Crispin took the light from Meade and fanned the beam into the high-arched ceiling, over fifty feet above them. "Napoleon designed the underground sewer."

"Mind if I skip the lesson this time, Professor?"

Meade moved his gun from its holster to his coat pocket. "If he's sold us out, we're sitting ducks."

"Holster your weapon, man."

"But—"

"Methane. A spark could—" Crispin returned the light to him. "Should we preserve the battery?"

Meade snapped it off and the most profound darkness settled over them. Crispin stared for some hint of light and found none. He held his breath until his lungs burned. He counted that effort as a minute. And again. Then, he guessed at the time. After what seemed like ten minutes,

Crispin pushed up his cuff and looked at the radium dots on his watch. Three minutes had passed. He heard a click that sounded like Meade's knife opening. Then, another three minutes passed and another two. Crispin thought he heard a thudding. Someone running toward them. A dim light glowed against the wall across the channel. The man turned the corner and the beam of his light bounced as he ran toward them.

"Meade! Keep our light off."

"I hear it."

After watching the light jolt and bounce, Crispin heard the footfall and said, "I do believe that it is our guide."

"How do you know it's him?"

"Look how low the light, the rapidity of the footfall. Snap on our torch."

Meade flashed the beam at the light, and Henrí shouted, "*Bien!*" Meade closed his knife and slid it into his pocket.

When Henrí was at their side, he leaned down and put his hands on his knees, panting. Crispin clapped him on the shoulder. "Thank you. *Merci.*"

Nodding, Henrí took the crutch, and Meade carried Crispin on his back. After a few minutes, Henrí vanished into a small side chamber. Meade pointed his light after him. Rusted iron rungs led up a small bricked chimney. Pinholes of light shone above them.

Henrí scrambled up the rungs of the ladder to the street with an agility that his stockiness disguised. He pushed the iron manhole cover above his head, then let it slide to the street. He scrambled out. A battered Peugeot delivery truck blocked the entrance to the alley. A tall man near it ran toward them. His black leather jacket flew open and showed a blue smock over heavy black trousers. He was a lean man with the angular face and prominent nose like those found on Roman coins.

Crispin put his hands on the cobblestones and struggled to push himself out of the hole. Henrí grabbed one elbow and the tall man the other. They jerked him onto his feet. The tall man draped Crispin's arm over his shoulder and walked him toward the truck. Crispin looked back. "*Merci.*"

Henrí reached his hand down for Meade, who handed him the crutch and swung up to the street easily. As soon as Meade was on his feet, Henrí dropped into the hole and tugged the iron cover back into place. Meade sprinted for the truck.

Crispin squirmed into the rear of the truck, which was filled with crates of vegetables and a side of rancid beef. Meade jumped up and crawled over the crates and fell next to him. The lean man threw a old canvas tarp to Crispin and slammed the back gate shut.

The truck jolted as gears ground. Crispin choked back a nervous laugh and turned toward Meade. "You know, old man, I have a new appreciation of the phrase *eau de toilette.*"

Chapter № 17

Sunday
October 29, 1916
Le Bourget Aerodrome, Paris, France

As the grocery truck jolted to a stop, Crispin threw the canvas over Meade and slid under it. A man with a thin voice asked, "*Ça va?*" The grocer answered. "*Bein, et tu?*"

"*Pas mal, Philippe.*" There was a shuffling of feet and a laugh.

Crispin exhaled quietly and listened carefully for any indication of risk. He flinched when someone pounded on the side of the driver's door. "*Nous sommes ici.*"

Crispin whispered, "Hear that, Meade? We have arrived."

Both Crispin and Meade slid off the back of the truck and were met by two stern French sentries in dark blue overcoats. One stood to the side of the truck and aimed a rifle at their feet while the other pointed a hand torch at their faces and extended his hand for their identification.

"*Papiers?*"

Crispin held his military identification for the guard's inspection. Meade pulled his passport from the inner pocket of his jacket and opened it. The guard looked at their photographs with a hand torch and directed the beam at their faces again before returning the papers. The guard asked Crispin something to which Crispin shook his head and laughed before responding.

Meade looked at Crispin, who shrugged. "He asked if you were enlisting in the Foreign Legion. I told him you were too old."

The guard smiled and motioned them to go to the cab of the grocery truck.

After Crispin squirmed into the cab, Meade climbed in and slammed the tinny door. The truck jolted past a sign. *Le Bourget, Aerodrome et Champ d'Aviation Aeropostal.*

The truck took a bend in the road and its headlights swept across the grass airstrip, which resembled an enormous soccer field. Huge sheets of canvas had been nailed over wooden frames to make hangars beside the airstrip. Meade stared at the dark green and black splotches on the canvas.

Crispin pointed. "Oh that? Painted to camouflage the buildings. They say it resembles a woods from the air."

The rain had slowed to a light shower. Philippe opened his window. Crispin detected the familiar aromas of cut grass, fuel, and the sweetness of burnt castor oil from a hot engine.

Electric lights in each hangar glowed above three French Nieuport 11 fighters and a British Sopwith. Men in dark coveralls repaired rips in the fabric covering the planes, tightened the wires between the upper and lower wings of the biplanes, or worked on the engines with a sense of urgency. A short mechanic painted a roundel on a new SPAD VII fighter while a man in uniform stood in the cockpit and installed a machine gun.

The truck drove past a dozen Avro 504 biplanes huddled beside the hangar under netting. They looked the worse for wear, but apparently were still in service.

Past the Avros, there were three Nieuport 17s without either roundels or guns.

The truck stopped in front of a stark wooden building which had been painted a dull brown. Meade thought it looked like the twenty by sixty foot shells that served as barracks for men in an oil field. The single-story structure was long and narrow with few windows and only one entrance, a small door near the center that was up two steps of raw planking. Meade opened the truck door and jumped down into a muddy track. Crispin followed him and had splashed most of the muck off of his boots before Meade helped him over it to dryer ground and retrieved the crutch from the rear of the truck.

"*Bonne chance.*" The driver ground the gears and drove toward the mess hall.

Crispin hobbled up the steps. "Well, Meade. Here we go."

The door flew open. A man ran past Crispin shouting, "Watch it, pal!" His shirt was unbuttoned, and his overcoat flapped behind him. He held a large flashlight like a relay runner's baton. Crispin watched the man as he sprinted into the darkness with a small brown dog yipping after him.

Meade took the stairs quickly and held the door for Crispin. As Meade shrugged out of his wet overcoat and leather duster as a unit, Crispin held on to the door and surveyed the room. The barracks interior was one large smoky room. The walls, whitewashed an oatmeal color, reflected what little light there was from the bare hanging bulbs. On either side of the living area were rows of cots lined up like pins on a paper.

Rainwater dripped from the dozen coats and jackets on the coat trees at the entrance. The fire in a small brick fireplace directly across from the entrance crackled. The mantel above it held several pewter tankards, a couple of bottles of Scotch and several glasses. Bookcases populated with coffee cups, footballs, several battered books by Zane Gray, a poetry anthology, and a small hand-cranked gramophone flanked the fireplace. Near the front door were three large tables, each with three or four bentwood chairs. There was a low hum of men talking and occasional laughter as they were occupied with chessboards, checkerboards, dice cups, and card games. Crispin stared at the men and searched for any similarity in their attire. Uniforms, it appeared, were but a starting point for individual expression.

A downy-faced lad wore his uniform trousers with a hand-knit sweater that sagged at the neck. A stocky man topped his plaid pajama bottoms with the blue shirt of a French Legionnaire. Silk ascots in black or white hung untied at the neck of several of the partially buttoned tunics. Two of the men at the card game in the center of the barracks were wearing pajamas, cardigan sweaters, and wooden shoes.

In front of the fireplace, a lanky man with straight dark hair, who was reading a letter, sat in one of the unmatched upholstered chairs. He alone appeared to be dressed properly. Blue trousers and shirt. But then Crispin noticed the man's wooden shoes. Yellow sabots. A slim Asian man was by the hearth. He took three logs from a neat stack of firewood and placed them with care on the fire.

Meade had just finished hanging up his coats when Crispin let the door slam. The lanky man folded his letter, slipped it into his pocket, and shouted, "New flyers? Spotted you, toot-sweet! You can tell an American at six hundred yards."

Crispin offered a faint smile as he pointed to his uniform cap. "Actually, I'm British."

The man smiled. "Meant him. Bet you're a Yank."

"Right. Jack Meade's the name. He's Will Crispin."

Abandoning his chair, he walked over to them. "Glad to meet you fellas. Jimmy Hall from California. You've already seen Alice, our mascot." He had a prominent nose and an easy wide smile.

Meade motioned toward the door. "Yeah. What's with that guy? He almost knocked us down."

Hall said, "He has taken the first watch on the field to signal Davis in. He's still in the air. Everyone else from today's mission is accounted for. Where do you get your mail, Jack?"

"New York until a couple months ago."

Thus ignored, Crispin placed his wet leather coat on the rack, continued to wear his overcoat, and looked for a seat.

Hall continued. "How are things in the States?"

"Unsettled."

"How so?"

Meade stomped his feet. "Can we get something hot to drink while we chew the fat?"

"Sorry. Grab a seat. Hot chocolate? Coffee?"

Crispin slid into the chair closest to the fire and dropped his crutch beside him. "Chocolate would be appreciated." Meade nodded agreement.

Hall turned. "Let me commandeer one of the *Annamites* to get it." He walked over to the lean man tending the fire.

Meade whispered to Crispin. "*Annamites?*"

Nodding toward the fireplace, Crispin said, "By definition, one who resides in or resided in the French colony of *Indochine*."

Meade scowled. "What's that in English?"

"Indo-China."

Hall returned to his chair. "These guys can find anything you want and fix anything you break, including airplanes. We call them the 'Oriental Wrecking Company.'"

Meade frowned. "Why? If they fix—"

"Our joke. Don't know how we'd survive without them." Hall looked at the new arrivals with a studied eye. "You boys aren't flyers, are you?"

Meade shook his head. "No. Just spending over."

"Have you checked in with HQ?"

"No. We just got dropped off here."

Hall reached toward Meade. "Look, you boys look pretty tired out. Why don't you gimme your papers? I'll take your credentials over while Tran gets your drinks."

Crispin pulled his identity card from his pocket and hesitated. "Are you certain that we do not need to present these in person?"

"Yeah." Hall grabbed a coat from the rack. "Still raining?"

Meade handed his passport to Hall. "Just a light shower now."

"Man, I hate this weather. Even worse up there." Hall pointed skyward. "I've been back an hour and still can't feel my toes."

Meade held up his hand to delay Hall. "Any chance you've got another crutch around here?"

"Sorry, no dispensary here. Just have a doc for emergencies." Hall motioned to the end of the room, past the row of cots. "You can wash up down there. Tran'll have your drinks in *un peu.*"

Meade and Crispin walked toward a group gathered around a man standing near the foot of the iron frame of a sagging cot. The flyer wore a fur-lined combination suit that was open to the waist. His hand motions were of a diving plane and another rolling after it. When his hand slammed into the palm of the other hand, a cheer broke out, and someone slapped the man's backside.

He noticed Crispin, and yelled, "Fresh meat, lads! We've got some fresh meat for the German sausage machine."

Crispin's head jerked. "Pardon?"

The airman faced Crispin, as if challenged. "So, you are the best Doctor Gros can find now? Bunged up guy on a crutch." He was lean, younger than Crispin, and his face was still flushed from the cold.

"Pardon me, but who is Doctor Gros?"

The man laughed, almost taunting. "The godfather of all us poor lads in the Lafayette Flying Corps. Looks out for our needs. Seems to have some magic to get parts to make new planes out of those we've managed to scatter into bits." The sneer faded from the flyer. "You'd know that if you were one of the boys. Just who are you?"

Meade stepped in front of Crispin. "We're just here overnight."

"Well, excuse me all to hell. Thought you might be the new trainees. They're late coming off their leave in Paris."

Crispin shivered. "Weather was beastly. That might have delayed them."

The flyer said, "Only good thing about it is that the Boche can't fly any better than we can in this much water. But it's starting to clear. We'll be in it tomorrow."

Meade waved at the man and walked toward the sign that said "Shower Baths – WC." Crispin followed, glancing at the occasional pictures of girlfriends or letters thumbtacked to the wall above the dozen cots.

Crispin and Meade had washed and pulled their chairs closer to the fire before Tran returned. He placed a tray holding two steep-sided bowls of hot chocolate and a large basket containing a torn baguette on the table near the fire.

Meade nodded. "Thanks, Tran." Bowing, Tran left the room. Meade handed the steaming bowl of chocolate to Crispin. "Have you had much to do with aviators?"

After a careful sip, Crispin said, "Met a few chaps from the Royal Air Corps in signal school. They were just there for the courses on wireless, flares, and Morse. Certainly saw more than my share of the aviators from the trenches." He pressed his shaking hands against the arm of the chair.

After taking a sip, Meade asked, "What do you mean?"

"A German *Albatros* would fly over the Somme every couple days and the machine gunner in the rear seat would unload on the trench or the men charging the wire. Bloody hard to hit it with gunfire."

"Why? Seems to me it ought to be like duck hunting."

"Meade! Think for a moment. Ducks don't dive out of the sky at eighty miles per hour, guns flashing at you."

Offering a faint smile, Meade said, "Got a point there."

"Heartening to see our lads answer in our biplanes. Boche would fly so low you could make out the faces of pilots and gunners, then our boys would take after them. 'Dogfights' they call them. Chasing after each other up in the air, twisting and diving. Once they got so low that I could see the smoke trail of their tracers. Bloody terrifying to watch."

Meade frowned. "Tracers?"

"Every fifth round is a tracer bullet. It is made of a special metal. Gives off a smoke trail and glows at night. It lets them adjust their aim."

Meade looked grim and asked, "How can they tell each other apart in the air?"

"They say it's by plane shape, but I look for the roundel on the side. The three-color circle for the French has a blue center, white middle ring, and red outer ring. The British planes reversed the order. Of course, the Germans have their black cross."

Hall let the door slam when he returned. He pulled a bentwood chair next to Meade and returned his passport. "So, Jack, what's your take on it? Coming in or not?"

"I think we'll be in the war soon enough, whether Wilson is President again or if Hughes wins. America can't turn a blind eye much longer."

"Yeah?"

Meade took a sip and sighed. "Tone's changing. Butchers in New York City don't sell German sausages anymore. Call them 'liberty sausages.'"

"Time to get in and get this over."

"Probably," Meade said, slipping his passport back into his jacket.

Crispin let them chatter. He took a deep breath and savored the faint scent from childhood. He took a small sip. It was not the watery bitterness of boardinghouse cocoa, but had the rich kiss of chocolate. He held the hot bowl in both hands and watched the steam circle. He dipped a chunk of baguette in the hot chocolate. The bread turned a brown that was almost black. Almost the color of the slurry of mud and blood in the rain. Suddenly a surge of nausea left him breathless. He closed his eyes and recited the Greek alphabet forward and then in reverse. A moment later, he forced himself to take another sip and then a bite of bread.

After a deep breath and another sip of the hot chocolate, he closed his eyes and started to relax. For once, he actually tasted something. He let the hot chocolate linger in his mouth. The warmth relaxed his throat. He blinked, watched the fire, and ignored their chatting until Hall reached over Meade to return Crispin's identity card. "A little warmer?"

Crispin nodded and took his card.

Hall looked at his watch. "Good. You've got about half an hour before dinner at the *Café des Aviateurs.*"

Chapter № 18

Sunday
October 29, 1916
Le Bourget Aerodrome, Paris, France

The rain stopped just before they left the barracks for dinner. The few remaining clouds were scattered around the moon and looked like lace. At the sound of a faint buzz in the distance, Hall spun and looked into the sky. Crispin heard the distant engine and turned toward the sound.

Hall glanced at Meade, "Stay here." He sprinted a hundred yards across the grass to the hand-cranked siren at the edge of the hangar and ground away until the siren's initial moan became an ear-splitting howl.

Crispin pointed just left of the moon. "There! See it?"

A red flare burst above the airfield. Meade ducked. "What the—"

Crispin shouted above the siren. "Signal flare from the pilot!"

The man with the dog sprinted to the end of the landing field and aimed his large flashlight toward the aircraft. A stocky man lumbered across the grass, stopped behind the signaling man, and lit white flares on the ground in a T formation.

Crispin squinted at the bright flares. "Wind directional signal."

The man shoved the flashlight into his coat pocket and scooped up the yipping dog. By the time the siren's wail subsided, the barracks had emptied and all the mechanics had stopped their work and run to the edge of the field with the flyers. Some held red fire extinguishers. Others carried pails of sand.

The sound of the engine grew louder and sputtered slightly as the craft circled the field. A man in uniform shot a white star flare above the center of the landing area. The entire aerodrome was suddenly daylight bright as the flare swung on a small parachute for what seemed a full minute.

A pale yellow Nieuport 11 biplane flew into the flare's light, swept above the earth by a few yards, slowed, and bumped unevenly across the grass. Before it had stopped, mechanics were running to it. The pilot jumped to the ground, picked up the small dog, which had been released, and kissed its forehead.

Hall waved at the pilot as he ran back to Crispin and Meade. "Davis is back. Now we can relax." Davis was surrounded by other flyers and hurried off to the headquarters building.

Hall walked his two guests past the sentry in the direction of a small two-story farmhouse.

Crispin lagged behind the others. "Just where is this *Café des Aviateurs?*"

Hall pointed to the stone farmhouse. "That's it."

"That?"

Letting his hand sweep over the landing field, Hall said, "All this used to be farmland. The farmer sold the farmhouse to Pierre, who used to manage the field hands. Anyway, Pierre and Marie live there and run the café. She cooks. He raises rabbits and takes our money. You'll see."

As he entered the *Café des Aviateurs*, Crispin was surprised to find an inviting open space. Huge hand-hewn beams crossed the ceiling and joined upright pillars in the dining room. Five scuffed wood tables, each occupied by four or five flyers, were scattered throughout the large room. Only one table was unoccupied. Flyers were drinking wine from short glasses and watching the stout woman at the stove. Complex aromas of smoky stew, rich soup, and baking bread filled the room. From the right of the room came the sizzle of meat hitting a hot pan in the small kitchen, half hidden behind a waist-high buffet.

To the left of the entrance, a sturdy long farm table held open bottles of wine, pitchers of water, a carafe of coffee over a candle, and trays of mugs and unmatched glasses. Silverware and napkins were in a tin box at the end of the table. A slate board had the day's entrées printed on it, which Crispin translated for Meade. "Looks like omelets, rabbit stew, and split pea soup." From the smudges on it, Crispin gathered that the menu had not been altered in some time.

Crispin examined the variety of uniforms in the room, frowned, and turned to Hall. "Say, old man. I thought this was an aviator's club. Isn't that chap in the red trousers and black tunic a French artilleryman?"

Hall nodded. "That was his old unit. Frogs just keep the uniform of their old assignment and tack the wings on the collar and wings and star on the right breast pocket."

Pointing at Hall, Crispin said, "But I thought your uniform was the aviator's uniform."

"For the Americans, yes. We get issued the horizon-blue French uniform when we join the Foreign Legion." Hall laughed when Meade looked surprised. "Got to be in somebody's army to fight. But the uniforms, you'll see anything here, from dress uniform to flying suits. One guy used to come to dinner wearing pajamas, a bearskin coat, and wooden shoes."

Crispin shook his head. "I believe I may have seen him. I must tell you that I am accustomed to an officer's mess where there is some decorum."

"Well, that's not here. Just need your wings to get in."

Crispin looked over the room again. "I thought we were going to the officer's mess."

Hall laughed. "Naw. The only rank here is aviation. Makes the older soldiers pretty nuts."

Crispin raised an eyebrow. "I can see why."

Hall motioned to the one empty table. Meade put the crutch under it while Crispin slid into a chair and turned to Hall, who was still standing. "So, tell me, I saw several fighter craft when we arrived. Do you fly any bombers out of here?"

Hall extended three fingers and said, "There are three kinds of pilots."

A stocky blond American at the next table interrupted Hall. "Dead, alive, or in Paris."

Crispin glared at the man, who laughed and went back to his wine. Crispin asked, "Most of the flyers seem to be American. Are they?"

"About half. Got some Brits, a couple of Russians, but most are French here. They usually eat at the aerodrome. Lots of Americans up at Champagne, northeast of here. As I started to say, there are fighters, observers, and bombers."

Another American pilot with pale green eyes walked to the serving table with an empty wine glass, laughing. "Or fighters and lovers."

Hall pulled out a chair, sat by Crispin, and shouted, "Knock it off, will ya? If any of you guys want to make yourself useful, get some wine for our guests!"

A lean pilot with straw-colored hair scuffed his chair back at a nearby table, got three short glasses and a bottle of red wine, and put them on the table in front of Hall. He stood straight and said, "When I was in the Royal Navy, we had a right good rum ration. A gill a day." Crispin looked at the man with a Cockney accent and a major's insignia on the collar of his French-blue shirt as he continued. "Officers got theirs neat. We got our rum as grog." He looked at Meade and Hall. "That is to say, one part rum and three parts water. Life always seemed better when His Majesty stood me to a drink at the end of a day."

Crispin found a kindred soul and stood, although uncertain what if any courtesy should be extended, as the man was neither in a British uniform nor in the service of the King. "Lieutenant William Crispin at your service, Major."

He extended a slim hand. "Ian Riley."

Crispin shook his hand robustly and sat quickly. "Why did you muster out of the navy for this?"

He shook his head. "I didn't. They invalided me out after my ship got torpedoed and sunk. Hurt me back. At any rate, when I saw what was going on over here, I couldn't stay at the shop. I thought if the Germans couldn't drown me, maybe I'd try flying."

As he turned to go back to his chair, Meade raised his glass to Riley. "Thanks."

Riley nodded. "Enjoy the *vin rouge.*" Riley pulled out his chair.

Crispin called after him. "Do you have a moment, Major?"

"Of course. It's grand to hear proper English for a change."

"Just what I was thinking. Join us?" Riley nodded and slid his chair next to Crispin.

Hall called from across the room. "Crispin, would you like stew or an omelet?"

Riley leaned close to Crispin. "Stew's quite choice tonight. Had two bowls of it, I did."

Crispin called, "The stew, please." He smiled at Riley. "Londoner?"

He took a sip before saying, "Was raised there. So was the Missus."

"So, you are an aviator now?"

Riley nodded robustly. "Went to the *Ecole d' Aviation Militaire* like every man jack of 'em here."

Crispin turned to Meade, who was listening. "That's a flying school."

Riley nodded. "Right you are, Lieutenant Crispin. We fly the Blériot system. You fly alone, not like England, where your instructor is in the plane with you."

"Alone? Where is your flight instructor?"

Riley pointed to the floor. "On the ground, watching!" Riley shouted to the next table. "Our instructor was not a shy old boy, was he, lads?"

Three flyers waved their hands just above their heads and shouted in unison, "*Pourquoi? Nom de Dieu! Jamais faire comme ça! Jamais! Jamais!*"

Crispin translated for Meade, "Why? In the name of God! Never do it like that. Never! Never!" Meade reached over and filled Crispin's glass.

Riley held his wine glass on his knee. "Penguins can't fly and neither can the three-cylinder Blériot airplanes they start us in. We call them 'Penguins.' These tricky little grass-cutters have short wings, so all we really learn to do in them is taxi about."

Crispin leaned back in his chair. "That shouldn't seem too difficult."

"Not sitting here, but I've seen little flocks of them crashing into each other. Saw a face-to-face collision once. Wood propellers in splinters all over the field. The instructor got right cheesed off, he did."

Crispin sipped his wine. "I can only imagine."

Riley laughed and choked on his wine. "You ought to see it when a new fella panics and gives it full rudder with full bore."

Meade shifted his chair and asked Riley, "What happens then?"

He drew circles on the table with his index finger. "Chases its little tail like a dog!"

Crispin scowled. "Why ever would they do that?"

"I don't think they intend to. Ever driven an automobile?"

"Certainly."

Riley smirked. "Then you know that in an automobile, your accelerator is under your right foot. But in an airplane, you have a rudder under each foot. That is the right and left control and the stick in your hand, that's the up and down control."

Crispin nodded and Riley continued. "If any of these fellas had driven an automobile, they have an instinct to shove in the right rudder to get speed. But that action spins them around."

"I am confused, where is the throttle?"

Riley reached up to an imaginary throttle at shoulder level. "Hand control. Some of the earlier planes didn't even have one. Just on or off."

The stout woman in a black dress appeared with three large bowls of stew, which she put at Hall's place. As he distributed them to Crispin and Meade, she returned and handed a basket of dinner rolls to Hall with a smile.

"*Merci, Marie.*"

Meade jumped up to get spoons and napkins. As they began eating, Riley continued to describe his aviation training in detail. Crispin only half heard of his progress from Penguins to the next craft, called "rollers", performing little hops into the air like chicks trying to fly. Riley ran his hand above the table and toward the ceiling, almost clipping Crispin's bowl. "Then we move to the *décoller* class. Learn to land with and without power."

Crispin blinked. "*Décoller*? Doesn't that mean 'to unglue'?"

Riley laughed. "Does it? I guess. You unglue yourself from the ground."

Crispin took a spoonful of the rich stew. "What then?"

"*Tour de piste*, circle the field at two hundred meters, then you get some altitude and learn to do spirals. Then hold altitude of two thousand meters for an hour. Then you take your brevet flight across country. That's flying two triangles of about two hundred fifty kilometers a side."

"And all this you do alone?"

Riley laughed. "Believe me, mate. Never felt more alone in my life."

Crispin was wide eyed and took a drink. "Amazing."

"Then after we do that, which is about as exciting as driving a bus once you have conquered it, we go to *Haute École du Ciel*."

Crispin translated for Meade, who was listening intently. "That's 'High School of the Sky' and not your American high school, Meade. This is an advanced course in military aviation."

Riley nodded. "Right you are. There we learn rolls and loops and the *vrille*. Nasty spiral down at full power. I can pull a five-turn spiral and drop three hundred meters in less time that it took to tell you about it."

Crispin blanched. "That all sounds ever so challenging."

"That's an understatement. Flying on a good day in summer is hotter than the hinges of hell. In winter you can freeze off...important parts if you don't pay attention– and that's before they start shooting at you."

Crispin dipped his spoon into the stew, seeking a carrot. "Then why do you all sound like it is such good sport?"

"It is. It's the most fun you can have with your pants on."

Crispin choked and was taking a deep drink of wine as the door crashed opened. A tall flyer came into the café wearing his leather flight suit, holding his gloves and goggles in his left hand above his head.

Hall nudged Meade. "That's Ben Davis from California. We saw him landing."

Crispin looked up from his stew. Davis' black hair was short on the sides but long on top. A comma of hair fell over his right eye. He blinked at the brightness of the room. His eyes were lake blue and looked even lighter against the smudges of oil on his high cheekbones.

Hall yelled at him. "Hey, Ben! Marie gets worried when you are late. Pull up a chair."

Chapter № 19

Sunday
October 29, 1916
Le Bourget Aerodrome, Paris, France

C rispin moved his chair closer to Riley's to make room for Davis at the table. His fleece-lined one-piece leather flying suit gave Davis an odd inflated look somewhere between an artic explorer and a teddy bear. Davis struck a pose as though waiting for applause and then broke into an ear-to-ear grin. "Did ya miss me, fellas? Or is it my Champagne?" He pulled a bottle from behind his back. A cheer exploded from the men at the tables. All the flyers immediately either drained their glass or ran to the table by the door for an empty wine glass.

A pilot near the door shouted at him. "Good hunting?"

"Got an *Albatros*." Davis leaned on Hall's shoulder and set the bottle on the table, harder than he intended. "Be a pal and open it, will you? My hands are frozen stiff."

Hall got up and slid his chair under Davis, who was starting to topple sideways. "Sure. Sit down. This is Meade and Crispin."

"Hi, fellas." Davis forced a smile. His hands were shaking uncontrollably. He laughed. "Colder than a well-digger's behind up there."

Meade got up and brought back a mug of coffee for Davis, who put his hands around it and pressed his elbows into his ribs to steady his arms. He closed his eyes for an instant. The grin returned and seemed less forced. By the time he had opened his eyes, all of the men in the café had come over to the table with empty glasses. Hall let the cork fly into the wall and splashed Champagne into each glass. Davis held the mug tightly as the flyers surrounded the table and pelted him with questions.

As he opened the neck of his suit, Crispin saw silver bars on his blue collar. When Davis held up his hand, the room grew silent.

"Freddy and I were up in our Avros on reconnaissance, needed to see where their artillery line was moving. On our way back, he was flying above me when his engine starts sputtering. He plants it in a field on our side of the line. I circled. He waves me off. I'm northeast of Amiens, so I write his location on a message streamer to drop there when I catch a glimpse of a couple of German birds. Two *Albatros* were running low and slow along our northern trench, where it takes a sharp turn."

Several in the room nodded. Crispin knew precisely where it was and clenched his jaw. Davis continued. "Gunners in the rear of both airplanes were strafing the trenches. There was a break in the rain. I came up from behind, fast, and clipped the rear one with a burst. It spun left and climbed fast. I stayed with it. Ran up its pipes. He returned fire and made a mess of my upper wing. Then he took a hard right. I fired low in front of him. Hit the block. All of a sudden it was nothing but black smoke around me. I looked for the other *Albatros*, which had gone toward Hautmont. It must have circled, because it had me in its sights."

Davis paused and sucked in breath. "But he just turned and hightailed it. Must have been out of ammo or had a jam. The first plane made a hard landing. I saw the pilot crawl away from it, but the gunner was still in it when the gas went up. Crashed near one of our tanks, and they captured the pilot. So, there I am. Running on fumes. I put in at Amiens, tell them where Freddy is, get gas and a patch. They wanted me to stay up there. But they don't cook like our Marie. Had to get home for dinner."

Hall raised his glass. "Gentlemen, I give you Davis. Hell of a flyer."

Many applauded and some shouted, "Hear! Hear!" Flyers returned to their tables as Hall brought a bowl of stew for Davis without asking.

When he slid the bowl in front of Davis, he asked, "Think he gave you a pass on purpose, because you didn't target the pilot?"

"Doubt it. Maybe Boelke's death yesterday had him rattled." Davis looked at Crispin. "Boelke downed over thirty of our planes. At the start, our contacts with the Boche were civil. We'd salute each other before we fired. Like gentlemen in a duel. We'd shoot to down the plane, not kill the pilot. Now it's a shake of the fist and tat tat tat. Blindside the guy. Throw a chain into his prop, that sort of thing. No chivalry any more." Davis poured another full glass.

Hall spoke quickly. "He's right. It's changed. I think it started in January of '15 when the Germans bombed Great Yarmouth from their Zeppelin. Now they've bombed London and Paris. Targeting factories is one thing, but women and children. Despicable."

Silence fell over the room. Hall cleared his throat, slapped his palm on the table, and said, "I'll tell you what is even more barbaric. Last April, a Zeppelin bombed a distillery in Rosyth. Sent a river of single malt Scotch flooding down the streets."

Riley shook his head. "Hadn't heard that. Nonetheless, their bombing of London has split England's aviation between home and here. Built a new aerodrome outside London to send up aircraft to stop them at the coast."

Crispin nodded. "Can they?"

Davis shook his head. "Good luck to them. The Zeppelin is five hundred feet long and has five machine gun ports, counting the gunner in the gondola. Prickly as a hedgehog."

Hall sat straighter. "Everything is vulnerable, you just have to know the soft spot."

Davis smirked. "What'll ya do? Drop a bomb on it from the sky? Can't. They have altitude advantage over most attack planes. Outrun them? Can't. They can turn off their motors and float to England on the westerly wind. If I run out of gas, splash into the sea I'd go."

Hall looked at him. "But you have speed. What's their maximum? Sixty and you can whiz around at almost a hundred miles per hour."

"Faster in a sharp dive. I'll bet you anything that I pushed well over a hundred today. It's a wonder the wings didn't peel right back."

Hall punched Davis in the shoulder. "Come on. Don't be such a sourpuss. Tonight is for celebrating."

Davis let his head hang and then brightened. "Well, at least I won't need my spare toothbrush tonight."

Crispin tipped his head. "Sorry?"

Hall patted Davis' shirt pocket. "Ben always takes his extra toothbrush up with him. Says if he gets captured, at least he is going to have his own toothbrush. Isn't that right?"

Davis pulled a toothbrush out of the pocket of the shirt he wore under the flight suit, displayed it with a grin, and returned it to his pocket.

Meade looked at Hall. "Do you fly with a toothbrush?"

"Naw. I carry a roll of hundred-franc notes. Figure that might get me farther."

Others in the room laughed at Hall's comment and started talking in smaller groups. Meade filled their glasses with red wine.

Riley turned to Crispin. "You know, the physics of flying are truly fascinating. Learning about all those scientists and their discoveries. Newton's Laws of Motion. Coanda's discovery that air bends over a convex surface let 'em design better wings. Bernoulli discovered that pressure decreases as speed increases in fluids, and that includes the air. So that the plane is actually *pulled* up, not held up, by its speed. Lieutenant Crispin?"

"Sorry, old man. I was distracted thinking of those blimps over England."

"They're not blimps," Riley said. "They are dirigibles, with a fixed inner frame. Blimps are just gas bags."

Crispin nodded. "Dirigible? From the French *diriger*, to steer?"

Hall shrugged. "Don't know. They're starting to come out of Belgium in the late afternoon. They can just float on the prevailing wind to England. Save their motors for the last."

Riley stood, raised his glass, and tapped it with his spoon. "Gentlemen! There have been legends in flying. *Icarus* and his father *Dædalus*. But now, Davis, you fly a plane and now you are your own legend." Cheers broke out again for Davis, who toasted them back, and sat to finish his stew.

Hall laughed. "Sure, Davis, you're the Hawk of Hautmont. The Falcon of France."

Crispin looked at Davis, who seemed embarrassed by the attention of the other flyers. "Tell me, Lieutenant Davis, what's it like? Not the mechanics, but the feeling of driving a plane in the air?"

Davis took a slow breath before answering. He spoke softly, "It is magic. Flying is imagination made manifest. I just think where I want to go. And I am there."

"Seems impossible. Like a child's story."

Davis smiled. "It is dreamlike at its best moments. There is no gravity and no time. It is indescribable. You'll see."

Crispin laughed. "Oh, I doubt that."

Lowering his voice, Davis said, "I got new orders when I was waiting for them to patch up my plane. I'm flying you and Meade to England."

Crispin raised his voice. "What?"

"Just listen a minute. Our old Avros are being ferried to England to use as trainers. The two-seater 504s will be perfect for them. It has a speaking tube so it's easy to talk between the two cockpits. Hate to see her go, but the newer German chase planes can outrun her now."

Crispin blinked rapidly. "I'm to fly? With you?"

"Yeah. You both are. Seems you guys are needed in England toot-sweet."

Crispin took a large sip of wine. They finished dinner and walked back to the barracks in silence. When they arrived there, Crispin went directly to his assigned cot, leaned his crutch against the wall, and sat. Meade, who had lagged behind with Hall, walked back to Crispin and sat on the opposite one.

Meade held a bottle of Scotch and two water glasses. "How about a splash?"

"I'd fancy that. Davis tell you?"

Meade poured a generous shot into each glass. "About tomorrow? Yeah."

Taking the glass, Crispin said, "Thank you."

"How's the leg?"

"Tolerable."

Each took a small sip. Crispin spoke into his glass. "My grandmother used to say some people had teeth in their eyes. Stahl had those eyes." Crispin drained his drink in one swallow.

Meade nodded and glanced back at the men in the sitting area. "Try to look sick, in case anyone remembers us." Meade chuckled. "You were in plays in school, weren't you?"

Scowling, Crispin said, "Meade. This is really quite unsettling. You know intimate details of my life as though we were chums, while, in actual fact, I know virtually nothing about you."

"What'd you wanna know? Ask me anything."

Crispin paused a moment. "Married?"

"No."

"Ever been in love?"

Meade poured a bit more into each of their glasses. "Yes." Crispin stared until Meade shrugged. "She was married, then."

"Then? Are you suggesting that she is no longer married?"

Meade answered slowly. "Her husband was killed a few years back."

"Have you seen her since?"

"I sent her a letter of condolence. Never heard back."

Crispin took a small sip. "Hard cheese."

"Is that Scotch taking the edge off the leg?"

"Slightly. Thanks."

"Want some more?"

Extending his glass, Crispin said, "Just a bit. Don't want to tempt the gods tomorrow."

"Get your leg up. Davis told me we won't go until mid-morning. I'll wake you in plenty of time to get ready. Hall said there's a dawn flight, so try to ignore that noise and sleep in if you can."

Crispin handed the empty glass to Meade. "What about you?"

Standing, Meade said, "Seems there's a running poker game. I'm gonna see if these boys are as good as they think they are."

Crispin took off his Sam Browne belt and uniform jacket. He looped both over the small metal bedpost at the head of the cot. He took off his damp boots, pulled a rough black wool blanket over him, exhaled, and found that he was restless.

He leaned up on an elbow and watched Meade and six other Americans at a large round table in the center of the barracks. They were juvenile and loud. Boasting and promising. Threatening and beseeching the god of poker to smile on them. Laughing, slapping cards on the table, and occasionally groaning. Crispin overheard snatches of conversations. Hall said he wanted to go to Tahiti or Moorea, where there was no winter so he would never be cold again. Davis was going back to his family's farm, near San Francisco. Someone wanted to work in his uncle's shoe repair shop. Another wanted to plant his own apple orchard in the state of Washington. When someone asked Meade where he was going after the war, he shrugged and said that he had a small ranch and some land in the Dakotas. No one knew he was *that* Meade, or cared.

Meade was with his tribe. An undisciplined group from a country without a real history. Crispin shook his head, punched the flattened pillow. He folded his hands behind his head and tried not to think of tomorrow, of flying, or of which of the pilots he had met today would not return tomorrow night. He forced his thoughts to the maps that the old man had held for Meade earlier that day. Crispin admired the antiquity of the documents and the intellect underlying them.

Crispin turned and laughed at himself. The shouts of the card players and his racing thoughts pushed sleep away. He found his journal and entered the numerous aviation terms the Americans had spewed. He returned the book to his jacket pocket, stood, checked his pockets for francs, pulled on his boots, and limped toward the poker game.

Chapter № 20

Monday
October 30, 1916
Le Bourget Aerodrome, Paris, France

Before dawn, Crispin pressed the blanket against his ears to muffle the clatter of the pilots stumbling out of the barracks. He returned to a restless sleep populated by mud-crusted ravens and flying gargoyles. One raven pecked at his own back, cracked off the dark shell of mud, and became a dusty yellow canary, which marched back and forth over tinned wires. A hand opened the latch of the bell-shaped cage and placed a gas mask, no larger then a thimble, on the floor of the cage.

The canary flew past the hand into the red sky. Crispin tossed on his cot. Trench rats clad in dress uniforms moved toward him in parade formation. The blanket brushed against his cheek. He swatted at his face, bolted up, stumbled, and grabbed the iron frame. Panting, he looked around the barracks. He was alone.

He fell back onto the bed and checked his wristwatch. He blinked and rubbed his eyes. Just a tick after six. As Crispin ran his hands through his sweat-soaked hair, Meade returned from the shower room with a towel around his waist. Meade dressed quickly. Tucking in his shirttail, Meade said, "Didn't mean to wake you when I left. You were sawing logs."

"I beg your pardon?"

"Snoring. Probably dreaming about your winnings from last night. Not bad for a beginner." Meade cinched his belt, pulled the map pouch from under the thin mattress, slipped the cord over his head, and tugged on his sweater.

"Are we leaving now?"

Meade shrugged. "No. Thought I'd go to the hangar and see if anything has changed."

"I'll perform my ablutions and join you shortly."

"Oh, Professor. After you turned in, Hall found a couple new razors for us. Left one on the sink for you."

"Very kind of you, Meade."

When Crispin arrived at the hangar, wearing both his greatcoat and the leather duster over his uniform, Meade and Davis were near the center of the hangar, leaning on a large workbench littered with hand tools and studying a silk flight map of France. A paper map of Britain was folded next to it. In the center of the hangar, three mechanics were working on a yellow Avro biplane. The tart smells of petrol and varnish were soon mixed with the complex aroma from the dirt floor that had once been farmland.

As Crispin walked past a table and two benches that could serve for a picnic in some park, under better circumstances, he peered at the plane. When he was near Davis, Crispin leaned on the crutch and said, "It is so much smaller than one would have imagined."

Meade put his hands on his hips and took a harder look at the craft. "Yeah. You could park two, maybe three of these on a basketball court and not even hit the net."

Davis looked up. "Don't sell her short. She's a peach to fly. Beautifully built. Oak struts for wing strength and framed in ash. Come here, let me show you where we're going. North to Amiens, fuel up, and get your gear from the train station." Davis turned the map toward Crispin, pulled the pencil from his pocket, and tapped each of the cities he had circled. "We'll fly this dogleg to the channel to avoid Archie."

Crispin turned to Meade. "German gun emplacements." Meade nodded quickly.

Davis tapped the blue on the map. "Jump the channel from here, just north of Calais. Strait of Dover is the shortest path over the water, only about twenty miles. Fly to Hendon, just north of London. I'm trading in two hundred pounds of bombs for one of you. Unless you have bricks in your bags, we'll have fifteen to twenty minutes to spare."

Meade watched him tapping the blue of the English Channel with the tip of his pencil. "What is it?"

His breath fogged the crisp air as Davis said, "The water. It's fine for bathing, but I hate to fly over it." He started ticking off the issues on his fingers. "There is no orientation, no clue where you are except the compass and your calculations. The reflection of the sun can be blinding. There are no trees to give you wind indication, just whitecaps. By then the weather is so nasty you shouldn't be flying anyway." Davis stopped counting. "Don't even let me think about trying to swim in my combination suit, or how cold that water is."

Meade laughed. "Any other good news?"

Looking sheepish, Davis said, "Café's open. You ready for breakfast?"

Crispin shivered and grimaced. "I'll wait for you here."

Davis looked concerned. "Did you get seasick on the boat over?"

Sighing, Crispin said, "Profoundly so."

Davis clapped him on the shoulder. "Then eat a light meal. Bread and a little milk. I was about to send Tran to bring back an omelet and a pot of coffee so I can keep working here. I'll have him walk you over."

Crispin glanced at the mechanics swarming on the plane. Two were on ladders stitching patches to the fabric. Another was tightening wires between the wings. A fourth man was replacing some metal canisters on the engine. "Is there anything we can do to assist?"

Davis paused. "Are you any good with a paint brush?"

Crispin looked at the canary-yellow craft speckled with pale canvas patches and nodded. "Just tell me what to do."

Meade said, "Count me in."

Davis pointed to the wings. "Paint all the fresh canvas patches. Go heavy on the seams."

Crispin's eyebrows elevated. "You want to paint it? At this temperature?"

"They thinned the paint so it'll dry fast, even in the cold. It's not just for looks. Seals the stitches. Makes it fly faster. Reduces the air drag."

Meade balanced on a ladder and painted the raw canvas on the upper wings and tail while Crispin painted the patches to the areas he could reach from the ground. When Tran returned with a large tray covered with a towel, they put aside their brushes. Crispin sipped the milk, forced down some bread, and tried not to watch as Meade and Davis wolfed down glistening cheese omelets and steaming coffee.

Shortly after ten, the painting had been completed and the mechanics had finished with the repair to the engine. Davis ran his fingertip over the edge of the two-bladed wooden propeller, inspected the hub, and patted the bolts. "Roll her out, boys." Patches of yellow paint sparkled on the wings as two mechanics pushed the plane to the edge of the hangar and began pumping fuel from a fifty-gallon drum.

Meade wiped the last of the yellow paint from his hands with a rag soaked in turpentine and looked past the plane. "How much of that field do you need to take off?"

"Only about twenty yards with a modest headwind. Landing the Avro is a dream. Stall speed is twenty-five miles per hour. You can come in really slow before you touch grass."

Crispin straightened his tie and asked, "Anything else we can do to assist?"

"Once we're up there, keep your head on a swivel. If you see anything, yell. And hang on."

Meade and Davis watched the sky in a way that Crispin envied. Flyers and outdoorsmen had some connection to the world that was beyond him.

Davis pointed to the horizon. "Pressure's going up. That line of clouds to the north shouldn't develop into much. Most of the weather is to the east of us, so it's time to tootle off."

Crispin and Meade followed Davis into the hangar and watched as he shrugged out of his overcoat, dropped it on a bench, stepped into the legs of his combination suit, tugged it up, and slipped into the arms. "Your suits and helmets are over on that bench. The mechanic will bring gloves out to the plane."

Meade took off his wool coat and leather duster, dropped them on the bench. He shifted his holster from his back to his side, wormed into his flight suit, and buttoned it. Meade rolled his fedora into a tube and slipped it into his briefcase. He held his hand out for Crispin's uniform cap.

Crispin hesitated.

Davis turned and stared at Crispin. "What's the problem?"

"I can not wear a flying suit. I would be out of uniform in a combat area."

Frowning, Davis said, "It's too cold up there for just a coat."

Crispin stood straighter. "I managed quite well in an open motorcycle for hours yesterday."

Davis shook his head, walked close to Crispin, and lowered his voice. "Look, it's thirty-seven degrees Fahrenheit now. The temperature drops three degrees for every thousand feet we climb. I hope to run at three thousand feet. So, you'll be sitting in a hurricane-force wind that's below freezing. It only gets worse if we go higher or faster. So, suit up." Davis laughed as he punched Crispin in the shoulder. "Who is gonna see you anyway?"

Crispin cleared his throat and handed his cap to Meade, who pushed it into the briefcase and latched it. As he slipped his swollen leg into the suit, Crispin said, "I see. We could leave the dusters for others, I suppose. But I do need to retain my uniform coat."

Once Crispin had buttoned his suit, he removed the belt from his greatcoat and turned to Meade. "Want me to bundle your coat as well?"

"Sure. Thanks." Crispin folded the coats together and cinched the belt around them into a tight parcel.

Davis laughed, took the coats, and handed them tattered leather helmets. "Say, you boys look like natural born flyers."

Crispin glanced at Meade and laughed. "I rather thought we resembled tots in those horrid snow suits. Barely able to waddle about."

They pulled on the helmets and goggles. Davis saw Crispin rub the scratched lenses. "Here's some gum, fellas. Chew it during the flight. It keeps your ears open."

Meade took a stick from Davis. "Thanks."

Shaking his head, Crispin said, "Thank you. I do not chew gum."

"Okay, if your ears hurt, swallow and yawn. Or yell."

Crispin suppressed a smile. "Certainly."

Davis turned toward the Avro. "Okay, let's get this show on the road." He walked to the center of the field where the Avro shone in the bright sun. He went to the left side of the plane, held the rear strut, and carefully put his feet into the metal foot holes in the fabric fuselage. He hoisted himself up, slid into the rear cockpit, and threw the bundled coats into the foot well of the forward cockpit. Davis looked down at them. "Meade, put Crispin in front of you. And don't kick a hole in my plane."

Crispin looked at the foot hole but did not move.

Meade whispered, "You okay?"

"I have to be. Orders, you know."

"Davis is good. I asked around."

Crispin watched a tall mechanic pull the wood wedges away from the wheels and carry the chocks back to the hangar. Glancing at Davis, Crispin said, "Yes, I see that. He's sharp as mustard. I just don't fancy myself in the air."

Meade looked at Crispin. "Grab onto the struts and take it slow."

After Crispin was seated, Meade handed up the crutch. As he squirmed in behind Crispin, he hit his elbows on either side of the cockpit and swore. Wide leather belts were nailed to the wood frame. Both men quickly buckled them over their laps.

Just as Meade and Crispin had settled into the cockpit, a big-bellied mechanic came to the right side of the plane carrying a large stained canvas sack, which he handed to Meade. He held up fur-lined boots which

Davis took. Meade opened the sack and pulled out an oilcloth the size of a small blanket, which he held over his head for Davis to see. "What's this for?"

Davis shouted to them. "Ought to be two in there! Wrap them around your feet and legs. And shove the coats deep into the foot well."

When Meade took a heavy canvas pouch with a brass buckle and a short leather belt at each corner from the mechanic, Crispin said, "That's our communications pack." Meade buckled the top belts to a spar inside the cockpit to his right. Crispin opened the bag and examined the contents. Message banners, grease pencil. Hand torch and signal flare packet. Binoculars. Crispin turned to Davis. "You do have a wireless transmitter, don't you?"

"No. They stripped it off last night to put into one of the newer spotters. Shouldn't need it. Our gunners have been advised of our flight."

The mechanic handed Davis thick fur-lined gloves as Meade gave well-worn gloves with long cuffs from the sack to Crispin and put a pair on his own lap. He held the empty sack over the edge for the mechanic.

Davis laughed. "Keep it. That's for Crispin. I can't fly if his breakfast is on my goggles." Davis suddenly turned to the mechanic and shouted, "Alice! Kiss my Alice."

The mechanic slapped his head in mock astonishment and whistled in the direction of the hangar. The small brown dog sped to the mechanic, who lifted her to Davis, who kissed her forehead and said, "For luck."

The mechanic held Alice up for a kiss from Meade and Crispin, both of whom obliged. The mechanic returned Alice to the grass. At the sharp whistle of a slim man in the hangar, she raced to his side.

Davis gave a quick salute to his mechanic. "*En l'air!*" He said, "That thing that looks like a funnel by your elbow. It's a speaking tube. Once we get in the air, I won't be able to hear you unless you yell into it." Crispin and Meade nodded.

Once Davis had seated his goggles, he offered a thumbs-up. The mechanic shouted, "*Coupe, plein gaz!*"

Davis nodded and turned a fuel valve. "*Coupe, plein gaz.*"

The mechanic dragged the propeller through two rotations to suck the mixture of gas and air into the engine. The mechanic grunted and shouted from the front of the plane, "*Contact, reduisez!*"

Davis answered, "*Contact, reduisez.*" He snapped a switch as the mechanic pulled down hard on the propeller. A balloon of blue-gray smoke enveloped them. A bone-shaking roar came from the exhaust tubes on both sides of the fuselage. The plane quivered and started rolling. It bounced and jostled. After the tail came up off the ground, the front wheels lifted. The ride smoothed. They were racing into the wind, directly toward a stand of trees.

As the biplane climbed, Crispin looked at his wristwatch and noted that it was 11:16. He calculated that if he could think about something else for an hour, he might not vomit.

Davis pushed the throttle to full power. Crispin's head slammed into Meade's chin. He shouted over his shoulder, "Sorry, old man!"

Suddenly, Crispin's head weighed four times what it used to and his chest was being shoved into his stomach. As soon as he became accustomed to the sensation of climbing, the plane leveled. When nothing unpleasant occurred, he breathed again and peeked at the clouds over Amiens. They looked different from this altitude. Like dots and dashes of cotton wool.

Davis banked the airplane into a slow turn to the east.

Crispin lunged for the tube. "What'swrong? Why are we going back to the airfield?"

"We're not. I'm gonna show you Paris!"

Chapter № 21

Monday
October 30, 1916
North of Paris, France

Davis continued the Avro's slow turn. Heavy clouds churned on the eastern horizon. Crispin pointed and shouted into the tube. "How far?"

Davis shouted back, "The thunderheads? They're over Champagne, about two hundred miles."

Crispin looked at the gauges and dials in front of him. The compass was shifting and showed due south. The silver needle on the altimeter hovered over the mark showing: two thousand feet. The dial went to twenty thousand. One dial counted revolutions of the engine and another showed airspeed. A foot-long tube of glass, with an air bubble in it, arched across the bottom of the panel. When they banked, the bubble shifted. He guessed that it imparted something of their angle to the pilot. A vertical glass tube at eye level seemed to be the fuel indicator.

Davis slowly dropped to one thousand feet and leveled the airplane. "Eiffel Tower on your right. I'm gonna fly almost even with its top." Crispin looked at the small pointed top of the tallest structure in the world and twisted back to hold the sight as they passed it. Davis held the airplane level and followed the Seine toward the island where Notre Dame Cathedral towered.

Meade pulled the binoculars from the communications pack and examined the cathedral. He held the binoculars in front of Crispin. "Want to take a look?"

Crispin waved him away, pulled his scratched goggles down around his neck, and peered over the edge past their wing. The city looked like a flea circus. Small matchboxes of carriages and automobiles moved on the streets. Insects dressed as miniature humans had fly specks for dogs. Tiny horses pulled carts made of matchsticks. The city plan was evident from this altitude. Small districts were connected by wide avenues. Squares where five or six streets converged were scattered throughout the city like starfish on a beach.

The wind stung Crispin's face as he looked over the edge of the cockpit. After they passed the cathedral, Davis began a turn to the right. Crispin pulled back into the sheltered cockpit and put his goggles in place.

The compass swung to the west, and moved again until they were going due north. Davis shouted, "In five minutes, she'll get up to thirty-five hundred feet." Meade put the glasses back in the canvas bag.

Paris was now behind them. Below them was a patchwork quilt of brown fields. Ahead, pale buildings clustered into small villages. Crispin searched for the plane's shadow among the irregular shadows cast by the thin clouds through which they flew. He found it, trailing and then passing a train traveling north. Soon the shadow became a mere dot as they continued their gradual climb.

The compass bobbled and shifted to the north north-east. Crispin was cold, and the air was getting colder. Beads of water from the clouds had frozen into pellets of ice that slid off the windscreen. There was a new sound. Crispin lifted the earflap on his helmet. The wires between the wings were ringing, like a harp. The airspeed dial in their cockpit had fogged over. Crispin leaned toward the tube. "How fast? Can you tell me?"

Davis took a moment before responding, "Almost eighty miles an hour."

Over the left wing, the slope of the Somme valley began and the river meandered west to the sea. Scattered clouds broke the symmetry of the landscape and soon grew into a thick blanket.

After a few minutes, they dropped down through an open spot in a layer of clouds and the miniature landscape of towns and villages took form. Columns of tin soldiers moved up ribbons of road.

When the plane rocked and slid sideways, Crispin grabbed the edge of the cockpit. The plane pitched forward as the sound thundered past them.

Davis leveled the aircraft and shouted into the tube. "Hobbits!"

Meade hit Crispin on the shoulder. "What's he saying?"

Crispin turned sideways and shouted. "Hobbits! Troops call the German Howitzer cannons 'hobbits'! Haven't the foggiest why. Nasty gun, that. Pounds itself into the ground as it fires."

Crispin looked to the right, where a plume of smoke swirled up from the ground. As the smoke drifted away, he saw charred trees. There were ruts in the land as though a race of giants had driven their wagons over it. He gasped when he recognized the turns and bends of ruts matched the inked trench lines on the situation map in the command bunker.

The hum of the engine changed to a growl as Davis started to descend toward a meadow flanked by tents. Canvas painted with black and green patches had been nailed over wood frames, 50 feet square and 15 feet high, to make hangars. A large command tent had been placed beyond the last hangar. To the left of the field, two rows of six-man tents served as the barracks. Crispin looked at his watch: 12:42.

They landed and jolted to a stop. A mechanic walked out to them and gestured some instructions to Davis, who throttled up again and bounced the plane to the west of the larger of the two hangars. Davis shut off the engine. The mechanic ran under the wings and shoved chocks on either side of the two front wheels.

Davis pulled off his helmet and goggles and left them in the plane. He hopped out of the plane and stomped his feet on the grass as though he were shedding snow from boots. He looked up at his passengers and shouted. "There's always food and hot coffee in the HQ tent. What are you waiting for?"

Crispin and Meade unbuckled their restraint belts and unstrapped their helmets. Crispin leaned forward. "Can you manage to squeeze out first, Meade?"

"Anything wrong?"

"No, just want a moment to get my bearings."

Meade pulled out the crutch and threw it away from the plane. He tossed his briefcase after it. "Sure, I'll wait for you at the bottom."

Meade crawled out, dropped from the last step to the ground, and stumbled. He got his balance. He waited to equip Crispin and then followed Davis.

Another flyer in a leather combi suit called to Davis from the hangar. Davis turned to Meade and pointed to the largest tent. "You guys go ahead. I'll catch up in a minute."

Meade held the musty tent flap for Crispin, who stopped in the doorway to look at the busy soldiers at desks along the far end of the tent. After a brief glance at their flying suits, the soldiers returned to their work. Meade stopped at a table near the entrance. The cold buffet consisted of plates of sliced beef, cheddar cheese, and a basket of crusty rolls. Coffee steamed in a glass carafe on a metal stand over a candle. A tray of mugs was next to it. Meade poured two mugs of coffee. Crispin motioned "no".

Davis came in, waved to one of the officers, ran a hand through his mussed hair, and took the offered cup from Meade. "The guy I was talking to just got in from the coast, near Dunkirk. Wind is calm now. We'll plan to leave about four when it picks up."

Meade took a sip and squinted at the heat. "Good. That'll give us time to get our luggage from the station."

Crispin suspended his review of the soldiers at work and looked at Davis. "Was it a crosswind? Was that why we weren't flying due north?"

Davis blew over the top of the mug and said, "Yeah. If we flew just by the compass, we'd have ended up ten miles off course."

"Thank you. I thought I had calculated that correctly."

Davis smiled. "You did fine up there. Get something to eat."

Crispin forced a smile and picked up a roll as Davis and Meade constructed thick sandwiches. Davis walked into the sun with his food and coffee. Meade and Crispin followed. Halfway to the benches at the gaping mouth of the hangar, Crispin pointed to a fifty-gallon oil drum in the sun at the corner of the hangar. "I'll take a rest there, if you don't mind. Make a few notes."

Davis motioned to the bench. "Sure. We'll be over here if you need anything."

"My cap. If you please, Meade."

After Meade returned the cap to Crispin he pulled out his fedora and slapped it against the leg of the suit. He tugged it down onto his head.

Davis sat down harder than he intended and splashed coffee on the browned grass. Putting the mug beside him, he motioned for Meade to sit. "Take a load off. We're gonna be here a while."

After he placed his coffee on the bench, Meade stood facing Davis and stretched as the sun warmed his back. Looking at a battered Ford Model A flatbed truck, Meade asked, "Whose truck?"

"Why?"

"I can drive over and get the bags." He tipped his head toward the mechanics. "They don't look like they need one more chore. And you ought to rest up."

Grinning at Meade and squinting as the sun hit his eyes, Davis said, "I'm fine." Davis ignored Meade, who was looking at his shaking hands, finished his sandwich in two bites, and took a long drink of his cooled coffee.

"Thought Crispin might want a distraction."

Davis unbuttoned his heavy flight suit to the waist and pulled a small packet of letter paper from the breast pocket of his uniform jacket. "Good idea. He seems a bit rattled by aviation."

Gesturing toward Crispin, Meade said, "But he managed it without a whimper."

Davis unfolded the paper on the bench. Meade asked, "More flight calculations?"

"Naw. Letter home. Add to it when I have a minute."

Meade watched the mechanic looking at a rack with a dozen keys on it as he asked Davis, "Where's home? Wasn't it near San Francisco?"

Grinning, Davis said, "Rutherford. Just north of the city. My dad and I have an orchard there."

Nodding, Meade said, "I'll be in San Francisco over the next few years. Got an oil field south of there, in Coalinga. We're trying out some new pumps. Maybe I could buy you dinner in the city on one of those trips."

"Don't get down there too much. But if you're in Rutherford, look me up. Ask anyone where the Davis orchard is."

"Apples?"

"Plums. Just my dad and me. While I'm over here, he's working at Mrs. Niebaum's winery. Hired hands tend our trees." He paused. "He thinks we can plant a small vineyard on the steeper hills where the trees won't grow. Every time I can, I go down to Bordeaux. Talk to 'em about how they plant and trellis their vines. If he's right that the cabernet grape will grow there, we'll replace the whole orchard with a vineyard."

The mechanic sauntered over holding a key on a dirty leather fob. Davis took it and handed it to Meade, who finished his coffee quickly.

Reaching for Meade's cup, Davis said, "I'll take it back."

"Thanks."

Meade started the truck and drove over to Crispin, where he left it running and got out. "Coming with me to the station?"

Without answering, Crispin reached toward Meade. "Your penknife. May I borrow it, just for a moment?"

Meade pulled his Buck knife from his pocket and handed it to Crispin, who opened it and carefully excised two pages from his journal. "I thought that inasmuch as you have shared your knowledge on the art of mapmaking, I could return the favor."

Taking the pages, Meade asked, "What's this?"

"A glossary of all the words on the face of your map. The text. You already know the few words on the reverse."

Meade looked at the pages.

Glossary for Meade (medu)
æt - at, near, upon, with, before, next to, toward
bēam - wooden ship
betwuh - between, in the midst of
ceaster - city, fort, castle, town, heaven, hell
cyning - king, ruler, God
dēormōd - bold, courageous
dryht - men, nation, body of retainers, people
ēadnes - inner peace, joy, ease
ēaststæđ - east bank of a stream
flōc - flounder
hafela - head
hord - treasure, hoard
metod - fate, god
micel - big, great, large, intense, large, many
Michæl - Michael
ne - not
ođberan - to bear away, carry off
ofer - over, beyond, above, across
on - in, on, upon
ond - and
randhæbbend - shield bearer, warrior
rēfmæd - reeve's meadow
tō - to, into, toward
twā - two
under - under, among, in the presence of
yđwōrigende - wandering the waves
ymbfæstnung - monument, tomb

Meade held the pages in front of Crispin's face. "What am I supposed to do with this?"

"It is the vocabulary you will need to translate the map's text in alpha order."

"And the two words. Didn't you call them 'the bookends'?"

He opened his journal and turned the page toward Meade, who saw the carefully printed letters: PQTXLM and QTSH. "I made a note of them to ponder."

"And?"

Crispin shrugged. "They remain an enigma."

"Professor, I need you to translate the whole thing."

Looking at the Avro, Crispin said, "Yes, but I really hate flying, if the truth were to be told."

"You did fine. I heard Davis say so."

"They seem to have the nerves of fishes, those flyers. But it is well-near impossible for me to consider mounting the foot holes in that craft again."

Meade narrowed his eyes. "Knock that off. I need you in England."

"I know that, Meade. But–"

Meade looked at the paper. "What's this *medu* thing at the top of the list?"

"It's your name in Old English. Mead, by definition, is a honeyed ale. They make it by–"

Meade carefully folded the pages and slipped them into his shirt pocket. "Thanks, you can explain this to me in England."

"Meade. I just can't. Look at me. I couldn't even fire up my pipe my hand was shaking so. Took me ever so long to write that simple glossary. Longer yet to place it in alphabetical order."

"It was cold up there."

Crispin looked away. "Not that cold."

"I can't leave you here. One way or another, you're getting on that plane."

Sitting taller, Crispin asked, "You are not threatening me, are you?"

"I don't threaten." Meade forced a smile. "When we get to the station, do you want some of the Calvados that Madeline gave us?"

Crispin looked at his hands. "Fool's courage? Thank you, no."

Peeling off his flying suit and leaving it next to the drum, Meade said, "Well, at least come with me to get the bags from the station." Crispin slid off the oil drum and stood looking at the truck. Meade helped him out of his suit.

Meade climbed into the driver's seat. "Hop in." Crispin tugged his uniform jacket into place and crawled into the cab of the truck. He sat silently as Meade drove along the outskirts of town. The windows of the truck had long been broken out and the wind whistled over the doorframe. When Crispin slipped his hands into his breeches pockets for warmth, he smiled when his knuckle scuffed against the limestone pebble, no larger than a collar button, that his mother had given him while they were still in India. He almost heard her voice when she gave him the pebble which she had kept in her small jewelry box, saying "Keep this bit of England in your pocket and me in your heart wherever fortune takes you." It was his good luck charm and anchor to the earth.

When Meade accelerated past the lane leading to the station, Crispin pointed at the street. "Meade?"

"Yeah, I know. I missed it." He turned onto the Rue de l'Oratoire. Homes on both sides of the street had been burned; only stalagmites of scorched brick walls remained. The acrid smell stung Crispin's nose.

At the end of the street, Meade braked hard and stopped. Crispin opened the door and craned his neck to see the top of the two towers wedging into the sky. Moments later, they were standing at the massive hand-carved doors. Crispin tugged at the center door. It did not move.

"Wait for me here." Meade ran down the steps and along the side of the cathedral.

Crispin looked at the figures carved in deep relief in the gothic archway above the door and read the tableau of the Day of Judgment as easily as one of his ancient texts. He examined the carvings from old scripture for a congregation that could not read in a time before books were printed by press.

Meade called softly from the corner of the cathedral, "This way."

Crispin followed him along the stone walkway along the side wall. The door to the south transept was open. Crispin snapped off his cap. Meade called after him, "I'll be back in about ten minutes. The labyrinth is octagonal. About a hundred feet to a side."

With an impatient frown, Crispin said, "I am certain I will find it."

"It's black and white. Almost hidden by the other mosaics."

Crispin nodded to Meade and entered into the dim cathedral. In a few steps, he was at the base of the sanctuary. The tap of his crutch was the only sound he heard. He stopped, looked up at the high altar, and let his eyes adjust to the dimness. The gold leaf on the statues glowed, and the ornate cross seemed to shimmer from the light cast by the small candles in ruby glass cups. Crispin turned and looked down the massive nave toward the locked entrance. Slashes of blue-gray smoke from the votive candles were illuminated by the daylight, which entered through the voids where the stained glass windows had been removed. Crispin shivered and inhaled deeply. He closed his eyes and inhaled again. Smoke and the scent of hot candle wax mixed with centuries of incense into a perfume that masked the stink of battle.

He turned, gazed at a tinted statue of Saint John the Baptist, and heard a soft scuffing to his right. A sandaled priest in a hooded robe was walking toward him. Crispin started to greet the priest, who walked past him as though he were invisible. The man stepped into the entrance of the labyrinth, which Crispin had not seen. The priest walked the twisting path in slow, measured footsteps. Crispin began walking on the white tiles and found himself at a dead end within a few paces. He looked at the priest in astonishment. The priest leaned down and touched the black marble where he was standing. Crispin looked down and saw that he was on the white border, not the path.

The priest spoke softly in French. "Walk the path. God won't let you get lost."

Crispin started again and soon abandoned anticipation of how the path would turn or what he would feel or find. He trusted that the path would convey him to the inevitable center and then return him to the world.

By the time he had exited the labyrinth, the priest had gone, and he was alone. As he walked toward the door, the tip of his crutch snagged on the protruding base of a column. The crutch fell behind him, he hopped two steps, and clung to a chiseled stone column. He straightened himself, faced the stone, and pressed his palms into it. He leaned his forehead against it and let the cold stone draw the poison of the war from him like a poultice.

When Crispin left the cathedral, he squinted at the brightness and put on his cap.

He joined Meade, who was transferring their bags from the cab to the rear deck of the truck. Meade tugged on the brim of his hat. "Ready?"

Crispin nodded.

Meade drove quickly and silently. Just after passing the sentry at the aerodrome, Crispin turned to Meade. "May I ask you something?"

"Sure."

"You have walked it. Am I correct?"

"Yeah."

"You knew how important it was for me, didn't you?"

Meade nodded.

Taking a deep breath, Crispin asked, "At the Verne estate, when Michel told us about that woman visiting the labyrinth–"

Meade's knuckles went white on the steering wheel. "What about it?"

"When did you tell her about the labyrinth?"

Meade did not look at Crispin. "When I was a surveyor for the railroad and she was married to a French Marquis who was rich enough to name a town for her. It was a long time ago." Meade braked at the hangar and was out of the cab before it had stopped rocking.

Davis trotted up to the truck, grabbed the bags, hefted each bag a second time, and handed them to the mechanic. As the mechanic loaded the bags into the Avro, Davis said, "Time to suit up, fellas. I left some gum by your goggles in the plane. We're going higher this trip, so you'll need it."

Crispin got out of the truck and stumbled. He steadied himself on the crutch and limped toward the hangar.

Davis looked at Crispin. "Did you have anything to eat besides that roll?" Crispin shook his head, and Davis said, "Eat a couple more while you suit up."

Meade turned and started to walk away from the hangar. "Go on, Professor. I'll get you something."

Crispin ate two more rolls as they got into their flight suits before climbing into the cramped cockpit. He called to Meade, who held the crutch on the ground. "Can't see how that will fit. Best you leave it here." Meade passed the crutch off to a mechanic and climbed into his seat.

Davis shouted to them as he slid into his cockpit. "Don't worry if it feels soggy when we lift from the field! We've got a lot more weight and fuel!"

Meade and Crispin both gave the thumbs-up signal they had adopted from Davis. As the pilot repeated the earlier protocol to start the engine, Meade shoved their hats into his briefcase, and they buckled their helmets. After starting the plane, Davis jolted over the grass, turned the craft into the wind, and gave it full throttle. The aircraft lunged forward. The tufts of grass passed under them faster and faster. The tail of the plane lifted, but the two front wheels seemed glued to the ground. There was a quick rattle and a ping when the wires between the wings tightened as the craft became airborne.

Crispin cinched his helmet strap one notch tighter and gnawed on the chewing gum. He counted the spotty clouds on the horizon to steady his stomach. As they went west, a patch of ground fog above the river engulfed them. Davis brought the plane up out of it. At a thousand feet, Crispin watched the fog below them sliding down the riverbank and spreading over the fields like cream over porridge. Crispin followed the train tracks leading into the fog, close to where he calculated Amiens would be hiding. At the center of his calculation, the spire and the two towers of the cathedral poked above the flat tide of fog.

The revolution counter shifted from fifteen hundred to seventeen-fifty and then to eighteen hundred rpm, where it stayed.

A light wind had come out of the east. Now, it was stronger than before. Davis turned the plane slightly to stay on course. At two thousand feet, the sky above them was gray. Crispin saw only the enormity of the foggy clouds, which billowed up from the earth and surrounded them. On the windscreen, small beads of water formed. The wind blew them over his head as though there were some invisible shield protecting him.

Crispin shivered. He lost the sense of speed and orientation that the ground provided. He started to breathe deeply and heavily, his shoulders heaving under the heavy flight suit. He leaned forward in the cockpit. All he heard was the droning of the engine.

The sound changed as the Avro banked slightly to the right and climbed. The gray clouds brightened to the whiteness of light fog. Then it became brighter still. There was a shimmering iridescence in front of them, a spot of intense brightness with a rainbow surrounding it. The millions of water droplets captured the sun and magnified it, threw it to another million droplets that magnified it further, and shot it through prisms.

Crispin blinked. The rainbow still surrounded him. He pulled down the scratched goggles and looked again. The world of white was edged with colors as pure as a child's paint box on Christmas morning.

He shut his eyes, but it remained bright. Magnesium and phosphorus bright. Flare at night bright. He pulled the goggles over his eyes again. The plane climbed higher, and the cloud tops below them became a field of white, an arctic landscape, and then a gently undulating white ocean under a deep blue sky.

To the east, thunderclouds loomed. Cloud balloons of white and gray became oversized mushrooms and then stretched into anvil tops. Then the tops sheered away, and the clouds looked like the stout marble columns of a Greek temple.

Davis spoke into the tube. "I'm going to stay just above the clouds. Harder to see us that way. Might be bumpy but it's safer."

Crispin shouted. "I thought you didn't want to go over three thousand feet."

"I didn't. But I've got to manage the weather and stay invisible."

The Avro was skimming just above the top of the flat layer of clouds at five thousand feet. When small holes appeared in the clouds, Davis dropped through them to verify locations. Crispin played Gulliver over the miniature landscape and let his imagination follow their journey on the living map of the earth. He looked west toward England but saw only lower clouds and an offshore fog over the English Channel obscuring his vision.

Far to the west of the river marshes of Amiens, the fog dissipated. The Somme River made a clear path for them to follow to Abbeville. Migrating birds flew below them in wedges.

At Abbeville, some ten miles before the river joined the ocean in the Bay of Somme, Davis turned due north for Calais. Crispin looked at his watch. Davis had turned five minutes before he expected it. As they flew north, two more large estuaries emerged on the coast. He consulted his map and confirmed the closest city to be Boulogne-sur-Mer, some ten to fifteen miles to the west, which made Calais just that far to the North. They flew over Calais and then up the coast toward Dunkirk. Crispin used the binoculars to look below them. He checked the compass heading before shouting into the tube. "The wind is pushing the trees due west!"

Davis banked west, and they picked up speed although the engine's tone did not change. As Crispin looked down, the land slid out from underneath them. Then he saw a thin white line of surf and knew that it was grinding at the round stones on the French shoreline. Davis yelled into the tube, "Keep your eyes open!"

The ocean appeared flat and solid. The Avro burrowed up into the high clouds. When they emerged, Davis cruised along rounded cloud tops in the bright blue sky.

Crispin looked at the altimeter. It read: eighty-five hundred feet. The water on the windscreen had frozen into dots and fused to the glass as hundreds of prisms. He scanned the sky above him quickly before he turned to Meade. "Keep a sharp eye above us and behind. I'll watch the margin of the clouds."

Chapter № 22

Monday
October 30, 1916
West of Calais, France

Crispin made a rapid inspection of the rounded tops of the heavy clouds. Vapor and wisps tangled into an undulating blanket, hiding the earth and all that was familiar. He designed a search pattern, a mental grid, and methodically scanned the top of the clouds. Starting at the far left, from cockpit to horizon and then back. Shifting slightly to the right with each sweep until every cloud had been inspected to the horizon on his far right. Again and again. Routine. He was the organized trained spotter. Disciplined. Focused on his task. He felt Meade twist to look behind them but kept to his own drill.

Minute after minute, until minutes had no meaning, Crispin was the sentinel on duty. Squinting into the brightness of the sun, low on the western sky, was like staring at a candle's flame. The top of the clouds spiraled up, rolled over, and became vapor again.

A cloud darker than others interrupted the pattern. Almost halfway to the horizon, slightly to the right. When the mounded cloud became darker still, Crispin pointed toward it. "There—"

Davis shoved the stick forward. The Avro dropped. Just as the wispy tops of the clouds started to cover the windscreen, the dark cloud became a mound of forest green and brown. Meade grabbed the rim of the cockpit. "No! It's a mountain!"

As the Avro plunged into the invisibility of the clouds, Crispin shook his head. "Camouflage! It's a Zeppelin!"

"Naw. They're silver."

"Gray below. Painted on top!" Crispin shouted into the tube, "How far away do you make her?"

Davis answered, "We're about a mile off its left side."

"Blast. They are going to England, aren't they?"

Davis did not seem to hear Crispin and yelled, "Cripe, we could have run right into it! Good job!"

Crispin's attention was riveted forward. Somewhere in that bank of white lurked the black sky rider from German folk tales. If it caught their scent, it would attack. It was already stalking along the pathway to inflict night terrors on England.

Davis leveled the airplane and tapped the tube. "Boys, I think we can take him, if you're game."

Twisting to see if Davis was kidding, Meade shouted, "We don't stand a chance!"

Davis shrugged. "They're not shooting at us."

Crispin leaned over to the tube and shouted, "We have the advantage and–"

Meade grabbed Crispin's shoulder and yanked him away from the tube. "Are you nuts? We don't even have a machine gun."

"We have a bomb. I saw the mechanic load it. A ten-pounder."

Meade shouted at Crispin. "A bomb! They will cut us to ribbons!"

"Not unless they see us. Didn't you listen to the pilots? Zeppelins have two blind spots. They can't see behind them or directly above them."

Davis called. "We can drop our egg on them and still make England for dinner."

Crispin did not hesitate. "We must have a go at it." Meade grinned and clapped him on the shoulder.

Davis plotted a new east-northeast vector and turned the Avro onto the invisible trail. After Davis verified the compass reading, he pushed the throttle to its maximum. The burst of speed pushed Crispin back into Meade. Davis leaned down to the tube. "I'll double back in the clouds. Got to do it now as they are thinning to the west. When we're directly behind it, I'll turn and climb to sixteen thousand. I'll swoop down over its back. You drop the bomb."

Grabbing the wood bracing in front of him, Crispin tried to remember the technical ramblings of Riley and the other pilots the prior evening. He saw from the dial in front of him that they were flying at nine thousand feet already. The frigid air felt thin.

Davis completed his calculations and yelled into the tube. "Its going to take a good ten minutes of climbing to get up to sixteen thousand, so that's eight more minutes of flying before we can turn! It's gonna be cold and hard to breathe."

Meade asked, "Do you want me to throw out our bags? Lighten the plane?"

"No! Might hit the tail."

After five minutes inside the clouds, Davis gently nosed up to the ragged upper edge. All three looked around quickly. Davis dropped down like a cautious rabbit.

"There, that way." Crispin yelled, pointing. They were miles away from it. Only a thin slice of the dark top of the Zeppelin showed above the clouds.

Crispin looked at the needle on the speed indicator. They were flying at just under ninety miles per hour. He yelled, "Davis? How fast can it go?"

"We're about there on the flat. We could push a hundred, maybe even one-ten in a dive. The rigging is tight, and the wires are good."

They were silent as the motor whined at its higher pitch. Davis popped the Avro up again to get his bearings. They were directly behind it now. The Zeppelin was just a speck. He banked, turned, and lined up on the dark dot now almost eight miles in front of them.

Davis checked the Zeppelin's position as he began his climb. As the nose went up and obscured the view of the Zeppelin, Davis flew off to the right to retain sight of his target. The late sun shone through the

Avro's yellow canvas wings and made them glow like buttercups on a summer day.

Davis shouted, "Crispin, get the binoculars on it! Any change in the swirl of the clouds on either side, you yell."

Crispin dug into the communications bag for the binoculars.

Meade yelled, "Why?"

Crispin pulled the caps off the glasses. "If they spin, we are in their gunner's sights." Crispin brought the binoculars to his eyes.

Davis yelled into the tube. "Meade! When you drop the egg–"

"Me?"

"Crispin's got a bum leg. I've got to fly. When I pass the bomb to you, take it by the rod between the fins. When you lean out to drop it, hang on to a wood strut, not a wire."

The Zeppelin was two miles ahead of them as Davis climbed to almost a mile above it. Crispin watched the dark top bob in and out of the clouds. Undulating, rocking slightly fore and aft like the sea serpent in Verne's *Twenty Thousand Leagues Under the Sea.*

The clouds parted uniformly at the bow of the airship and gently swirled in its wake. The engines on both sides were engaged.

"Meade. We're closing on them at about sixty miles an hour. A mile a minute. Get ready for it."

"Is it armed?"

"No. Uses a pressure fuse. So don't drop it in the plane."

Meade put a hint of a laugh in his voice. "Ten pounds? Ought to manage that easily."

Calling back, Davis said, "Ten is the explosive charge. Weighs closer to thirty-five pounds."

Meade unwrapped the oilcloth blanket from around his legs. Crispin did the same, folded the oilcloths, and shoved them under the disconnected rudder pedal. His eyes darted between the instruments as Davis yelled, "We're at sixteen thousand. I figure them at ten. Bit over a minute away. Crispin? Any change in their wake?"

"No. But the clouds are thinning."

"Meade? Drop it when we are just barely over the tail. That ought to angle it toward the gondola in the center. Got it? Repeat!"

Meade yelled back his acknowledgement. "Drop at the tail. Like leading ducks before you shoot. Anything else?"

Davis yelled, "After you drop it, grab the wing strut with both hands and stay there until Crispin can help you back in! Got it?"

"Yeah."

"And for God's sakes, don't hit our wing!"

Crispin held Meade's legs as Meade stood in the cockpit, reached back, and took what looked like a big black milk bottle with sharp fins on top from Davis. Meade slipped his glove under a rod welded between two opposing fins and pulled the heavy bomb into his chest.

When Meade had wormed back into the cockpit, Crispin motioned for him to stay seated. Meade started to argue, but Crispin held up the flat of his palm to silence him. "This is my duty from here out." He squirmed up into the wind and lashed his injured leg to a spar with the belt from his overcoat. He grabbed the bomb from Meade. He held a strut and leaned over the edge of the cockpit. Meade braced Crispin as the wind buffeted them.

Davis eased the stick forward into a forty-degree dive toward the tail of the Zeppelin.

As they sped toward the Zeppelin, Crispin had the oddest sensation of being weightless while the wind ripped past him at a hundred miles an hour, sounding like a railroad engine. He fixed his gaze forward. His goggles pressed into his cheeks. The Zeppelin had doubled in size. It looked as big as the landing strip at Amiens from the air. Davis started to pull out of the dive. For an instant, Crispin imagined that Davis was landing the plane on the back of the Zeppelin.

Crispin held the oak strut with his left hand and lowered the bomb to the trailing edge of the lower wing. His glove started slipping off the wooden strut. He lunged forward and caught the strut in the crook of his arm.

The wind grabbed the bomb and pulled Crispin's arm straight behind him. His shoulder started to pop. He tensed his back and leaned against the pressure.

As Davis reached the bottom of his arc, his Avro was a hundred yards behind the Zeppelin's tail and perfectly positioned to run straight along its spine.

Crispin released the bomb as they passed over the tail.

In the next breath, the plane started arcing up. Crispin bent over the lip of the cockpit. The once distant blur of camouflage was now distinct patches of paint, like serpent scales. Seams on the back of the Zeppelin were visible as Crispin watched the bomb pierce the Zeppelin's skin and a flap of material flutter slightly. The bomb had entered at least one of the many hydrogen compartments in the floatation structure.

Davis pulled harder on the stick. The plane climbed higher. Meade reached his hand out for Crispin, unbuckled the belt around Crispin's leg, and hauled him into the cockpit. A moment later, the plane was climbing at a sixty-degree angle. They counted and waited for the explosion.

The motor sputtered. Davis adjusted the mixture of gas and air and the engine noise smoothed. The Avro could not sustain the angle of climb. Davis had to bring the nose down, fly level, or roll and drop. Flying level would soon expose them to the gunners in the gondola attached to the underside of the Zeppelin. A low roll would put them in front of the side machine gunner.

Still, there was no explosion.

Crispin braced himself on the cockpit rim and waited for the flash. He struggled to find the buckle and fasten the wide belt.

Nothing.

Three seconds later, Davis looked down at the shifting Zeppelin, swore under his breath, and yelled, "Dud!"

Crispin looked at the Zeppelin in disbelief. It was intact.

He clung to the rim of the cockpit as the Avro leveled out of the steep climb. The Zeppelin rotated slowly but decisively. The German pilot had reversed one engine to start the turn. Now a combination of thrust and a hard right rudder rocked the Zeppelin and one side began to lift.

Suddenly, the sky around the Avro was full of pencil-straight gray lines. Davis flew through the web of tracer smoke. He banked hard to the right. Meade's head slammed into the edge of the cockpit. The acrid smoke blew over Crispin, who glanced back and saw flashes of light coming from the side gunner's basket. Davis rolled the airplane down to the right.

Flashes of light came from the gondola as well. More lines across the sky. The gunners adjusted for the information from their tracers and shot again. A wire pinged on the plane's right wing as it was sliced in two by a bullet. Hearing small pops to his left, Crispin turned and saw scorched streaks and fist-sized voids in the pale yellow fabric. The sound of flac-flac-flac accompanied fabric tearing to his left. Wood splintered under his feet and beside Meade's shoulder.

Davis shoved the stick forward, aiming for the cover of the clouds. The tangles of webbed smoke floated above them as they dropped fast. They were a smaller target now, showing just their tail.

The soft patting of shredding fabric started again to Crispin's left. Tracers scarred the sky with spikes of smoke, running alongside them. They were shooting past them. The clouds were wispy and thin below them to the left and thicker to the right. Davis slammed the plane to the right and then into a *vrille*. The spinning, full-power nosedive peeled away altitude faster than gravity would have allowed. He pressed the engine, and it shrieked.

Davis tightened the spiral. Crispin looked back at the blur. They were corkscrewing toward the thicker clouds. The canvas communications pack swung out from the cockpit spar, and the edge of the brass buckle clipped Crispin's chin. The deep cut bled immediately. Crispin shoved the bag against the wall of the cockpit. The safety strap dug into his hips, and his head was slammed sideways. He turned, put his hand under the makeshift seat to clutch the ash framework, and felt the nails on the left side of the seat pulling free.

The strap dug the pebble in his pocket deep into his thigh. He twisted, and it dug deeper. As they spun down, Crispin watched the day go from light to dark, sky to earth, as though there were instant sunsets and sunrises.

Six spiral turns in less than three seconds. They were not yet to the clouds. Another wire pinged. Fewer of the dark webs floated near them. The clouds were seconds away. A wire snapped and the ends whistled in the air.

Davis leveled the Avro after he entered the cloud cover. He gestured to the red-hot exhaust pipe and screamed, "Smoke!"

Crispin yelled back after looking at the engine. "No smoke!"

"*Make* smoke! Oilcloth or a rag."

Crispin unbuckled his restraint belt and dug into the foot well. He grabbed an oilcloth and leaned past Meade but was inches shy.

Meade grabbed the cloth from Crispin and jammed it against the red-hot pipe. It flamed. The speed of the wind blew out the flames. Meade shoved it back onto the side of the pipe and held it there. A plume of thick black smoke trailed after them and floated above the clouds. The rag was scorched and charred. Bits broke off and passed by the tail of the plane. Meade's glove flamed. He slapped it into his chest, and the fire went out. Davis banked hard into the thickest of the clouds, slamming Crispin into the rim of the foot well. Davis tightened his turn and dropped through the clouds. Meade shook off the charred palm of his glove. Crispin clawed his way into his seat and held the wide belt.

The dark sea was coming at them, and smoke was still coiling off the exhaust pipe. Crispin slammed his hands over both ears and tried to clear the pressure by opening his jaws in a silent scream. The altimeter read twelve hundred feet. Davis was still dropping fast. He was trying to pull out of the dive, but the wings were bending. Crispin looked at the left wing and wondered if Davis or the immutable law of gravity would prevail. Two wires on the left wing snapped.

Davis was flying as smart and hard as anyone could. Now it was down to luck. Too hard a pull on the stick at their speed would rip the wings off. Too slow a recovery, and they would slam into the sea at full power.

Davis was still diving at a thousand feet above the sea. When the altimeter pass five hundred feet, Crispin braced for the impact.

Suddenly, Davis pulled the plane out of the long left turn toward the sea.

The plane leveled and started to climb. Crispin looked at the altimeter. The needle hovered at one-fifty. Crispin held his breath and calculated to calm himself. He guessed their speed at over a hundred so the nine thousand foot drop took under a minute. He exhaled and thought it seemed like a lifetime

Davis shouted into the tube. "Throw stuff out! Make it look like we crashed."

Crispin passed the coats back to Meade and yanked his duffel from the foot well. "Meade! My uniforms—"

Davis turned right so the clothes would not foul his rudder. Meade threw the coats into the air and then opened the duffel bag. Meade tossed Crispin's hand-tailored uniforms into space, where they fluttered like dull birds. He threw the duffel bag after them and saw the debris hit the water.

Davis circled lower. "More smoke."

Meade took the second oilcloth from Crispin and reached out to ignite it. As Crispin looked back, he saw Davis pull a cork out of a wine bottle with his teeth, spit the cork over the side of the plane, and laugh.

Davis held the bottle as if offering a toast. "Gas to burn the plane if I'm downed behind the lines." He arced the bottle out of the cockpit. When the glass shattered, iridescent circles undulated on the sea. Meade dropped the flaming oilcloth, igniting a blazing island on the sea's surface.

Meade shouted, "They've got to look for us, don't you think?"

Davis pointed above him. "Sure. They're coming down now. They'll need to confirm the kill to get their medals."

Crispin turned to Meade. "The petrol slick and my uniforms should meet their needs."

Davis climbed fast and was in the clouds before the Zeppelin began its search. He adjusted the throttle, started climbing, and shouted, "We're ten minutes from England, fellas!"

Chapter № 23

Monday
October 30, 1916
Northeast of Dover, England

The wind tearing at his helmet, Crispin reached for the communications pack and secured it. He shouted at Meade. "They'll be over England before we can warn anyone!"

Meade grimaced and shrugged as he wiped his goggles.

Crispin saw that Meade was splattered with blood. "Are you—"

Meade pointed to Crispin's chin. Crispin pressed the back of his glove against the gash. "Meade, think man. There must be a way."

"How? Stab them with my Buck knife?"

Crispin pitched forward, searching the cramped cockpit for an answer. The strap of the communications bag dug against his legs. He shouted, "Our pistols!" He ripped off his gloves and reached for the pack. "If we disable the Zeppelin's engines or flight controls or make a spark, the gas—" He opened the flap. "Tell Davis to fly back. We've got to have another go at it. Think of the Londoners!"

"We've only got three pistols—"

Crispin grinned as he pulled the flare pouch from the pack. "Four. The Very pistol. That's the key."

Meade looked puzzled.

Crispin pulled a stubby brass pistol from the pouch and held it in front of Meade's face. "The flare gun!"

"How many flares can it shoot?"

"One."

"Distance?"

"A hundred feet, for accuracy."

Looking stricken, Meade said, "Swell."

"We can do it, Meade. I'm certain we can. We begin with our pistols. Puncture the gas compartments. Then the flare will ignite the gas."

"You want to kill a five hundred foot monster with a couple pistols and a flare? Professor, that's a David and Goliath fantasy."

He grinned. "David won."

Crispin leaned over and shouted directions into the tube. He listened as Davis shouted back, "You're batty! We might be able to out run the debris but not the munitions when they go off. I'm trying to get us to England, our cloud cover is vanishing, and you come up with this stunt!" After no more than a heartbeat, Davis banked the plane sharply. "Oh, what the hell. I say we pull a Steve Brodie and go for it."

A few minutes later, Meade shouted to Crispin, "What if we get it to explode, think it's going to kill us?"

"What makes you think we'll last that long?" He leaned to the tube. "Davis? Can you get off a shot?"

"No. Got my hands full."

Davis turned the Avro until it faced due east and was skimming the upper edge of the clouds over the Strait of Dover. Searching for the Zeppelin, Crispin peered below them.

Meade peeled off the remainder of his charred gloves and threw them into the foot well. He undid two buttons on his flight suit and reached for the grip of his .38-caliber Smith & Wesson. The front sight snagged on his sweater. He jerked it free and looked around the cockpit. Meade tugged up the leg of the flight suit and shoved his gun into his boot top for easier access.

Crispin methodically examined the Webley & Scott Mark III flare gun. "I want to be sure it didn't take any damage in that spin." The fat brass barrel looked dull in the diffused light of the cloud. Crispin held the gun in both hands, snapped the barrel forward, looked down the empty chamber, pointed it away, and dry fired it. He smiled as he dug into the pouch, which held five signal flares. They looked like oversized shotgun shells with a dot of white, red, or green paint on the end of the brass casing. Two magnesium white, two red, and one green flare.

The clouds were higher now. They climbed again, not as far or as fast, but up to twelve thousand feet in ten minutes. Crispin yelled into the tube, "What flare you want to use?"

Davis answered, "Save the white stars. If we need to land short—"

Crispin held up two of the large shells in front of Meade. "Red or green?"

"Which is hotter?"

"Same. Five second burn-time for each."

Meade smiled. "Always liked green."

"Green it is." Crispin snapped the four-inch brass barrel forward to load the green flare. The airplane jolted as he tried to align the flare with the barrel. On the third try, he chambered it and snapped the barrel closed. "Ready."

Crispin dragged his goggles down around his neck, put the binoculars to his eyes with his left hand, and popped above the windscreen to search the sky. He needed to find an anomaly, any deformity in the cloud pattern that would give away the location of the Zeppelin.

At nine thousand feet, the lower gauzy clouds swirled. Crispin pointed to where the Zeppelin was leaving a wake of swirling moisture.

Crispin tapped Meade's arm. "I may not be able to aim the flare properly if I take a pistol shot as well. Afraid you'll have to try to puncture the chambers, Meade."

Meade pulled his .38 from his boot and slid off the safety catch. The plane jolted and the blued barrel slammed into the back of Crispin's left wrist, cracking the crystal of his silver-cased Omega. "Sorry, Professor."

"Least of our worries." Crispin handed the Very pistol to Meade. "Hold this a moment."

Less than a minute later, Crispin had strapped himself to the spar again and was facing toward Davis. Meade wormed up, put his knees on the seat, and held on to the rim of the cockpit.

Crispin wrapped his left arm around the oak strut at the right edge of the cockpit and braced the Very pistol on his wrist. Davis began the approach to sweep over the Zeppelin's back again.

Crispin yelled at Davis, "Dive as soon as we fire!"

Davis looked at Crispin and shrugged.

Meade screamed, "He can't hear you!" He leaned down to the speaking tube and shouted Crispin's directive to Davis.

Meade emptied his pistol into the Zeppelin. Crispin waited until it seemed that Davis was about to crash into it before firing.

The Very pistol jerked when Crispin squeezed off his shot. The flare hissed and left a wobbly corkscrew tail of smoke until it hit the crest of the painted canvas and spun like a top on the dark hull. Meade tightened his grip on the rim of the cockpit as the nose of the airplane dropped down.

Crispin grabbed the strut and unstrapped his leg. He saw the machine gunner twist toward them as they sped past.

Nothing.

Meade pulled Crispin down into the cockpit. Davis accelerated in a straight power dive to escape. They both looked past the Avro's tail and saw the Zeppelin looming above them.

Crispin was counting the seconds but did not trust himself. At three, he heard a small cracking in a wing strut. At five, the entire skin of the Zeppelin suddenly brightened like a lampshade over a bulb. The chambers of hydrogen ignited, almost in unison. The sound followed an instant later. It began as a chest-pounding rumble like surf on stones and quickly became the high-pitched howl of bending iron. The skin of the Zeppelin seared and burning sheets flaked off. The glowing framework slowly collapsed inward.

Heat hit them like an open oven door on a cold morning. The rear of the gondola twisted free as the framework above it failed. Smoke belched from the armory in the gondola's bay. When the first of the munitions exploded, the concussion slapped the plane's tail like a bear paw.

Hundreds of machine gun rounds blew at once and filled the sky with smoking tracers corkscrewing in all directions. The rain of hot metal fragments singed the wings. The smoke and the smell of scorched fabric blew into the cockpit. Several bullets tore through the wing next to Crispin. It was like a dozen Guy Fawkes Days rolled into one. The sounds were magnified. High-pitched, fast-popping strings of firecrackers, the shrill whiz of Roman candles. Drum-deep booming.

The gondola shredded when the racked bombs exploded. Even before the crushing sound hit them, huge iron shards peppered the sky in front of them. Davis banked hard to the left. They were jolted inside the cockpits as a jagged piece of shrapnel clipped something on the belly of the craft. Crispin saw fragments of yellow wood fly past the wing.

Davis wrestled with the controls to return the airplane to its dive path when something sliced across his forehead. Blood streamed from the cut over his left eyebrow and stained the pale fuselage. He tipped his head back and rubbed his goggles clear.

Meade looked up. The fire had faded into a dark column of smoke that filled the sky above them like a thunderhead.

The nose of the Avro wobbled and dropped. Crispin checked the altimeter when the whine of the wind against the wires was all that he heard. The needle flew past six thousand feet. They were less than a mile above the sea when he realized that the engine had stopped. He glanced over his shoulder. Davis was tugging at the controls to change the fuel mixture. Then Davis hit the contact lever. There was a sizzle and two pops but no engine noise.

Crispin looked at the dial in front of him and saw the needle slide past five thousand.

Not a sputter.

Meade braced lower in the cockpit. Crispin looked back to see Davis snapping a switch on the left side of the cockpit, near his elbow.

They plummeted through the thin veil of coastal clouds. The needle passed twenty-five hundred.

As it passed twelve hundred feet, the engine coughed twice and then gave a throaty roar. An oily cloud belched from both exhaust pipes.

Davis made a slight downward arc while he balanced the fuel mixture and tested the controls. Then he danced on the rudder and wrestled with the stick to level the plane.

Crispin looked toward England as the Avro sped north, out from under the falling debris.

Chapter № 24

Monday
October 30, 1916
Northeast of Dover, England

Davis pushed the plane up to five hundred feet and flew north for just over a minute before Crispin pointed back. Davis nodded, turned, and circled over the debris. The only movement was the pulse of the dark sea. Large sheets of the Zeppelin's scorched canvas skin gleamed on the dark water.

Crispin used the binoculars to look for any sign of survivors. He saw only fragments of tattered uniforms on still forms surrounded by unidentifiable charred debris. When he panned his glasses along a strip of coast seeking coastal defenses, he saw a shore as barren as when the Vikings sailed these waters. He put the glasses away.

As Davis turned to the west and flew toward the setting sun, Crispin leaned forward to the speaking tube. "Davis? We got hit."

Davis wiped his goggles with the back of his glove. "You or Meade?"

"Not us. The airplane."

"Yeah. Lots of rips, but she's holding together. Thought they hit the engine when it stalled. But it's okay."

Crispin persisted. "Davis! Listen to me! I think we lost a wheel. I saw...."

He wiped his goggles again and nodded. "I'll check later."

Crispin turned just as Davis tapped on the glass tube in front of him. Crispin looked at the fuel tube in his cockpit. It was empty. He hit it harder. Some fluid entered the indicator.

After less than five minutes, Crispin looked past the left wing and saw London in the twilight. Davis flew just above the treetops and over fields, inspecting them for potential landing sites.

Meade turned and motioned up to the sky.

Davis answered, "Can't climb. Got to save fuel."

Crispin shouted into the tube. "The wheel?"

Davis veered north. When the low sun cast their shadow on a bare field, Davis saw the shadow of only one wheel. One wheel and the small skid that should have been between the wheels were missing. He shouted into the tube, "What'll it be? Wet or dry?"

Crispin was not sure he heard Davis. "Sorry?"

"I can set it down in water now. Won't flip, at least. Or we can try for the landing strip."

Crispin shouted. "How much petrol?"

"Not enough to burn if we crash."

"Try for Hendon. I can signal about the wheel. Have an ambulance at the ready."

As Crispin pulled the hand torch from the pack, Meade shouted into the tube. "What else do you need, Davis?"

"Couple things. First, load the Very gun with a white flare now. If I need to set down in a field, I'll need the light. Then get a red one at the ready to signal if we make the airstrip."

Meade verified the directions. "Load white now. Red over airstrip?"

"Right. Crispin fires only at my command."

Meade clapped Crispin on the back and relayed the orders.

The light in the cockpit was dim. Crispin yanked off his goggles and threw them at his feet. He held the brass casings of the flares up to the late sunlight to distinguish one from another. Crispin loaded the Very gun with a white-tipped shell and handed the red-tipped one to Meade.

Crispin called to Davis. "Shall I signal for an ambulance as we approach?"

"No. Signal for a skid."

"A skid?"

"Right. Just one word skid. S K I D. Point it at the wind direction flares on the ground. Should have a signal man there."

Crispin was silent as he held the flare gun. After flying for about fifteen minutes in the dark, Davis shouted, "Load the red!"

Meade grabbed his shoulder. "Professor! Red. Load the red!" Crispin passed the hand torch to Meade and traded out the white for the red flare. Crispin aimed the Very gun off to the side and looked back at Davis for his command.

Crispin muttered, "*Dominus Illuminatio Mea.*" And then whispered the translation of the motto from the Oxford crest to himself, "The Lord is my Light."

Davis nodded fast and shouted, "Now! Fire it now!"

Crispin shot the red flare away from them. A white flare answered and illuminated the field. Davis took a slow circle while a mechanic lit the wind flare.

Meade took the Very gun from Crispin and handed him the flashlight.

The wind indicator was lighted at the east end of the airfield. Crispin slid the locking latch on the light with his palm, aimed for the flares, and tried to depress the signal button, but his fingers were too cold to respond. He made a fist and pounded the button with his knuckles to make the signals. Long light for dashes, short lights for dots in Morse code. Meade identified the three short dots as an S. Then the dashes and dots all ran together into some flashing light pattern that illuminated a part of their wing. Crispin was spelling the word "skid" over and over. Three dots. Dash dot dash. Two dots. Dash two dots.

A small signal light by the wind flare answered.

Crispin shouted, "Signal received! Their message: Contact at wind flare."

Davis yelled, "Got it! Hope they've practiced a skid landing recently." He circled an open meadow to line up with the airstrip. The engine sputtered on the turn and then smoothed when he straightened for the landing. The speed indicator dropped from forty to thirty-five and then hovered at thirty mph as they approached the field.

When they were about fifty feet above the airfield, a second white flare illuminated the landing strip. A flatbed truck sped toward the wind indicator. Dirt and grass shot from under the rear tires and it slid turning onto the field. It ran just ahead of them and to the right.

A man, hanging on to the back of the truck cab, shouted to the driver and gestured to Davis. The truck bounced and slid sideways on the grass while dragging a ten-foot square sheet of wood. Davis slowed to just less than thirty miles per hour. Crispin looked at the indicator. He saw that the silver needle hovered just above a straight line scratched in the glass at twenty-five. The truck pulled ahead of them.

Davis dropped the left wing slightly. The left wheel hit the grass and bounced. The plane tipped to the right and the stub of the landing strut settled on the moving wood skid. Crispin held his breath for what seemed forever. The tail hit and bounced once before Davis cut the power and the strut splintered under them. They slid for another fifty feet on the skid before the plane slipped sideways and stopped.

The man on the back of the truck jumped off and joined the other men who had run from the hangar to position a small wagon under the stump of the landing strut. Two ambulances at the edge of the field jolted toward the plane.

Meade took off his helmet and goggles. "Congratulations, Professor."

Crispin undid his restraint belt and reached for the communications packet. "For what?"

Meade rubbed the palms of his hands together before reaching for the buckle. "I think you and Davis just earned a Victoria Cross."

"A V.C.? Hardly."

"Hey, pal. You're a hero. You might even have a dashing scar on your chin. Extra something to brag on."

Crispin handed the pack to Meade. "To brag on? I want none of that. All I want is a quiet life. I am no hero."

"You could have fooled me."

Crispin grabbed the splintered rim of the cockpit and twisted back to face Meade. "Do you think that I want my students wondering how many men I killed today, or if they were my German cousins? I will not be called out in parade dress on holidays with medals flashing to join some ostentation of peacocks."

"But—"

"This is no path to glory. I don't want anything that could come from their deaths, Meade. Can you understand that?"

Meade leaned back to make way for Crispin, who was straining to see Davis. "What about him?"

"We simply rub out our involvement in the matter. I'm going to be invisible, as though I wore the Ring of Gyges the Lydian. All credit to Davis."

"Are you sure? Getting a V.C. is—"

Crispin took the communications pack and leaned over Meade. "Davis?"

Davis was slumped over the control stick but looked up. He pulled his goggles down with his left hand and blinked.

"Davis? Can you hear me?"

The pilot nodded. Crispin dropped the communications pack next to him, "Listen carefully. Your report of this flight must indicate that you were on a solo flight, ferrying the Avro back as a trainer. You saw the Zeppelin and downed it with your one bomb. Clear?"

Davis frowned. "But it was a dud—"

Crispin glanced toward the approaching ambulances. "Listen carefully. First, I want to thank you for all you did. We shall be forever in your debt." Davis leaned forward and listened to Crispin intently. "Second, I must tell you that we have a sticky wicket here."

Davis shook his head. "A what?"

"A difficult situation."

Two dark-haired men wearing the white tunic of the British medical corps over their uniforms jumped from the back of the first of the ambu-lances and ran toward the Avro.

The heavier of the two climbed up the foot holes and looked at all three men.

"Crispin?"

Turning away from Davis, Crispin said, "Yes."

"I'm Wallace. That's Brown. We're here to collect you two."

Crispin motioned Wallace to lean closer. "Who sent you?"

He whispered. "RLS."

Crispin gestured for them to wait on the ground. "A moment."

When Crispin looked at Davis again he was shaking his head rap-idly. "No, this was a team effort, fellas."

Crispin was abrupt. "Davis! Remember, you were alone! That is an order."

Meade squeezed beside Crispin. "He's right. It's gotta be a secret."

Davis pleaded with Meade. "No. We did it together like Tinker to Evers to Chance." Turning to Crispin, he said, "Best triple play artists in baseball."

Meade grinned. "Sorry. But you'll have to suffer the glory alone. Women wanting to meet you. Your photogravure in the paper. It's going to be rough for you to be a national hero, but shoulders back, stand tall."

After Davis nodded agreement, Crispin called down to Wallace. "Attend to Davis first. He's got a nasty slice on the forehead. We shall make our own way down."

Wallace climbed up quickly, reached into the rear cockpit, and un-buckled Davis who was still gripping the stick with his right hand. Blood was splattered over his goggles and streaked his cheeks. Wallace touched his shoulder. "Do you think you can stand, sir?"

Davis was using his left hand to pry his right from the stick. "Give me a minute."

Wallace stood behind Davis in the cockpit, freed his cramped hand, lifted him by his arms, and called down to Brown. "Ready for him?"

Wallace lowered him down the side of the Avro to Brown and then jumped to the grass.

Crispin pulled himself out of the cockpit by his arms and swung his legs over the side. He held onto the rim of the cockpit and slid down the fuselage. When he dropped to the ground, his left leg gave way. He fell on his back. By the time Meade had thrown their bags and the cane out of the cockpit, Crispin had pulled himself up by the wing strut and was leaning on his cane and patting Davis on the back.

Davis asked, "Think they have Champagne here?" He stuttered from the cold. "I owe…owe you a drink."

"Sorry, old man, we have another engagement." Crispin unbuttoned his suit and dug into his jacket pocket. He took out a packet of carefully folded French francs and handed it to Davis. "Buy the lads one on us, when you get back over there."

Wallace and Brown each took an elbow and walked Davis to his ambulance. After turning him over to the medical staff, they trotted toward their own ambulance as Meade helped Crispin up its steps. The interior of the ambulance had a canvas cot attached to each side wall. A small aisle led to the cab. Crispin pulled the blanket from the cot and wrapped it around himself before he sat.

Wallace hopped in and sat on the cot facing Crispin. He opened the cabinet on the wall and pulled out a gauze-wrapped dressing of cotton wool, which he pressed against the gash. "Press this here gamgee on your chin, sir."

Crispin complied and looked at Wallace. "From Birmingham, are you?"

"Indeed, I am. Do I know you?"

"I think not, but Birmingham is the only place where one refers to that particular dressing as a 'gamgee.'"

Meade slid his Gladstone bag, briefcase, and Crispin's tan suitcase under the other cot and climbed into the ambulance next to Wallace.

Crispin removed the compress from his chin. "Meade, how bad is it?"

"I've cut myself worse shaving. Put it back. You're making a mess."

Wallace looked at Meade's hand. "Let me get some ointment on that burn."

"That can wait."

"Actually, it can't. We've got the time now and if we get the salve on it immediately and wrap it, you might not get infected." As Wallace wrapped the burn, he asked, "Any other injuries?"

Meade pointed to Crispin's knee. Crispin asked, "How far to the hospital?"

"Under a half hour."

"Best we leave here as promptly as possible. I'll get it attended to there."

Brown latched the rear door as Wallace started the ambulance. Crispin and Meade stretched out on the cots. They were asleep before the ambulance had driven past the aerodrome's security gate and turned on the road leading to the recovery hospital.

Chapter № 25

Monday
October 30, 1916
North of London, England

Wallace braked the ambulance abruptly. Swearing softly, Brown braced against the window and looked back to see Crispin sitting upright in the dark compartment and squinting at his watch. "Sorry, Lieutenant. Dog bolted across the road. Late for his supper, I fancy."

Crispin leaned against the cold metal wall of the ambulance. "Where are we?"

"Almost to the recovery hospital."

Looking at Meade sleeping on the cot, Crispin wondered if he appeared as worse for wear. Blood had splattered the chest of Meade's filthy flying suit, and oil had smudged his face. His hair was matted. Their boots smelled of the sewer. The only thing that appeared to be clean was Meade's gauzed right hand. When the ambulance braked hard and turned right, the smooth hum of the tires on the tarmacadam road was replaced with the clatter of gravel being tossed up against the wheel wells. The driver slowed and Meade propped up on one elbow to look out the windscreen.

The manor house at the end of the oak-lined lane was stately. As they approached, amber lights glowed from windows on all three floors. The dark stone looked almost black in the dim light. Crispin tapped the driver's shoulder. "I thought you said we were going to a hospital."

"This is one now, sir. The Earl was killed early on. His widow has taken rooms on the upper floor. The rest is a recovery hospital. Converted the grand dining room on the first floor into a dormitory for those in pushchairs. Ambulatory cases go to the second floor. Nursing staff all live on third with the family. Kept on all the staff what's not at the front. Almost twenty rooms it has."

The manor house was situated on a slight rise. The ambulance drove past the front entrance. Where the driveway branched, the ambulance followed the smaller path down a slight slope to the rear of the house, where there was a receiving dock. In better times, merchants could deliver produce directly to the kitchen and storage rooms. But today, there were four other ambulances lined up awaiting transfers. Brown swore softly and wheeled sharply, retracing his path to the front entrance.

Upon arrival at 6:47, Brown acquired two wicker pushchairs from the hallway of the hospital. Crispin winced as Brown helped him toward a chair that creaked when he fell back into it. He watched Wallace hold the other pushchair for Meade.

Brown handed the bags to Meade, who balanced them on his lap. Wallace threw a heavy blanket over Meade's baggage and draped a second blanket over Crispin's lap for the journey.

As they were wheeled down the long oak-paneled corridor, a scratched phonograph recording of Mozart echoed around them. When they passed a large sitting room, Crispin saw the patients in light blue pajamas and dark blue robes sitting quietly in pushchairs, but failed to find a familiar face. Most had a length of white gauze covering their eyes. Those without bandages appeared to be staring at the ceiling or toward the curtained window. A nurse in an ankle-length white uniform and apron read to herself beside the gramophone.

At the end of the corridor, Wallace held the brass gate while Brown pushed the chairs into the large elevator. Before Wallace turned the control, he pointed to the oak door opposite the elevator. "Administrator Jamison's office is there. He and the night Matron know you are here, but not why."

Brown leaned down to Crispin and whispered. "Got your desks all set up for you, sir. Orders from *himself* are there."

When the elevator shuddered to a stop in the basement, Wallace opened the gate. Crispin and Meade remained in their chairs while they were pushed past various storerooms. Wallace stopped at a door with "ANATOMY" painted on it in neat black letters. He unlocked it and pushed it open. "Here we are then. Your new home."

Bright light flooded into the hall. Crispin peered into the room. Walls, floor, and ceiling were all tiled in white, which increased the intensity of the two rows of electric bulbs, each under a bright metal reflector. The echo from the creaking wicker back of the chairs and the squeak of the hard rubber tires on the tile was shrill.

Meade pointed at the lights as he tossed off the blanket and placed the bags on the floor. "Where's the switch?"

Wallace put two keys on the small table next to the door. "Might be one in there." He motioned with his head in the direction of the left wall. "There's a bath and loo. Uses the same key. You need to throw the bolt after I go."

Meade leapt from his pushchair and grabbed the door before it shut. "About dinner—"

Wallace said quietly, "When I notify the Matron of your arrival, she'll get it ordered straightaway. Fancy an ale if I can manage it?"

Crispin smiled and nodded. "That would be most welcome."

After Meade locked the door, Crispin looked around the room in silence. Good sized. Thirty feet to a side. But stark. Meade deposited Crispin's tan bag beside his own Gladstone bag and briefcase between two freshly made hospital beds along the right wall. Extra blankets, black fabric slippers, pajamas, and a robe rested on the foot of each bed.

Crispin wheeled toward the two desks, which faced each other over a large floor drain in the center of the room. They formed a rough facsimile of a partner's desk. The wooden desks had been painted white some years before and were badly chipped. Matching painted metal chairs sat neatly in the kneeholes. The chips in their paint coincided perfectly with dents in the desks just above the thin center drawer.

Two small rough wooden crates tied with heavy twine and a finished chest were on one desk. On the other was a large tan envelope which Crispin held up for Meade to see. "Mind if I open it?"

"Go ahead. He seemed to think this was your party anyway."

Crispin slid his finger under the glued flap and pulled out one unfolded page of onionskin, which was signed with the letter "C" in green ink. Crispin tried to hold the paper still, but his arms shook as though they were still jolting in the Avro. He placed the page on the desk and read the three typed paragraphs quickly.

Leaning forward on his desk, Meade asked, "Well? What does it say?"

Crispin pushed the thin page across the desk toward Meade. "Seems they are sending us reinforcements."

Reaching over the desk for the page, Meade asked, "What do you mean?"

"An archaeologist. A Doctor Lee. Best you read the details and memorize the contact information."

While Meade read the orders, Crispin unbuttoned the chest of his flight suit, drew his Webley from the holster, and put it into the center drawer of the desk.

Meade returned the orders to the envelope and opened the latch of the chest. "Just as you packed it at the Verne estate."

Crispin examined the office supplies in the drawer. Paper. Pencils. A hand sharpener. Dip pens and a bottle of black ink. "My joy. Now, I can watch you peering at all of them again."

"I just want to examine the *Seller Atlas*. If any of those pages match—"

"Fine. But must you bang on about each and every map?"

"Sorry. I thought—"

Crispin pointed to the row of examination screens which had been placed end to end, forming a false wall. The fabric that stretched between the dented metal frames was faded and stained. "Anything past them?"

After Meade looked behind the screens, he called, "Nothing but junk." Past the small table and two side chairs was an abandoned sofa. A four-by-six foot slate board on wheels sat at an angle to the wall. Behind the furniture was a row of deep sinks and wide counters that looked like a commercial laundry. Above the disorder, the ceiling was lined with rows of white-painted pipes.

Meade turned and walked back toward Crispin. "Looks like they gave us a storage or laundry room."

Crispin shivered violently and leaned over. "Could it possibly be colder in here than the out of doors?"

"Might just be. Want another blanket?"

"If you don't mind."

Before Meade could get it from the bed, there was a tapping at the door. He spun toward the sound and looked at Crispin. "Yes?"

The door muffled a woman's voice. "Tea!"

Crispin opened the desk drawer and let his hand fall over the grip of the Webley. He nodded. Meade opened the door slowly.

A stocky, square-faced woman in a well-tailored chocolate tweed suit held a tray with a large brown teapot and three matching mugs. She was in her mid-sixties and of medium height. Her wavy white hair was gathered at her neck in a brown velvet ribbon. The edges of her hazel eyes crinkled as she smiled when Meade stepped aside. A strand of faceted jet beads and a thick gold chain holding a small watch fell from her neck and were almost hidden by the large loose bow of her ivory silk blouse. Her skirt, hemmed just above her ankles, showed sensible walking shoes.

Crispin wheeled over to the door. "Thank you, Matron." Staring at the glazed teapot, he said, "That Brown Betty is a most welcome sight."

She smiled in the manner adopted by nurses, nuns, and grandmothers to calm children. Before she could say anything, Crispin pointed to the table next to the door. "If you will leave the tray, I'll pour." She lowered the tray to the table and leaned over it. Crispin elevated his voice ever so slightly. "Thank you, Matron. I am certain that you have other duties calling you."

She glanced at him. "Several." She peeled back the top layer of a folded cloth on the tray, picked up a glass thermometer, and shook the mercury into the bulb at the tip. "But your health is paramount." She smiled and her voice rolled easily with a confidence that assumed no contradiction. "Let's start with your temperatures, before the hot tea."

She aimed the tip of the thermometer at Meade, who reflexively opened his mouth. She glanced at his bandaged hand. As she shook the mercury down in the second thermometer, Meade closed the door. After she placed the thermometer, she leaned down and took Crispin's chin in her palm to examine the gash. "Wallace said you were both severely chilled and somewhat the worse for wear. I want to be certain that you do not require immediate treatment for hypothermia before we get to the other matters." She crossed her arms and looked at the men. Puffy flying suits. Bandaged hand. Cut chin. Reddened faces under smears of oil, blood, and soot. Blued lips. The stink of old sweat and sewage. She shook her head and poured two mugs of tea and left them on the tray.

Meade took out the thermometer and asked, "What's the treatment, if we have, whatever you said?"

"Warming food and blankets. No brandy or spirits." She sniffed. "Soak in a warm tub, which wouldn't hurt either of you. Warm, not hot."

She read Meade's thermometer and frowned. "I suppose it would be a waste of my time to inquire how long you were at extreme altitude, or if that slight burn on your faces where the goggles didn't protect your eyes was from the sun or an explosion, so let me be clear. You need to get that hot tea in you." Meade walked toward the tray. "Drink it all promptly. Do not sip it."

She bumped Crispin's leg as she reached for his thermometer. He inhaled sharply. She looked at Crispin and then at the thermometer. "Well, what's that all about?"

Meade answered quickly, as he handed a mug to Crispin. "He hurt his knee."

She watched as both men quickly drank their steaming tea. "Help me get this flying suit off him, if you will." Meade assisted Crispin in standing and sliding out of it. Crispin straightened his jacket and wobbled as he stood.

She frowned. "Good Lord, your knee is the size of a basketball! I'll get my shears."

Crispin sat quickly. "That will not be necessary. I can just unlace the leg of my breeches for the doctor when he arrives."

"I will be attending you while you are here. I am a licensed physician, both here and in America." Crispin stared at her. She stared back. "University of Michigan— with honors."

Crispin blushed. "My apologies."

She put her hand on her hip. "Lieutenant. You needn't disrobe; just sit up on the desk. Now."

After Meade helped Crispin onto the desk, she positioned his leg straight out in front of him and held his booted ankle. He watched the confidence with which her square hands worked. Her fingernails were short and well buffed. The only ring on her short fingers was a single gold band.

She rotated the foot first to the right then to the left, watching Crispin's face. He flinched. Then she placed one hand on the edge of his knee and the other on his ankle. She pulled gently on the side of the ankle. The throbbing became a searing pain. She looked up just as he grimaced. She released the pressure immediately. She patted the inner surface of his knee, just above his calf. "When did you hurt it?"

Looking at Meade, he said, "Saturday. Wasn't it Saturday night?"

Meade nodded as he poured two more mugs of tea.

She let her hand hover above the top of his boot before unlacing it. "The bruising tells me that you are continuing to tear your median lateral ligament. We need to get that pressure relieved and this leg immobilized or you are going to have a limp for the rest of your long life." She opened the case of her watch, looked at the time, snapped the case shut, and let it fall back on the chain around her neck. "Let me get my things and attend to your leg. Best we do it before you eat."

Crispin hopped back to his wicker chair. "Won't you be noticed, scurrying in and out of here?" After he sat, Meade handed him a mug of tea.

She laughed. "One of the advantages of being an old lady is that I'm invisible."

Crispin said, "Thank you–"

She took one of the keys from the table near the door, slipped it into her pocket, and turned. "I should have introduced myself, as we will be working together. I am Doctor Catherine Lee."

Crispin choked on his tea. "You? I thought he was an archaeologist."

She smiled and sighed. "Can you manage a bath before I return?" Crispin nodded as she shut the door without waiting for his answer.

He unbuckled his Sam Browne belt and put it in the side drawer.

Meade grabbed Crispin's small tan suitcase and started for the door.

Crispin slammed the desk drawer. "And just where do you think you are going with my case?"

Startled, Meade turned. "The bathroom. Thought you might have a change of clothes in here."

Crispin unbuttoned the jacket of his uniform. "No. You were good enough to scatter my entire wardrobe over the channel."

"Then what have I been dragging around in here?"

"Books."

Meade slid the suitcase back to the bed. "Books!"

"My books."

"Great. All I have with me is an extra sweater and a pair of trousers–"

Crispin pulled off his right boot. "Kind of you to offer, but I doubt if I would get a proper fit. Could you be so kind as to gather up the night-clothes from the foot of the bed?"

Meade got the robe and pajamas and started to hand them to Crispin, who was struggling to remove his left boot. Instead, he laid them on the desk, knelt, and eased the boot off while Crispin held his knee and grimaced. Crispin grabbed the key from the table as Meade maneuvered the pushchair into the hallway, holding his hospital attire under his arm.

Once in the large bathroom, Crispin handed the key to Meade. "Thank you. I will knock when I need you to open the door." He thought a moment. "Do you recall my signal for the skid?"

"How you flashed the light?"

"Yes. The 'S' is three dots 'K' is a dash, then—"

Meade threw up his hands. "I'll never remember all that."

"Then make it three raps, a pause, then one. Can you remember that much?"

Meade's lips went thin. He nodded and shut the door.

By the time Crispin tapped on the door, Meade had maps scattered over both desks. He laughed as Crispin wheeled into the room. "Enjoy your bath?"

Crispin ran his hand over his wet hair. "Immensely. What seems to be so humorous?"

"Sorry. You are steaming like a boiled lobster."

"I shouldn't wonder. It's cold as a cave in here."

Meade blew a slow breath and saw it fog in the harsh light. He opened his briefcase and pulled out their crushed hats and dropped them on the desk. "We might as well wear—" Crispin motioned for him to be quiet as the lock on the door turned.

Doctor Lee wheeled in a new pushchair with an extension to elevate Crispin's leg. Crutches were balanced on it. The seat held a large tray with a tapestry-covered knitting bag, a fresh pot of tea, a small kidney-shaped white enamel basin, and a large metal bowl, both of which were covered with towels. Meade took the crutches to the bed and moved the tray to the desk.

Pointing to the wicker chair, she said, "Lieutenant, if you can sit in the new chair and hike your pajama pant leg up above mid-thigh, I can begin."

Crispin complied and tried unsuccessfully not to look embarrassed. Once situated, he tugged the cord of his robe tighter. "Certainly."

Meade smirked as he picked up his Gladstone bag and walked to the door. "Unless you need me, I'll get cleaned up now." He locked the door from the hallway.

Doctor Lee slid the desk chair over to Crispin and looked at his knee. "We need to reduce the pressure caused by fluid in the joint before it does any more harm."

Crispin looked at his swollen knee. "Are you proposing to lance it?"

She put on gold-rimmed glasses from her pocket and uncovered the basin, exposing two large hypodermic syringes. "I prefer a less-invasive technique to draw off the excess fluid. You will experience immediate relief."

Crispin tried not to wince as she swabbed the area just beside his kneecap with alcohol. "You have performed this procedure before, haven't you?"

"Yes. Lieutenant, you might wish to look at the far wall for a few moments."

Crispin counted the white tiles on the wall and listened to the pipes at the end of the room rattle and clank. He exhaled when he heard her place the full syringe in the enameled pan and swallowed hard when she took the second syringe to his knee.

Moments later, Crispin looked at his knee. "Thank you for repairing it."

"In about an hour, I'll cast it." She ignored Crispin's frown. "That should allow us the opportunity to have you and Mister Meade review your findings with me. Mansfield should be here. He loves this sort of a challenge."

"Mansfield?"

She said slowly, "Captain Mansfield Smith-Cumming. Signs his letters with green ink."

Crispin froze.

She stood, covered the basin with the towel, and looked at Crispin. "You do know the Director, don't you?"

Before he could answer, Meade opened the door slowly and peeked into the room. Crispin motioned him to hurry. He padded into the room in his stocking feet and carried his boots. He was wearing charcoal trousers and a crew neck sweater. He carried the pouch under his wet towel and put it into the map case while she stared at Crispin.

Meade walked to Crispin's side. "What's the matter?"

Crispin pointed to the large envelope and whispered, "The challenge. We should have asked her the question."

Meade stared at her and shrugged. "Is it too late?"

Sitting straighter in the chair, Crispin glared at her. "Without meaning any offense, I should inquire who sent you?"

"I must admit, I was shocked that you had not posed the query prior to this."

Crispin cleared his throat. "And, who sent you?"

She said clearly, "RLS."

Crispin shook his head in disbelief. "Well. You are indeed the genuine article, but just how did the Director think you might assist us? Do you translate Anglo-Saxon or have some background in cartography?"

She had an easy, deep laugh. "Oh, no. My husband and I met the Smiths on an archaeological dig one summer. His wife was particularly keen on such things. You know he had been retired from the Navy for several years before he was called back to serve in London."

Meade extended his hand. "I'm Jack Meade. Glad for any help."

"Yes. I know who you are. Much better looking than your image in the newspaper."

Crispin looked at her, not certain what to make of what she had said.

Meade laughed and sat on the edge of the desk. "That's not saying much."

She said, "Something of a map collector, I gather."

As he put his hands in his pockets, Meade nodded. "How'd you get interested in archaeology?"

"My husband, Stewart, and I spent several summers on an Indian reservation in North Dakota. Archaeological expeditions always need medical personnel they can't afford. We began volunteering on digs after he closed his medical practice. When we weren't attending to twisted ankles, snakebites, broken legs, or the like, we became rather good amateur archaeologists."

Meade crossed his arms. "How'd you end up here?"

She paused before answering. "After the war started, I decided I could be of better use in a hospital than picking up pottery shards from a saltern near Yarmouth. That's where I was when it began. I contacted the health service and was assigned to a surgical hospital in Edinburgh, then to the recovery hospital here."

"Where are you from, Doctor?"

Crispin sat back and watched for Doctor Lee's reaction to Meade's abrupt American way.

She smiled. "Chicago. I left to attend the University of Michigan. After I was graduated, I was fortunate enough to return and find a post in a laying-in ward. My husband had his surgical practice at the same hospital. That is where we met."

"Is he with you now?"

She shook her head. "He passed away. It will be nine years in March."

Crispin looked at her strand of jet beads and wondered if they were for mourning or fashion.

Meade pointed to Crispin's knee. "How is it?"

"He has a torn ligament. Drained nicely. If it does not fill right away, I'll cast it."

Crispin cleared his throat. "If you will permit me, whatever did he envision your role to be, Doctor Lee?"

Meade held the desk chair for her. She remained standing and put her hands on her hips. "Lieutenant Crispin. How long have you been out of England?"

"Just over five months. Why do you ask?"

"Things have changed considerably in that time. Your hospitals are swamped with the war-wounded. Hotels and private estates like this are being converted into auxiliary and convalescent hospitals. Midwives are assisting in the surgical theaters."

Crispin stared at her in disbelief as she continued. "So, Lieutenant, for your government to allow you the use of any hospital space and to curtail my medical services to help you suggests that they think more highly of my abilities to assist you than a simple task definition."

"I meant no offense."

"None taken. Let's get to work. I have no idea how long they can allow the Anatomy to remain available to us."

Crispin looked at her and squinted. "Anatomy?"

"The sign outside this room says 'Anatomy.' Do you understand what that is?"

"Of course I know what anatomy means. By definition, it is the study of—"

She laughed a deep booming laugh. "You're bluffing, Lieutenant. In America, we call it 'the morgue.' It's where we do postmortem examinations. They cleared out the laundry room that had been converted into an autopsy theater just so you boys could work in secret. Good thinking. No one likes to come here."

Crispin looked stricken. "Autopsy? From the Greek to see for one's self. Well, perhaps that might explain why it has been so blasted cold in here."

Meade choked on his tea. Doctor Lee poured a mug for herself. "I want to see the Baldwin. Then I want to know what you have done and what's missing. Who wants to brief me first?"

Meade took the pouch from the map case and carefully extracted the Baldwin portolano which he placed in front of her. She started to reach for it and stopped.

"Go ahead. Pick it up and have a good look." He pulled the chair from his desk, straddled it, and leaned his elbows on the back.

She picked up the portolano and balanced it on the fingertips of her left hand as she examined it. She turned it over and repeated her careful review. After placing it on the desk, she traced the cracked edge of the seal with the tip of her index finger. She gazed at the seal silently for a moment. When she looked at Meade, she smiled. "Amazing. Simply amazing. There are some things that transcend time." After a pause, she asked, "Are you ready to tell me your thoughts on the map's meaning?"

Meade told her that he was examining historical maps from museums and the Verne map collection to learn what the sea level was between 500 and 1000 A.D. Once he found that, he would adjust a modern map of the English coast to find the coastline which matched the portolano. Crispin showed her his translation of the text from the face of the Baldwin portolano and the list of items on the reverse.

She pointed to the two words Crispin had not translated. "And these?"

Crispin shrugged. "Nothing that I have seen before. A code or cipher, perhaps."

She asked a few clarifying questions and finished her tea. After a moment of reflection, she said, "It seems to me that the information you need is locked in that map. All you need is a key from the same century to unlock it. That's Mansfield's plan to find the treasure."

Crispin smiled. "If only it were that simple. You see, this map was once a part of the *Codex*."

Doctor Lee looked at her watch and glanced at his knee.

"Best that discussion wait for a bit, Lieutenant. I think your knee is ready for the cast."

She uncovered the large bowl and took out gauze, a packet of dry plaster, a large wooden spoon, and a knit tube resembling the top of a stocking. She handed the bowl to Meade. "I'll need about a pint of water." She slipped Crispin's bare leg into the tube.

When Meade returned from the bathroom with the bowl, she moistened half of the towel, mixed the remaining water with plaster to the consistency of a pancake batter, and pushed the roll of gauze into it. "Mister Meade, would you assist me by elevating his heel about ten inches above the extension platform?"

"Sure."

She positioned his leg. He held still as she wrapped the plaster-soaked gauze around his lower calf and then wound it at an angle to the left then to the right so by the time it had reached his upper thigh, a herringbone of V's ran down the center of his leg. She ran her hands over the edges of the cast at the ankle and mid-thigh to smooth away any roughness. As she wiped the excess plaster from her hands onto the wet towel, she said, "Hold as still as you can until it dries. About thirty minutes."

"Certainly."

Crispin looked at the wrapping and squirmed slightly. "It feels a bit warm."

"Perfectly normal as the plaster cures."

Crispin looked down at his leg with an academic interest as though it were an alien attachment. It resembled a battering ram or the prow of a ship.

Doctor Lee cleared her throat. "Lieutenant? I believe you were about to tell me something about a codex?"

"Yes. A codex, by definition, is a collection of bound materials. A form we know as a book, as opposed to a scroll or unbound pages. But the *Codex* to which I refer is a special one collected by Sir Robert Cotton. It is a collection of exceptional handwritten manuscripts. It contains *Beowulf*, religious texts, a letter from Alexander the Great, a partial biography of Saint Christopher, and the poem *Judith*. All are on parchment or vellum and predate the printing press. As I started to say, I believe that the map you just examined was once a part of that *Codex*."

Doctor Lee looked at the Baldwin. "How could this have been bound in a book? It's uneven on the edges. Was it torn out, somehow?"

Meade pointed to the stain on one edge. "The Professor thinks it was glued to a strip of parchment that was sewn into the book."

"Why would they put a map in a collection of manuscripts?"

Crispin leaned back on his elbows. "When Henry VIII disbanded the monasteries, their libraries were pillaged. Golden covers studded with gems were purloined. Bound manuscripts were torn apart, parchment pages were baled up like so many hides, and sold by weight in Europe."

Doctor Lee looked at the map and then at Crispin. "By weight?"

Crispin nodded. "Butchers wrapped meat in them. Bookbinders in Europe used these parchments to stiffen book backs. Every now and again, someone will discover a fragment of an old parchment."

She looked hopeful as she asked, "Still? I can't begin to imagine what knowledge has been forever lost."

Crispin nodded. "Fortunately, some saw the preservation of any parchment as very important. The manuscripts in the *Codex* were saved by Laurence Nowell, the archivist who began the first Anglo-Saxon dictionary. Later, Sir Robert Cotton came into possession of the bound volume in the mid-1600s, when Puritans in England burned ever so many books here before sailing to America."

Meade laughed. "Those upright pilgrims?"

Doctor Lee pointed her index finger at Meade. "Mind you, they were not the first to try to control knowledge or diminish the power of books. Look at Girolamo Savonarola. The anti-Renaissance Italian who started the wholesale destruction in 1497."

Meade laughed. "What?"

She nodded. "They called the madness 'the Bonfire of the Vanities.' They burned books, paintings, mirrors, gaming tables, and journals. Anything suggesting pride or vanity was destroyed in an effort to return to pure religion and eliminate vain excesses."

Crispin looked stern. "Quite so, Doctor."

"But how could your *Codex* have survived that?"

"At the height of the book burning, Sheriff Bromfull of Blunham grabbed the *Codex* and stored it at Stratton, Bedfordshire. He hid it in a barn."

Meade paced and shoved his hands deep into the pockets of his trousers. "How'd you ever learn all this? You're still a kid."

Waving his hand to dismiss the question, Crispin said, "That is not important. What is important, however, is that you understand that this is a national treasure. The map alone, even if it never leads to anything, could make you a very, very wealthy man."

Meade chuckled. "Really?"

Doctor Lee noticed that Crispin was shaking.

Crispin smiled. "It's nothing. Just a bit of a chill."

Meade pulled a folded blanket from the bed and walked toward Crispin.

Doctor Lee held up her hand. "Drape it over his shoulders just until the cast dries." She turned to Meade. "Tell me, Mister Meade, was it common for maps to look like this?"

"Yeah. Just a hide, usually not this good, with a couple of holes punched on the edge to lash it to a stick."

Before Meade could continue his thought, there was a sturdy rapping at the door. A man called, "It's Brown and Wallace, sir."

Meade slid the Baldwin into the chest and dropped the pouch on it before he opened the door. Brown entered carrying a tray of food with two large bowls of stew and two empty water glasses. He placed the tray on the desk closest to the door. Wallace set two opened bottles of Bass ale next to the tray.

"Sorry it took a bit. Wallace stepped out to get your beverages. Thought you chaps might like a bit of England's best."

Crispin looked at the steam swirling off the food. "Thank you, chaps. Appreciate it. Any possibility you could get some heat down here?"

Brown said, "I'll see what I can do, sir."

Crispin offered a casual salute. "Thank you."

Wallace said, "Lieutenant, Mister Jamison will check in on you in the morning to see if you need anything. Goodnight."

Meade locked the door and put the *Seller Atlas* on his bed. Crispin slid his pushchair up to the edge of the desk and paused for a moment of prayer, a silent grace of thanksgiving for the food and their deliverance. He looked up at Meade and nodded.

"Professor, don't let it get cold."

"Indeed. It looks…warming."

Doctor Lee looked at Meade and smiled. "As neither of you appear in any danger of hypothermia now, I am canceling my order prohibiting spirits."

Meade poured a glass of ale and offered it to her.

"Another time, Mister Meade. I still have a few patients to look after tonight."

She stood. Meade opened the door for her. "Your bag."

"Oh, my knitting bag. Best I just leave it here. I'll be attending a seminar all day tomorrow. I regret that was planned well in advance of Mansfield's call. I will join you on Wednesday morning as early as possible."

Meade nodded to her. "Goodnight."

She called to Crispin. "Oh, Lieutenant?"

"Yes?"

"While I do not expect your leg to pose a problem if you stay off of it, if you have any undue pressure from the cast or significant discomfort anywhere in your leg, I want you to have Meade go to Jamison's office immediately. He or the Matron will have another physician attend to you."

Holding up his hand in protest, Crispin said, "But this is a—"

"A secret mission. Yes, I know. I've already discussed with Jamison how he could bandage your face and wheel you up if you required attention. Your cast should be dry enough in about an hour for a blanket."

Crispin nodded and smiled. After the door shut, he took a long drink, looked at the stew, which had the appearance of boardinghouse swill. Knowing that he must eat, he prodded it with his spoon.

Exhausted, they ate and drank like strangers at a café, silent, staring vacantly at their food. Crispin looked at his bowl. "I had no idea I was that famished."

Emptying the remainder of the bottle into his glass, Meade chuckled. "For once, I'm glad you Brits serve your beer warm."

"Warm? I had it on good authority that you Americans serve it far too chilled." He pointed to the open envelope. "Could you pass it over?"

Crispin read the contact information again and turned the page toward Meade. "Do you have it memorized?"

After Mead nodded, Crispin pulled his silver match case from the drawer. He put the flame to the edge of the page and watched it singe and crackle before he dropped the ash into his empty bowl.

Meade glanced at the smoke swirling from the paper. "Think we can bust the map's secret tomorrow?"

"One can but hope. If not, Doctor Lee may indeed be of some use. But for the life of me, I cannot see how. All I know is that I'm spent."

Meade drank the last of his ale. "Yeah, I've got about ten steps left in me."

"You're ahead of me. I'll be lucky to get standing again."

Meade pulled back the covers and helped Crispin maneuver his cast onto the hospital bed.

"Thanks, old man."

Meade put the two extra blankets over him and returned the *Seller Atlas* to the desk. He stumbled the few steps to his own hospital bed, yanked back the sheet and blanket, sat down harder than he intended, and rolled his face toward the wall.

"You know, Meade. I had a thought…."

Crispin listened for a response but heard only Meade's deep breathing.

Moments later, Crispin fell into a deep sleep that lasted until midnight.

Meade rolled over and punched his pillow twice. He squinted at

SHARON O. LIGHTHOLDER

Crispin's empty bed and then toward the door. Crispin was balanced on his crutches, holding the doorknob and twisting it slightly.

Meade blinked hard. "You going out?"

"No."

"I'm sure I locked it."

"Yes, I thought as much. Just checking." Crispin leaned on his crutches and limped back to his bed.

"Goodnight, then." Meade rolled over to face the wall.

Meade woke to the tapping of the crutches against the tile as Crispin walked to the door and tested it again. Meade looked at his watch. It was not yet two.

Meade sat up and ran his hand over his face. "What is it, Professor?"

"Just checking the security here. One can never–"

Meade swung his legs over the side of the bed. "Do you want me to stand watch, like on the train?"

"Awfully good of you to offer."

Meade stumbled to his desk chair and rubbed his eyes. "Okay. I'm up. Get some shut-eye. I need to look at the *Seller Atlas* anyway."

When Crispin had pulled the blanket over his head, Meade opened the atlas and turned the thick pages slowly. All he needed was for one of these marine charts to have the same pattern as the Baldwin portolano's three rivers. Then, he would simply look at the title on the map plate in the *Seller Atlas* and wake Crispin.

At 3:18, he examined the last of the plates and closed the heavy leather binding. Frustration pushed away sleep. Meade reached into Crispin's crate of books and took out an English translation of *Beowulf*. He slouched in his chair and opened it.

Chapter № 26

Tuesday
October 31, 1916
North of London, England

As he shivered and tossed his head, Crispin dreamed of hail falling on a frozen lake. Then the drumming of ice on ice became the staccato sound of steel on steel as a hundred bayonets snapped into their mounts on the Lee-Enfield .303s. From the far end of the trench, an infantryman gave a shout that was relayed down the line, past Crispin, to the end of the trench. "Hop the bags! Hop it!" Troops scrambled up the ladders, out of the trench, into the dark, and became moss green rabbits in forest green uniforms bounding about in a grassy meadow.

Flares had the meadow glowing crimson and silver as the rabbits chewed on strands of licorice barbed wire. The chatter of chewing became the chirping of machine gun fire. The ringing of cartridges hitting cement became the chiming of Big Ben. Three rabbits with furry feet marched toward him and goaded him toward a deep hole in the center of the meadow muttering, "Hop it, hop it." They pushed him into the crater. The metallic clanging grew louder as he fell faster.

Crispin woke, choking, to the rattle of the overhead steam pipes. "Infernal pipes!"

Turning from his desk, Meade saw Crispin squint at his wristwatch and try to read the time. "Almost six, isn't it? I thought you'd have awakened me."

"Why? You seemed to be sleeping well, for a change."

Blinking and shading his eyes, Crispin asked, "Isn't there a switch for these lights?"

"Not in here. There's one in the bathroom that might turn them off."

"I saw it. Wouldn't it be completely dark in here?"

Meade shrugged. "Want me to unscrew some of the bulbs?"

"No. What little heat we have appears to emanate from them." Crispin stretched and sat on the edge of his bed. "I'll stand watch now."

Meade took the key from the table by the door. "Be right back."

As the echo of the door bolt seating dissipated, Crispin reached under his bed and pulled his leather-bound missal from the tan bag. He had adopted his mother's habit of moving the purple ribbon forward to mark the next reading and folding the bottom tag of ribbon between other pages to avoid wear. It opened to All Hallows Eve. All Saints Day was tomorrow. He should sit vigil, as he had done with his mother, and wondered how he could manage it in these odd surroundings and with the pressing mission. He finished the reading for the day, opened the front cover, read the inscription to him on the occasion of his first communion, and let his finger trace his mother's delicate script.

Crispin slid the book under his pillow as Meade unlocked the door. He started to stand and sat down abruptly.

Meade saw Crispin slip as he reached for the crutches on the floor beside his bed and asked, "You okay?"

He took the crutches that Meade handed him. "Yes, thank you."

"Sure."

As Crispin walked past the desk, he noticed that the old atlas was closed. "Discover anything in that last night?"

"Wish I had. Go get washed up."

When Crispin returned, he had shaved, and his hair was wet. Although unsteady on his crutches, he walked to the desks and untied a crate.

"Take a look, Meade. These must be yours as well." Crispin looked through the contents of the box and made a stack on Meade's desk of Ordinance Survey maps of England, navigational maps of the German and English coastlines, road maps of Holland, Belgium, and France, and other small maps of the British Isles. He looked at Meade and chuckled.

"What's so funny, Professor?"

"We look like castaways."

Looking at Crispin's hospital attire and then his own, Meade laughed and said, "We are."

Handing Meade a large modern world atlas bound in a blue cloth binding, Crispin said, "Well, I for one can't abide these nightclothes for much longer."

"Jamison should be here soon. He should be able to get you a new uniform."

"Yes. That's right. I can have one tailored, now that I am in England."

Meade dropped the atlas and glared at Crispin. "Hold on, Professor. You can't get a uniform made. You are not in England."

"I most certainly am."

Glaring at Crispin, Meade said, "Your file will show that you are still in a hospital in France. You can't just show up here."

"That is merely the sham which you and others have concocted. The reality is that I am here, and I see no reason why–"

"This is a secret! Remember?"

Tugging at the tie of his robe, Crispin muttered, "Of course. Of course, you are right."

"Professor, you're stuck with me, here, in quarantine until we can find out where the treasure is buried."

"Quarantine, you said? Quarantine, by definition, oh, well, you know the common usage, I assume. It is derived from the Italian for forty days–"

"Come on, Professor. We don't have that long."

Crispin scowled and looked into the other crate on his desk. Pencils, a box of paper, and books. He slammed his hand on the desk. "What the devil is this, Meade? This crate is chockablock with translations of *Beowulf!*"

"You said there were alternate meanings to the old words. I asked Thompson to get them for—"

Crispin took a book from the crate. "Translations into Victorian English verse, indeed. These simply add another subjective layer to the interpretation." He tossed it on the edge of the desk and dug out another. "And this, a summary for schoolchildren." Crispin dropped it on the first volume. He fanned through a leather-bound book and sneered. "An Italian translation by Grion, *Beowullf: Poema Epico Anglo Sassone del VII Secolo*. Honestly, they don't even have the same climate, let alone culture."

Crispin sorted through the remaining volumes. Most went to the right of the box with the Italian translation and a few to the left.

Meade folded his arms over his chest. "What are you doing?"

"I am simply separating the wheat from the chaff. Are you familiar with that phrase? The concept?"

Narrowing his eyes, Meade said, "Yeah. Hey, I was just trying to help."

"I did not ask to be here, Mister Meade. When this war is over, there shall be two clubs in England. Those who served King and Country and those who failed to do their duty. I had intended to be in the former."

"You already are. Your service—"

"What tales do I tell over a pint at the pub? That we had a hard go of it at the Somme, and I just went missing? Shall I brag that I read a book or two while hiding in the cellar of a manor house?"

"Simmer down. This work is important."

Crispin unpacked the remaining books by slamming each book onto one stack or the other. He squirmed into his pushchair and was unable to find a comfortable way to sit. He opened a volume from the shorter stack and tried to read it and was distracted by the smell of the place. It was almost like a hospital tent. Sterile. Chemical. Off-putting. Not like a barracks of men, a pub, not dog or drink or food but of something less defined. He tried again to read.

Meade worked silently at his desk.

At seven, there was a knock at the door. A deep and husky voice said, "It is Jamison." Meade answered the door quickly. Crispin looked up from his books and saw an older man with a pronounced paunch standing outside the door beside a hospital cart. His ruddy complexion seemed even darker compared to his white hair and pale goatee. Crispin looked at the man's wool suit, tiepin, and spats. A minor official, he surmised, not a physician.

"Jamison, at your service. Floyd Jamison, administrator of this hospital."

Crispin refrained from making introductions. "Yes?"

Pushing the small cart into the room, he said, "Your breakfast, gentlemen. I understand from London that you desire a minimum of contact with my staff. Therefore, the hospital Matron or I will deliver your meals if the doctor is unable to do so."

Crispin looked at the silvered domes on the cart with interest. "Thank you."

"I regret that we can but offer these Spartan accommodations. However, rest assured that I shall personally see to any instructions you might have for staff."

Crispin tugged at his robe. "Awfully good of you. Have you a laundry here? And some clothing we could wear while our soiled attire is done up? I fear that what remains of our wardrobe has suffered unspeakably during travel."

"Of course. I am afraid that all I have to offer are added sets of pajamas and robes."

Crispin sighed. "Is there a telephone, should I require it?"

"In my office."

Crispin nodded. "Near the elevator, isn't it?"

"Yes. At least no one will pay you any mind if you are in your robe. Enjoy your breakfast. I'll be back in about an hour to collect the tray and your laundry."

Breakfast consisted of overcooked porridge with a small jug of heavy cream, a rack of charred toast, and a large pot of tea. Crispin was grateful for the fact that the meal, which he found to be entirely devoid of taste, was not completely cold.

Just after eight, Jamison returned with additional sets of blue pajamas, robes in a darker blue plaid, and slippers. He had placed two large laundry sacks on the top of the folded attire. "Our hospital laundry is quite able, you'll see."

Meade nodded. "I am sure they are. Any chance you could have our boots cleaned as well? Been in some rough areas and—"

Holding up his hand, Jamison said, "Say no more. I have a cobbler in town who is wonderful at managing the odd repair of leather goods. He has salvaged more than one pair of boots for our patients. The hospital has a standing account with him."

Meade jammed the boots into one of the sacks. He pulled his wallet from the desk drawer and slipped a five-pound note into his boot. "That cobbler is gonna earn his money." He shoved their dirty clothing into the other sack.

Jamison was discrete enough not to pay any notice to the stench that emanated from the bags.

Crispin launched into reading his assigned books and spoke infrequently during the remainder of the morning.

For lunch, Jamison brought plates of tepid slices of beef that quickly chilled. The fat in its juices congealed into yellow islands at the margins of the plate. The oven-roasted winter vegetables held the heat only slightly longer necessitating a rapid consumption and a minimum of discussion. The tea, however, was adequate. Crispin held the teapot. "Care for a bit more?"

Meade pushed his mug across the desk, thanking him absently while shrugging to loosen his neck muscles. He resumed his review of the older maps in the Verne collection that they had packed in haste. Throughout the day, Crispin continued to read *Beowulf* in the translation of others.

After dinner, he considered the day and felt that he had made little progress.

After Meade had changed into his fresh nightclothes, Crispin watched him tug back the blanket on his bed. Pointing to the stack of translations, Crispin asked, "Would you object if I stayed up reading? The sooner I read those, the sooner we may be to the end of this."

Meade laughed as he pulled the blanket over his head. "Sure. Wake me if you solve it."

Less than five miles from the recovery hospital, the Dancing Dog Inn had fewer than the usual complement of patrons. The night barman, Edward Wilson, attributed the slow evening to it being All Hallows Eve. For once, he could take a moment and admire his favorite hunting prints on the far wall. He had washed all but six of the pint glasses and considered wiping down the bar for the evening. It was well before ten when he rolled down his sleeves, buttoned the cuffs of his white shirt, and took off his black half-apron. He looked over the few hardy patrons, all older men, and guessed he would be able to close early.

As the Jones brothers left, Max Jamison finished his pint and pulled on his coat.

Only Martin Long remained, sitting alone in the corner. Wilson went to the fireplace and poked at the embers of the three pine logs. Sparks and smoke answered the insult, and the fire sputtered lower. He shoveled ashes on the embers.

Long lifted his glass of stout and called, "Ed, you trying to get gone of us? Turning us out on All Hallows Eve?"

"Nothing of the sort. Getting up on me chores, that's all."

A minute later, after the barman picked up the glass and was wiping down the small table, the door opened again.

A short man with white hair came through the door, dropped his overcoat on a chair, and stood at the end of the bar. He wore a stained

SHARON O. LIGHTHOLDER

cobbler's apron over his dark shirt and trousers. His hands were shoved deep into his trouser pockets. The barman pushed the towel along the bar. "How is it tonight, Sandy?"

"Fortune smiles."

"And how is that?"

"A double whiskey tonight, if you please."

Wilson leaned an elbow on the bar and lowered his voice. "Now, Sandy, you know. Your account—"

Long glanced over from the corner table, emptied his glass, and made an unsteady course for the door. "Well, I had better be getting on. Good night."

"See ya, Martin."

The cobbler slapped a five pound note on the bar. "Right as rain, it is now."

"A double. That more than pays it off."

"Put the remainder to my account, if you will."

He pocketed the note. "So, did a rich uncle die?"

The man laughed. "Naw. Been working on boots for Mister Meade, himself, the American tycoon."

The barman placed a glass on the bar. "You actually met him?"

"Not exactly. But I did up his boots and got five quid for it."

"Just for a pair of boots?"

"His and a pair of officer's boots. But custom made, they were."

The barman grinned as he poured. "So, of all the cobblers in all of England, Meade came to you—"

"Naw. Jamison brought the items to me on his behalf. Wants the boots back tomorrow. Boots for his patients don't usually have no rush to them."

Wilson poured another drink and winked. "Here's to a good day's work, then."

After his third drink, the cobbler glanced around the pub and saw that he was the last customer. "Best I be on my way, so as you can lock up." He put on his overcoat and lurched for the door. He almost bumped into the tall man in a dark suit who was entering the pub. The man went straight to the bar and rapped on it.

Wilson smiled as he wiped his hands on a small towel. "Be right with you, sir."

After the door slammed, the man asked softly, "Anyone else about?"

"Not now."

"Well, then. Got any news for me? Anything unusual?"

Nodding toward the door, Wilson said, "The man what just left told me that he did up some boots for Mister Meade, the American."

"Where is he?"

"Lives over his shop—"

"No. The American?"

"Hospital, I gathered." The barman tipped his head. "Just down the lane a piece. You know, there was something odd. I forgot to mention it when you were in late last night. A new ambulance driver stopped in for a pint—"

"Hardly news, that—"

"Asked for two bottles of Bass. Took them with him."

"What's so—"

"Asked me to leave the capper on the bottles. Said he'd open them his self. Odd thing, as they don't allow no drink at the hospital now that the army's taken it over."

The tall man put two ten pound notes on the bar, pushed them across the scarred walnut, and left.

Chapter № 27

Wednesday
November 1, 1916
North of London, England

When Crispin squirmed in his pushchair, the plaster cast thudded into the desk. Meade rolled over in bed and glanced at him. "You okay, Professor?"

"Sorry to wake you. Even with the blankets over my lap, I've been shivering for the past half hour."

Meade crawled out of bed and pulled on his robe. He rubbed his hands together and pulled the blanket from his bed and tossed it to Crispin. "It was colder in the airplane, and we lived through that."

"Barely. What time is it?"

Meade started to unbuckle his watchband. "Here. Take it."

"No. I was quite fond of mine. But I cannot read it clearly through a cracked crystal."

"It's five twenty-five, in the morning."

Crispin opened a new book, pretending to read. "Thank you."

After half an hour, Crispin shut the book, pushed the wicker chair away from the desk, and stretched his neck. He muttered under his breath as he dug in the pocket of his dressing gown for his briar pipe and tobacco pouch. "Nonsense. Utter nonsense."

He packed his pipe and watched Meade leave for the bathroom. Under other circumstances, he might be interesting company. But he was tired of Meade. Tired of watching him examine maps with a hand lens that he always seemed to drop on the desk. He had reflected, more than once, how profoundly he objected to the manner in which Meade had him press-ganged into service.

He sighed and focused his attention on his pipe, tamping it and finally lighting it. Through a cloud of good Cavendish, he glared as Meade returned to his desk and opened yet another map. At least the smoke from his pipe tobacco masked some of the acidic stench of the room.

After Crispin finished his pipe, he rolled the pushchair alongside his desk and joined Meade in grinding away at their research materials under the harsh light. They slouched over their respective desks, glowering at their work.

When Doctor Lee knocked and unlocked the door at six thirty, she laughed. They each looked up with matching frowns. Crispin stared at her dark garnet suit and matching hat, which was much more formal than her traveling suit. Yet her only adornment remained the gold watch dangling from its chain and her jet beads.

She pushed a cart holding two plates of small sandwiches and a large pot of tea. "You fellows look like an old married couple over your newspapers."

Crispin grimaced. "Sandwiches for breakfast? Is that an American custom?"

She chuckled. "No. They count the breakfast trays for the daily census. This was all I could manage."

In her absence, Meade had rooted through the clutter of furniture and pulled out a square table and a chair, which he had butted against their facing desks. He had placed her knitting bag on it. The beginning of a small lap robe in pale blue had escaped from the bag. She pushed it back in.

"Doctor Lee? How's this for a work table?"

"That will do very nicely, Mister Meade. Thank you."

As Crispin stared at her hat, he asked, "Are you leaving us?"

She opened the door. "Briefly. Services in the chapel."

Meade poured two mugs of tea, brought them to the desks, and handed Crispin a plate of sandwiches. They continued their silent examination of their materials while they ate.

About an hour later, Doctor Lee returned with a fresh pot of tea, on a large cart draped with a sheet. She poured a mug for herself, and took it to her table. Meade went to the side table by the door and poured tea for Crispin and himself. Doctor Lee sat, removed her hat, stuck the long hatpin back into it, and placed it carefully on her knitting bag. She picked up her mug of tea and blew across the top. "Let's work on the sea-level problem. I thought of a city that might meet your needs."

Crispin held the warm mug between both palms and listened to the Americans.

"Okay, Doctor, which city?"

"Venice. I thought of it because of an article I read some months ago about their continual battle with *acqua alta*, as they call high water, to preserve the crypt of Saint Mark. You see, the plaza in front of the cathedral regularly floods. The cold *bora* winds come from the northeast and the sirocco winds blow out of Africa. Both generate waves that push water into the lagoon of Venice."

Meade sat down, his tea splashing on the desk. He wiped up the drop with his hand. "That is a storm condition—"

Nodding, she asked, "But if it is happening more frequently now than in the past, wouldn't that suggest a fundamental change in the sea level?"

Meade sat back with his sandwich. "Maybe."

She smiled. "In the fifth century, they built interconnected islands on pillars in the bay for defense. You see, they were trying to avoid invasion by the Huns and Goths. The approach by land was across a marsh and difficult to cross. The Adriatic Sea, which meets the bay, is fairly shallow. Deep draft warships could not get close to Venice, but the shallow draft trading ships could."

Crispin took a small bite of his sandwich and muttered, "Clever. But don't you mean that they built *on* islands?"

"No. I mean precisely what I said." Meade choked slightly on his sandwich as she continued. "Thousands of alder trees were cut from the surrounding countryside and their trunks pounded into the mud to make the foundation on which the city was built. It is not on naturally occurring islands."

Meade took a sip of tea. "Is there any record of how high they built above the water?"

"Not that I know. But the article did say that the crypt of Saint Mark was six feet above the waterline when it was built."

Meade leaned toward her. "When was that?"

Crispin returned his attention to his sandwich as she said, "I'll need to check, but I recall that it was shortly after 1000." She looked around the room. "Don't you have any reference books down here?"

Meade pointed to the materials on the desks, "Just some maps and–"

Crispin snickered as Meade pointed to his case of books and said, "And more translations of *Beowulf* than one can shake a stick at."

Doctor Lee frowned at Crispin and turned to Meade as he asked, "How far above sea level is it now?"

Before she could answer, Crispin finished the last bite of his sandwich and slid the plate across his desk with a flourish. "Aren't you overlooking one thing?"

Doctor Lee asked, "What would that be, Lieutenant?"

"Could Venice be sinking?"

Doctor Lee sighed and looked into her tea mug as though an answer were awaiting her there. "I don't know. It is a relative matter, isn't it? We need a constant, not a variable."

Meade said, "Doctor Lee. I think you've got the right idea–"

She nodded. "But the wrong city. I'll try to find another example without those variables. Any ideas, Mister Meade?"

"I'm looking for an island of rock. Something that is *not* going to sink, or have sediment collect in an estuary that turns into a delta. I don't want land that crumbles like the chalk cliffs at Dover."

She nodded once. "That's what I needed. Guidelines."

Meade slid his chair away from the desk and started to pace.

"Between 1300 and 1400, Europe got colder by a couple of degrees a year."

Crispin snapped, "How do you know–"

"Tree rings are thin in cold years and thicker in warm ones. Some guy studied the grain of wood on violins made over a couple hundred years and matched the dates to the ring size. As glaciers grew, the sea level dropped. The fragments of coastal maps from the 1300s show the change in sea level."

Doctor Lee's eyes brightened as though she were a student finding the answer to a difficult math problem. "In that extreme cold, crops would have failed and a malnourished population would provide an opportunistic target for disease."

Meade stopped pacing and stood near her. "Makes sense."

"How dramatic was the shift in crops?"

Meade leaned his palms on the desk. "Before the cold, wine was being produced in England and Vineland, what we now call Nova Scotia in North America. Then the change drove the growing areas south, to France and Italy."

Crispin lifted his hand to interrupt. "Vineland? Named for grapes?"

Glancing at Crispin, Meade said, "Precisely."

Doctor Lee crossed her arms. "Wine from northern Canada? I will have to think on that for a bit."

Pointing to his crate, Meade said, "I have good maps of the wrong times. Few maps ever existed of the time I need, so I have to back into this information somehow."

Doctor Lee sighed. "I see your point. You assume that today's sea level would be different than it was on your portolano. Higher or lower?"

"Don't know. But I can't find a coastline that matches it on a modern map of England."

Crispin finished his sandwich and stretched. "Even if Meade finds the place on the map, how would we ever locate a buried ship? Dig about for a few years?"

She said, "I doubt if it was buried completely. I would expect something like that to be a monument, not a secret. Most likely there will be a small hillock. A barrow."

Meade turned to her. "Barrow?"

Crispin sighed. "By definition, a barrow is an earthen mound under which one may find archaeological artifacts."

Doctor Lee nodded. "Occasionally, they are a foundation to a building, but more often burial mounds of persons or things."

Sitting straighter in his wicker chair, Crispin asked, "Would you expect it to be heaps of rock or would it be grassed over?"

"Wind would carry soil that would have settled on it. I would expect a mound, a small hill. What is or is not growing in that soil is another matter."

Crispin leaned forward. "So then. We would be searching for a place where man has interrupted the natural landscape. An anomaly, by definition, a break in the normal expected pattern."

"Yes. For example, your trenches in France will probably be scars on the land for a couple hundred years, unless someone plows them over." She thought a moment. "But then, that would alter the earth yet again. Land has a memory. It holds history. Mister Meade, did you know that you can still see the tracks of the covered wagons that crossed the American prairies?"

Meade started to say something when Crispin interrupted. "How long were the ships?"

She spread her hands apart. "A hundred feet or so."

"Might we see a point for the bow of the ship at the end of a barrow?"

Doctor Lee paused for a moment before reaching for a sheet of paper and taking the pencil from the top of Meade's desk. "Here. Let me show you." She sketched the profile of a Viking ship on the sea and then from above. She tapped the pointed stern of the craft. "Viking ships were pointed at *both* ends, so there might be an elongated barrow shape. Possibly an oval. But it would be a first."

Meade looked skeptical. "A first? What do you mean by that? There are records of other ship burials."

She said firmly, "Not in England."

Meade looked frustrated as he picked up the sketch and stared at it. "But if it is under a mound, why hasn't someone dug into it by now?"

"Mister Meade, you assume it is in an area where it would be noticed. What if it is in a woods or in a bog somewhere? And even if it were known, some of these mounds are nothing but trash heaps of broken pottery and refuse. Some of the barrow diggers didn't know how to excavate and might have missed the treasure."

Crispin leaned forward in his chair and challenged her. "Why would they miss it?"

"The barrows that interested the wealthy amateur diggers in the 1800s were often on their own estates. Their treasure hunting is what spurred the current discipline of archaeology. But if someone started digging and just found rubbish at the margin of the mound, they might stop before they got to the treasure."

Meade stood and paced the length of the room. He put his hands behind his neck and twisted his back as he walked.

Crispin laughed. "What irony if that were the case."

She smiled. "There was little science to it. A gardener or hired help performed the actual digging, more often than not. Certainly some of the barrow diggers were not much more than treasure hunters or artifact collectors. They had no regard for the time of an artifact or its relative location to other materials. We have become a lot smarter on how we approach a dig today."

Crispin rubbed his eyes. "Aren't there some reference books we can go to on this damnable water-level issue with which Meade is consumed?"

"Not that I know. We are just at the start of our knowledge of these things. But thank you for reminding me, Lieutenant."

Crispin raised his eyebrows. "Pardon me? I don't seem to follow—"

She pointed to the empty counter at the rear of the room. "Reference materials. I did not see either an encyclopedia or authoritative dictionary down here. So I borrowed them from the manor's library."

"You did what?"

"Just put the largest dictionary I could find and the complete 1911 *Encyclopedia Britannica* on the cart's lower shelf. Covered the cart with a sheet and disguised it so well, I nearly forgot it." She turned to Meade. "Could I impose on you to unload that cart, Mister Meade?" She pointed to the end of the room.

Meade pushed the cart. "Of course."

"Lieutenant, I looked up the answer to when Saint Mark was encrypted. It was actually 1094. I was close but not precise in my recollection. As I researched this, I thought, why not bring the encyclopedia down here?"

Crispin muttered more to himself than in response. "And precisely why would I need either reference?"

"Scientific methodology. I have found that the referral back to original source documents such as Gray's anatomy, or even my own clinical notes, can often serve to give me a new perspective on a problem or refresh my recollection in a way that offers fresh thinking."

Meade glanced up from putting the black cloth-bound volumes of the encyclopedia in order as Crispin raised his voice. "So you think I need a dictionary? Well, which is it?"

She tipped her head. "Pardon?"

Crispin demanded, "Which dictionary? I certainly hope that it is the *OED*."

Meade looked at the spine of the red cloth bound book. "It's *Routledge's New English Dictionary*."

Crispin ignored Meade and said to Doctor Lee, "I want the *OED*, if anything. That's the *Oxford English Dictionary*, you know."

"Yes. But I am certain they will not have the full edition."

Crispin interrupted her. "Which has grown to well over a dozen volumes."

She continued, "I will see if they have a shorter edition."

"I would prefer the one edited by Sykes."

Doctor Lee glanced at him and raised an eyebrow. "Apparently, beggars *can* be choosers."

Crispin looked away from her and blushed. He cleared his throat. "I mean no offense. I simply was requesting the appropriate authority on which to base my work. That is my field of study, after all."

"I was making an observation on method, not ability. I'll see if they have the *OED* you want."

Crispin made an exceptional effort to sound calm. "Well, perhaps you are correct. It could not be a hindrance, could it?"

"No, Lieutenant. It couldn't. Here's my thinking. Poetry does not always say what it means or mean what it says. It operates at a level either above or below what you might ordinarily understand. So maybe an allegorical or poetic meaning might be what we are seeking, not the literal truth of each individual word on Meade's map. Like calling the sea the 'whale's way.'"

Crispin relaxed. "That is called a 'kenning.' Each kenning has a specific translated value. But they are all logical if you know your history. 'Breaker of rings' is a kenning that means 'king.'" When he saw Meade's confusion, he continued. "Kings wore gold bracelets on their upper arms, called 'rings.' They might take a few rings off, the gold bracelets that is, and give them to warriors who pleased them as an honor as well as a monetary reward."

Meade paced back to the desk and stood behind Doctor Lee. "What's another one? Try me!"

"'Raven harvest'?"

Meade answered quickly. "A battlefield. War. Too easy."

Crispin smiled wickedly. "What is the meaning of 'Bane of Baldur'?"

Meade threw up his hands. "Got me there."

Doctor Lee started to answer. "Baldur was a mythological god. But what was his bane? Okay, I surrender. What is it?"

"Mistletoe. Myth has it that all plants and creatures swore not to harm Baldur, all but mistletoe, which was overlooked, so when Loki uses it to trick Hodur to bring about Baldur's death, mistletoe becomes the Bane of Baldur. Easy— if you have the key."

Doctor Lee said, "Just like those two mystery words on the map."

Crispin scowled at Meade. "I did not initiate this fool's errand. Meade stumbled on a map, has a half-baked translation of the Old English from some writer, and now thinks the words in second-rate translations of *Beowulf* are the key to the treasure. Tell me that's not ridiculous? Going off at a half-cock—"

Doctor Lee slapped her hand on the desk. "Lieutenant—"

The veins in Crispin's neck stood out and he jutted his face forward. "What? Are you defending him? You just arrived, and yet you seem to have the notion that this is some Sunday-paper puzzle that just needs a pencil and a cup of tea—"

Meade stood away from Doctor Lee and moved toward Crispin. "That's enough, Professor. Knock it off."

"Why? Because I think your theory is laden with *lacunae*, that is to say it has a few holes in it?"

Doctor Lee adopted a calming tone. "Not necessarily. There are other examples of archaeological finds predicated upon commonly available written works."

Crispin's eyes narrowed. "Such as?"

"Heinrich Schliemann taught himself Greek and translated Homer on the fall of Troy."

"As I have done."

"But, based on his translation, he calculated where Troy was located, and ultimately found it. Of course, the story is a bit more complicated. He used some good sense looking for disturbance in the surrounding landscape, but—"

Crispin gave an artificial laugh. "Not all of these little plans have been successful, have they?"

She said, "Of course not. Constantine the Great sent an expedition to Palestine to find the tomb of Jesus. That did not prove fruitful." Crispin shrugged, and Doctor Lee continued. "Chance discoveries have been much more common. Pompeii was discovered by a peasant in 1748. The Rosetta stone was discovered by one of Napoleon's captains in Egypt in a military campaign. That led to an understanding of hieroglyphics and other ancient lost languages."

Crispin smirked. "So, are you saying that any pig can find truffles?"

"Hardly. I'm certain that there are exceptions to any rule. Like the rule that officers are gentlemen."

Lowering his eyes, Crispin said, "I am most deeply apologetic. I did not intend that as it sounded."

"I understand the pressure you and Mister Meade have been putting on yourselves to resolve this. Fatigue can be damaging. But I think that we do need to retain some civility, or this is going to be even more difficult if you continually criticize."

He nodded toward her and extended his hand toward Meade. "Quite so. Dreadfully sorry." Meade shook Crispin's hand. Each of the three retreated to their reading and note-making in silence.

By two thirty in the morning, Crispin was staring into his empty tea mug and Meade was stretching to stay awake.

Doctor Lee closed a volume of the encyclopedia with a thud. "Well, I say we call it a day and get back to this in the morning. Remember, I have rounds, so I should be joining you about midmorning. Anything you want me to smuggle down tomorrow? Crackers and cheese?"

Crispin nodded. "Capital idea, if you can manage it. Thank you."

Abandoning her desk, she said, "Goodnight, fellas." After she left, Crispin and Meade stretched out on their hospital beds wearing their robes for warmth and wrapped themselves in blankets.

Crispin covered his head with the blanket, the way he had done as a boy in the boardinghouse to keep away the sounds. He sighed and began his ritual before sleep. At home, it began with *The Lord's Prayer*. After he translated it into Old English, he recited it to himself in that mysterious and ancient tongue. Now, as a whisper for himself, in place of the vigil which he would have preferred before All Souls Day. A prayer for the departed not yet in heaven. For the named and nameless.

Fæder ure þu þe eart on heofonum si þin nama gehalgod. To becume þin rice, gewurþe ðin willa, on eorðan swa swa on heofonum. Urne gedæghwamlican hlaf syle us todæg, and forgyf us ure gyltas, swa swa we forgyfað urum gyltendum. And ne gelæd þu us on costnunge, ac alys us of yfele. Soþlice.

Chapter № 28

Thursday
November 2, 1916
North of London, England

After what seemed to Crispin to have been only a few minutes, there was a rapping on the door. He looked at his watch, gave up trying to read it, and let his arm fall on the blanket. "What time is it, Meade?"

"Just after five."

Meade disentangled himself from his blankets and padded toward the door while tying his robe.

Crispin called after him. "Morning or night?"

"Morning."

"Still can't tell in this bloody cave. Got my times twisted about staying up the other night."

Meade opened the door. She was wearing a dark gray tweed suit. In addition to her watch on a gold chain and strand of jet beads, she also wore an amethyst pin at the throat of the stand-up collar on her crisp white blouse. She pushed a large cart carrying a tea tray and two large platters covered with tin domes. Meade took the cart from her and pushed it up to their desks.

Remaining in the doorway, she called to them, "Breakfast, boys. Your own clothes are on the bottom shelf, as well as fresh bed linens. I'll be back later to see what you really look like."

Meade pointed at the cart and laughed. "Did you steal the breakfast trays?"

"I am ashamed to say that larceny is starting to suit me. I simply delayed reporting two discharged patients, so the tray count will still be correct. And Lieutenant, they did have your *Concise Oxford Dictionary of Current English*. It's on the cart."

Crispin sat up on his bed. "Thank you."

As she pulled the door shut, she said, "Eat while it is hot. We'll need our brains today."

Within the hour, Crispin and Meade had eaten. Meade changed the sheets on their beds. Crispin sorted the clothing, put his freshly laundered uniform on his lap, and wheeled to the bathroom. After dressing in his fresh undergarments and slipping into his uniform shirt, he attempted to negotiate his wool breeches. He unlaced the cuff just below the knee and pulled it over his cast. Lacking his high boots or leggings, his right calf was bare. Crispin buttoned his breeches, sat back in the pushchair, tied his tie, and struggled into his jacket.

When he returned to the workroom, Meade was still in his nightclothes. He looked at Crispin and started laughing.

Crispin sat straighter. "Sorry?"

"Either you just gained about fifty pounds, or they shrunk your uniform."

Crispin examined his cuff, which was now well above his wrist. "It seems to have compressed."

Meade picked his sweater off the desk and pushed his hand through a gaping hole in the side. "No hope for my things either." Meade threw the sweater toward his bed, where he had left his tattered trousers.

Tugging the cuff over his wrist, Crispin said, "Still, this is superior to wearing my nightclothes. I wonder when we'll get our boots back? At least I could wear the one."

"Should be soon."

Crispin flipped through the pages of the new dictionary and made notes for a few minutes before dropping his pencil on the desk and stretching. "Well, Meade. I have to tell you that I certainly have avoided the obvious."

"How's that?"

"The Doctor had it spot on. My return to source material has provided a fresh perspective."

Meade pulled a blanket from Crispin's bed and handed it to him. "How so?"

Crispin wrapped it around his bare leg. "I simply looked up the definition of some of the key words within the poem's burial scenes. Specifically, the words 'salvage' and 'flood.'"

"Okay, what did you find?"

"As you had mentioned that you thought that the ship may have been adrift and then salvaged, I researched that word. In the context of the poem, 'salvage' is an intransitive verb in modern English. However, the distinction was not as clear in the past between verb forms. Given that fact, I am enlarging my consideration of that word."

"Meaning what?"

"Well, by definition, it has several meanings." Crispin made a fist and rolled out his thumb to begin the count. "As a noun, it could refer to the compensation paid someone who saves the ship from the perils of the sea." He extended his index finger, saying, "The act itself of saving the ship and its cargo where there was no duty to do so, verb. Or the property itself, noun. If it were a verb, it would mean that someone actively tried to gain control over an abandoned vessel."

"Professor, I'm sorry. I just don't see the point you are trying to make."

Crispin rushed on, ignoring Meade, "Well, then I looked at other words near it in the listing of the *OED* and came upon, 'salvage man.' Assuming that might refer to the person who performed the act of salvaging a ship, I read on and much to my surprise—"

Motioning for him to come to the point, Meade asked, "And?"

"'Salvage man' comes from the Middle English word *sauvage*. Initially, I thought there was confusion between 'salvage' and 'savage,' but there wasn't."

Meade leaned on his own desk. "Well, you have me confused now."

"The salvage man is a person living in a primitive state or belonging to a primitive society. A savage, if you will."

"How does that help us?"

"Well, I really don't know, yet. The word is from a later time, but it caused me to think on the state of moral development reflected in the poem."

Meade shook his head as he returned to his chair and reached for a map. "Let me know what you decide."

At noon, Doctor Lee knocked before letting herself into the workroom. She carried a tattered paper box to her table and began removing the contents. Crispin watched her as she pulled out a dented teakettle with a small whistle on the spout. He crossed his arms over his chest and scowled at her. She took a small tin of tea from the box and slid it over to him. He raised his eyebrows and nodded. "Fine blend. But–"

As she pulled rubber tubing from the box and let it drop like a snake on her table, she said, "I, for one, am tired of fetching tea for us–" She dug into the box and pulled out a metal rack and several tea towels.

Crispin feigned concern. "How can we make tea down here when there is no stove?"

She glanced at Crispin, rested her hands flat on the desk, and examined his uniform in detail.

Crispin tugged at his collar. "What is it?"

She shook her head and pointed at him. "Your jacket!" She laughed. "It could fit an organ grinder's monkey." She shook her head and pulled a squat metal tube on a flat base, which she held in front of her as though it were a trophy. "We'll use a Bunsen burner. Every lab has them, and if you do any research, you learn to make a meal on one. If I can do that, I am confident that you gentlemen will be able to make tea."

Meade smiled as he accepted the teakettle she held for him and went to the deep sink at the back of the room to fill it. She followed him and connected the tube to the gas jet on the wall above the counter, attached the Bunsen burner, and placed the metal rack above it. She struck a match and turned the valve on the wall. The burner whooshed, and an amber and red flame shot up a foot in the air. She adjusted the flame until it was an almost invisible blue. Meade put the kettle on the rack carefully, poured the cold remains of the teapot down the sink, put the sodden tea leaves into the waste bin, soaped and rinsed the pot, and left it next to the kettle.

Doctor Lee settled into her chair and took some notes from the box before she dropped it to the floor. "Well? Are you boys ready for a summary of the digs that I think might be relevant while the water heats? Each, Mister Meade, is firmer *terra firma* than Venice."

Crispin leaned back in his wicker chair and laughed. "Good one."

Doctor Lee started laughing again at Crispin's attire. The gold setting around the amethyst sparkled under the bright lights. Crispin watched the light dance on the stone and thought how well it would have looked on his mother.

"Lieutenant? What ever are we going to do with you? And, Mister Meade?" Turning toward Meade, she asked, "I gather your clothing was similarly compromised?"

"Yes."

Doctor Lee returned to her notes. "Let me try to summarize some information that may start our thinking, Mister Meade. That is, if I can keep from laughing."

Meade tipped his head toward Crispin. "Good luck."

Crispin squirmed in his chair. "Doctor Lee? Would you be kind enough to excuse me for a few moments—"

"Just pull up your blanket, Lieutenant. You can change later. I need to go over this with you now, while I have a break in my duties upstairs."

The kettle started to boil and water splashed on the counter. Doctor Lee jumped from her chair, took the kettle from the rack, and immediately turned off the gas.

Crispin laughed at her haste. "Some fine tea-wallah you are going to make. Look how fast you—"

She took a towel and mopped up the hot water. "Don't think for a moment that I don't know what a tea-wallah is. There were a good plenty of older soldiers who had served in India who used that phrase when I was in Edinburgh. I'll not be the only one down here making tea, I'll have you know."

Crispin chuckled. "Can't get ahead of you, can I?"

She warmed the pot with hot water. "I had neglected to put the whistle on the spout. If the flame had extinguished, the gas would have—"

Crispin gestured broadly. "Say no more. We shall cap the spout from this moment forward." The shoulder seam of his jacket ripped, and a flap dangled over Crispin's bicep.

Meade pointed at the seam. "It looks like it's back to your PJs and a robe."

"Meade, if you think I plan to work through the remainder of the war in my nightclothes, you are sadly in error." Crispin smiled at the absurdity of the situation and then laughed with the others.

Meade shoved a sheet of paper over to Crispin. "Professor, I don't think we have much of a choice for a day or so. Jot down your particulars."

"My what?"

"You know. Waist and inseam for trousers. Collar. Sleeve length. I'll call my tailor and see what he can do."

He wrote quickly. "Splendid idea. Splendid." Crispin pushed the paper back to Meade, who slipped it into his pocket.

After Doctor Lee had emptied the pot, added tea leaves and hot water, she returned to the table. Crispin put his robe on over his uniform, leaned back, and gave her his full attention.

"I think my work at the Birka dig is going to be the most helpful."

Meade pulled the modern atlas from the chest and searched the index. "Where's that?"

"Oh. It won't be in your index since it disappeared. It's outside of Stockholm. The closest town is Björkö, Birch Island."

Meade settled in his chair. "If it disappeared, how…never mind, go ahead."

She pointed to a spot on Lake Mälaren. "Once, this connected to the Baltic Sea. Birka operated as a major trading center from about 700 to 900 A.D."

Crispin nodded. "Well, that certainly is a good match for the time."

Meade sat forward. "How'd you figure those dates?"

"We found dated Arabic silver coins called 'dirhams' in our dig. Prior excavations unearthed pearls from Russia, Chinese silk, and Rhineland glass."

Meade scowled. "What did they export? Fish?"

"No. Other Baltic ports specialized in fish or salt, which was worth its weight in gold, literally, in the twelfth century. Essential for food preservation and thus trade and exploration."

Meade said, "You make it sound so rare."

"It was, until our age. I've read accounts of caravans of thousands of camels carrying salt across the Sahara. It was the mainstay of the spice route."

Crispin turned to Meade. "She's right. The *Atle Salzstraße*, Old Salt Route, ran from the mines at Lüneburg to Lübeck, where it was shipped throughout the Baltic. Their salt trade is what made Lübeck such a formidable power in the Hanseatic League."

Doctor Lee said, "Birka had little to do with the salt trade either. They exported Swedish iron and furs. We found numerous smelters, crucibles, and molds of stone for casting bronze bars and rods. And we also found delicate molds for making pendants and fine jewelry."

Crispin asked, "Did you find any of the actual jewelry?"

She shook her head. "Not while I was there. All of that was discovered and catalogued long before I got there. Remember, this was a dig that had been in process since 1871. It started when Hjalmar Stolpe was looking for fossilized insects in amber to assist in his bug work."

Crispin laughed. "What?"

She pointed to the teapot on the counter. "Most likely, it is ready now, Mister Meade." Without pausing, she said, "He was an entomologist who knew that insects got trapped in sap that turned to amber. Well, on Birka he found a huge amount of amber, and deduced that it was not from the local pine and birch trees, but a trading cache. He figured Birka for an important trading location and shifted his field of study to archaeology. Changed his life's work in an instant."

Meade carried the brown glazed pot to his desk and poured hot tea for them. "Just like that?"

"Yes. For the next twenty years, he trenched the island and cataloged his finds. By the time I left, there were four hundred sixty-three inhumations, multi-generations in family plots, a rather advanced society."

Crispin glanced at Meade who looked puzzled. "Inhumations are, by definition, human burials." Crispin's hand shook as he tucked his blanket around his bare leg.

"Yes. This was a transitional society. The early Viking tradition was cremation with the remains buried inside a rock-ringed area."

"Did they use boats?"

"We did not find any. Just the ship outline in rock. Later, Christian burials adopted the Muslim practice, which forbids cremation. They began using coffins. Frequently, we found both a symbol for the hammer of Thor and a rudimentary crucifix in the same coffin."

Crispin scowled. "Foreign influence? Intermarriage?"

"You might be right. By 970, they abandoned the village of Birka and moved to Sigtuna. We have a good historic date on it. They just packed up and moved."

Meade asked, "Why?"

"We think it was a shift in sea level. The trade ships could not get to it as easily as to Sigtuna."

Meade slapped the desk. "Did you hear that, Professor?"

She held up her hand in caution. "It is not that simple. As commerce got more complex, larger ships were used. This was one factor. But it seems that the sea level did subside at some time to the point that even smaller ships cannot sail to Birka today."

Crispin stared at her over his mug of tea. "Any indication of Birka sinking like Venice?"

"No. It is a rock island. We also know there was a shallowing of the Södertälje water route. It was a bay. It is a lake now."

Crispin nodded. "That's certainly a step in the right direction. Interesting that they had trade coming to them. I don't think of them as traders."

Meade asked, "Who? The Vikings?"

"Yes. By the way, do you know the derivation of the word 'Viking'?"

Meade clasped his hands behind his neck and stretched. "No. But I'll bet you can tell me, Professor."

"Actually, the history is a bit fuzzy, but 'Vik' seems to mean harbor or port in Saxon. The letter 'A' creates a negative. Thus to go A-Viking is to be out of port, out of town, at sea, and thus raiding. The 'ing' is just the verb form."

Doctor Lee looked up with a glare. "Gentlemen, that is far too simplistic a perspective on those people. They didn't just pillage monasteries and farms. They used contractual agreements and treaties. A great deal of what we credit as English common law comes directly from the Viking codes of conduct."

Meade sat back. "Really?"

Doctor Lee nodded. "For example, look at how the Duchy of Normandy was established. The Vikings rowed their longboats up the Seine River from the English Channel to Paris. They held the government of Charles III under siege on the island where the Cathedral of Notre Dame is today. Finally, they came to terms in 911 and signed the Treaty of Saint-Clair-sur-Epte. The French bought their peace. The Vikings got a lot of cash and the Province of France they called 'Nuestra.' We call it 'Normandy' today."

Crispin frowned, winced, and looked away.

"Lieutenant? The leg?"

"Oh. No. It is fine. I was just thinking of the price that France and her allies are paying now." He shook his head as if to toss the thought away. "Doctor Lee, you said the raids started in a monastery. How long had it been there? Could it be a tide marker?"

"Monks brought Christianity to Ireland and then Irish monks took it to England. The Lindisfarne Monastery was established in the early 600s, on a rocky island. Viking raids were documented at the monastery in 793. This is the first reliable record of a raid. Of course, there may have been others which were not recorded."

Crispin sat straighter and asked, "Doctor Lee? Did you know that there was a prayer related to the Northmen?"

"Yes, if you will forgive my Latin.... Let me think. *A furore Normannorum libera nos, Domine.*"

"Nothing to forgive there– perfectly recited."

Meade coughed. "Anyone going to translate for me?"

"Certainly, Meade. 'Protect us from the fury of the Northmen.' That is the customary translation. Doctor Lee, you might want to review the Viking conquest of England for Mister Meade."

"Well, the Vikings launched two simultaneous invasions at the death of Edward the Confessor. Now, as though history wasn't hard enough to get right, Harold of England marched against Harald of Norway, who had landed at Yorkshire. In a battle at York, the English Harold won, stopping the Norwegians. But then he learned that William from Normandy had landed in southern England. Harold had to march two hundred forty miles in thirteen days to get to Hastings in Sussex on the east coast, where William was camped. You know, William won the Battle of Hastings."

Opening a book, Crispin said, "Of course, to become William the Conqueror." He retreated to his reading. Meade paced while Crispin read at what seemed to be an irritatingly slow rate.

Meade reached across the desks and tugged at Crispin's book. "Not so fast, Professor. You can't just vanish into a book when you want to. You've said William brought French words. Is that any help in looking at our two odd words on the map?"

Shaking his head, Crispin huffed before answering. "Not that I can see. Even the French require vowels, often far too many for my taste."

Meade stalked around the desk toward Crispin. "Then how the heck are we going to figure out what these two words are?"

Crispin stared at the letters. "It is encrypted, encoded, or an abbreviation. Simple enough."

"If it's so simple, what is it?"

Crispin slammed the translation shut. "I don't know yet. I'll work on it after I finish the translations you have ordered me to read. Unless, of course, you want me to stop this nonsense and start work on the encryption. I remain at your beck and call."

Meade stopped a pace short of his desk. "Knock it off. When are you going to be through reading the translations?"

Crispin opened the book again. "Sooner, if you leave me be. Later, if you keep at me."

"Do I need to get a code breaker in here?"

Crispin leaned forward and smirked. "Are you acquainted with any code breaker, as you call them— particularly one who knows Old English?"

Putting his hands on his hips, Meade grinned. "Sure isn't me. I don't know code at all."

Crispin looked up and laughed. "Of course you do, by definition. You speak. That's an encoded message. You write. That is a very complex coded system of communication. Transmission of thought to sound and then to symbols is quite an achievement."

"You know what I mean. Morse code and ciphers."

"Meade, be clear when you speak." Crispin began writing. "Come look. A code is a representation of one thing by another. As one example, our artillery code uses a combination of letters and numbers to correct artillery fire. The numbers one through twelve are directional, with twelve as north—"

Meade looked over Crispin's shoulder. "South being six, I'd guess."

"Right. The distance is in letters, for example 'Y' means ten yards, 'zed', what you call 'zee' represents 25 yards. I need not disclose the entire pattern. But if our forward radio man saw our artillery falling short by twenty-five yards to the south, he would call in a correction of—"

Meade looked at the paper and grinned. "Twelve zed. Okay. I get the difference."

"Splendid. In the future, should you mean 'cipher', then say it."

Meade clenched his jaw and shook his head as he walked back to his desk.

Doctor Lee looked up from her papers. "Lieutenant, do you consider puzzles such as crossword or acrostics to be ciphers or codes?"

"Neither. Although they use some of the same logic. Their intention is to tease first and then convey information to anyone who is able to resolve the puzzle. Encoded messages are usually intended for a select and often secret reader."

She took off her glasses. "If I recall, there were parts of the *Bible* that were encoded as well."

Crispin nodded. "Quite so. The *Book of Revelations* being the obvious reference."

Meade crossed his arms and leaned back in his chair. "Can someone let me in on the secret?"

"Doctor Lee is quite correct in her recollection. The Number of the Beast and the '666' references found in the *Book of Revelations* were early Christian code for the Roman government and, some say, to Emperor Nero in particular."

"Why use a code?"

Doctor Lee said, "Being a Christian was punishable by death. Not until Constantine removed that penalty were Christians able to practice their faith in the Roman Empire without reprisal."

Meade asked, "Is that what we have here? Someone going outside the traditions—"

Crispin smirked. "If you were hiding, as you so delicately put it a few days ago, a 'boatload of gold', would you be so stupid as to leave directions just lying about? This scramble protected the treasure as well as the king's burial site."

Meade pushed back from the desk and stalked toward the door. "No. I'm not really *that* stupid."

The slammed door bounced open. Doctor Lee got up, locked the door after Meade, and said to Crispin, "Lieutenant!"

Crispin chuckled. "He'll not go far in his nightclothes."

Chapter № 29

Thursday
November 2, 1916
North of London, England

Doctor Lee marched directly toward Crispin. "Lieutenant, I want to speak with you candidly, as a physician."

He continued making notes without looking at her. "What now?"

"Lieutenant! Is this how you usually behave?"

Jerking his head, Crispin recoiled as if slapped. "What ever do you—"

Her hands were on her hips. "Belittling Mister Meade."

"Was I short just now?"

"You bait him, looking for a fight. I am sure that you do not intend to be unpleasant." He shrugged, but she continued. "Your demeanor is not my concern."

He tossed down his pencil, which bounced off the desk and hit the floor with a snap. "What is?"

"The cause of your discomfort."

Crispin tightened the tie on his robe and fussed with the blanket. "Damn leg throbs constantly. Should I just go on about it?"

"I believe that there is another reason for your outbursts."

He folded his arms over his chest. "You do, do you?"

She pulled the chair from her table and sat closer to him. "Lieutenant, I cannot begin to imagine the things you must have experienced in France. Those memories are haunting you. Am I correct?"

Crispin searched the inside of his mug.

She let silence hang in the room before she said, "War is more than a conflict between nations. It creates a rift between what you were taught was right and what your country requires of you. Trying to reconcile those differences can be wearing on the mind." Crispin tapped his index finger on the arm of the wicker chair and looked past her. She adopted a level tone. "When I was at Edinburgh, I met Doctor Rivers. He was visiting one of my patients scheduled for transfer to the Craiglockhart War Hospital."

Crispin laughed too loud. "That's the loony bin in Scotland for the shell shocked, isn't it?"

Doctor Lee frowned as she leaned forward. "At first, they thought the symptoms of shell shock came from physical damage, like someone hitting their head in a fall. But it's a bit more complicated than just exposure to concussive shocks from the new artillery."

"Wouldn't that suffice?"

She nodded. "It was *one* of the causes of injury. But some officers who were never exposed to artillery had the same symptoms."

"What symptoms?"

"Anger, shaking, loss of appetite—"

Crispin waved his hand and hoped that she would stop. "I'm tired, that's all."

"But your sleep is not refreshing. Is it?"

Crispin forced a laugh and carefully placed his mug on the desk.

She leaned her elbow on her knee and pointed at him. "Let me continue. Sleep interruption. Nightmares. Loss of perspective. Small things seem overwhelming. Is any of that familiar?" She sat back and folded her hands in her lap.

Crispin was silent. He shoved his hands under the blanket and clenched his fists to stop the shaking.

"Lieutenant, even if you refuse to answer me, I want you to understand that this is not a new malady, and you are not alone." She looked at his flushed cheeks and narrowed eyes. She took a deep breath and looked at her hands. "Had I told you that my father was a doctor? He left his medical practice to serve in the Union Army during our Civil

War. Just as I was starting elementary school. What I remembered most about him was his laugh." She looked at Crispin. "But, the war took it from him. For the longest time, I thought he was angry with us. As I got older, I saw other men with the same empty eyes sitting in front of the post office. Some looked fit. Others had lost a leg or an arm. All the life had been drained from them." The pipes overhead rattled. She let the sound pass before she continued. "In medical school, they called it 'Da Costa's syndrome' or 'irritable heart.' The symptoms are almost precisely what is now called 'shell shock,' 'war neurosis,' or 'neurasthenia.'"

Crispin closed his eyes.

She watched him. "Doctor Rivers is developing a talking cure. In London, they are trying electric shock to reorder the nerves in extreme cases."

He rubbed his eyes and glared at her. "Electric shock? Isn't that a bit like tossing petrol on a fire?"

She shook her head slowly. "I think that we are a wonderfully complex organism which is capable of the most glorious actions and the most horrific. Lieutenant, we can make our own decisions on how we live and what we think about the world we encounter."

Crispin glanced away.

She watched his hands gripping the arm of the pushchair. "If you want to confront your discomfort, I will do all I can to assist you to mourn your loss. Lieutenant, you are a young man, you have a long life ahead of you, and this will plague you until you address it. You can try to ignore it, but it won't work. Drink or powders from the pharmacy can only delay your healing."

Crispin blinked quickly before he looked at her and let his shoulders droop. "It will pass."

"You seem to pick at your food. How about taste and smell?"

Crispin looked at his pencil on the floor.

"Lieutenant, what do you want to change now?"

Crispin grimaced "I just need a rest. Once we finish our chore here–"

"Most patients ask how long it will take. I tell *my* patients that it will linger however long you want to punish yourself for doing your duty."

"How dare you—"

She looked at his shaking arms. "Lieutenant, I have seen men free themselves from this pain by forgiving themselves, by serving others, or by rediscovering their faith. Whatever pathway takes the poison out of the memories is—"

Crispin's hand drew a wild arc above his desk. "Just how does one do that? Wave a magic wand? Take a rest cure at a spa? Declare the First Age of mankind over and move along?"

"Some pray. Some draw. Some write. Siegfried Sassoon and Wilfred Owen have been publishing their poems, just as Walt Whitman did after our Civil War. He wrote of his nightmares after working in the army hospital that was treating his brother:

> *Thus in silent dream's projections,*
> *Returning, resuming, I thread my way through the' hospitals,*
> *The' hurt and the' wounded I pacify with soothing hand...."*

Crispin's clenched fists shook. "Absurd. How could one control a memory which arrives unbidden?"

"Master it. Convert it to one that you summon and control. I see how at times you hold your breath. I think I know why. But, exhaling can purge that thought and bring fresh oxygen to your brain to let you think. When you think, *you* can decide how to feel and not just react on reflex."

Crispin started to answer but she held up her hand. "Your intellect serves you well, but it does not make you whole. We also define our world through art and faith. They protect our spirit, like cotton batting against life's harder knocks."

Crispin waved his hand as if brushing away smoke.

"Lieutenant, I know that you are a man of faith. I saw your prayer book by your pillow, where I keep mine, and—"

"My missal."

"Is that what you call it? A soldier in Edinburgh gave me a prayer that is a great comfort to me. He came upon it in France, in a church paper. I copied his translation for you."

Doctor Lee reached over to her table, opened the knitting bag, and placed a half sheet of paper in front of Crispin. "There are many answers, Lieutenant. You need to find yours." He started to respond, but she held up her hand again. "Perhaps you recall the saying. *Paritur pax bello.* I will leave you with that to ponder."

"Simple first-year Latin phrase. *The peace is made by the war. War makes the peace.* Are you suggesting that this war will define my life?"

"I know that you were willing to die for your country. But you alone can decide if you are brave enough to live your life fully."

The lock crackled as the bolt turned. Crispin swept the paper into his desk drawer before Meade entered.

Doctor Lee picked up Crispin's pencil from the floor and returned it to his desk before she pushed past Meade. "Be back later, boys."

Crispin took a sip of his cold tea and shuddered. He nodded to Meade, picked up the first English translation, Sharon Turner's partial work of 1805, and read it quickly. Then he compared it to her 1823 revision. He skimmed John Kemble's 1837 translation, breezed through J. J. Earle's translation from 1892, and chuckled at the German translation of Wilhelm Karl Grimm. Occasionally, he made notes or thumbed back to reread a page before going on to a new translation. He was unusually quiet as he worked.

Late in the afternoon, Crispin put aside the last of the books and started organizing his notes. "Meade, when you have a few moments, I am ready to review my findings from the translations with you."

"Well?"

Crispin grinned. "Meanings which are blurred in one translation are sharp in another."

Meade leaned forward. "How do they stack up to the one you did in school?"

Chuckling, Crispin said, "I must admit, I have learned a thing or two in reviewing these."

"Do you want to wait for Doctor Lee?"

"Certainly. She might enjoy this. I loaned her one of the better translations last night." He pointed to the stacks of books. "Someday, I really should publish a sound translation of *Beowulf*. There are so many errors in these."

Crispin prepared a summary of his findings and was as ready as a tenured professor for an honors lecture when Doctor Lee opened the door at five and pushed in a cart holding two tinned domes.

Meade got up and pulled her chair around to face Crispin. "Have a seat. I'll get dinner."

Pointing to the cart, she said, "Thank you. Sorry that it's just a cold plate tonight. Didn't want to linger around the kitchen too long."

Crispin looked at the sliced meats, cheeses, and hard rolls. He nodded as Meade put the plates on their desks but ignored the food and instead picked up his papers.

She arranged her gray tweed skirt with care and crossed her legs. "Well? What are you up to?"

Meade popped a slice of cheese into his mouth, chewed, and swallowed it quickly. "The Professor is about to give us his review of the translations by lesser mortals. We'll see if he found anything that can help us solve the puzzle of the text. Can I grab a mug of tea for you?"

"No, thank you."

Crispin reordered his pages of notes. "I'll try to be brief. The poem is the oldest in what was to become our English language. Albeit, older poems exist, like the *Epic of Gilgamesh* from Mesopotamia almost 5000 B.C. Structurally, *Beowulf* is constructed of more than three thousand lines and alliteration is common, as it is in *Sir Gawain and the Green Knight* as we transition into Middle English. Rhyme is incidental in the double line structure."

Before taking a bite of cheese, Meade asked, "Is that good or bad?"

"I mention it only as a marker as rhyme was introduced by the French in the fourteenth century. Kennings are the literary device we most commonly associate with—" Crispin glanced at Meade who was looking at the ceiling. "As you may recall, the whale's way is—"

Doctor Lee and Meade answered simultaneously in flat voices. "The ocean."

"Other poetic forms, such as the simile are rare." Crispin looked at his notes, "Ah, here it is. Similes are found six times. Shall I give you the line numbers?"

Meade shut his eyes tightly and shook his head.

Doctor Lee said, "Maybe that's a little more detail than we need. I was thinking you might be discussing *themes* within the story that might relate to the map's text. Burials. Boats. The like."

"I am trying to get to that, but you must realize that these were clever people. They commonly used litotes, ironic understatement, and riddles."

Meade said, "Professor, let's stick to the stuff that's going to help, since I wouldn't know a litotes if it bit me."

"That would be no small problem."

"What would?"

"That's a litotes. A negation of an opposite for emphasis."

Mead shook his head. "What else?"

"Themes? Well then. All of the translations are generally consistent in their reporting of the story. It is the saga of a people, starting with their first king, Shield Sheafson, his death, sea burial, and the appointment of his son as king. This orderly transfer of power is the start of the rule of law. At any rate, Beowulf takes up a quest to help King Hrothgar, whose mead hall was being menaced by the monster, Grendel. The men huddled in the darkness of that mead hall waiting for Grendel's attack, *under sceadu bregdan*, that is to say, under the shadow of fear and evil. Not so very different than in the trenches today."

He paused and then continued. "Beowulf assumed this quest to repay the Danish king who had paid a debt owed by Beowulf's father. Now here is where the translations vary." Crispin paused to flip between two pages of his notes. "Most described Grendel as a troll-like monster, but a few describe him as someone outside their society, an outcast, an outlaw. Beowulf stands night watch in the hall and defends it from the monster's attack by ripping off his arm. Grendel escapes, only to die elsewhere."

Meade shrugged. "Simple morality tale. A war story."

Crispin held up his sheaf of notes. "Not so fast, Meade. Grendel's Dam, his mother, arrives to take revenge. But Beowulf is not in Herot, the mead hall."

Doctor Lee turned to Meade. "He was given better quarters for the night as a reward."

Crispin spoke faster. "You see, Beowulf was invited into their society. He goes on to fight Grendel's mother in her cave, where she has hidden looted treasures. A horrid battle ensues, his sword breaks, he grabs a sword, named Hrunting, from her treasures, and kills her. And then the dragon—"

Meade held up his hand to stop Crispin. "Any references to Michael? Big cities? Flounder?"

Crispin laughed. "In Canto Eight, there is a reference to a wraith of sea-fish and in Canto Twenty-three, a mention of meadow-ways trod. No other references to words in our map's text or to locations that help us."

Doctor Lee took a deep breath. "Let me see if I understood the ending, Lieutenant. Beowulf dies when he fights a dragon, but other warriors are emboldened by his selfless heroism and manage to finish off the dragon. At the end, his community rallies around his funeral pyre, which is his ship that has been brought on land. Next to it, they build a monument of stones."

Crispin smiled at her. "Quite so. A tower into the sky that travelers could see from land and sea. They declare him the greatest of their people, and twelve riders go forth to spread the fame of Beowulf."

Meade raised an eyebrow. "Three battles and he lost the last one—what's the big deal?"

Doctor Lee started to answer when Crispin raised his voice to Meade. "The big deal, as you say, is that this one poem represents ten percent of all known Old English poetry and almost all we know of the customs of the northern invaders to England from their own tales. It offers a portal to the past."

As Meade started to get up, Doctor Lee interrupted Crispin. "You can see their values in their system of rewards, using things of intrinsic value such as gold coins and jeweled swords, but also things of symbolic value, such as the invitation to the king's residence. And finally the burial. A cremation on the ship and a stone tower. That's what interests me."

Crispin asked, "How is that?"

She cleared her throat. "When I read it, I was reminded that Christianity was introduced at Birka before 1000. You can see the duality in the poem as well with its Christian references and pagan rites."

Crispin sat back and stared at her before saying, "Fascinating! I don't believe that I've heard that analysis before."

Doctor Lee reached for her knitting bag and resumed work on a dark blue muffler. The long needles ticked like an old clock as she spoke. "At Birka, a Benedictine Monk, Saint Ansgar, introduced Christianity. Missionary inroads were being made in England as well. In Norwich, where I worked on an archaeological project, there was a vibrant Christian community well before the Norman Conquest. Beautiful cathedral there."

Crispin asked, "Was your work related to the cathedral?"

"Oh, my no. Nothing so glamorous. Just collecting shards from the marsh area we called 'North Town.' Some went back to the 900s."

Meade stood and stretched. "Wasn't there a Viking raid on a monastery earlier than that?"

Crispin nodded and pulled his plate toward him. "The raid at Lindisfarne was in the 700s."

Meade whispered, "Lindisfarne." After he leaned over his desk and opened the atlas, he said, loud enough for Doctor Lee to hear, "Where is it?"

"Off the north coast of England, just before Scotland. Why?"

Meade sat and ran his finger down the index. "If the Vikings raided it, maybe there is a three-river pattern after I adjust the shoreline. Where the–"

"On the northern coast." Doctor Lee said, getting up and looking over Meade's shoulder at the map.

He flipped pages and squinted at the small type. "I can't find it in the index. Is it an island in another group?"

She said, "Look up Holy Island."

"Why?"

Doctor Lee went to the encyclopedia on the counter and picked up a volume. "That's what it is called now. It's on a bay, and there is a causeway connecting it to the coast."

Meade looked up Holy Island in the index of his atlas. "There are three Holy Islands. One in England. One in Scotland, and another in Wales. Which is it?"

She pointed to one in the index. "That's the one. The English one. On Budle Bay, just off the town of– The print is so small." Doctor Lee squinted. "What is that? Beal."

Meade looked at it. "Yes."

She closed the volume of the encyclopedia she was holding and opened another. "Got it. Sir Walter Scott's poem, *Marmion*. Written in 1808. Describes the monastery there in which one of his characters is held as a prisoner. Let me quote it to you:

> *The tide did now its floodmark gain,*
> *And girdled in the saint's domain:*
> *For with the flow and ebb, its style*
> *Varies from continent to isle;*

Dry shod o'er sands, twice' every day,
The' pilgrims to the' shrine' find way;
Twice' every day the' waves efface'
Of staves and sandaled feet the' trace'.

Meade smiled. "I get it. The monastery is on an island part of the time and connected to land the other part."

Crispin choked on a bit of cheese and cleared his throat. "By definition, a causeway provides passage over a marsh or a flooded area. Middle English *cauciwey*, French *cauci*. Related to the Latin *calx*, a limestone used in paving roadways. It's rather like a road, across a marsh or into the sea that goes underwater with the flood tide. Like Saint Michael's Mount in Cornwall."

Meade shouted. "What?"

Crispin said, "The Benedictine monastery—"

Meade stood. "There's one in England? Why didn't you tell me?"

Crispin waved a chunk of cheese at Meade and said, "Common knowledge. Thought you knew of it."

Meade spun the atlas to face Crispin. "Show me. This could be the Michael—"

"Oh, Meade. Relax. There is an island off Ireland called Skellig Michael, 'Michael's Rock,' where monks have been copying texts since 600 A.D. Our country is simply littered with the sightings of saints." Crispin pointed to Saint Michael's Mount and turned the atlas for Meade to see.

Meade pounded his fist on the map. "Tell me about this one!"

"The one in England is called 'Saint Michael's Mount,' named for the appearance of Saint Michael on an outcropping at the shore."

Doctor Lee put on her glasses. "In France, there is one just like it. Larger, of course. More dramatic tide."

Crispin slapped the desk. "Our two Michaels? When were they built?"

She walked to the counter, returned one volume of the encyclopedia, and selected another. "Stewart loved the one in France. But it is a treacherous place. The tide rushes in so fast that you can actually see it change. I think it was something like a meter per second so that in a period of five seconds it can be fifteen feet higher than it was just moments before."

Meade stared at her. "When was it built? Does it say?"

She took a minute to find the answer. "From the eleventh to the sixteenth century."

Meade's shoulders slumped. "Too late. It had to be before the millennium for our mapmaker to have known about it." He shoved his chair away from the desk and stalked to the rear of the room. He filled the kettle from the tap and started the Bunsen burner.

Doctor Lee looked up from the book. "Thank you, Mister Meade. That will be most welcome."

As he paced back to the desks, Meade said, "Please continue. I didn't mean to interrupt you."

She looked at the open book and adjusted her glasses. "In the year 708, Saint Michael appeared to the Abbot and directed him to build an appropriate edifice. When he failed to do so promptly, Saint Michael tapped him on the head and burned a hole in his skull. Shortly thereafter, others commenced construction, although it took a couple of hundred years to complete. Today, there is a beautiful Benedictine abbey and church there."

Meade crossed his arms and snorted. "I don't see how that helps. But at least it puts that location in the first millennium. What about the one in England?"

Doctor Lee balanced the book on the corner of her desk, pushing her knitting bag to the edge of her worktable. "Now, in England, there also was a sighting of the archangel Michael in the fifth century at Cornwall near Land's End."

Leaning over his desk, Meade turned to a map of England's southwestern area.

Doctor Lee adjusted her glasses. "Julius Caesar replaced the sailors with merchants when he was there shortly before Christ was born. This rock was a trading center for tin and copper in the fourth century. Then, a fisherman saw Saint Michael there in 495 A.D. Pilgrimages began promptly thereafter." She looked up from the book. "So from 500 A.D., the English site has been visited regularly."

Meade ran his finger along the southern coastline. "Where is it again?"

Crispin sighed. "In Cornwall, across the bay from Penzance. I believe you are familiar with *The Pirates of Penzance*."

Meade frowned and then turned pages, stopping at a map showing all of the British Isles and the coast of France. He grabbed Crispin's pencil from his desktop and started to circled Saint Michael's Mount in Cornwall with it. He swore under his breath when he discovered that the lead was broken.

Crispin pulled another pencil from his desk and leaned over to circle it for Meade, who was looking at the map with his hand lens. "Damn! Nothing here called 'Mount Saint Michael.' I'll have to go to a larger scale."

Doctor Lee stood and looked over Meade's shoulder at the coast of France. She placed her fingertip on a bay on the French coast south of the Channel Islands. "See the city of Avranches? That is where we stayed when Stewart and I visited the abbey. Try the French spelling." She pronounced it very slowly. "Mont Saint-Michel."

Meade circled Avranches and looked at Crispin. "Are they the right Michaels?"

Crispin opened the drawer to his desk, pulled out a metal ruler, and drew a pencil line from Cornwall to the black circle on the coast of France. He tossed the pencil on the desk with a flourish. "Meade? Hand over the Baldwin for a moment, if you will. I want to refresh my memory of that line at the bottom of the portolano."

As Meade pulled it from the map chest, he asked, "The rhumb

line?" He slid the portolano in front of Doctor Lee to Crispin, who then turned the portolano until the straight lines on the atlas and portolano were parallel to each other. "There! That's the line!" By circling the two locations on the atlas, Crispin had mimicked the straight line on the portolano with small dots or asterisks at each end.

Meade stared at the line on the atlas and ran his finger between the two circled locations as though feeling the cool of the sea. He shook his head, got a crooked grin, and laughed. "All this time, I thought that line was a wind line or a directional line. I never for a minute considered—"

Crispin said, "But you called it a 'rhumb line'! By definition, a rhumb line is any of the points on a mariner's compass, from the Spanish—"

Meade looked up. "I don't even know if the guy that made this map even used a compass. What else was I going to call it?"

Doctor Lee walked behind Meade and put her hand on his shoulder. "Congratulations appear to be in order, gentlemen. You seem to be unraveling it." She turned to Crispin. "What's the line in the verse again, Lieutenant?"

Crispin looked at the portolano on the desk in front of him. "Literally, head two Michael over. Or as we might say, above the head of the two Michaels. Singular or plural were not nearly as definitive in Old English as today."

Meade tapped the atlas. "The treasure is buried above this line. Above the line connecting the two abbeys, the two Michaels."

As Doctor Lee passed the portolano to Meade, Crispin reached for it and asked, "May I see it again? I wonder if…."

Chapter № 30

Thursday
November 2, 1916
North of London, England

As Meade turned the pages to a more detailed map of the coast of France and found the French abbey's small island, Crispin examined the portolano with a hand lens and grinned. Pointing to Meade's atlas, he asked. "Mind if I have a second look at our line?"

Meade flipped back to the larger map and turned the atlas toward Crispin. After placing the portolano above the pencil line on the atlas and copying the two asterisks with care onto the ends of the new line, Crispin removed the portolano and placed the ruler's edge against the longest of the points of the asterisk on the French coast. The straight-edge went north into the eastern coast of England. He swiped a pencil lead against the ruler's edge. The line pierced the southern coast near Brighton and the northeastern coast by Great Yarmouth. He quickly repositioned the edge over the longest line in the asterisk, which had been made near Cornwall, and drew a line. It skimmed along the southern coast and ended on the shore near Dover.

Doctor Lee stared at the lines Crispin had scribed on the map and tapped the point, south of London, where they crossed. "Here? You think it could be near here?"

Crispin frowned. "Seems unlikely. Don't you think that's a bit far inland for them to have sailed?"

Shaking his head, Meade said, "I don't see anything close to your three-river pattern near there."

Tossing the pencil on the desk, Crispin said, "I thought they might have used their knowledge of geometry to leave us directions, as the compass was not in common usage. They were a pragmatic and clever bunch."

Meade smiled. "You still might be on to something."

Crispin pointed to the portolano. "You see, there is one line on the top of each asterisk which is longer than the others. If it were *intentionally* drawn longer, and if I got the angle right. And if—"

At the far end of the room, the water in the kettle sputtered and the whistle over the spout emitted a soft middle C which then ascended to an ear-splitting high E.

Meade jerked his head toward the noise. Doctor Lee jumped up and started for the kettle as Crispin pitched himself from the wicker chair, pressed flat against the floor, and covered the back of his head with his hands. He glanced up at her. "Silence that blasted thing, can't you?"

As she ran to the kettle, she saw Crispin struggle to stand and Meade grab his elbow just in time to stop him from falling. She yanked the shrieking kettle off the rack and knocked the whistle from the steaming spout with the small towel. After extinguishing the burner, she glanced at Crispin, who leaned into the desk. She poured some water into the teapot to warm it, taking longer than necessary.

Crispin saw her glance at him. "Forgive the bother. I just was going to excuse myself for a moment." He was shaking and felt a trickle of sweat at the small of his back. He touched the scab over his cut chin and was relieved that it had not broken.

Doctor Lee emptied the warmed pot, added tea leaves, and filled the Brown Betty. She returned to Crispin. "I had no intention of ignoring the kettle that way. I am very sorry that—"

He waved his hand in the air as if pushing away insects. "Meade? Seems I do need those crutches after all. Could you pass them over?"

As Meade retrieved them from the bed, Doctor Lee opened the door. "Time I take a pause as well. Tea should have steeped by the time we all return."

Crispin took the crutches from Meade and smiled thinly. "Splendid."

Meade held the door for Doctor Lee and waited for Crispin. After he tested his footing, Crispin called to Meade, "Go ahead. I'll visit the facilities when you return."

When he was alone, Crispin leaned over the center drawer, pulled out his silver match case, and put it on the top of the desk. As he reached for his pipe, he noticed the half sheet of paper Doctor Lee had given him. He turned it and read slowly.

From La Clochette, 12 December 1912:
Lord, make me an instrument of your peace.
Where there is hatred, let me sow love;
Where there is offense, pardon,
Where there is wrong, right,
Where there is doubt, faith,
Where there is despair, hope;
Where there is darkness, light, and
Where there is sadness, joy.

Grant that I may not so much seek to be consoled as to console;
To be understood as to understand,
To be loved as to love
For it is in giving that we receive
It is in pardoning that we are pardoned,
And it is in dying that we are born to Eternal Life.

Sweat prickled on his forehead. He breathed deeply and tried to focus on the words.

As he heard the door start to open, he grabbed his pipe and slid the paper into the drawer. He looked up at Meade. "Dare I take time for a smoke?"

"If you hurry. You know how she is."

Crispin grimaced as he filled his pipe. He put it in his robe pocket and walked to the door. "Blast."

"What is it?"

Crispin turned and started toward the desk. "My vesta case."

Meade was pulling out his chair. "Your what?"

"Matches, for my pipe."

"Stay there." Meade picked up the monogrammed silver box and tossed it casually in his hand as he brought it to Crispin. "You called your matchbox a what?"

"'Vesta case' or box. Vesta, fire, vestal virgins of mythology, you know."

"Say, Professor. What if those words aren't code? What if they are just odd words, like 'vesta for matchbox.' What if it is a word you don't know or a local dialect?"

"Vowels. It still needs vowels. Let me smoke my pipe in the other room before 'she of the stern look' returns."

Meade smiled. "Is that a kenning?"

"No, but it should be."

After his pipe, Crispin returned and the tip of a crutch snagged on the hem of his pajama leg as he slid into the wicker chair. Meade grabbed the crutch before it clattered to the floor, took the other from Crispin, and leaned them into the bed.

Crispin opened the dictionary and stared at a page. He blinked and the words of the prayer interrupted his plan to look up the origin of several more words in the riddle.

He was relieved when he heard the door open. Doctor Lee entered with a small tray with a plate holding slices of cheddar cheese and soda crackers. She left it on the desk and brought over the pot of tea from the counter.

"Did you enjoy your pipe, Lieutenant Crispin?"

Crispin ignored her question, shifted his glance as a truant schoolboy might, and then smiled broadly. "Tea. Good of you to keep us in postprandial tea."

Meade took the pot and poured for them. "I suppose that means 'after dinner'?"

Crispin nodded without looking up from the dictionary.

Doctor Lee sat and opened her knitting bag. Soon, there was a soft clicking of her knitting needles. Then the tapping became the chatter of machine guns and ringing of casings on concrete. He shut his eyes and tried to remember the prayer he had just read. After a few moments, Crispin turned a page and then another and pretended to look up words. He repeated the words of the prayer and turned pages randomly until he was able to gather his wits and begin his research in earnest.

After a few minutes, Crispin breathed deeply and leaned back in the creaking chair. "Meade?"

"Yes?"

"I've been thinking of the flood tide only as related to the ocean. You know the line in the text about flood. I've been contrasting ebb tide to flood tide, and contrasting flood tide to spring tide. The Old English is *flod*, and the old Norse is *flōd*. An archaic usage is meaning a body of moving water. Perhaps, this could be a river flowing or shifting with the tide."

Meade turned his attention back to his map. "And?"

Crispin persisted. "Then, I looked at 'tide,' yet again. In the Middle English is *tyde*, as we see in time such as Eastertide. Granted, it is a later sample, but–"

Meade scowled. "What's your point?"

"Perhaps there is another use of the phrase 'flood tide' that relates not to ocean or rivers but to the spread or the development of Christianity, calling it a 'rising tide.'"

Doctor Lee stopped knitting. "Well, Christianity was on its ascendancy then. Birka certainly had a blend of pagan and Christian–"

Crispin spoke slowly, "What if some of the King's followers had converted to Christianity? It was possible by that time, wasn't it? Perhaps the mapmaker or king had even made pilgrimages. At the very least, they knew of the abbeys honoring Saint Michael." Doctor Lee nodded as Crispin continued. "What if the king had converted and wanted a burial with Christian symbols as well as a ship burial?"

She said, "Possible, I suppose."

Meade asked, "Doctor Lee? Have you been on a dig with a buried Viking ship?"

"No. They are quite rare. They have only been found in Scandinavia. There is a museum in Norway that Stewart and I visited that had artifacts from the burial ship at Gokstadt. A farmer plowed into a small mound in his field in about 1880. Fortunately, he notified the Norwegian Historical Museum."

Crispin stared at the two scrambled lines of letters on the map and rocked slightly as Meade talked to Doctor Lee.

Meade asked, "Was it the whole boat?"

"Much of the wood had rotted away, as you would expect, but the shape was clear enough in the photograph. Stewart and I boarded a modern replica of it at the Columbian Exposition in 1893. Let me think. It had at least sixteen oars per side, that's a crew of thirty-two plus added passengers. Or cargo."

Meade laughed. "You really went on it? How big was it?"

"Huge, compared to Stewart's twenty-five-foot day boat. It must have been seventy feet long and just under twenty wide. I remember that there was only about eight feet between the water and the top of the rowing stations. It was actually sailed from Norway to Chicago for the Exposition."

Meade said, "Burying something that big must have been like digging a basement for a house."

Crispin leaned forward on his desk and gestured for Meade's attention. "I don't mean to interrupt, but I've been pondering those two word-like oddities to the right on the map."

Meade smirked. "Figure it out?"

Smiling broadly at Doctor Lee, Crispin said, "Well, I have been reviewing my cipher training. I could tell you a dozen things it is not."

Meade looked exasperated. "Do you have any idea what it is?"

"Perhaps it is a simple cipher. Substituting one letter for another."

Sitting straighter, Meade asked, "How do we test that?"

Pointing at the jumble of furniture, Crispin said, "We shall begin by putting the Old English alphabet upon the slate board."

Meade tugged it from the pile of furniture and dragged it toward the desks, in spite of wheels that had rusted in place.

Crispin struggled to his feet and hopped to the slate board, using only one crutch. He picked up the chalk from the tray but became unsteady when he put more weight on his leg than he had intended. Doctor Lee started to get the second crutch but stopped as Meade helped Crispin back to his desk.

Crispin relinquished the chalk to Meade and tightened the sash on his robe. "Thanks, Meade. Here's what you do. Write the modern alphabet. Use lowercase for simplicity."

Meade wrote:

a b c d e f g h i j k l m n o p q r s t u v w x y z

"Now we need to adjust the twenty-six letters of the modern alphabet to form the Old English. Erase the consonants 'J' and 'V.' You see, in Old English the letters 'I' and 'U' function as the vowels we know them to be as well as the consonants 'J' and 'V' which you have removed."

The line now read:

a b c d e f g h i k l m n o p q r s t u w x y z

Crispin looked at the board and muttered. "Now add three new letters at the end. Ash, eth, and thorn."

Meade turned and put his hands on his hips, awaiting further instruction.

Crispin raised his voice. "I said add ash, eth, and thorn."

"I would if I knew what you were asking me to do."

Crispin pulled paper from his desk. "Come over here. Look how I make them." He exaggerated making a letter. "*Ash* is the name of the letter that combines the 'a' and 'e' letters that you already know." Crispin drew "æ" for Meade. "This is *eth*. It resembles a modern 'd' with a bar through the top, much as you would cross the letter 't.'" Crispin drew the "đ."

As Crispin drew "þ," he said, "And this is *thorn*." He handed the paper to Meade, who went to the board and copied the three letters.

a b c d e f g h i k l m n o p q r s t u w x y z æ đ þ

Crispin smiled. "Splendid. All the letters are accounted for. Now, there is something else to consider. The letters 'K,' 'Q,' and 'Z' are rarely used. Should we keep them or not? It will influence the count, you know."

Doctor Lee quickly said, "We definitely need the 'Q.' Both words have a 'Q' in them."

"So they do. Well, let's hold on to all three."

Meade looked at the board. "Okay, I've got the alphabet up here, now how do you undo a substitution code—"

Crispin snapped. "Cipher." He referred to his notes. "As a part of signal training, we received instruction on ciphers. Now, the more modern polyalphabetic code and the Alberti dual disks system for—"

Doctor Lee waved her hand at him. "Stop. Just focus your attention on the substitution—"

Crispin looked hurt. "I was merely explaining that the more complex code systems were not used until the middle of the 1400, so this must use a simpler one." He took a deep breath. "So to create a cipher, if the shift is three, you count three from your true letter to determine the letter you want to use in your encrypted message. Three to the right is the cipher Caesar commonly used, so it is called the 'Caesar cipher.'"

Doctor Lee frowned. "Let me see if I understand. You write a message, send it to me, and I just reverse the process to write down the correct message."

"Yes, that is the deciphering part. All you need to know is how many letters in which direction to shift, on what alphabet."

Meade smiled. "That seems simple enough."

She stared at Crispin and canted her head. "Lieutenant, why are you so convinced these are not just odd place names or abbreviations?"

"Because we have a 'Q' in both words and no vowels. That's a tease, almost."

Meade took a sip of tea and returned to the chalkboard. "Please spell them for me, Doctor Lee."

After looking at the Baldwin, she said, "The upper one is 'P Q T X L M.' The lower letters are 'Q T S H.'"

Meade wrote the letters under the alphabet on the board and turned.

Crispin looked at the board. "Oh. Did I mention frequency analysis? We know vowels are usually in a first or second place in a word. Certain vowels such as 'E' arise with greater frequency than others. Letters in order of appearance are 'E, T, A, O, I, N, S' for modern English." He shrugged. "It may offer a starting point."

Doctor Lee smiled. "Stewart and I used to do acrostics and crossword puzzles. He loved those mind teasers. Have you ever read Poe's *The Gold Bug?* The story hinges on a secret message."

Crispin looked irritated. "No. I haven't."

Doctor Lee adjusted her glasses. "Or the Sherlock Holmes story with the little stick figures as code? *Adventures of the Dancing Men,* wasn't it?"

Crispin brightened. "I do know about that one. The matchstick men are a symbolic substitution code. Not like here, where letters seem to be letters."

Meade tapped the board. "Fine, so looking at the first word, I take the 'P' and decide to go left or right any number of places?"

"Exactly."

Meade snapped, "Come on, Professor. We could be here forever."

Crispin stared at the Baldwin and smiled. "Unless the direction and shift are a part of a riddle."

Meade shouted, "A riddle!"

"The odd phrasing. The use of 'Q.' Quite unlikely. Thus, I am reminded of *The Exeter Book*, which has a variety of riddle poems in it. Many were from the time that *Beowulf* was written."

Doctor Lee rubbed her eyes. "Well, Lieutenant Crispin, it seems that you are our riddle expert, aren't you? When you are through looking at the portolano, would you please hand it to me? I wonder if there is anything I missed."

She looked at it and tapped on her desk next to it.

"Lieutenant, could you translate this block again for us? Mister Meade, write it on the chalkboard as he speaks, please."

Crispin looked irritated. "Meade, the first line is simply what it is. I can fancy up the translation if you wish, but I feel the better course is to put it up word for word. Come here and take my paper."

Meade took the translation that Crispin shoved toward him and began to copy it on the board. Crispin was irritated at his slowness and struggled to his feet. He used the crutches to go to the board, where he stood until Meade relinquished the chalk and helped him balance. Crispin quickly wrote a line of the Old English and put the translation under it, slightly offsetting it to the right.

Dryhet oðberan dēormōd cyning ond hord
    'Retainers bear bold king and treasure'
Randhæbbend tō metod ond ēadnes
    'Warrior to God and joy peace'
Ymbfæstnung under flōc
    Monument under flounder
Hafela twā Michael ofer
    Head two Michael over

Twā micel ceaster betwuh
Two great cities between
Ēaststæđ æt rēfmæd
East bank of stream at reeve's meadow
Ne yđwōrigende on bēam
Not wandering the' waves in wooden ship

Crispin snorted as he handed the chalk to Meade. "Not centered, but you get the idea."

Doctor Lee went to the board and read the translation. "It seems to me that we have solved the first, second, and last lines. They intended to bury the king, and not let the boat remain at sea. Agree?"

Crispin nodded as he resumed his seat.

Doctor Lee took the chalk from Meade and put a check mark in front of those three lines. She turned to Crispin. "The Michael clue. We decided that was the pencil line between Saint Michael's Mount in Cornwall and Mont Saint-Michel in France, so we needn't fuss with that any longer. Right?"

Seeing Crispin's doubt, Doctor Lee put a question mark by it and tapped the chalk on the word "cities." "Two cities? Is that what is behind our scrambled words?"

Crispin crossed his arms and a smile started to build. "I believe it might well be."

Chapter № 31

Thursday
November 2, 1916
North of London, England

Meade stalked to the far end of the room and back, flexing his tight shoulder muscles. He stood at his desk and tipped his head. "If you are right, Professor, what we need here on the bottom of the map is a four-letter word for a great city in the first millennium."

Doctor Lee chuckled. "Sounds like one of the clues for the Sunday crossword puzzle."

Crispin rubbed his palm across his forehead. "Or a five- or six- or ten-letter word. You have failed to consider that there is a hole in the parchment."

Doctor Lee watched him as he sat back. "On which coast would you expect to find the cities, Mister Meade? We cannot assume that the right of the map is the east, can we?"

Meade nodded and spun the atlas so that north was closest to him. He held the portolano over the inverted image of Great Britain.

Crispin stretched his arms over his head. "Starting over, are we? Random rooting about like a hog for truffles again?"

He saw Doctor Lee frown and wheeled his chair closer to his desk. Meade leaned over the page and tried to see the inked rivers flowing to the east or south, not the northwest of his imagination. Meade rubbed his eyes and then tried to match the pattern of the portolano to the southwest coast of Britain. He pointed to a bay that had a large river and smaller tributaries fingering inland. "Hey, take a look, what's that?"

Doctor Lee adjusted her glasses. "Bay of Bristol. Just above Saint Michael's Mount."

Crispin tapped the map just inland from the bay. "Look there, Meade. Gloucester and Tewkesbury both were occupied by Saxons. Certainly those towns are as old as the portolano. The Cathedral at Gloucester grew from a seventh-century abbey. However, the construction of both the Tewkesbury Abbey and the Gloucester Cathedral started just after the turn of the millennium. Still–"

Doctor Lee took off her glasses and rubbed her eyes. "What else might match our directions? Above the two Michaels–"

Crispin snorted. "Almost all of Britain is above that pencil line on the atlas, if 'above' means 'north.' And nothing matched that pattern if we were to look to the south."

Doctor Lee pointed to the bright blue bay and the large river. "The bank. Does the river turn to have a, what was it, an east bank?"

Meade read from the atlas. "Rivers Avon and Severn are the most likely. Have their confluence near Tewkesbury and snake all over the place. They've got lots of east banks. Between two great cities? There's the rub. We do not know which coast."

Crispin turned the atlas and pounded the top of the map. "If we are correct and my line connected the proper two Michaels, and the lines off the asterisks were even close to correct, it must be the eastern coast. North is up here, for God's sake!" Crispin froze and stared at the upper portion of the English Channel. "The flounder! That proves it up!"

Doctor Lee started to say something as he shoved his finger toward Cornwall to the south. "Down here, the sea to the west, out from Bristol or Penzance quickly becomes deep water. Not at all suited for flounder."

Meade frowned. "But what's that–"

Crispin tapped the map just north of the English Channel. "The shoals in the German Sea, here, above the English Channel, are flounder fishing grounds. Been so forever. Just as herring inhabit the Baltic, and deep-water fish are off the southern coast. Look here, at the Gabbard Shoals."

Meade leaned closer to the atlas to read the names. "Show me, Professor."

Crispin tapped the map. "Here, just off the Suffolk coast. By Southwold. The Battle of the Gabbard was fought here."

"What's that have to do with–"

"We took a real drubbing from the Dutch Navy in the 1600s. Almost a hundred warships were lost."

"And?"

"The other name for the naval engagement is the 'Battle of Sole Bay.' Sole and flounder are flat fish which reside in these shallow waters."

Meade went to the chalkboard and tapped next to the line. "Professor, can the word 'under' in this line mean the same thing as 'below'?"

"It seems as though it does. Change the question mark on the Michael's line as well."

Meade put a check mark beside her question mark and a check beside the line.

Ymbfæstnung under flōc
Monument under flounder

Doctor Lee looked at the board. "Two lines left to solve. Which are the two great cities? Where is the east bank?" She ran her finger along the eastern coast on the atlas. "I think it is fair to assume that one of the two great cities would have been London. Mister Meade? Could you write 'London' under that lower set of letters? I'd like to see where that takes us."

He went to the slate board and wrote:

QTSH
LONDON

Doctor Lee stared at it for a moment, "Okay, if 'Q' is 'L,' then that's five letters to the left—"

Crispin pointed at the board. "Modified Caesar cipher using five. Meade, go five to the left of the 'T' as well. That is an 'O.' We might have just broken it."

Meade wrote the 'L' under the 'Q' and an 'O' under the 'T.' "Well, those seem fine, now the 'S.' Five back from that is 'N.' Finally 'H.' Five back from that is 'C.'"

Crispin snapped, "It should be 'D. Did you miscount? It's five back."

"I can count, look." Meade tapped the chalk on the letters as he counted backwards and it landed on 'C.' "It says LONC."

"Eth!" Crispin shouted. "Meade. Try the alternate placement of 'ash,' and 'eth.'"

Meade let his arms hang limp. The chalk dangled from his fingers. He continued to face the board. "Where?"

"There are two ways to order Old English letters. We tried the more common, which simply clusters the added three letters at the end. Would you please place the letter 'ash' after 'a,' 'eth' after 'd,' and leave 'thorn' as it is, at the end."

Meade adjusted the alphabet and wrote:

a æ b c d ð e f g h i k l m n o p q r s t u w x y z   þ

Doctor Lee applauded. "By inserting the 'eth,' counting back from the 'H' gives us a 'D.' 'Lond.' It *is* London. Lieutenant, you are brilliant."

Crispin sniffed. "More than likely the word on the Baldwin was *Londinium*. The Romans called it that from their arrival in 43 A.D. until their departure some four hundred years later."

As he recounted the other letters and confirmed that they still matched, Meade grinned. "*Londinium?*"

Meade tapped the board as he counted letters and applied the same five-letter shift using Crispin's revision to the Old English alphabet.

PQTXLM

"'P' is 'K.' Any ideas of a town starting with 'K'?"

"Be a good chap and run the whole word out for us. We know that 'Q' becomes an 'L.'"

Tapping back five places for each remaining letters, Meade said, "'T' is 'O.' 'X' is 'R.' 'L' is 'F.' 'M' is 'G.'"

Meade spelled out the letters. "K L O R F G. At least it has a vowel now. Ring any bells with anyone?"

Crispin slouched in his chair and let his head fall back so he spoke to the overhead lights. "That cipher has gone dud on us."

Doctor Lee picked up the portolano and looked again. "Mister Meade, did maps of this age use astrological signs? Sun, moon, stars."

Meade rubbed his eyes. "What?"

She motioned to him. "Come and look at this."

Meade looked at the circle above the text that Crispin had translated, the crescent moon next to the upper word, and the star by what Crispin now believed to be London.

"Are these symbols usual?"

Meade rubbed the stubble on his chin. "I have no idea. They were made by the navigator for personal use. Some even made intentional mistakes so nobody else could find the place."

Crispin pointed at the map. "Meade, what if this star was not a star?"

"What else could it be?"

He stared at Meade. "Would you mind adding these three symbols on the board?"

Meade grumbled as he tossed the chalk between his hands. "For what good that might—"

Doctor Lee tried to assist. "What are you thinking, Lieutenant?"

As Meade drew the circle, he asked, "So, what do you think it is, Professor? A circle, a wheel, or nothing."

Doctor Lee persisted. "What else could it represent?"

Meade muttered. "A sun?"

Doctor Lee frowned. "And the next one?"

Meade drew a crescent moon, with the arc pointing to the left. "Obviously, it's a crescent moon."

Crispin pressed Meade for another answer. "What else could it be?"

Tossing the chalk on the tray, Meade said, "A banana or a slice of cantaloupe."

Doctor Lee intervened. "Fine then. Put up the star that was over London or should I say, 'Londinium.'"

Meade snatched the chalk from the tray and drew four childlike wedges, connected them, and turned around. "Happy?"

Crispin snickered. "Not really. The star here is different. Look."

Meade stomped back and scrutinized the star on the portolano. "Huh! Sure is." He erased his star and redrew it.

More to herself than to the others, Doctor Lee asked, "What is it, if it is not a star?"

Crispin leaned forward on his elbows, staring at the board. "A pentagram? A five-sided...we shifted letters five to the left to make the word 'London.' Think! The five points on that star are the key to the cipher. There are no points at all on the circle. It is not the sun or moon."

Doctor Lee asked, "Then what is it?"

"Meade had it right! It's nothing. A zero. A null." Crispin smiled. "That large block of text simply was not encrypted."

"Yeah. You were able to translate it just like it was."

"Well, for once, I think you are right, Meade. There is a *code* here, not a cipher. The shape of the sun and moon and stars telling us the number of letters to shift. Meade! There are two points on the crescent moon, try shifting only two places."

Meade glanced at the letters "PQTXLM" and began tapping on the revised alphabet and writing the letters quickly. "'P' back two is 'N.' 'Q' is 'O.' 'T' is 'R.' 'X' back two is 'U.' 'M' back two is 'K.'"

Doctor Lee looked puzzled. "So what have we now? 'NORUK.'"

Crispin hit the arm of the wicker chair. "Meade, you have skipped a letter. Go back."

"Sorry." Meade tapped on the "L" that he had omitted, went back two places on the alphabet on the board and found the letter "I." He corrected the name to "NORUIK."

Crispin slammed his hand on his good knee. "Substitute 'V' for the 'U,' please."

Meade made the correction. The word became "NORVIK."

Doctor Lee laughed. "Norvik! That's what King Athelstan called it in the 900s. North Town. North Port. Norvik."

Crispin turned to Meade. "It's Norwich! The modern name is Norwich."

Meade went over to the translation on the board and put a check next to the line.

Twā micel ceaster betwuh
Two great cities between

Meade was quiet as he returned to his desk and stood over the atlas. He ran his finger from the sea at Great Yarmouth inland to Norwich. "This can't be right. It is over twelve kilometers inland. Almost eight miles. Portolanos don't usually show inland locations. London works because it is a port."

Doctor Lee leaned over the atlas and pointed to a river. "The River Yare is still navigable today."

Crispin slid the metal ruler across his desk. "Meade, circle Norwich and put a straightedge between it and London. Where's the halfway point?"

Meade answered quickly. "Inland from Ipswich by eighty kilometers. That's about fifty miles. That doesn't make any sense."

Crispin shifted the northern end of the ruler to the sea east of Norwich and the straightedge came closer to Ipswich. "You have said how the portolano did not bother with interior geography, so why not assume it is a *coastal* town halfway between the two cities? Both towns are as accessible from the sea as they were a thousand years ago." Crispin tapped it and looked at Doctor Lee. "And both have twisting rivers with banks that might match our text. But why here? Why would you want to bury someone halfway between two great towns on a river bank?"

She said. "I can only guess. Privacy? Maybe that is where they had their kingdom. Maybe it is just somewhere on that imaginary line, not really halfway."

Crispin said, "In actual fact, that word in Old English does infer the half-way point, but I do not think it need be inland." He looked at her and fell silent when he saw her holding he fingertips over her mouth and staring at the back of the room. "Are you ill? What is it?"

Doctor Lee took off her glasses and let them dangle in her hand above the desk. She frowned and then said softly, "Mister Meade, per-haps I have been working on the wrong question. I have been trying to help you find the ancient sea level anywhere. Italy. Sweden."

He nodded. "Right, so I can adjust the coastline."

"Perhaps it's the lateness of the hour. Perhaps, it is a faulty proposi-tion, but I have an idea." She put her glasses down. "From the pottery shards we were collecting in the marsh. We know that Romans had a saltern on the marshland."

"A what?"

Crispin said, "A salt works."

"Right, Lieutenant. The Romans build an earthen dam at the shore with a gate. They would leave it open and let the tide flood it. Then they would close the gate and let the seawater evaporate. They would repeat that flooding and evaporation process day after day until there was enough salt to rake up and harvest."

Crispin muttered into his tea mug. "Indeed, the origin of our mod-ern word 'salary' is from the Latin *salarium*, salt. One being worth his—"

Doctor Lee frowned at him and continued. "We can trace the Roman saltern to about 425 A.D. Then it just stops. The shoreline changed as the sea level went—"

Meade's hand was shaking. "Higher or lower?"

"Higher. The marshland flooded, so they couldn't use it for salt making. But that let boats have better access to the wool market upriver. They abandoned the saltern at the shore from 400 to about 700 A.D. Then it started being used after about 750."

Meade grabbed his pencil. "Guess how high the water would need to be to let the trading ships into Norwich. Guess!"

"Just a few feet for the Viking ships."

Meade looked at Crispin, who seemed to be counting the ceiling tiles. "Hey, were you listening?"

"Oh. Sorry. I was trying to recall a paper I wrote while at King Edward's School about a gristmill somewhere on a river in Suffolk. Give me a minute."

Meade looked astonished and fell back in his chair. "What's so important about a paper you wrote as a kid?"

"The waterwheel that turned the grinding stones was fed from a mill pond not a river or stream."

"I still don't see—"

"It was a *tide* mill. At high tide, the miller opened a lock and filled a pond, like the Romans at the salt flat. Then at low tide, he'd open a gate, sending the water through a waterwheel, which then powered the grinding stones and ground corn into meal."

Meade stared at Crispin, waiting for him to sort his facts.

After Crispin blinked several times, he said, "Built in the twelfth century. Operated by the Augustinian Canons of the Woodbridge priory until Henry the Eighth seized it."

"Twelfth century. That's the 1100s. Do you remember where it is?"

"Oh, I thought I said. The Woodbridge priory owned it. They are at Woodbridge." Crispin pointed to the atlas. "If the tide rose high enough to fill the mill pond, a Viking ship could have gone that far just after the turn of the millennium. So, I say we look to the riverbanks at least as far inland as Woodbridge and Norwich."

Meade grabbed a pencil and started shading the map at Great Yarmouth shifting the coast halfway to Norwich and widening the river.

Crispin turned to Doctor Lee. "Pots. I thought you were collecting shards of cooking pots in the marsh."

She said, "The Saxons used large clay pots to boil off the last of the water from the brine. It proved to be a much more efficient process than waiting for natural evaporation."

Crispin touched the scab on his chin. "Doctor Lee, the French still use the evaporation method in the œillets, the shallow salt beds in the south at Noirmoutier on the Atlantic, and in Camargue, south of Arles."

Meade resumed penciling a new coastline at the Norfolk broad. "I don't get it. How could the sea level at Birka drop when it went up here?"

Doctor Lee adjusted her glasses and thought a moment before answering. "All the papers that I have read on the place were in translation. Perhaps the translator placed too great an emphasis on the sea level and not enough on the simple fact that the larger trade ships needed a deeper waterway to sail to Birka. We do know that the channel dried up but not exactly when."

Crispin pointed to the atlas that Meade was shading. "Meade, as you move south, there will be an area of cliffs in Suffolk, so you wouldn't alter the coast there, would you?"

"No. Professor, you know the coastline better than I do. Can you point them out for me?" Crispin leaned over the atlas.

The two constructed an ancient coastline, mile by mile. Small inland movement at hilly areas. No alteration at cliffs. Substantial shading where flat lands or marshes joined the sea.

After Crispin had assisted in pointing out the elevations at the coast, he leaned back and stretched. Meade widened the river running from great Yarmouth to Norwich and moved his pencil south. He shaded the rivers north of Lowestoft, on either side of Southwold, and near

Aldeburgh. After Crispin tossed him a freshly sharpened pencil, Meade widened the rivers flanking Felixstowe and was about to take a sip of cold tea when Crispin grabbed his wrist. "Stop, Meade."

"What now?"

Crispin released Meade's wrist. "Look at what you just did. Sit back. Look where you just shaded."

Crispin reached for the Baldwin and placed it next to the atlas.

Meade stared. "It's. It's almost...."

Crispin tapped across the map where the Deben, Orwell, and Stour rivers met the sea. Doctor Lee squinted at the atlas and then at the portolano. "There is your upper river coursing to the sea. The Deben, isn't it?"

Meade nodded and let his eyes dart between the shaded atlas and the Baldwin.

Crispin sat back in his chair and smiled. "Meade! This might be it!"

"The island...there is no island on the atlas—"

Crispin leaned forward. "A minor detail! Didn't you see it on that map of Suffolk? I packed several."

Meade fanned through the box of maps and pulled out one which he handed to Crispin, who looked skeptically at the map. "No. Not this one. There was another map. Hand me that chest. I'll find it myself." Crispin flipped through several maps before he pulled one from the chest. He examined the Latin inscription *SVFFOLCIÆ comitatus cuius Populi Pagos et Villas.* "Here is the one. Pieter van den Keere in 1617." Crispin placed the fragile paper map on the table next to the atlas. "The Dutch one. Look, there's your island. I wonder if he copied his map from your Baldwin?"

"Congratulations, gentlemen. This is a huge step forward." Doctor Lee walked to the chalkboard. "All we need to do now is find the place on one of these three rivers that is on the east bank of a stream in a reeve's meadow."

Meade looked at Crispin "I've been meaning to ask you, what is a 'reeve'?"

Crispin sighed. "By definition, it is the official charged with protecting the property of the shire for his lord. You have that word in America. There you call a Shire Reeve, a 'Sheriff.'"

"Okay. Professor, where do we find his meadow?"

Before he could answer, a knock on the door startled them.

Chapter № 32

Thursday
November 2, 1916
North of London, England

Meade waited for Crispin to slide the Baldwin into the drawer. At the second barrage of knocking, Meade called, "Who is it?"

"It's Jamison."

Meade waited for Doctor Lee to turn the board to the wall before he opened the door. The administrator held a pair of boots in each hand. Meade reached for them.

Crispin looked at Jameson, who appeared distressed. "What is it?"

"A gentlemen rang up just as I was bringing your boots down. He insisted that I fetch you, Mister Meade. Quite demanded it."

Crispin motioned Jamison into the room, and Meade slammed the door. Crispin asked firmly, "How did you respond to the caller?"

"I made like it was a bad connection and asked him to repeat himself while I got my wits about me. I think I asked him what he was talking about, as I did not recall a patient by that name."

Crispin forced a calming smile. "Good man. Did he give his name?"

Jamison shook his head and breathed rapidly. "No, sir. I didn't think to ask."

"That is just as well. Did he say anything else?"

"Yes. That he wanted to talk to Mister Meade about their mutual friend, a Mister Baldwin, and that he would call again in fifteen minutes."

Meade clenched his jaw as he heard Crispin say, "Could you excuse us for a moment?"

Jamison asked, "Want me to wait outside the door?"

Crispin nodded. As soon as Meade shut the door, he slid the boots toward their beds and ran back to where Doctor Lee and Crispin were whispering to each other.

Crispin said, "Well, Meade. Someone knows where we are."

Holding up his hand, Meade said, "Where *I* am. He didn't ask about either of you. Do you think he led them to our door?"

Crispin shook his head. "No. They'd be here by now if that were the case."

Nodding, Doctor Lee said, "The manor house is small enough to find us if they wanted to root us out."

Meade leaned forward. "Then why didn't they?"

Doctor Lee tapped the desk. "They think we have better sense than to have the Baldwin with us. They want the map, not Meade."

Crispin's eyes narrowed. "Quite possibly. We should have secured it in a bank box, but we needed to refer to it for—"

Meade turned to Doctor Lee. "Is there anyone armed up there? Are there any military police or guards?"

She drew back in shock. "This is a recovery hospital— not an army garrison!"

Crispin pushed his chair away from the desk and rubbed his chin. "It will take hours to get help from London. I say we play the bluff."

Meade stood and stared at him. "You want me to take the call?"

"Yes. Arm yourself, Meade. I'll stay the watch here with Doctor Lee. We are well entrenched, and there is only one way to get to us, which I can defend."

Meade grabbed his holstered Smith & Wesson from the desk drawer, verified that it was loaded, and slipped the holster on his belt at the small of his back. "Is your revolver loaded?"

Crispin nodded. "Doctor Lee will remain under my protection until your return." As Meade turned to go, Crispin cleared his throat. "Advise the London contact of this event. You do recall the number, don't you?"

Frowning at Crispin, Meade left the room. Doctor Lee locked the door behind him and spun to face Crispin. "What's this all about?"

"The Director would have used a code if he called, just as you did. No one else should know that we are here."

"What now?"

"We wait."

"Lieutenant! While we await Mister Meade's return, may I inquire if you have reflected on our prior discussion?"

Crispin pulled his revolver from the drawer and placed it on the blanket on his lap. "This is not the time." He looked at the door anxiously and pulled the portolano from the drawer. "It's worth a king's ransom." He paused. "But it is not worth a hair on that man's head."

"Lieutenant? What are you thinking?"

"Would you be kind enough to toss me the pouch? I think Meade left it in the drawer of his desk." She found it and handed it to Crispin. He put the cord over his neck and slipped the portolano into its case. He pulled his robe over it and cinched the tie. "Best I keep it on my person."

Doctor Lee sat next to Crispin. They were silent for a few minutes, each watching the door. He checked the Webley again. Released the cylinder lock. Counted the cartridges. All were seated properly. He snapped the cylinder home. The sound of metal on metal echoed in the tiled room. The sound of bolts on rifles snapping to the ready echoed. Behind him, there were the mortar shells exploding and small arms fire. The snapping chatter of a machine gun sounded in the distance. He blinked hard and wiped the sweat from his forehead.

"Lieutenant?"

Crispin sat motionless. Sweat trickled down the small of his back. Doctor Lee stood up from her table and walked in front of him. She looked closely at Crispin. His eyes were fixed on the doorknob, and his hands were trembling.

"Lieutenant! Say something!"

Crispin blinked twice and focused past her.

"Lieutenant? What is it?"

"Nothing. Nothing at all."

"You may think that it is all well and good for you to close up like an oyster when I try to talk to you. But it is not. You have changed. The war has changed you. And will continue to—"

Crispin stared at her. "Not now!"

Doctor Lee cleared her throat. "Lieutenant, I mean no offense, but you can't just leave these memories undigested."

He forced a smile. "Didn't that fellow in *A Christmas Carol* blame his ghosts on a bit of beef or a blot of mustard?"

"As much as you try to dismiss it, this is not folly. Talking helps. I am available to listen. As either your friend or as a physician."

Crispin glared at her. "I shall take that under consideration at a later time. I know that I am not at all myself."

"But you are, you see. You are fully and completely yourself. Your decisive action and extended wariness, which was troublesome when the kettle steamed, are precisely what kept you alive over there and what puts you on a keen edge now."

Crispin started to smile.

"You are one of the lucky ones. You can use your intellect to harness some of those emotions."

He started to say something but stopped.

"Lieutenant? What do you want to say?"

He blinked away the thought. "Is that what they taught you at your training day?"

She chuckled. "Taught me?"

"Yes. You were going to be trained—"

"Oh, no. I was the instructor. I am sorry if I was unclear."

Crispin turned to the door and was silent a moment before he asked, "How long has Meade been gone?"

Doctor Lee opened her watchcase. "Fifteen minutes."

"Could you put it there where I can see it?"

Doctor Lee unhooked the gold chain from around her neck and opened the back cover. "Stewart had his favorite prayer engraved for me. By Basil the Great, the Eastern Orthodox Saint of the fourth century." She handed her watch to Crispin.

He read the engraving to himself.

Steer my ship, good Lord, to your quiet harbor.
There may I be safe from the storms of sin and conflict.
Direct my course and shelter me when the waves are high.
Guard me when the sea is rough, and
In every danger grant me your comfort and peace;
Through Christ our Lord. Amen.

He opened the front cover to show the watch hands and balanced it on the desk where he could glance at it easily. He stared at the door. "Doctor Lee, what if the king were leaving the pagan world? What if this were a Christian burial? How far back could that take us?"

"Do you think that is possible?" She walked to the encyclopedia on the counter. "Let me check some dates." She returned to her table and leafed through the volume. "That would take us all the way back to the Wuffing kings." She ran her finger down the page. "King Rædwald was called, by some, the first Christian king of what has become England." She looked up. "Not king over all the land, but a king to whom other regional kings owed allegiance. 'First among equals' might be a way of putting it."

"In the 600s, wasn't it?"

She read from the book. "Very good. King from Anno Domine 616 to 627."

"Buried where?"

She flipped back a page and frowned. "It doesn't say."

"Tell me again, wasn't the sighting of Saint Michael in France in the 700s?"

"The year was 709 A.D."

Crispin frowned. "But that is after Rædwald—"

"If you assume that was the one and only sighting. We have a written record of that moment, but all that is true has not been written, has it?"

"Then this might—"

"I think we don't know a hill of beans about what saints do and don't do. What if there was a sighting in the fifth or sixth century or a week before the mapmaker drew the map? If everything else points to a Christian king, why discount that possibility?"

Crispin returned the watch and sat in silence. Doctor Lee closed it and tipped her head as she hooked the chain.

Crispin looked past her to his writing on the chalkboard and gasped.

Doctor Lee looked behind her. "What?"

"An acrostic. Odd. I hadn't noticed that before. The first letters of—"

Doctor Lee jumped up and went to the text of the map and tapped on the first letter of each of the lines in Old English.

"What do the letters 'D R Y H T E N' spell?"

" 'Dryhten' has only one meaning."

She stared at him. "And that is?"

" 'The Lord God.' The Christian God. They were—"

A soft knock at the door interrupted him.

Doctor Lee's eyes darted to Crispin. "Meade?"

Crispin shook his head and whispered, "It's not his code." He shouted toward door, "Who is it?"

Although muffled, Crispin heard a man with a slight Irish accent say, "It's Father Mullins. Hospital chaplain making my rounds."

Doctor Lee shook her head and whispered. "The hospital chaplain is Reverend Johns. He's out of town this week."

Crispin shouted. "A moment, if you will!" He slid the Webley under the blanket and wheeled his chair to face the door. He took a firm hold on the pistol's grip and nodded. Doctor Lee whispered in his ear, "Do you think this wise?"

He whispered, "Step aside quickly after you open the door."

A thin, older man with wispy white hair stood in the doorway. He wore a black suit. At his throat, the white priest's collar seemed to fit well.

Crispin spoke firmly. "Father Mullins?"

"Yes. Seeing as the hospital's chaplain is away for a few days, I am making pastoral visits to the infirm." As he shifted in the doorway, his suit jacket opened showing a thin white stole around his neck. Crispin tensed, slipped his index finger past the guard, and rested it lightly on the trigger.

The priest blinked at the brightness of the room. "Might I come in?"

Crispin forced a smile. "Of course. *Commemoratio omnium Fidelium Defunctorum.*"

When the man was three steps into the room, Crispin calmly pulled his pistol from under the blanket and pointed it at the center of the man's chest. "Put your hands above your head, now!"

The man complied and stared at Crispin under heavy lids.

Doctor Lee turned to Crispin. "What are you thinking? He's a priest!"

"Not a very good one. Latch the door and stand behind me."

The priest puffed with indignation as Doctor Lee scurried to Crispin. "What is the meaning of–"

Crispin asked, "What day is this, *Father?*"

The man answered cautiously. "It's the second of November."

"And yesterday was?"

"Wednesday."

"I take it you have not consulted your missal or you would not be wearing that stole."

"Stole?"

Crispin continued aiming at the man. "That white stole is worn on All Saints Day. That was yesterday. A green stole would be appropriate for today. It's All Souls Day, which you failed to recognize in Latin."

The man tore off the stole and threw it to the ground.

Crispin cocked the Webley. "That puts paid on it. Go to the wall. Lean your hands against it."

The man turned slowly as Crispin said, "Be clear, my revolver is aimed at your spine, and I have no qualms about firing should your hands come off that wall."

Doctor Lee leaned over the back of Crispin's wicker pushchair and whispered, "What now?"

"We wait." He motioned for her to come closer to him and whispered. "Please go to the burner and be prepared to ignite it for illumination. He may have a colleague who could switch off the electricity."

Chapter № 33

Thursday
November 2, 1916
North of London, England

Meade followed Jamison into his office. With its high ceiling, old walnut paneling, and the dark calm of a reading room in a gentlemen's club, the room retained its place as the manor library, in spite of the addition of metal file cabinets and the clutter of medical files balanced ten high in uneven rows on the desk and credenza. The curtains were closed. A strong rain beat against the windowpanes.

"Take my desk chair, Mister Meade. The telephone is on the far side. Sorry for the clutter, we're booking at five times our capacity and are somewhat awash in paper."

Wondering if he could do as well if his work suddenly increased fivefold, Meade nodded. "It's fine. Thank you."

After Jamison departed and closed the door, Meade sat on the edge of the high-backed chair as alert as a guard dog. He jerked when the telephone rang and smiled at his reaction. He let it go to a third ring before lifting the earpiece from the candlestick base and holding the mouthpiece close to his face. "Meade, here." He sat straight in the chair and listened very carefully to a calm voice. "How are you?"

"Swell, thanks." Meade had heard the crisp diction and deep voice before.

"And your friend? How is he getting on?"

Trying to place the voice, Meade stalled. Someone he had met recently. "What friend?"

"Don't be coy, it's too late in the day for that."

"Coy?" Meade feigned shock. "I've been called a lotta things, but never coy."

"We know where you are. And we know that you recently acquired a portolano."

Leaning back into the desk chair, Meade nodded as he placed the voice as the one behind him at the auction, bidding against him. He smiled and slowed his speech, trying to sound calm. "I've got a lotta maps. I collect them for a hobby."

The voice was firmer now, deeper, almost cross. "Are you trying to play with me?" Meade still did not have a face to match the voice.

"What? Not at all."

"I want the Baldwin."

Meade wedged the earpiece against his shoulder, grabbed a sheet of paper from the wastebasket, and crumpled it near the mouthpiece. "The what? I didn't hear you. Static."

The caller spoke louder and faster. "The Baldwin. It left the auction house in your box of maps. It has his red wax seal."

Meade paused before asking, "Who are you?"

"I am a very unimportant detail—"

"I disagree! How do I know you can afford the Baldwin, if I still have it?"

"Will money persuade you to part with the map?"

Meade paused and tried to hear anything in the background to indicate the location of the caller or if anyone was speaking to him. Nothing. He clenched his jaw before saying, "Money always interests me."

The man snickered. "What about a trade. The map for your friend's life? Lieutenant Crispin, isn't it?"

Meade held his breath and felt his stomach tighten as though expecting a punch. He waited for the caller to threaten Doctor Lee. Nothing. After counting to three to himself, Meade said, "Why would I care about a guy I just met?"

The caller snapped back, "Don't lie to me. I know Crispin was with you in Amiens." Meade said nothing and listened as the caller swore almost imperceptibly. The earpiece crackled with his voice. "I take it you are interested in selling the map?"

"Depends on your offer."

"And what would you desire?"

Meade looked at the ceiling. "I won't know it until I hear it. The map is of museum quality, but I would expect a premium as well. Something large enough to cover my disappearance from England forever."

Meade stretched his neck as he strained to listen. The caller said, "I'll need to discuss that with others. We'll talk tomorrow at this time."

Meade looked at his watch. It was after seven. He deepened his tone. "No. At six tomorrow. Where do I call you?"

"I will call you at this exchange. At six."

"Fine. If your offer interests me, I will need a few days to secure the map and make other arrangements."

"Certainly."

The connection had ended. Meade returned the earpiece to the candlestick telephone and rocked back in the chair.

Meade had the hospital operator call the London contact's number.

The man answering the telephone did so with the one word. "Kell!"

"My name is Meade, and–"

"Say no more. Cumming said you might be giving me a ring. Is there something you care to ask me before we chat?"

After Meade queried and Kell provided the proper recognition code response, Meade gave a detailed account of the call and threat to Crispin. Kell's response was quick. "I shall send one of my best men, Kenneth McLean, to collect you and your associates. Have your personal effects packed within a half of an hour."

"You work for Cumming?"

After a short chuckle, the man said, "We are colleagues. I manage matters interior to the country, whereas he is the foreign branch."

"I see. Oh, there is one other thing. We are having some clothes delivered."

"By whom?"

After Meade provided the details, Kell said firmly, "I shall have someone intercept the parcel for you."

"Thanks. Want us to wait in the hospital workroom or go somewhere else?"

Kell asked, "Do you have side arms?"

"Yes, we both have pistols."

"Then stay deep in your burrow. I'll have him find you. When he arrives, challenge him with the recognition code."

"Same question and three letters?"

"Precisely."

Meade listened for more but Kell had clicked off the line. He left the office, ran down the back stairs to the workroom, and listened at the door. Hearing nothing, he tapped the agreed-upon sequence and put his key into the lock.

When he opened the door he saw Crispin pointing his pistol at a man who was facing the wall. Doctor Lee stood at the end of the room, by the Bunsen burner she had lighted.

Crispin spoke without looking at Meade. "Confirm the door to the loo is locked and then get in here, fast."

Meade rattled the knob and ducked into the workroom. "It's locked." Doctor Lee extinguished the flame and leaned on the counter.

Crispin nodded. "There is cord in my desk."

Meade locked the door, sprinted to the desk, and returned with the rope that had bound the crates. Meade stood to the side of the man and tied a tight hitch on one wrist. He nodded to Crispin, who aimed the gun away from Meade as he snapped the man's arm behind his back and tied his wrists together.

Crispin said, "Tie him to the chair and keep him facing the wall."

Doctor Lee pushed a chair over to Meade, who then tied the intruder to it. Meade patted the man for weapons and grinned at Crispin when he pulled a revolver with a short barrel from the man's calf-high boot.

As Meade moved aside, Crispin returned his aim at the man's back.

"One last thing, if you will," Crispin said to Meade. "Would you be kind enough to remove the clerical collar from that imposter?"

Before Meade could comply, Doctor Lee snatched it from the intruder's neck and threw it on her table. She brushed her hands together as though removing dust. "If you gentlemen would like to chat in private, you will recall that I am not unfamiliar with pistols. I would be pleased to watch this scoundrel."

"In a minute," Crispin said and turned to the man. "How did you find us?"

The man sneered. He caught sight of the boots by the beds and laughed.

Meade pulled his Smith & Wesson from his holster, clicked the lever above the trigger guard. Doctor Lee sat expectantly at her table. Meade handed it to her. "Safety's off. It's a hair trigger."

"Take your time, gentlemen. We're not going anywhere."

Crispin said, "We'll be just outside the door."

Meade pushed Crispin's wicker chair into the hall, closed the door behind them, and left his key in the lock. Meade spoke quietly. "The caller. It was a guy who was at the auction. Pretty sure he's German. He wants the map."

"So that was that the imposter's job? To steal it while you were out taking the call?"

Meade shrugged. "Maybe. The guy is calling me tomorrow with an offer."

Crispin tipped his head toward the room. "What do we do with him?"

"I've already called the–"

From inside the room, Doctor Lee shouted, "Stop!"

Meade bolted through the door as Doctor Lee raised the pistol and aimed at the man, who had freed his arms and was cutting through the cord that held his back against the chair. Crispin wheeled in and aimed at him as well.

The intruder cut the last of the restraints. Slicing an arc in front of him with a razor blade, he lunged at Meade. Meade backed up toward the door.

Crispin held his blanket up for Meade. "Wrap it on—"

Meade flipped the blanket around his left arm, used it as a shield, and charged into the man, knocking him into the wall. Meade pressed his left forearm into the man's throat and grabbed his right wrist as he tried to bring the blade up into Meade's chest.

The man slammed his head from side to side and found no escape. He lifted his knee as Meade turned sideways and the blow glanced off his hip. Meade pressed until the intruder's face flushed almost purple and he went limp. After he dropped the blade and Doctor Lee had kicked it away from them, Meade slowly released his pressure and let him slide down the wall to the floor.

Meade panted and shook the blanket from his arm. He pointed to the desk. "Rope!"

Doctor Lee got the ten feet of tangled cord and unsnarled it as she hurried back to Meade. He flipped the unconscious man on his stomach and tied his wrists together at the small of his back with one end of the cord, pulled off the man's boot, and tied his bare ankle to the wrists. He put three hitches on the bundle of joints and stood panting over the man.

Crispin said, "Telephone London again. Our contact needs to know of our guest. Change your entry code in case we have been overheard. Knock twice and twice again before entering so I will know it's you."

"Two and two." Meade coughed. "Not three pause one."

"Right. Off with you."

Meade sprinted toward the stairs, made his second call, ran back to the workroom, and knocked as Crispin had requested before he opened the door. He glanced at the man, who remained hog-tied on the floor, walked to Crispin, and motioned for Doctor Lee to join them. Meade whispered, "They'll send men for him and have a car for us here in half an hour." He nodded to Doctor Lee. "That includes you, too."

"I can't leave my—"

Meade patted her arm. "A replacement is on the way."

Crispin held up his palm to stop her argument. "You must get everything together quickly. Everything. Now, get cracking."

Meade gripped his Smith & Wesson in his trouser pocket and opened the door for Doctor Lee. Nineteen minutes later her suitcase and a trunk had been taken by two orderlies to the front hallway, and she had returned to their workroom where she grabbed her working notes and slipped them into her knitting bag.

Meade erased the chalkboard, scrawled over it, and erased it again. He returned all the maps to their chest. Crispin said, "Don't forget the kits in the loo."

"Right. The reference books?"

"Leave them. They belong here."

Meade looked startled at Crispin and asked, "Where's the—"

Crispin patted his chest and smiled.

Meade slipped the atlas with his notes into his bag and left the encyclopedias and dictionary on the counter. In less than the projected time, there was a knock on the door, a series of short taps. Meade drew his gun, went to the wall next to the door, and whispered. "Who sent you?"

A deep voice said softly, "RLS."

Meade opened the door and three burly men in brown suits, overcoats, and hats entered quickly. Two men untied, handcuffed, and removed the intruder without any discussion. The tallest of the three remained.

He took off his hat. His hair was short and black. His eyes were dark under heavy brows. Although a bear of a man, he had a gentle voice and an easy smile. "McLean, at your service. All packed, I see. Let's get you into better quarters."

Chapter № 34

Thursday
November 2, 1916
North of London, England

Crispin stood in the entrance wearing a greatcoat which Doctor Lee had purloined from Jamison's laundry to put over his night-clothes. In the coat's slash pocket was his Webley pistol. He leaned on his crutches and watched Meade and McLean load the luggage into a large Panard touring sedan with its canvas roof in place. Once the car was packed, Meade waved for them. Crispin and Doctor Lee walked over the wet gravel in the drizzle. Meade opened the door for her to sit in the spacious front seat beside McLean.

"Thank you, Mister Meade. But I'll accompany you in the rear."

Crispin maneuvered his plastered leg into the automobile with care. Once he had slid into the driver's seat, McLean said, "Please keep your pistols available, gentlemen." McLean slipped the sedan into gear and smoothly sped away from the hospital. Crispin turned to see how the boxes and bags were riding between Doctor Lee and Meade. Meade had brought the two blankets from their room along with the bags and the cane that Verne had given Crispin. Doctor Lee handed the top blanket to Crispin and leaned back against the window of the automobile. "Sorry my things took up so much room." She pushed the other blanket across the luggage to Meade, who toweled his wet hair with it before wrapping it around his shoulders.

Meade smiled at her. "Not a worry." The canvas top billowed and crackled in the wind as McLean steered the large automobile along the dark highway and through country traffic circles with skill in spite of the rain. Wrists the size of Crispin's forearm extended past his cuffs as he gripped the wheel. Partway through a traffic circle, Crispin looked out his streaked window and noticed lights far behind them. He turned to McLean, whose dark eyes glanced past Crispin out the side window. The suitcases shifted as McLean accelerated through a curve.

McLean asked, "How are you getting on back there?"

Meade braced himself against the front seat. "Can you take it easier?"

"Sorry. Trying to get you tucked in before the storm gets any worse. I figure it is about an hour out."

Crispin looked at the rapidly approaching traffic circle. "Never knew there were so many roundabouts in this part of the country."

As he braked hard, McLean said, "I don't want to make a beeline to the place, you know."

Doctor Lee laughed. "Not nearly as bad as that big one in Paris. Around the Arc de Triomphe. I got into a snarl there just before the war. Our taxi cab driver just turned off the automobile and walked away. Imagine our surprise. Buggies and automobiles do not manage well together."

McLean pressed on the accelerator. The car began a slide. He slowed only slightly. Doctor Lee looked at Crispin staring out the side window and followed his glance. "Is that a light from an automobile?" When no one answered, she persisted. "Are we being followed?"

Meade turned. "Looks like it."

McLean asked, "The portolano? Where exactly is it?" McLean noticed Crispin shift slightly and tighten his grip on his pistol. "Relax, Lieutenant. I'm Kell's special assistant. He has informed me of the nature of your mission so that I may offer any assistance which you require."

"I see."

"I simply wanted to know where it is to best protect it should we encounter any difficulties."

Crispin pointed to his chest. "It is secure."

"Good." McLean elevated his voice. "You might want to brace yourself back there. I will be turning to the left in a few moments to go behind a small summer cottage."

Meade looked out the rear window. "Do you think we're being—"

"Don't know what to think about the vehicle that is behind us. Pistols at the ready, if you please. We'll just see if it goes on its way or follows us up a blind lane."

Doctor Lee braced for the turn. Meade pulled off the blanket and drew his gun.

McLean swung down a small rutted lane, drove to the far side of a stone cottage, and pointed the dim headlamps across an open field. Meade and McLean jumped from the auto and ran to the corner of the small building. They heard the automobile pass the lane and chug into the distance.

McLean got back into the Panard. "There's a blessing."

Doctor Lee noticed the long knife cuts in the blanket as she handed it back to Meade. "What scoundrels! What perfect—"

Crispin's laugh startled her. "I beg to differ. No one is perfect. Meade, you've talked to him. What's his weakness? What can we use against him?"

Meade pulled the blanket over his shoulders. "Pride and greed."

Turning the Panard back onto the main road, McLean nodded. "You are quite right. That's Grimes for you."

Crispin stared at McLean. "Who?"

"Grimes."

Doctor Lee asked, "How could you—"

"We queried the telephone operators at the central London exchange after getting your message, Mister Meade. Any call to a military facility is written down. And the recovery hospital is now considered a military facility. The call originated in a cheap hotel near Whitehall. Desk clerk there thought a fellow calling himself Grimes used the telephone cabinet in the lobby at about the same time."

Crispin laughed. "That is astounding luck."

"To the contrary, we have been watching him for some weeks now. One of our soldiers on leave thought he was a bit too friendly and far too inquisitive about troop movements. He mentioned it to his superior, who passed the concern on to us."

Crispin held up his hand. "How does that connect him to this?"

"He's been visiting antiquarians all over the city. Seeking old, pricey maps. Asking after Mister Meade. Suggesting he knows you."

Crispin frowned. "By name?"

McLean nodded. "One of the antiquarians thought he bore a resemblance to a German archaeologist who purchased a Greek amulet from him before the war. Recalled that he taught at Heidelberg."

Meade looked at Crispin and saw a new set to his jaw. "Just what are you thinking, Professor?"

Crispin smiled and turned to Meade. "He hasn't seen it."

"But he described it."

"Think. Did he really?"

Meade frowned. "He never said what it looked like. He just called it 'the Baldwin.' I'm pretty sure he said it had the seal. But, he never really described the text on the portolano."

Crispin leaned his elbow over the back of the seat. "Did I recall correctly that there were several types of maps with the Baldwin in that collection?"

"Yes."

"If he had seen it, he could have described it to be certain that you had what he wanted. The text is certainly a distinctive feature."

Meade said softly, "Maybe—"

"Didn't you set up a return call tomorrow?"

"Yes. I told him I wanted to hear his best offer at six sharp. I was just stalling, of course. Had no idea he was sending a guy to steal it."

Crispin grinned. "Why not sell it to him?"

Meade choked. "Are you nuts?"

Boosting himself higher over the back of the seat, Crispin said,

"Why not sell him an altered facsimile of your Baldwin. Couldn't we make another map?" When Meade sat in silence, Crispin asked, "Meade? Do you think the intruder in Amiens—"

"You mean Stahl!"

"Yes. What could he have overheard?"

Doctor Lee listened intently.

Meade asked, "Weren't we talking about the ship's logs and the travel journals before Madeline—"

"Right. And one had a map in it."

"Yeah. What are you thinking?"

Crispin laughed and then became very somber. "We send him on a hare and hounds. Make a map and doctor the log to create its own provenance."

Meade chuckled. "You sly dog."

Braking, McLean said, "You might want to ready yourself for a sharp turn. We're almost at the vicarage." After he pulled to a stop at the heavy iron gate, he said, "The estate is quite secure, I assure you."

Meade started to open his door. "Want me to get it?"

"That won't be necessary." McLean turned to Crispin. "We never use the estate's proper name. Code name is 'vicarage.' Joke is, that it really was one. When Victoria was queen. A Member of Parliament owns it now. He turned his country house over to Military Intelligence to use as needed. Set up to manage quite a crowd and almost any contingency. Even has an infirmary just off the kitchen. Converted from the staff's sitting room."

A sturdy man in a black rain slicker came to the inside of the gate and gave a half salute to McLean who nodded in reply. He threw the bolt and pulled the gate open.

"Country estate, is it?" Crispin asked as the car crawled through the opening. He looked back to see the man shut the gate and retreat to a small stone guardhouse located beside the gate.

The sinuous road to the house snaked through a half mile of overhanging oak and sycamore trees. The earlier rain had ripped the last of the golden leaves from the sycamores, and the wet leaves on the pavement glistened in the headlamps of the automobile.

McLean cleared his throat before asking, "Excuse me, might I ask if any of you are experienced in forgery?"

Crispin laughed. "Unfortunately, no."

Meade said, "That's not true. Crispin's written with quills on parchment before. He could write the Old English on the map. I can draw a coastline."

Crispin looked back at Meade. "Probably good enough to get past a first look, but as to French journals…"

Doctor Lee asked, "Wouldn't you need to write it in French? Older French?"

Shrugging, Crispin said, "She's got a point. That is a level of criminality which is beyond us."

McLean asked, "How critical is a forger to your plan?"

Crispin sounded surprised. "A forger?"

"Perhaps I misunderstood what you were suggesting."

Crispin said, "No. You got it right. What are you thinking, Mister McLean?"

"That the more people knowing a secret, the less secure that secret becomes."

Crispin nodded. "Meade? What would you think if we could find some old parchment and make a go of our own forgery of the map and abandon any thought of creating a log of Verne's travels? After all, he is already convinced of the portolano's authenticity. I say we use an original hide, not a palimpsest. Let the map stand on its own feet."

"Let me think about it." Meade fell silent and looked out the window.

As the finger of light from the headlamps swept over the grounds, Doctor Lee gazed at beds of rosebushes pruned for the winter, the ornate hedging near the house, and a stand of trees surrounding a large rolling lawn. She noticed a small glass building some fifty paces to the side of the main building. "Is that a greenhouse?"

McLean answered, "A solarium. Built it for his wife. Fancies herself a sculptress. He reads while she attends to her art. Loved their travels in the tropics, they did. Filled it with palms and ferns."

"How lovely."

Crispin chuckled. "Under other circumstances, perhaps."

The road opened onto a broad graveled area at the front of the large two-story brick house. The dark slate roof was a dull black in the rain. Five brick chimneys loomed over the roof. Smoke curled up from only two. The windows were heavily curtained. No light escaped from the house.

Doctor Lee looked at the expanse of the graveled drive as they slowed at the front door. "There must be space for twenty cars to park here."

"In one of the bedrooms upstairs, there is a drawing of the house with the whole drive filled with carriages. No doubt some parish social." McLean stopped the car and turned to Doctor Lee. "The upper floor has six bedrooms and could comfortably manage a dozen guests for an extended stay. The main floor has rooms for a staff of five, a large study and sitting room, as you would expect of a vicarage, a large kitchen and formal dining room. All at your disposal. We've made up two rooms. Hope you gentlemen don't mind sharing. We try not to heat it all unless we are fully occupied. And you are our only guests."

After a pause, Meade said, "That's great."

"You'll have to make do with just the cook and me during your stay."

"A cook?"

"Among his other talents. We never know how many are going to need to vanish for a bit."

Crispin got out of the car, adjusted his crutches, and opened the car door for Doctor Lee. As they all walked up the bricked pathway to a double door that had been painted black, the door opened and a slim man in a black suit holding a pistol aimed skyward stood in the doorway. After McLean nodded to him, he holstered his pistol, held the door for his guests to enter, and walked to the Panard.

In the entryway, Crispin was silent as he surveyed the Victorian floral carpet and red velvet wallpaper. To the left was the study. A large mahogany desk with a high-backed chair dominated the room.

Doctor Lee said, "I feel like I've fallen back in time."

McLean said, "The present owner has gone to great pains to retain it in its original condition." Pointing to the two matching candlestick telephones on the desk in the study, he said, "Except for the modern conveniences, that is." After the cook brought the bags and crates into the hallway, he walked briskly past Crispin toward the rear of the house.

The sitting room opposite the study had a robust fire snapping in the fireplace. Clustered near it were a red velvet settee and four matching side chairs. On the opposite end of the room sat an upright piano. The warmth from the room penetrated the chill of the hall.

To the left was an enormous dining room. Doctor Lee stood in the doorway. "Honestly. You could easily seat two dozen guests at that table."

McLean pointed. "It seats eighteen now. But there are extenders and chairs in the cellar which allow us to seat thirty."

Crispin had never seen a rosewood dining set this intricate outside of a museum. The table had massive legs that were carved to resemble sinuous vines twined around them. The credenza and sideboard with a glassed case on top echoed the same botanical design and added birds in flight. Each of the chairs had the same carved legs but a distinctly different bird had been carved into the peak of the chair back at the diner's neck. The back and seats were overstuffed and covered with red velvet to allow a comfortable extended stay at the table.

Looking at the three crystal chandeliers in the dimly lighted room, she asked, "Would you be kind enough to turn on the lights for me, Mister McLean?"

He flipped one switch and the room was bathed in a soft light. The faceted drops of crystal cast rainbows on the dark red velvet wallpaper. He flipped a second switch and the room was illuminated brightly.

She blinked quickly. "Good Lord, I could do surgery in here."

Crispin smirked, "Let's hope that won't be necessary."

Pointing at the table, McLean said, "Although the entire residence is at your disposal, this might be the best location for your work."

Crispin nodded. "Indeed. Meade, perhaps you and Mister McLean could bring the crates in here?"

Meade turned back toward the hall and said, "Sure."

Crispin and Doctor Lee shifted the ornamental silver tea service to the end of the credenza, found a tablecloth in the top drawer, and folded it to protect the credenza from the rough wood of the crates. As Meade and McLean brought in the crates, Crispin turned to McLean. "Any chance of a pot of tea in the sitting room to take the chill off? Our hospital attire is entirely unsuited for travel."

Chapter № 35

Thursday
November 2, 1916
West of London, England

Crispin had relinquished his wet greatcoat by the time he joined Meade and Doctor Lee in the sitting room. Sliding into the red velvet chair that put his cast leg closest to the fire and the tea tray within reach, he sighed and tugged the belt on his robe tighter. Without asking, Meade slipped the needlepoint-covered footstool under his ankle and handed him a cup of tea.

Meade stood and put his hands on his hips as he faced Crispin. "Yes, Professor. Let's do it."

Looking startled, Crispin asked, "What?"

"During our drive, you suggested that we could forge another map. I think you are right. I think we should make a new Baldwin portolano to sell to Grimes."

Crispin rubbed his hands together in front of the fire and smiled. "My only concern is the materials and the location."

Meade sat on the small settee, putting his elbows on his knees. "Can we get enough parchment? I remember you saying the letters can't really be erased, so how would–"

Crispin laughed. "I can manage to get enough clean stock to make your map. We could use some from a nearby church. That's what Thomas Chatterton did. He stole old parchment from a church archive."

"Chatterton?"

"He was a lad who aspired to be a poet in the late 1700s. Couldn't sell his work, so he invented a fifteenth century monk who he named

Thomas Rowley. The monk's poetry, all written by Chatterton of course, had quite a popular following for a time."

"But you said the Baldwin's parchment didn't look like the parchment used by monks. And it sure is better than the hide I've seen on other portolanos."

"Right you are. Yours is of a much finer grade, a vellum, in fact. But Grimes won't know that. Any hide should suffice."

Doctor Lee grimaced. "Besides stealing from church archives, where else could one find it?"

Crispin smirked. "Do as William Henry Ireland did."

Meade stretched his hands toward the fire and then picked up his teacup from the table. "Another crook?"

Crispin nodded. "The very definition of one. A total scoundrel. He apprenticed himself to a lawyer to gain access to old deeds and property conveyances. Simply stole sheets of parchment from very old legal documents, sliced off any areas with lettering, and wrote on it afresh."

"You are kidding."

"Not in the least. Interesting chap. He started his life of crime by drafting a few autographs and then a promissory note that appeared to be in Shakespeare's hand. He went a bit mad, I think. He wrote an entire play which he then attributed to Shakespeare, *Vortigern and Rowena*. He actually had it performed about 1800. When he got found out, he confessed."

Meade rubbed his chin. "Old legal documents? Deeds? Indentures? Wills?"

"That's right. Just what are you thinking?"

"I know several antiquarians who separate documents. They frame the fancy parts with the big letters and wax seals and sell them as wall hangers. I'd never thought about what they did with the remainder of the parchment. I can make a list of them in a minute."

Crispin pointed to the desk in the study across the hallway. "Good.

If a church fails to yield any suitable parchment, your source surely will. There should be paper over there. What say we start McLean's shopping list now?"

Meade left his cup on a side table and marched to the study.

Crispin raised his voice. "The ink won't be an issue. I can mix up modern Indian inks to fool all but the best."

Meade returned to the sitting room, balanced several sheets of paper on his knee, and began to write. He looked sideways at Crispin. "And you've really done this before?"

"Certainly. I mocked up certificates and the like in school. Easy enough to simulate age with a bit of lemon juice to give the letters a rusty halo. That is the first thing that one looks for on such a document."

Doctor Lee asked, "Will a dip pen suffice?"

"I'd rather a quill. But if that proves too daunting, I could file the nib square. I'll put both on the list."

She shook her head. "We are in the country, for heaven's sake. There ought to be a quill somewhere. A feather duster, at least."

Crispin reached for Meade's list and pencil. "I'll complete drafting the materials list for McLean tonight, if we are all in agreement. Then we can fabricate it tomorrow afternoon after he has secured our materials."

Doctor Lee looked concerned and put her empty teacup on the table with a clatter. "Mister Meade? Don't you need to be at the hospital to-morrow to receive your telephone call?"

Folding the list, Crispin answered for Meade. "No. Kell is sending a man to the telephone exchange to redirect the call here. It is called 'switching over.' I did it all the time with the field telephones in France." Crispin was silent and looked at the floor.

"What is it, Lieutenant?"

Crispin looked up and chuckled slightly. "I was just thinking where we could send them on their merry adventure—"

Meade said, "Hell is not an option, Professor."

Doctor Lee looked at Meade. "I was thinking that a really good lie is very close to the truth so why don't we start with what we know about our location and then see what of that information we want to twist?"

Meade took the pencil back from Crispin and balanced a fresh sheet of paper on his knee. "Where do you think we should send him on his wild goose chase?"

Crispin looked at her when she did not answer.

She threw up her hands. "I'll need to sleep on that, Lieutenant. It has been a long day and my age is telling."

Meade pressed the matter and wrote a number one on his paper. "We want them to know that there is a treasure." He wrote one through ten along the left margin and filled in behind the two as he spoke. "Of significant value. From the Viking age."

Crispin nodded his approval. "We need it to be near a coastline for our facsimile to work."

As Meade wrote "coastal" behind number four, she yawned and looked at her watch. "But why would they believe us?"

Meade stood and stretched. "Because they want to."

Slapping his good knee, Crispin said forcefully, "Actually, I believe that Meade has not made the case strong enough. Plato understood our longing to be a part of something larger than ourselves. He divided the soul into three elements. Reason. Eros. And *thymos*. It is *thymos*, that need for recognition and belonging, that will compel them to accept our forgery as authentic."

"Even so, do you really think Grimes would take our bait and believe it?"

Crispin leaned back and smiled. "Ever heard of a Frenchman in the late 1800s named Professor Chasles?" He spelled the name for her.

She shook her head, and Crispin continued. "He was one of France's best mathematicians, in the century past. He wanted France credited for major scientific discoveries. The man rooted about for old documents to prove up his theory. Another wayward law clerk, this time in France, forged a letter from Isaac Newton that he sold to Chasles. In it, Newton gave the credit for discovering gravity to Pascal, a Frenchman."

Doctor Lee shook her head. "That's hard to imagine. How did he get discovered?"

"The greedy sot wrote letters from Galileo long after the man had gone blind. Then when challenged, he happened on a letter from Galileo explaining that he was just pretending to be blind."

Meade laughed. "You're right. Grimes has no other choice, now that his man failed to rob us."

Doctor Lee said, "Or worse. And now he thinks that we have vanished."

Crispin looked shocked. "Does he? His assailant who posed as a priest has gone missing, but Meade will still be able to receive his call tomorrow. I think we can continue the ruse that we are still at the hospital, just not in the same room."

Meade shook his head. "I think that's a long shot, but I'll try it that way."

Crispin nodded. "Thank you, Meade. Now, Doctor Lee? Where would you suggest locating the treasure? What undiscovered or unexplored site holds promise for a greedy archaeologist?" Meade added "undiscovered site" to his list.

Doctor Lee stretched. "Gentlemen, I need to reflect on it." She looked at the fatigue hanging on Crispin and felt her own shoulders sagging. "A good night's sleep is not going to hurt any of us."

Crispin took a long sip, which emptied his cup. "Ah. Best counsel is found on a pillow."

She pointed to his cast. "Any swelling after today's travels?"

Crispin held up his hand. "Nothing to be concerned about, thank you."

She stifled a yawn. "That is good to hear." She stood and touched Crispin's shoulder. "Give us all a last look at the Baldwin, will you? Something on which to dream."

As Meade pulled the pouch from under his sweater, Crispin said, "We thought it best to keep it on Meade, as he is far more ambulatory than I." Meade began unwrapping the cotton wool from around the seal. He handed the portolano to Doctor Lee.

Crispin looked at her and went pale. "The seal."

Meade listened to McLean's heavy footfall approaching as she handed it back. "Yeah, I'll put it away carefully."

"Mister Meade. I think the Lieutenant means that we have overlooked the seal in our planning."

Crispin watched McLean remove the tea tray from the small table next to him. "Excuse me. Would you know if there is any sealing wax in the house? Preferably a deep red."

McLean tipped his head toward the study. "I believe there is some in the desk."

"Splendid."

Meade asked, "Is there any plaster of Paris in your infirmary?"

"I am certain we have some. Would you care for me–"

Crispin looked startled. "What are you thinking?"

Meade opened his arms. "We just take the imprint of the real seal and–"

"Meade, plaster generates significant heat as it cures. I do not want to chance any damage to the authentic seal."

Meade looked at the ceiling and paused. "Any other ideas?"

Doctor Lee pointed toward the curtained window. "Clay. We could make an imprint on clay. Mister McLean? Didn't you say the owner's wife sculpts in the solarium? Could you secure some modeling clay for us from the studio?"

"I regret that I cannot. She works in marble."

Crispin unfolded the list and wrote as he said, "Well then. We'll simply add modeling clay to our list."

Doctor Lee sighed. "I am so glad that you considered that now."

Crispin folded it again and said, "See you both for an early breakfast, say six? I need to see the wax and speak with Mister McLean for a moment before I retire. I believe that we should have him inform his superiors of our plan in person to retain the utmost security. Agree?"

The others nodded.

Chapter № 36

Friday
November 3, 1916
West of London, England

In Crispin's dream fractured shards of stained glass and ripe apples pummeled him as he swam the backstroke in black mud under a sky of azure streaked with gray smoke. He whimpered in his sleep and grabbed at his pillow. He rescued an apple encased in a silver wristwatch and dropped it into a steaming bin.

Meade prodded Crispin's shoulder. "Hey, Professor."

Crispin sat up in the single bed and cocked his arm to swing at the shadowed face. "What–" He glanced around the room, saw the gaudy Victorian wall coverings, and fell back on his pillow.

"Is it your leg?"

Crispin propped himself up on one elbow. "My what?"

"You were yelling, so I got up and woke you. Is it your leg?"

"Oh. Yes. It must have gone a bit crampy. Sorry for the bother, Meade." Crispin said, tugging the covers over his head and trying not to shake. "Oh, Meade–"

Meade looked at his watch. "It's not even two yet. Go back to sleep." Meade punched the pillow and sat up. He walked into the bathroom.

Crispin called after him. "Wake me before six?" Then he recited, quiet as a sigh. "Our Father…*Fæder ure þu þe eart on heofonum….*"

Crispin returned to a fitful sleep. His moaning increased as the night wore on. Meade finally turned on the light and looked at him. A gloss of sweat covered his face and the collar of his pajama top was soaked with sweat. Meade called his name. When he failed to wake and moaned louder, Meade put on his robe and went to fetch Doctor Lee.

Crispin jerked awake at the touch of her hand to his forehead. He cocked his arm back and made a fist. His wrists were quickly restrained by Meade's large hands. "Easy, Professor! I got Doctor Lee for you."

Meade released Crispin once he had fully awakened. Crispin looked past Meade to Doctor Lee, who had retreated to the chest-high dresser near the door. The blue hem of a nightgown escaped from under her long dark plaid bathrobe. Doctor Lee poured a small glass of water from the carafe on the dresser, seated her glasses, and took a small brown bottle from the pocket of her robe. After squeezing and releasing the rubber top, she unscrewed the cap and carefully held the medicine drop-per over the glass of water. When she had finished squeezing two drops of a dark liquid into it, she recapped the brown bottle, swirled the glass, and brought it to Crispin. "For the pain."

He started to push it away. "No. I have to be sharp in the—"

She held the glass in front of his face and was stern. "It is a quarter of the usual dosage of laudanum. It is just enough to allow you some relief so you can rest."

He took the glass, bolted down the bitter liquid, and returned the empty glass to her. After she left, Meade turned out the light and listened to Crispin's breathing until it took on the slower pattern of deep sleep.

In the morning, Meade had dressed and returned to the bedroom for his watch. As he buckled the strap, he looked at Crispin, who moaned softly. Meade pulled the blanket from Crispin's face to look at him. He woke and blinked several times as Meade asked him, "Leg again?"

Propping himself up on one elbow, Crispin said, "Good Lord! Look at you."

Meade was attired in a new black and white tweed jacket, black sweater, and charcoal trousers— exact replicas of his attire when Crispin first met him. Crispin looked for boots, but saw that Meade was wearing black leather slip-on shoes. "How?"

Meade nodded to three large parcels wrapped in brown paper on the chest of drawers. "Delivered last night. McLean just brought them up. You were still asleep. Hope your stuff fits."

"Thank you, Meade."

Meade paused, waiting for Crispin to ask for the time. When he did not, Meade looked at his wristwatch. "It's almost five."

Stretching, Crispin said, "Good. That should let us get a start on our connivance before breakfast."

Meade nodded. "I'll go see if I can find some tea for us, before she gets up."

After Meade left, Crispin stood and hopped unsteadily to his crutches. He then decided to use his cane and pulled it from the wardrobe. He bathed, shaved quickly, and returned to the bedroom in his robe with a towel around his neck. He put the large parcel on his bed. Water dripped from his hair onto the brown paper, and he toweled his hair again. An odd anticipation came over him, not unlike getting the parish parcels at the boardinghouse.

Crispin pulled the tag end of the string. The knot released, and the string fell away. New clothing. Not something from the charity barrel.

He pulled back the brown paper and found neatly folded packets in crisp white tissue paper. Gently unfolding the first packet, he discovered two shirts. White. Starched crisp. Button cuffs and wing collars. A smaller packet held ties. One was silk and the other a jaunty knit. Both were in shades of chocolate. He selected the knit one. The next packet held a sweater vest. Argyle over a tan background. A bit sporty.

He picked up the largest of the bundles. A jacket of fine wool and two sets of trousers. He held the coat by the shoulders, and it unfolded immediately. Chocolate brown, tailored. Refined. A gentleman's suit. He laid the coat and trousers flat on the rumpled covers.

He tore open the smaller of the two remaining brown paper parcels on the dresser. Underclothes, stockings, and shoes. He examined the caramel brown shoes. The soles were fresh and the waxed laces thin. The leather was so supple that it shifted under his lightest touch. The final parcel held a deep brown overcoat, which he spread out on his bed.

Crispin sat on Meade's bed looking at the clothing on his own. He held the shoes and looked at the knee-high pile of tissue paper that surrounded him. He started laughing, like a child at Christmas.

The trouser legs were wide enough to slip over the cast. They fit as though they were spun of spider webs just for him. He wrapped the extra trousers, shirt, tie, and underclothing in sheets of tissue paper and placed them on the top of the bureau. He gathered and folded the extra papers and left them on the foot of his bed.

He combed his hair, looked for his revolver in the drawer of the bed stand. Not finding it, he went downstairs. Meade was dropping the atlas on the table as Crispin arrived in the dining room. "Professor, you look just like a country gentleman after the shoot."

Crispin leaned his cane against the buffet table and forced a smile. "Do you have my revolver?"

Meade nodded to the top of the buffet. "Over there. You look well enough to manage it, now."

He leaned back against the buffet, crossed his arms, and discreetly stroked the soft fabric with the tip of his index finger. "Quite a fine fit, if I do say so. Thank you. This is most kind of you."

Meade noticed the lace to the left shoe was untied and leaned over to tie it. "Better than looking at you in your pajamas."

"Thank you, Meade." He turned, opened his crate, and pulled out his Sam Browne belt. "Any word from Mister McLean?" He removed the chest strap, buckled on the waist belt, and holstered the Webley.

"He said things were going well, then rushed off to get the tea. Oh, here he is."

McLean carried a large silver tea tray which he placed on the buffet. He turned to go, then spun to face Crispin. "Oh, Lieutenant Crispin. I am pleased to report that the lads were able to get the parchment last night. Almost all the other materials on your list are collected and the remainder should follow later today."

"Splendid. Would you be kind enough to bring in the parchment for us to examine?"

"Certainly, sir."

Meade filled two cups and handed the first to Crispin. When McLean returned holding a parcel wrapped in dark brown paper, just over a foot square and half a foot high, Crispin motioned to the center of the table. "Thank you. Just set it there."

McLean put the parcel down and left.

Meade pointed at it. "I thought you needed a parchment that was a couple of feet in all directions."

"It is. Honestly, have you never seen a folded sheet of it before?"

"I guess not. Just framed documents or flat maps."

"Well, before sheets were cut to size and bound in books, the custom was to fold them for filing. Here, let me show you." Crispin ripped off the brown paper, picked up the pale ivory parchment, and slowly unfolded the stiff hide. First, turning over the top sheet to the left, as if opening a book. Then, unfolding it to the right. He continued to carefully unfold it and slid the open sheet to the center of the table. The folds created a wrinkled "H" on the pale dappled hide. Lettering ran across the upper quarter of the long edge of the parchment. Above the lettering the parchment was deeply stained and abraded.

Crispin turned it over and smiled. "Good. Plenty for our use."

"What was it?"

"A will." Crispin easily read the curls and flourishes in the bright room. "It begins, 'In the name of God Almighty.' Just look at the detailing on the first letter. That almost looks like a 'Y' or a flower, but you see the 'N' after it is almost one you or I would write today. 'This be the Last Will and Testament of one John of Colby, County of Norfolk, In the year of Our Lord, One Thousand Five Hundred and Fifty.' Astounding, isn't it?"

"How did it last this long?"

"Who can ever know these things? I am simply pleased that he didn't blather on. Simple will. Primogeniture. First son got it all." Crispin turned the parchment over and inspected lettering in pale ink in a finer hand. "*Probatum—*"

"What?"

"This Latin inscription simply validated the implementation of his will. Probated, we would say, after his death."

"Latin? But the front, were you translating?"

"No. It is English on recto. Latin on verso. The front probably was drawn up by some law clerk, and the notation on the reverse written by someone at court."

Meade reached for his tea and clattered the cup against the saucer. "A magistrate?"

"Who knows? At least they left us enough to use. Look at it; you could cut two, possibly three maps from the uninked areas."

"Why several? What are you thinking?"

Crispin grinned. "That you could have spilled your tea on it."

"Come on, Professor. I'm not gonna spill on—"

"But you should, Meade. Look at it. It's virtually pristine, but for the stained top. The true Baldwin had been knocked about at sea. Stored in the heat of Jerusalem. It shows the use and the effect of time. So must our fraudulent portolano."

Crispin turned at the sound of footsteps in the hallway.

Both men stood quickly when Doctor Lee arrived.

"Well, look at you two fashion plates."

Meade held the chair for her. She watched Crispin as she sat.

Crispin leaned on his cane and glanced at her brown tweed traveling suit with a high-necked, cream-colored blouse. He stared at the faceted amethyst pin at her neck. Doctor Lee kept her eyes fixed on his face. His brows shifted into a frown as he squinted at her pin. She asked, "How are you this morning?"

Embarrassed over his nightmares and unable to meet her eyes, he cleared his throat and looked away. "Much better."

Others might think his discomfort was from his leg, but she knew the truth of his anguish and the depth of his pride. "Good to hear. By the way, if you insist on using the cane, rather than crutches, please do it properly." She picked up the cane to demonstrate. "Hold the cane on the side of the good leg. Shift your weight to the good leg. Next, swing the bad leg and cane forward simultaneously. While leaning most of your weight on the cane and using the injured leg for balance, bring your good leg forward. By widening your stance and using this method, you are much less likely to fall." She returned the cane back to Crispin's right hand and remarked, "I see Mister McLean was successful. Good sized parchment, isn't it?"

Crispin pushed the parchment closer to her. "Yes. But you can see, not nearly as fine a skin as was used for the Baldwin. I was about to request that Meade take on the task of cutting blanks from the parchment. Then he can tint and distress them."

Meade put a steaming cup of tea in front of Doctor Lee and asked, "Want me to use the outline of our portolano?"

Crispin nodded. "We need our facsimile to be as similar as possible to the Baldwin. Torn edge and holes. Of course, we will only use one, but best make as many as you can, should we have any mishaps in our work as amateur forgers."

Meade nodded, pulled the Baldwin from its pouch, and placed it at the lower edge of the will on the rosewood table. The Baldwin glowed a deep amber on the pale ivory of the larger sheet. He opened his Buck knife.

Doctor Lee gasped. "Stop! What if that knife slipped? We need to protect the original map and this beautiful table. Isn't there a better way to go about this?"

Crispin handed a pencil to Meade, who took it after he had folded and pocketed his knife. He traced two outlines of the Baldwin on the will. After he returned the map to its pouch, he tapped the will. "Hard as a board. We could soak it—"

Crispin shook his head. "No. I did that in school. It takes forever to dry. Try to get a bit of grime or tea stain on the edges, but keep the center as dry as possible so the ink will lay down properly."

Meade darkened the light pencil lines. "I'll get McLean in a minute. They've got to have a saw and a barn or workshop here. I'll figure out a way to make a couple good blanks for your words, Professor."

"And your cartography, Meade."

Meade laughed and turned to Doctor Lee. "The Professor thinks it looks like it needs some age on it. We're going to use tea. Any other ideas?"

"The tannin in the tea should bind well. How about some soot or fireplace ash? You could get your hands a bit grimy, tallow or meat drippings, and rub on it. What do you think?"

Before he could answer, McLean came to the door. "I know it's not quite six, as you had requested, but the cook has the porridge ready if you would like your breakfast now."

Meade followed McLean toward the kitchen. "I'll help you." But Doctor Lee put her hand on his arm as he walked past her.

Meade leaned down. She said softly, "Would you be kind enough to bring a large glass of water as well?"

He nodded.

When they were alone, Doctor Lee looked at Crispin. "I want you to drink it all, immediately. It will help clear your head."

"If you insist." He smiled as he held up the parchment will and then slid it to the far end of the table.

"What possesses you this morning, Lieutenant Crispin? You seem—"

"Myself, in a word. First morning in an age that I awoke without that blinding fear and…." He gazed at the parchment. "The most interesting dream came to me. I imagined how the portolano was made and who made it. I saw it clearly as though I were at the cinema. Yes, just like a day at the cinema."

Before he could continue, Meade wheeled an ebony serving cart into the dining room and asked, "What's like a day at the cinema?"

"I was just recounting a dream I had."

Meade nodded. "Oh. There's a woodshop in the cellar. I'll tackle the parchment after breakfast."

"Here, let me help you, Mister Meade." Doctor Lee put the glass of water on the table near Crispin and arranged the silver serving dishes and plates on the buffet. When she had finished, the toasted bread stood with military precision in a silver rack. Steam swirled from the porridge in a silver chafing dish after she removed the lid. A tray held pots of butter, marmalade, berry jam, and a pitcher of cream.

Doctor Lee took two pieces of toast and a dollop of jam and sat next to Crispin, who had emptied his glass. She watched Meade ladle porridge into a bowl. "Mister Meade. I thought on your comment about pride last evening after I retired."

He poured a small amount of cream on the porridge and placed a slice of dry toast on a plate. "Oh?"

"It occurred to me that the German archaeologists I have known are enormously proud of their discovery of the fossilized remains of a human in the Neander Valley."

Crispin sipped his tea and tried to ignore the film of sweat on his forehead. "Oh. The Neanderthal Man. When was that?"

"About 1860, maybe a bit earlier. I was thinking that in your negotiations, you might want to mention that the discovery on your map would be even more important to German history than the quarryman's discovery."

"Capital idea. Remember that, Meade."

"Sure. Any ideas on where we send them?"

She spread a bit of jam on her toast, as slowly as possible. "Hedeby."

Meade turned to carry his breakfast to the table and stopped.

Crispin leaned forward as though he had not heard her properly. "Hedeby? I fear that I am not acquainted with the town."

Meade asked, "What can I get you, Professor?"

"I'll have just the same as you. Looks grand." Meade placed his breakfast in front of Crispin and made another serving for himself.

She said, "It was a trading port, not unlike Birka. It operated from the seventh century until the millennium."

Crispin smiled. "That certainly would please the Germans, taking their national identity back to the 600s." He swiped a bead of sweat from his temple with his knuckle as it began to trickle toward his cheek.

Meade brought his food to the table. "Where is it?" He took a bite of toast.

She pulled the atlas across the table, opened it to the German coast, and put on her glasses. "When I was at the Birka dig, I read a journal written by a Moor named Ibrahim ibn Yabub al-Tartushi. He was a trader from Cordoba who had traveled to Hedeby in the tenth century."

Crispin turned to Doctor Lee. "Before the war, the Huns were bragging that their national identity went back to the ninth century. Some nonsense about the Teutonic tribes defeating the Roman army. They cobbled that into the notion that the Aryan race was ancient and superior to others. We can pander to that distorted logic."

Doctor Lee flipped two pages, found a more detailed map, and pointed to the eastern shore of the Danish peninsula. She tapped her finger on the atlas.

Crispin craned his neck to see the location. "Where?"

"Just below the border. At the narrowest part of the peninsula. Here, near Schleswig."

He stretched over the book and frowned. "Sorry. I don't see it." A drop of sweat fell on the map and he wiped it away before the others noticed it.

"It's not going to be marked on a modern map. Hedeby was burned to the ground in 1066 by the Slavs. It was never rebuilt."

"Good idea for the map, but the name—"

"There are several older names we could use on our map. I've made a list." She pulled a paper from her jacket pocket, unfolded it, and adjusted her glasses before continuing. "'Heithabyr' is the oldest known name. 'Hedeby' is the Old Danish. It means town on the heather. That was used at the same time as 'Birka.' Then there is 'Heidiba' in Latin. 'Haithabu' is the Old Norse and the name used in many of the archaeological papers. If we wanted to be devious, we could refer to the Saxon—"

Crispin raised his hand slightly. "We need to be simple and consistent with the time. We use 'Hedeby.'"

Meade looked at Doctor Lee and then leaned over to see the atlas, which Crispin had pulled in front of him. "It's a ways inland, isn't it? Up river?"

"Yes. The 'Schlei' in German. 'Slien' in Danish. And here." She drew her finger across the narrow part of the peninsula just south of Friedrichsberg. "The Danes built an earthen wall around Hedeby, then extended it across the entire isthmus to defend against invasion by Charlemagne."

Meade asked, "When was that?"

"In the early 800s."

"Would a German archaeologist know about it?"

Nodding, Doctor Lee said, "He should. Hedeby served as the gateway to Christianity as it moved into Scandinavia. In 823, a monk by the name of Ansgar went there, the same monk who ended up in Birka. It might tempt Grimes, as it has never been excavated."

Meade asked, "Why not?"

"Excavations cost money, and there's never seemed to be anything really compelling about the site. Remember, Ribe operated at the same time, just a few miles away, and is still inhabited."

Crispin pointed to the map. "I think she's on to it, Meade. Just look at the location."

He shrugged. "So?"

Crispin looked disappointed. "Meade! The Second War of Schleswig was fought over this boundary. Germany and Denmark both claim this area. If Grimes were to discover something to strengthen their claim, wouldn't that sweeten the prize?"

As Meade started to respond, McLean entered the room with a wooden serving tray with inch-high sides. "Lieutenant Crispin? I believe all of the remaining materials which we could purchase are accounted for and in good order here. Although it was not on your list, I have taken the liberty of adding several dip pens and a fountain pen."

Crispin gestured for McLean to place it on the table. "Thank you." When he had gone, Crispin looked at Meade and Doctor Lee with a half smile. "Well? Are you ready to commit forgery?"

Chapter № 37

Friday
November 3, 1916
West of London, England

Crispin removed the heavy ivory oilcloth from the tray and handed it to Meade. "Would you please cover our end of the table with this? Just put it over the tablecloth. I would not want to damage their antiques with our experimentation." Once Meade covered the table, Crispin removed the other items from the tray and placed them on the oilcloth.

Doctor Lee stood and looked over each of the items. "We're missing something, aren't we? I do not find the molding clay. Didn't you put it on the list last night?"

"I did. But I have directed Mister McLean to secure something else. Be patient. If it fails to materialize, he will provide the clay."

"But how—"

Crispin held up his hand. "Meade? Any ideas on how to make our map of Hedeby?"

Opening the atlas on the oilcloth, Meade said, "I was just thinking about how much of the coastline to include."

"Meade, I propose that we include the area from Kappeln on the north to Kiel on the south. That should offer enough to orient Mister Grimes, if that is indeed his name. 'Grimes.' Sounds like *Grimma*, mask, a masked fraud."

Meade adjusted the size of his paper draft to match the size of the Baldwin portolano. At the top of the draft, he drew the bulbous Danish peninsula jutting into the Baltic near Kappeln and the wide harbor near

Eckernförde. From there, the river crawled inland toward a city that no longer existed. Then he inked the bay labeled 'Kieler Bucht' in the atlas. Sea to the right. Land to the left.

"Want me to write 'Hedeby' somewhere?"

Doctor Lee walked leaned over Meade's shoulder before pointing. "It's here. On the southern shore of this lake. Or is it a bay?"

Before Meade could complete the word, Crispin slapped the table. "No. Not 'Hedeby.' Write the Latin, what was it?"

Doctor Lee handed her list to Meade to copy the spelling. "*Heidiba.*"

Meade looked at the draft paper map and sighed. "If we do, I can't use 'Kieler Bucht' for the bay, can I?"

Doctor Lee sighed. "No. The names need to be from the same era. But as we are providing the town name, even an amateur should be able to locate it without the bay being named."

Crispin leaned over Meade's draft map and drew a pencil line through Kieler Bucht. "We have decided on the where, but not the why. Why would they bury a treasure?"

Meade arched an eyebrow. Staring at Crispin, he stood, picked up the parchment, and folded it into a neat package. Crispin canted his head to the side. "Just where do you think you are going?"

"The cellar. I'll let you two figure that out. I better get going on this in case it needs to dry for a while before we can write on it."

Crispin watched Meade leave and envied his easy confidence that he could do what he had never done. He shrugged and turned to Doctor Lee. "To protect it from an invader."

She slid into the chair beside him. "From whom? The Vikings?"

"No. Charlemagne."

"Lieutenant? What if we modified the Lindisfarne prayer? Can you change 'Northman' to 'Charlemagne?'"

Crispin took a new sheet of paper from the stack. "Easily. He is called *Carolus Magnus* in Latin."

"What do you suggest?"

He spoke as he wrote. "*A furore Carolus Magnus libera nos, Domine.* Protect us from Charlemagne." Crispin hit his cast with the palm of his hand and winced. "Treasure is *thesaurus.* Treasures plural is *thesauri.* Protect our treasures as well! *A furore Carolus Magnus libera nos et notra thesauri, Domine.*"

She frowned. "*Thesaurus?* That's a book, isn't it? "

"Indeed, Peter Roget's *Thesaurus of English Words and Phrases.* First published in 1852, added a new definition to the word in the English language. It means 'treasury or storehouse of words,' yet the Latin remained unphased by all this modernity."

"Shall we sign it 'Ansgar'?"

Crispin stopped and cocked his head to the side. "When was he born? Was it 800 or 801?"

"About then."

"Blast. Either way, Saint Ansgar was but a boy at the time King Hemming signed a treaty with Charlemagne in 811."

She leaned back and crossed her arms. "Well, that is a problem, isn't it? Any other ideas?"

"We could use the back of the map. The Verso. We simply address it to Queen…whatever her name might have been. If he sunk his treasure in the harbor, he would send the Hedeby map to his Queen in exile."

"Of course. Like a passbook at the bank. She'd need to know where her funds were on deposit, as it were."

Crispin looked at her. "Would you happen to know the queen's name?"

She shrugged. "Not a clue." She chuckled to herself. "But we wouldn't want King Hemming."

"Why not? He signed the treaty."

She laughed. "Exactly! He survived. We need his predecessor, the king who died."

"Godfred. He was killed by Charlemagne. *Godofredus,* in Latin. Do you concur?"

"Yes. I like that."

Crispin tapped on his paper with the tip of his pencil. "Perhaps we have the map sent to *Godofredus* by someone in his court rather than being signed by him. No need then to research how his actual signature might appear."

Crispin looked at his notes and read to her. "Here's what I have now. The salutation…*Godofredus Rex*. Then the message. *A furore Carolus Magnus libera nos et notra thesauri, Domine.* Shall I write in a Latin hand?" He muttered, "Insular script or Carolingian miniscule?"

She leaned forward. "Was that a question?"

"I was mulling over the hand to use. Some of the insular scripts would not be understood by all scholars today; whereas, the Carolingian miniscule would. Ironic, that."

"I don't understand, Lieutenant Crispin."

He smirked, "It was Charlemagne who made the miniscule the universal form of writing throughout his kingdom. It is the precursor to our lettering, you know. Before his decree, each region had its own lettering. You could make a life study of the variations in script and grammar by region and time. Now tools to write–" He reached for the large flight feathers that McLean had found.

She asked, "When you prepare the quill, may I assist?"

Crispin picked up the five goose feathers from the table and held them for her selection. She pulled out the largest.

He smiled. "That one would have been my choice as well."

He dug into his trouser pocket and brought out his small silver pipe tool. He opened the thin blade and left the reamer cased.

Doctor Lee held out her hand for the knife, ignoring the flat tamper at the end. "I vaguely remember my father trimming a quill nib that he used in a silver holder. I wonder if I remember how he did it. We had steel nibs by the time I got to school."

Crispin watched her hold the small knife. "It's like sharpening a pencil. Cut away from yourself at about forty-five degrees."

She sliced across the barrel of the first quill. It shattered. Crispin extended his hand. She relinquished the knife and feather. Crispin stripped away the side barb, exposing more of the shaft of the feather. He examined it for cracks and nodded. "No harm."

Meade bounded into the dining room holding two map-sized parchments and proudly placed them on the table. Doctor Lee and Crispin picked one up and sat back from the table to inspect the blanks.

"Spectacular, Mister Meade. How did you–" She dropped the one and picked up the other parchment blank.

Meade sat across from them and clasped his hands behind his neck. "Tea, splashed and sprinkled randomly. But there was enough grime and stain in the woodshop to mix up quite a disgusting brew."

Crispin nodded. "But the edges. A saw could not have produced this delightfully ragged effect?"

"I sawed out the blanks and then wet the edges. Once soft, I filed them with a wood rasp and beat them with a hammer. After all the rush of the past days, it was quite relaxing."

She said, "I can't decide which I like best. They are so…authentic looking."

On both blanks, Meade had sliced a parallel cut at the lower left and slipped a very dark and abraded ribbon of parchment through the slit. The ends extended past the edge of the parchment, awaiting the hot wax and seal.

Meade looked at the cut feather. "Were you making your quill pen now?"

Doctor Lee said, "I was trying to and made a mess of one."

"Not at all, Doctor Lee. We just need a bit more preparation."

"Perhaps you should just make it and let me observe."

He nodded and handed the feather to Meade. "Would you be kind enough to run this quill out to the kitchen and hold the bare end in boiling water for a few seconds? When it is about as limber as a fingernail, hurry back."

Meade tried not to scowl. "Want me to take the others too?"

"Not yet. Let's salvage this one."

After Meade left, he turned to Doctor Lee. "The brittle base of the feather is hollow so a point will naturally emerge when you cut across the shaft at a steep angle with my–" He interrupted himself and grinned. "As they would have called it, my *writseax*."

"The pen knife?"

Crispin smiled and continued. "The blade for writing. Starting at the point, slit the barrel carefully in half. Old English called the quill pen a *writingfeðer*, 'writing feather.' By putting the point of the knife into the center of the barrel and pressing down, it should leave an open cut that will hold the ink nicely."

She nodded. "Ink, what was it called?"

"'*Blæc*.' Black is our–"

Meade rushed back into the room with his hand under the dripping feather and handed it to Crispin, who made a quick cut across the shaft and slit the end. Without turning to her, he said, "And then, Doctor Lee, one simply shapes the nib by taking a slice on either side of the slit. How close you are to the center cut determines how broad the nib will be."

Meade looked at the quill and nodded. "Nice job, Professor."

He said harshly, "I am not through, yet. Just letting it firm up a bit before I finish off the nib." Crispin placed the top of the nib against the oilcloth and took a small slice at a shallow angle from the underside. "That way I'll have a smooth nib where it meets the parchment so the ink lays down nicely."

Meade glanced at the three bottles of ink. "I see that you got your black India ink."

He glanced at Meade before correcting him. "'Indian ink,' we call it. Indeed, McLean gathered up the black as well as the red and brown I requested."

"Why not use just the black?"

"Far too deep and uniform a color. One would expect hints of oxidation. By mixing several pots using various proportions of red, brown, and black, I will develop several shades to use and then use a touch of lemon juice to fool the eye."

Meade asked, "Is that to replicate the rusted edges that you said the gall nut ink would have?"

"Amazing. You did listen. Yes. They also made an ink of a mixture of soot, egg white and honey, but that was also much lighter than modern ink. They won't be able to tell what ink was used on a simple inspection."

Before noon, Crispin had copied the text from his draft to the parchment.

Godofredus Rex.
A furore Carolus Magnus
libera nos et notra thesauri,
Domine.

After the ink dried, he slid the parchment and an inkpot with a lighter hue to Meade, who copied his adjusted eastern coast of Denmark and Germany from the paper draft. The choppy series of dashes looked a bit more rustic than his Baldwin portolano. When it was completed, Meade balanced the quill across his teacup, stood, and walked behind Crispin to watch him mix another blend of ink. Once blended, he handed the quill to Crispin, who dipped it in his darkest ink blend and held it toward Doctor Lee.

She pulled her hand back. "Whatever are you handing that to me for?"

"I thought you should be the one to bury the treasure under the dot you are about to make."

"With pleasure." She took the quill and pressed lightly on the parchment until a pool of ink formed at the southern edge of the bay below the word *Heidiba*.

Without moving the parchment, Crispin looked at it with Meade's hand lens. "Ruddy good work, if I do say so myself. This Hedeby map is a smashing good fraud."

Meade slapped Crispin on the back and laughed. "You'd make a good crook if it weren't for your scruples."

"Thank you for the compliment, I think."

Meade took the quill from Doctor Lee. "Too bad we can't make a duplicate. I'd love to have one in my office!"

Doctor Lee looked at it and said, "Once the seal is in place, it will look like a million dollars. Don't you think, Lieutenant Crispin?"

He laughed. "I doubt that even Meade could strike that steep a bargain."

Meade stretched his neck. "How much should I ask for the phony portolano?"

Looking stern, Crispin said, "First, he will not know it is 'phony,' as you so quaintly put it. Think back to that Jules Verne book. The balloon one. Didn't you say that the Bank of England had been robbed and they thought that was why the man vanished?"

"You mean *Around the World in Eighty Days*?"

Crispin waved his hand. "If you say so. What was considered the princely sum that they stole?"

"I think it was fifty-five thousand pounds."

Crispin was steely. "Double it for the faux Baldwin we want to fob off on him."

Meade choked. "Over a hundred thousand pounds? You can buy a new house in America for a thousand bucks, so—"

Crispin glared. "You are not selling him some bungalow." Crispin lowered his voice. "You are offering the Baldwin for sale. You must call it what he thinks it is."

Doctor Lee held up her hand to get Meade's attention. "What is the exchange rate now? Four to one?"

Meade answered quickly. "Five to one. Dollars to pounds. Why?"

"A few days ago I overheard several nurses chattering about Charlie Chaplin's new contract in Hollywood."

Meade said, "I heard that Mutual Films had signed him, but I never heard the figure."

Doctor Lee said, "I am almost positive they said six hundred seventy thousand dollars for next year's—"

Crispin's eyebrows arched. "For a film actor?"

She nodded. Crispin silently calculated the exchange rate and then grinned. "It is not all that much more than my proposed offering price."

Meade rubbed the stubble on his chin. "You both might be right. Maybe a hundred and ten thousand is a good number to throw at him." After pushing back his cuff, Meade said, "Quarter of. Almost time."

Crispin grabbed his cane and lurched to his feet. "Best we get situated for the call." He cast a stern look at Meade, who was not following him toward the study.

Chapter № 38

Friday
November 3, 1916
West of London, England

Crispin walked toward the study alone, pausing briefly in the hall-way to test the scent, which seemed to be roasting beef. He took the side chair next to the telephone, dropped his cane, leaned his head back, and blew imaginary smoke rings at the ceiling. He glanced at the spines of the books lining the shelves and lost interest when they seemed to be only histories and popular fiction.

Meade walked past Crispin and motioned to the chair behind the desk. "Sure you don't want the big chair? To put your leg up?"

Crispin shook his head and sat straighter on the edge of the side chair. "You know, as an American, you are not as restricted as I am in your travels. Have you considered a neutral country for the exchange?"

Meade moved the chair closer to the desk. "Hadn't thought that far." He slid several sheets of paper across the desk toward Crispin and put some on the blotter in front of him. "In case you have any other good ideas during the call."

Crispin motioned to the desk drawer. "See if there is a pencil there, would you?"

Doctor Lee followed, carrying two teacups on saucers. She placed one in front of Crispin and took the other side chair.

She put her cup on the desk. "Where to meet that is safe—"

"Professor, where would you set up a meeting?"

"A public place. Not in the open, though."

"Like?"

Crispin slid the paper in front of him and centered the pencil on it. "Some location where any furtive move would garner attention. A bank, perhaps."

Meade checked his watch, stretched his shoulders, and drummed the paper with the pencil until the telephone rang. He let it go to a second ring before nodding to Crispin, who lifted the earpiece from the hook of the second telephone at exactly the same moment and turned the telephone so the mouthpiece faced away from them.

"Meade, here."

The reception was free of static and Meade heard the caller say, "Good evening. I have an offer."

"And?"

"Eighty thousand." Crispin wrote the figure on his paper and Doctor Lee looked at it.

Meade smiled at her and began the dance of negotiation. "Pounds sterling? Interesting."

"No. In dollars."

Meade paused. "Dollars? You've got to be kidding! That's just twenty percent of what I thought you offered. That's way too low for the portolano and the annoyance."

"Annoyance?"

"You have tried to take it from me twice. I find that very annoying."

"Would I do such a thing?"

Meade ignored the bait. "It doesn't matter. What matters is that an offer of eighty thousand in dollars is too low. I need to hear a much much better price."

Quickly, Grimes said, "One hundred fifty thousand dollars…in gold."

Meade smiled. Grimes was trying the gambit of agreeing on a payment method before the price was set. "Closer, but not in gold. Too bulky." Meade looked at Crispin, who nodded. Grimes was still negotiating in dollars. Meade had him going.

"What do you want? Bearer bonds?"

Meade leaned back in his chair. "What kind of a chump do you take me for? That's the same as cash. I want a wire transfer to my account in London."

Grimes sounded tired. "Done."

Meade pushed Grimes. "Of one hundred ten thousand—"

"Done."

" —pounds sterling, not dollars."

"That's preposterous!"

Meade paused before saying, "Think for a minute. There is no other map like this in the world. It will guide you to a treasure in a city lost from memory. Who knows the value of the treasures which may lie there?"

Crispin listened carefully and heard Grimes' breathing quicken. He printed "NEANDERTHAL" and held the paper in front of Meade, who grinned as he said, "You could be known as the scientist whose work eclipsed the discovery of the Neanderthal man."

Crispin listened carefully. There was a muffled sound, perhaps a hand covering the mouthpiece.

Finally, Grimes cleared his throat. "Agreed. Pounds sterling. One hundred thousand even."

Meade lowered his voice to suggest a hint of disappointment. "Agreed."

Grimes spoke quickly. "But the funds do not transfer until after my inspection."

"Okay. And I'll release it to you after I have proof of the deposit to my account."

"We'll transfer the documents in Berlin."

Meade noted the deal points of the negotiation on his paper. "It's so hard to travel now. Why not London?"

Grimes was agitated. "Do you want to play or do business?" Meade made a face as though he tasted something bitter. Doctor Lee nodded.

"Do business, but in comfort. Make it Stockholm."

"Stockholm. Opera steps at—"

Meade interrupted him. "Too cold."

"Your idea?"

"The Grand Hotel?"

Grimes said, "No. Too public."

"Svenska Handelsbanken. The main office on Kungsträdgårdsgatan, near the Grand Hotel."

Grimes did not hesitate. "Certainly. When?"

"I'll need a few days to retrieve the portolano and travel. I assume you'll need time to put the funds on deposit in that bank for the transfer. Make it Friday the tenth. At ten."

"The tenth at ten. Certainly." Crispin nodded, indicating Grimes' acceptance to Doctor Lee.

Meade said too forcefully, "Ask for Director Lund. I've used the bank for other transactions." Meade waited for the objection. Hearing none, he said, "I should mention that the map is very fragile."

Grimes said, "Yes, I would expect you to transport it with care."

"Oh, I will. But if you try to take it from me, I will destroy it. Is that clear?"

Crispin thought he heard a small gasp before Grimes said, "Yes. Very clear."

"See you Friday. Alone."

Crispin motioned for Meade to hold the earpiece a moment longer. Once they heard Grimes click off, Crispin placed the earpiece on the hook and Meade did the same.

Meade turned to Doctor Lee. "He bought it hook, line, and sinker."

Crispin tried to sound calm as he tapped the arm of the chair. "Good of him to donate German funds to England's war effort."

Doctor Lee brushed invisible lint from her skirt. "Now all we need to do is finish making it."

Meade looked at them and smiled.

"What's so funny, Meade?"

He laughed. "Well, we got what we wanted. Our map should keep him occupied for a—"

Crispin turned toward the thud at the front door. The brass knocker hit again. McLean walked past the study.

A deep voice boomed from the hallway. "Lieutenant Crispin. Where is he?"

Crispin wedged himself out of the side chair and stood stiffly. McLean quickly escorted a slim, dark-haired man in formal evening attire into the study and stood at attention behind him. Rain dripped from his black evening cloak.

The man reviewed Crispin's military demeanor and new suit. Crispin stood all the straighter. "Take your seat, Lieutenant." The man turned and gave Doctor Lee and Meade short nods. "Doctor Lee and Mister Meade, I presume?"

She nodded, and Meade said, "Yes."

He extended his hand to Meade and said, "Good to meet you in person."

Crispin said, "Director Kell! Thank you for coming, sir. I hope you will forgive my request. We seem to have interrupted your evening."

Meade and Doctor Lee looked at Crispin with surprise.

"Not at all, Lieutenant. Yours is quite an extraordinary assignment."

"Sir! You should know that we have narrowed our search for the burial mound and treasure to an area north of here. I have a proposal —"

Kell continued to stand. "Very well then, be quick about it, Lieutenant."

"We need an airplane."

He chuckled. "Are you barking mad?"

Crispin made a small gesture with his hand to stop him.

Kell stared at Crispin. "Something to add?"

"We need to borrow an aircraft."

"Borrow?" Kell smiled. "Are you a pilot?"

"No. I'll need one of those as well. You see, the best way to locate the buried ship and treasure is by finding anomalies in the natural landscape. Having an airplane for a few hours could save us months of trudging over the countryside." Doctor Lee and Meade stared at Crispin.

Kell shook his head and then grinned. As he walked to the desk, he pulled his fountain pen from his tuxedo jacket, unscrewed the cap, and then scratched a few lines on the stationery on the desk. He signed it and turned the page for Crispin to read. "Do you believe that will suffice?"

Crispin read the directive on the paper, and his eyebrows elevated. "Yes, sir. Thank you, sir."

Crispin smiled.

Kell did not smile in return. "Lieutenant Crispin, you have a full commission to proceed, as you deem appropriate. Mind you, I have neither funds for this operation nor the approval of others. I'll have McLean serve as liaison with the aerodrome for you."

"Thank you, sir."

"And should you manage to peddle this false document to the enemy, I have no way to account for the proceeds. But HMG will expect the British public to benefit in some manner."

"Yes, sir. We'll push on, then. Thank you, sir."

Kell reached into his coat pocket and retrieved a small black velvet bag. He dangled it in front of Crispin, who took it with care. "I believe this is what you requested."

"Thank you."

"Send it back through McLean." Kell turned to Meade and said, "Be clear, Mister Meade, HMG can have no part of your impending dealings with the enemy. Particularly if it goes badly."

Meade nodded. "Understood."

Kell shook Meade's hand again. "I do so wish that my staff were half as clever as you three." Kell turned to Doctor Lee and bowed formally. "May I extend our deepest gratitude for your sacrifice and for your service to our nation, madam."

Meade followed Kell from the study.

Doctor Lee turned to Crispin. "Who is HMG?"

"His Majesty's Government."

The massive front door slammed shut and the bolt was thrown. Meade returned to the study and looked at the bag Crispin was gripping. "What is that?"

Crispin smiled as he said, "Baldwin's seal."

Chapter № 39

Friday
November 3, 1916
West of London, England

C rispin cleared his throat when Meade continued staring at him. "Perhaps you did not hear me. I said it is Baldwin's seal. His *royal* seal. Or by definition, his seal-die or stamp which was pressed into warm wax to affix his wax seal to a ribbon or document."

Crispin placed the black velvet bag on the desk, released the draw-string, and let the velvet crumple. Surrounded by velvet sat a tapered rod of dented ebony which rose three inches atop a brass disk slightly under an inch in diameter. A dark green patina stained the rim. Crispin picked up the handle and examined the face of the stamp. The bright reddish copper showed the reverse image of the wax seal on the Baldwin portolano.

As Crispin handed it to him, Meade grinned. "How the—"

"I took a chance and asked McLean to inquire if it were in the collection of the British Museum."

Meade carefully passed the seal to Doctor Lee and looked at Crispin in disbelief. "Like some lending library?"

"In a manner of speaking. Clearly, they would not just release it to anyone, but Kell appears to be the man of the hour."

Doctor Lee held it by the ebony handle and rotated it so the light bounced off the face of the die. She stared at it, sat back, and held it on her lap. "It's the real…."

Crispin got to his feet, balanced on his cane, started to weave, and held on to the back of the chair. He forced a smile as Doctor Lee and

Meade looked at him. "Indeed. Well, now we can press on, if you will pardon the pun. Meade, would you mind getting a candle from McLean?"

"Sure."

By the time Meade joined Crispin and Doctor Lee in the dining room, Crispin had pulled the Hedeby portolano in front of him and overlapped the ends of the ribbon of leather just past the bottom of the map. He looked at Meade. "The colors and textures of the map and this strip are not at all similar. Brilliant touch, Meade."

"Thanks. I cut it from the stained area just above the lettering. Is the wax going to stick to it okay?"

Crispin cast a glance of irritation at Meade. "It will adhere to almost anything, including the die."

"How are you going to keep it from—"

"Quite simple, really. In school, lads with signet rings would usually just spit on them. One chap with a particularly shiny forehead, I recall, would pass his thumb over his forehead and then rub the oil on his ring."

Doctor Lee said, "As unhygienic as those juvenile practices may have been, it appears that the goal is to have some barrier between the metal and the hot wax. Would a cup of cold tea serve? Or butter?"

Crispin struck a match. The candle's wick flamed. "Tea. Let's give it a go on a test seal on paper first. Lay out several pages, if you please. Don't want the wax to burn the table through the oilskin cloth." He held the stick of dark red wax next to the flame and turned it slowly.

Meade pointed. "Put it over the flame, or we'll be here all night."

"I will do nothing of the sort." Crispin glanced sideways at Meade and lowered his voice. "That would leave streaks of soot. A keeper of the seal never would have made such a shoddy seal for a king." He rotated the wax rod slowly. "Look again at yours. Are there any traces of black in the wax?"

Doctor Lee watched Meade's jaw tighten. She put on her glasses and looked at the seal on the Baldwin portolano. "He's right."

When the wax started to droop slightly at the tip, Crispin removed the stick and held it above the stack of papers. A few drops of hot wax dripped on the paper. Before they cooled, he pressed the end of the wax stick into the pool of wax and twisted off the melted end, forming a larger puddle.

Meade held the copper seal for Crispin. "Now. Professor. Stamp it– now."

Crispin blinked rapidly as he dipped it into his cold tea, shook the die once, and steadied his hand over the wax. "Not so fast, Meade. I need to let the hot wax form up, or it will not hold the impression."

Crispin waited until the wax lost its liquid sheen, pressed the copper die into it, and seemed to count to three before rolling the seal off the wax.

Doctor Lee looked at the wax seal. "Perfect."

"Indeed. Too perfect, if you ask me. After it cools, we can discover how best to crack some off and get a look of age on it."

Meade tapped the side of the cooling wax carefully before picking up the paper. He felt the underside. "Still warm."

Touching the wax quickly, Crispin said, "But the wax has set. This is more brittle than the usual wax one would find in stores now. Try to snap it in half." Meade did so easily and handed the half that came away from the paper to Doctor Lee.

"Interesting texture. Glassy. We need to get some suggestion of dirt or age on it."

Crispin pointed across the hallway and said, "Ash from the fireplace. Wouldn't that be fine enough to lay on it?"

She asked, "But will it stick?"

Meade went to the sitting room and returned with a small pile of white ash on a paper.

Crispin sprinkled it on the cold wax and pressed on it. "There. Looks old enough."

Meade blew on it. The ash swirled over the table and left the seal shining brightly.

Doctor Lee asked, "What if we put the ash on immediately after you remove the stamp?"

When they pressed the ash into the warm wax, it imbedded itself and looked furry. Next they pressed the stamp into the ash rather than the tea. It created a smudged seal, and half of the wax stuck on the die. After five minutes of carefully removing wax with a toothpick, sweat had beaded on Crispin's forehead. He brushed his brow quickly as Meade applied a small amount of grease to a handkerchief and dabbed it on the cooled wax seal. After wiping most of it off, Doctor Lee blew ash across the surface. It fused with the grease in the fine lines of the lettering. It had a look of age that did not rub off immediately.

"Ready?" Crispin smiled and handed the seal to Meade, who held it while Crispin prepared the wax and dripped it on the intersection where the two leather strips crossed.

Handing the seal-die to Crispin, Meade said, "Here. Have the honor."

Crispin lowered the stamp into the wax and steadied his arm against the edge of the table as he lifted the die. When the wax had cooled, Crispin broke the left rim away in small chips and added the ash in the lightly greased crevices. He turned the Hedeby map for Meade to inspect the seal.

Meade whistled. "Hard to tell which is which." He chuckled and patted his chest. "I'd better keep the Baldwin in its pouch so we don't sell the wrong one."

Crispin's eyes narrowed as he looked at Meade. "Did the pouch accompany it from auction?"

"Yes. It's not as old as–"

"Clearly not. But if the Germans know of the pouch, shouldn't we transfer our Hedeby map to it? Judging a book by the cover, and all that."

Meade nodded quickly. "Where should I–"

Crispin raised his voice. "Keep the Baldwin?" He then whispered, "I might suggest my bank box in Oxford. I rang them up and am able to put you two on the authority card, if I should–"

Doctor Lee said, "But Grimes knows about you." She turned toward the door as she heard someone approaching. "Shouldn't I get a box for it?"

McLean knocked on the jamb of the open door of the dining room and pushed in a small cart holding a faceted decanter of claret and matching cut-crystal glasses on a silver tray. "Dinner will be served in about half an hour." McLean poured three glasses and left them on the tray.

Taking a glass offered by Meade, Crispin offered a toast as he glanced at the map beside the tray. "Congratulations. Splendid bit of work."

Doctor Lee took the glass but did not raise it. "We still haven't found the site, Lieutenant."

Frowning at her, Crispin said, "Well, we solved the riddle of the Baldwin portolano and found its location in the atlas. It is no longer a needle in a haystack."

Meade choked on his wine and then laughed. "All that means is that we know where there might be a haystack."

Crispin sipped the claret, held the rim at eye level, and examined the glass. "But she knows that the haystack should resemble the burial mounds at Uppsala, so she can point them out to us as we fly."

Doctor Lee was about to take a sip but stopped. "*Fly?* You expect me to *fly in an airplane?*"

Crispin said, "Certainly. I think we all should. Meade and I are old hands at this, you will–"

She snapped. "Will what? We know so little about the effects of flight–"

"Didn't seem to hurt us at all, did it, Meade?" After placing the forged map on the tray, Meade laughed.

She took a drink of wine, sighed, and held the glass. "You know, Lieutenant, if we must fly, I believe that the best time to find the mound would be quite early or late on a clear day. The sun would cast a longer shadow."

Crispin smiled and looked at Meade. "You game for another flight?"

Meade shook his head. "Afraid not. I'll leave it to you. I've got lots to tie up before I meet with Grimes."

Crispin said, louder than he intended, "Such as?"

"I have work papers to sign. Got to go to the Embassy and vote. Presidential election, you know." He chuckled. "Can't let them decide between Wilson and Hughes without me."

Doctor Lee traced the rim of the glass with her finger. "How long will we continue governing with only half our brains? How can we think that a president elected by only part the citizenry can represent the entire nation?"

Crispin looked confused for a moment and then said, "Oh, I see. You're on to women's suffrage. I follow you now." Crispin paused then boasted, "In that regard, Britain may be a bit ahead of you Americans. We do allow our women to vote in many of the smaller elections."

Doctor Lee shook her head. "Allow? How can you *allow* someone their God-given right?"

Crispin blinked rapidly. "I am certain that I could have found a better word." He cleared his throat twice and turned his full attention to McLean as he came to the door. "Yes. What is it, Mister McLean?"

"Weather might be breaking. They are on the telephone now, wanting to know if they should stand by to fly you tomorrow."

Doctor Lee looked at Crispin and asked, "Tomorrow? So soon?"

He nodded to McLean. "Tell them we shall be ready."

After McLean left, Crispin raised his glass to Doctor Lee. "Well, you will find flying quite the bracing adventure." He gestured at her suit. "Is that the warmest you have?"

"Yes."

"I must say, that is a smart looking traveling-suit. However...."

Doctor Lee stared at him. "However?"

"It may be unsuitable for flying. Do you realize that we shall be flying at well over seventy miles per hour? It will be like standing in a gale."

She shrugged. "I'll have my overcoat."

"If I may be so bold as to inquire, what do you wear on your expeditions? Do you have any other attire? A riding habit?"

"I do have riding attire and boots in my trunk upstairs. Is that what you think I should wear?"

He finished his claret, nodded, and reached for the decanter. "And bring your passport."

Doctor Lee put her empty glass on the tray. "I have a question about flight–"

Pouring, Crispin said, "I must assure you, it is quite safe and–"

"Oh, no. It is not that at all. I am concerned about your knee. A sudden reduction in barometric pressure may–"

Crispin held up his hand to stop her. "I must accompany you on this flight. Be clear on that. There is no alternative."

She scowled at Crispin. "Yes, I understand that. I am trying to determine whether leaving the cast on your leg and risking a blood clot or swelling would warrant the removal of the cast before we fly. But without the support offered by the cast, your leg–"

Crispin's neck reddened. He tugged at his collar and put down his glass. "I see your quandary. At height, it is very cold. Wouldn't that reduce the opportunity for swelling?"

Before she could answer, he glanced toward the door, canted his head to listen, and lowered his voice. "Is he gone?" Meade looked out the door and nodded. Crispin continued in a whisper. "I believe that the Baldwin portolano should remain hidden until the treasure is above ground and in safe hands." Doctor Lee started to say something, but he held up his hand. "There is too much afoot just now to rely on a verbal assurance, even from Kell or Cumming, that all is well and pass the Baldwin off to the museum."

Doctor Lee nodded quickly. "I agree. Any idea how much of our conversation McLean overheard before he brought in the claret?"

"Unlikely that he overheard me say I had a bank box. But he must have heard you saying you could get one. I'm sure of it."

She leaned closer to Crispin and asked, "Yours is—"

"At Oxford. Family papers. Had to keep them safe. Had no one with whom I could leave them."

Pulling a blank page off the buffet, Crispin dug through the tray of forgery materials until he located the fountain pen. He wrote a few lines on a fresh page and handed her the pen. "What's this, Lieutenant?"

"This note will provide authority to allow you or Meade to access the box if anything should happen to me. You need to sign and date it as I have indicated."

Meade scowled. "Nothing is going to happen—"

"I expect that I shall be issued orders back to the front when my leg is better. We three need to be its guardians."

Meade watched her signing. "Will the bank honor it?"

"Yes, even without a key. They have agreed to attach this to my authorization card when I deposit the map."

"But why there?"

Crispin grimaced. "Oxford is less of a target than London. Now please sign it."

Doctor Lee dated the line Crispin had drawn on the paper. Meade signed and dated it. He handed it back to Crispin with a somberness Crispin had never seen.

"What bank is it?"

"Barclay's Oxford branch."

"Want me to drive it over tomorrow when I leave?"

Crispin shook his head. "No. I'll have McLean drive me after you go."

Meade pulled the pouch from under his sweater and held it for Crispin. "Well, then. Professor. Guess I need to give you the portolano."

"You're not just passing along some old book, Meade. Where's the ceremony?"

Doctor Lee stood and reached out her hand. Meade relinquished the pouch to her. As she stood somberly in front of Crispin, she held the pouch at arm's length in front of her and said, "By the powers vested in me–"

Crispin struggled to his feet and bowed to accept the cord over his head. He swayed and grabbed for the back of the chair. He missed it and crumpled to the floor, landing on his left side. Meade leaned over the motionless Crispin and reached for his shoulders.

Doctor Lee shouted, "Leave him as he is!" She knelt and put her fingertips to his neck. "Fainted. He's burning up." She slid the knot on his tie down and unbuttoned his collar. "Go get McLean. We need to get him to the infirmary and get his cast off."

"His cast?"

"Now!"

Meade sprinted toward the kitchen, slipping the cord over his neck as he ran.

Following her instructions to support the cast, McLean, Meade, and the cook carried Crispin through the kitchen into the wing that had been converted to an infirmary. They placed him on an elevated hospital bed in the center of what once was the staff's sitting room.

Doctor Lee followed the men into a large examination and treatment room and said, "Get his trousers off and a sheet over him." While Meade untied and removed Crispin's shoes, McLean lifted Crispin's waist, and the cook tugged on the cuffs of his trousers.

As Meade threw the trousers over a side chair, she searched the tall white cabinets. "McLean? Any idea where they might keep a hammer and heavy shears?"

He pointed to the closest row of a bank of drawers under the sink. "Second or third drawer."

She opened and slammed two drawers before she found a small chromed hammer and scissors with blunted tips. McLean unfurled a sheet over Crispin, leaving only his face uncovered. After folding the sheet back to expose the cast, which ran from mid-thigh to ankle, she tapped a straight line in the plaster where the outer seam of trousers would have been. The rapidity of the strikes made one blend into the next in a chatter. Chalky dust covered the skirt of her suit as she reached for the shears and cut the now-flexible gauze. She looked up at the two men staring at her. "McLean, see if you can find some smocks and gloves for us. I'll need your help in opening the cast, and there may be an infection."

Crispin moaned. She went to the head of the bed and put her hand on his forehead. "It's fine, Lieutenant. You just fainted. I'm removing the cast to make sure you haven't started any infection. Relax; it won't be long." McLean removed three white smocks from the large wardrobe and found gloves in a drawer under the counter. McLean and Meade put the white smocks over their attire. McLean held the smock for her to slip into as soon as she completed knocking the second line along the inseam area of the cast. She took the scissors and snipped the gauze free at the top and bottom of the inner leg. "You two, go to the far side of the bed. I'm going to open the top of the cast like a clam's shell. Your job is to pivot it up and toward you and not let it drop on his leg. Hold it. I'll snip it free and then you take it off."

Once the top of the cast was gone, she probed the leg, leaned over the knee, and sniffed. "No infection here. Meade, take the ankle and lift his leg when I do. McLean! From his ankle, pull the rest of the cast from under his leg." She examined the back of his leg as Crispin groaned and turned his head to the side. She shook her head. "Splints?"

McLean opened a door that led to a storeroom. "In here." She easily found finished wood splints and lengths of sheeting with which to affix them. She started to say something to Crispin but noticed that he was snoring quietly.

Meade looked at her. "Never seen wine hit someone like–"

As she tied off the last of the binding, she looked at Meade and said softly, "It's more than that. Slurred speech, flushed face, sweating, and rambling are also signs of a dangerously high fever."

After his knee was again protected, she found a thermometer and put it under his tongue, leaving her gloved knuckle between his upper and lower teeth. She read the thermometer, put it down, and pulled the sheet off Crispin's shoulders. She tugged him into a sitting position. "Help me with these, now!"

The men wrestled Crispin's jacket and sweater free before he fell back against the sheet. She unbuttoned his shirt and tugged up his undershirt. "Damn."

Meade looked at Crispin's pale skin and saw red dots covering his belly and lower chest. "What's he got? Measles?"

"Unless I miss my guess, it's trench fever." She looked at Meade, who was staring at Crispin's sweat-covered face. "First thing is to cool him down fast with an alcohol bath. Then we'll deal with getting him well again." She turned to McLean. "I'll need a basin and alcohol."

As McLean hurried to the cabinet, he asked, "Is it contagious?"

She took the bottle from him and poured a hefty splash into the enamel basin and grabbed a gauze pad the size of a hand towel from the counter. "No. This must have started while he was still over there. It's about a two-week span from contact with infected lice to symptoms."

Meade looked at her. "I think we should cancel the flight, don't you?"

She nodded. McLean removed his gloves and smock. "I'll ring them immediately."

Doctor Lee and Meade stripped off Crispin's shirt and undershirt. She dipped a gauze pad into the basin of alcohol and swabbed his arms and chest. He shivered as it evaporated and started to lift his head. She put her hand on his shoulder. "Lieutenant?"

"Wha—"

"Listen to me. I want you to open your eyes and look at my finger!"

Crispin squinted into the searing light as he followed her moving finger.

She barely touched his shins through the sheet. He flinched and moaned. She glanced at Meade. "Has he complained of a headache to you?"

"He never complains about important stuff."

"Leg pain, fever, headache, that rash. All indicators of trench fever."

She swabbed his chest again. The stark, pungent scent stung Meade's eyes. He stood back from the bed. "How long?"

"Until his fever breaks? An hour. Maybe all night. I'll need to chart his readings. Can you bring in some paper? And a pencil."

As Meade returned with several sheets of paper and pencils, she dumped the alcohol into the sink. Meade asked, "Why'd you pour out the alcohol? I thought we needed to–"

She ran tepid water into the basin. "I'll keep swabbing him with water until the fever breaks. Pyrexia, a persistent fever, can cause heart failure."

She picked up a small hand towel from the stack on the counter and dipped it in the water. "He started shivering during the alcohol bath. That reaction can elevate his temperature. I'll just keep mopping his arms and chest with tepid water. Slower but safer."

Meade took the basin from her and squeezed out the towel. "Like this?"

Chapter № 40

Saturday
November 4, 1916
West of London, England

Shortly after three in the morning, Meade brought two mugs of tea into the infirmary. Doctor Lee looked at Meade with curiosity as he left his on the counter, handed her one, and took the basin from her. "Can I ask you something, Mister Meade?"

"Sure."

"How can you leave when we are this close? What can be so important?"

He squeezed most of the water from the towel. "I run a business." He swabbed Crispin's arm.

"Meade Oil. I know. But your employees have been able to operate it for you for some time."

"It's not that. I need to disappear after the sale. It's part of the deal." He dipped the towel into the basin and wiped Crispin's chest. "British Military Intelligence thinks it makes me look like an even bigger crook."

"I see. Does Lieutenant Crispin know that?"

"I don't think so. What about you? Gonna stay in England?"

"As long as I can. I applied for a paying position at the hospital at Ipswich."

Meade left the towel in the basin and took a quick sip of tea. "Why there?" He resumed swabbing Crispin's legs.

"They are opening a clinic for the shell-shocked. I applied for teaching and clinical positions. I can't just volunteer forever. I hope they will have me."

"They'd be lucky to get you. Your talks, when I was out of the room, certainly seemed to help the Professor."

She scowled at Meade. "Did you listen at the–"

Meade looked stricken. "Of course not! He changed for the better in the short time I've known him, and I credit that to you. It had to be you."

"Lieutenant Crispin's case is mild," she said softly. "He is recovering from his nightmares on his own by turning to his religion. He is challenging the dominion of his dreams by confronting the demons and looking toward a more normal time. I think that is the key– returning to those things which make us who we are. Whatever reconnects us with our community and our character."

Mead put the basin on the counter and picked up his mug. "The shooting's got to stop soon."

Crispin moaned. She stood and looked at his face. "The war won't really be over for years after that."

"What do you mean?"

She sat again and slumped. "War is an aberration, Mister Meade. Women and children go hungry to feed soldiers so they can kill each other. The weak and injured are prime targets for disease. And the lads in the thick of it. It will haunt them to their last days. This war's even given us a new name for an old disease: shell shock."

"Old?"

She pushed a wisp of hair away from her forehead. "I thought I told you of Doctor Da Costa's findings after the Civil War. Perhaps I didn't. But you can see symptoms of the injury we now call 'shell shock' in the behavior of Odysseus. And I don't recall any mention of artillery fire in *The Odyssey*."

Meade chuckled and nodded toward Crispin. "He'd be the first to give you the history of artillery." Meade picked up the basin and turned to her. "You'll be close enough to visit the Professor, won't you?"

"If he stays in London or goes to his beloved Oxford."

Meade stared at her. "Have you discussed *The Odyssey* with him? That might be a way to break through his hard shell."

She peeked over the rim of her mug. "I don't know if he is ready."

"Try. Trust him to see what he needs to see."

"You care for him, don't you, Mister Meade? Like a brother."

"A very irritating little brother. He can be so smart at some things and thick as a short plank other times."

She took his temperature again. "Reminds me of you in some ways. You think you are opposites, but you are just two faces of the same coin."

"Really?"

With a shy smile, she said, "Same metal and mettle, if you will forgive me a pun Crispin might have made. Tell me something?"

"What?"

She paused to read the thermometer and smiled. "It's dropping." Shaking the thermometer, she said, "Why is the map and this discovery so important to you? That hooey about you being a wildcatter was true once, but no longer. You're rich as Croesus."

"Dress it up all you want, but being an oilman is still digging in the dirt. That's the difference between old wealth and new money."

She returned the thermometer to its place on the counter and charted the reading. "That woman you have mentioned, was her name 'Mina'?"

"'Medora.' She's in Cannes now. Thought I'd pay her a call, after I sell our map."

She walked past Meade and patted his arm. "About time."

Crispin tossed in bed. She adjusted his pillow to keep his head elevated.

Meade looked at sweat glistening on Crispin's forehead and picked up the bowl. "He's weak as a pup. Think he'll be able to fly?"

"It may be a few days before we can evaluate that question."

Just before four, Crispin whimpered, tossed, and squirmed. Meade looked at him and then at Doctor Lee, who was asleep in the chair. Her chin bobbed against her chest. He took a towel and dabbed the sweat from Crispin's brow before getting the bowl and swabbing him again. Crispin squinted at Meade and smacked his dry lips. Meade got a tumbler of water and held the glass straw for him.

After two sips Crispin motioned Meade to lean closer. "Paper and a pen. Get me some paper."

Mead patted his shoulder. "Go back to sleep. Plenty of time later for that."

"No. I've thought it all out." He tried to look around the room but fell back on the pillow, exhausted. He whispered, "Are we alone?"

Meade said, "Doctor Lee is over there. Asleep. Want me to wake–"

Crispin winced. "Take the Baldwin to Stockholm."

Meade shook his head. "No, you've got it wrong. I'm taking the fake–"

Crispin grabbed Meade's sweater and pulled him closer. "Take both. Get a bank box there." He was panting. "Put the Baldwin in it. Sell the Hedeby map like we planned."

Meade whispered, "Why?"

Crispin continued. "Until they excavate the site, the Germans still could find the map and claim the treasure as theirs. I say we have McLean deposit the blank parchment to my box in Oxford."

"He'd know–"

Crispin sputtered as he stifled a laugh. "You need to wrap it. He wouldn't dare open it."

Meade turned and called softly, "Doctor Lee."

She jolted her head up and hurried to the bed. "What is–"

Meade put his finger to his lips to quiet her. "He's better, just a little loopy. He's got an idea you need to hear."

Meade recounted Crispin's plan, and she nodded slowly. "It does have merit, but McLean seems to be everywhere!"

Crispin pointed to her. "Then we'll task you to occupy McLean and the cook while Meade wraps the blank parchment."

She nodded. "Certainly. I am sure I can think of some chore for them. Mister Meade, will the bank up there honor the three signatures, as his has promised to do?"

"I'll phone and check."

Crispin grabbed his arm and said, "No. They found Grimes through the operators. Call after you leave here."

"Sure." Meade pulled a sheet from the stack of paper on the counter and quickly replicated the format of the authorization letter that they each had signed the prior day. He held it for Crispin to sign, which he did. "The date, Meade?"

"It's November four. Saturday morning."

After signing, Crispin passed the paper to Meade. "When are you leaving?"

"As soon as I can. I need all the pieces in place if this is going to work."

Crispin nodded and fell asleep against his damp pillow.

Chapter № 41

Wednesday
November 8, 1916
West of London, England

The late morning sunlight in the vicarage gardens seemed exceptionally bright to Crispin after his confinement in the infirmary. As he sat on a cold stone bench smoking his pipe, he pulled his brown overcoat over the splint that had been affixed outside his suit trousers. He tapped out the ember, ground it under his heel, and slipped his pipe into his coat pocket as Doctor Lee approached. Her jacket and ankle-length skirt were of tweed in shades of chocolate. The jacket was fitted close at the waist and flared over her hips. The apron skirt was buttoned up the front. Only the toes of her boots were visible as she walked over the gravel. But for the heavy wool sweater under her jacket and coat over her arm, she seemed perfectly suited for a fox hunt.

He started to stand as she approached, but she motioned for him to remain seated. She dropped her coat on the bench and sat beside him. "Meade did find you before he left last night, didn't he?"

Crispin nodded and whispered, "Yes. We made the exchange before we said our goodbyes."

"Good. I shall miss him."

"Clever fellow. By cutting the Hedeby map a bit smaller, both just fit in his pouch. Our plan is in motion."

She leaned close to Crispin. "McLean?"

"He's off to Barclays to deposit the blank parchment in my box. Meade wrapped it quite well, even used wax to seal the string while you were distracting McLean and the cook last evening. But enough on that. We don't want the cook to see us whispering like schoolgirls out here."

She turned her back to the house, as though looking over the grounds. "Could they know there is another blank from the remnants of the will?"

Appearing to smooth his moustache, Crispin let his hand cover his mouth as he said, "Oh, didn't Meade tell you? He burned the scraps in the furnace."

She patted his arm and smiled. "Well done. You boys have thought of it all."

He pointed to his hair, which was blown by the light breeze and laughed. "Not everything. I neglected to give him my hat size back there. As he left this morning, he noticed and offered to have his man at Harrods send over a Borsalino fedora. Can you imagine? I declined, of course, as we will be in other headgear up there."

She stood, nodded, faced him, and spoke louder. "Lieutenant, I have to tell you how excited I am."

After a deep breath, Crispin said, "And well you should be. How many people have flown above the rooftops of England? Today, you will see her lakes shimmering like sapphires. See birds flying under us. It is a marvelous thing."

"You make it sound so inviting."

Crispin's hand soared in front of her. "You will be flying just like Wendy in *Peter Pan*."

Doctor Lee looked him over with a critical eye and smiled. "That attire suits you."

"Meade chose well. He is a generous chap, isn't he?" Crispin touched the fabric again and shook his head ever so slightly. "Won't be buying togs like these on a teaching salary. Best they last." He flexed his ankle.

"Leg bothering you?"

He shook his head. "In actual fact, the splint is much more comfortable than that plaster." Crispin looked past the garden and was pleased that the clouds were clearing. He stood and shifted slightly on the pathway adjusting to the feel of his new shoes and the splint. "May I ask the time?"

Doctor Lee opened her watchcase. "Five of. The driver should be here soon."

"If you don't mind my asking, are you certain that you will be warm enough in just that long skirt and jacket?"

She chuckled as she stood. "In actual fact, I'm roasting right now. This is my winter expedition attire."

"Expedition?"

"Yes. About ten years ago, when Stewart retired, we began travelling to archeological digs. First in America and then we went to Cairo for the museum there and found out about a dig in Mesopotamia. Met the most interesting people. Our good friend, Gert, designed this getup. We met her on our first dig. She rode her stallion astride, as you would, while I rode sidesaddle as I had been taught. She talked Stewart into having his tailor run up an outfit like hers for me when we got back to Cairo. In linen, of course, as it was summer. She had determined that it was ever so much safer to ride astride when she trekked out on horseback and convinced Stewart of that. She was quite forceful when she took a notion to something."

Crispin gazed blankly at her rambling about fashion, but tried to concentrate on what she was saying. "You know, Lieutenant, I thought it quite daring at the time until I saw their perfect logic. Trousers or riding breeches were out of the question, and a skirt simply wouldn't do." She grasped the waistband of the skirt. "Here's the genius of it, I can unbutton the skirt, ride how I wish, and the skirt falls into place when I dismount."

Crispin smiled uncomfortably and blushed.

Doctor Lee laughed. "Oh! Didn't I mention that my skirt is *over* a matching pair of jodhpurs, rather like your uniform breeches, but roomier." He nodded and cleared his throat nervously. He watched a small winter wren take a dust bath in the dry soil under the stark canes in the rose garden. Several other birds arrived to scratch and flutter in the dirt. They scattered at the sound of an approaching car and then reunited in the field past the garden.

Gravel snapped under the tires of the unmarked black sedan from the Hendon Aerodrome. A corporal exited the car.

Crispin walked toward him. "I'm Lieutenant Crispin. I believe you are driving us."

The corporal saluted Crispin. "Yes, sir."

"At ease, corporal. I don't believe the usual courtesies are appropriate, as I am not in uniform."

"Yes, sir. My apologies, sir."

The corporal quickly opened the rear door of the sedan. Crispin held Doctor Lee's elbow as she slid into the seat. She held his cane as he hopped on one leg and then backed into the car.

The driver asked, "The airfield directly, sir?"

"Yes, straightaway."

Less than five minutes after passing through the gate from the vicarage, Crispin's head fell back against the high seat and he slept soundly until the road changed from smooth tarmacadam to rutted gravel and then cobblestone. When he woke, the landscape had changed from the scattered oaks and gently rolling countryside around the estate to a small village. As they drove past the row of homes on the main street, Crispin noticed that more than half of the homes had a small black crepe bow tied to the door knocker. Saddened, he turned his face away from the row houses and tried unsuccessfully to sleep. After the village, there were a series of small towns. Factories with tall brick smokestacks lined the roads north of London. Crispin used the plumes of black smoke as a wind gauge noting that there was only a slight breeze.

Crispin watched the people walking on the narrow sidewalks or to the side of the road as they passed through the small towns and villages on the way to the aerodrome. It was not the same as when he visited during his college days. There were few men of his age and those few were in uniform. Old men swept the sidewalks in front of shops. He was hoping to see children with their parents. Instead, heavy blackout curtains covered the windows. He shut his eyes again and leaned his head into the rear of the seat. Soon his head rolled easily with the rocking of the car and he was deep in sleep.

The driver slowed as they turned from the road to a long graveled lane leading to the guarded gate of the aerodrome. Doctor Lee nudged his arm. "Sorry to wake you but–"

Crispin sniffed and sat up quickly. As the car slowed approaching the guardhouse, he held out his hand. "I'll have your passport, if you please."

At the gate, Crispin handed his identity card and Doctor Lee's passport to the guard, who matched photos to the occupants of the vehicle, returned the documents, and waved them through the gate. The driver stopped next to the white timbered building Crispin remembered as the headquarters.

"Please remain in the vehicle or next to it until I locate your pilot."

"Certainly," Crispin said.

He opened the door and got out. He surveyed the aerodrome and was relieved at how much larger the landing field looked in the daylight than under the light of a landing flare. By the first hangar, there were rows of Avros. He searched but could not find his yellow craft. In front of the far hangar, two massive planes were being swarmed over by blue-clad mechanics. Bombers, no doubt. Incredible to believe they could become airborne.

Doctor Lee left her coat in the car and stood beside him. "Wouldn't you like to have one of your pipes before flying?"

"I won't receive your gimlet eye?"

"Not this time."

Crispin pulled his briar pipe out of his pocket and filled it quickly. He lit it and looked at the sky again. The smoke drifted gently and the breeze ruffled his fine hair. The sky was clear above them, although a few high clouds were forming to the far north.

"You know, Doctor, we might even make some history of our own when we discover it."

"How is that?"

"You may well be the first aviator to conduct aerial archaeology." He stopped himself and took a quick puff of his pipe and frowned. "Rather, I assume the proper word would be 'aviatrix,' wouldn't it?" Crispin looked at her as she cocked her head and smiled. He blew the smoke away from her. "May I ask you something rather personal?"

"Certainly. I might not answer you, though."

"Why stay here? You're an American."

"I know where my home is. But I can be of use here."

He said, "Meade seems less convinced of his place in the world."

She nodded. "In some ways he is still looking for his home."

Crispin chuckled. "Well, good luck to him if he thinks it is in France."

"Why are you so bitter about France? Is it because of the war?"

"I loved it, once. But its beauty has been lost to me after the sights of the past year. I can see every place I passed through or was billeted with the clarity of this bright day." He took a puff and laughed slightly. "The troops had a beastly time with the language, even worse than Meade. They were always finding some odd way to remember a place. Étaples was called 'Eat Apples.' Auchonvillers was called by troops 'Ocean Villas.' Ferme de Mouquer was called most rightly 'Mucky Farms.'" Doctor Lee laughed, and he continued. "There were wonderful moments, though. Amiens in July. There were blue cornflowers and red poppies in the fields at the edge of town. Some places, I recall with great affection." He paused. "But when we were ordered back to La Boisselle, we found it only by compass."

Crispin paused and looked at Doctor Lee. Her face was calm. He continued. "The town had been obliterated. There were children huddled there that reminded me of this one town, Beauval, that's it. Their eyes looked so old. Nothing but skin and bone. We left what we could of our rations with their mothers."

Crispin felt, as much as remembered, how the sweltering sweat-soaked days of July became the cold mud in autumn, smelled the fungal stench that clung to their wool uniforms, saw the splintered towns, and began to see the men die, one by one. Soon their names became a litany. He sucked in a breath.

She put her hand on his arm until he exhaled. "Lieutenant, I can understand why that would be particularly difficult."

Crispin tamped his pipe ash to pull away. "And why should you as-sume that?"

"Consider the childhood you had. Losing your parents so early. You had little of your own childhood. Look, you need the imagination and time of childhood to be a complete adult. If fate stole that from you, take it back. Be whimsical, allow your imagination to play on its own."

Crispin clenched his jaw and looked out to the airfield. "Why did you come here for some dig? Aren't there any in the Americas? Away from this war?"

"My son is in France."

He raised his eyebrow. "Now?" He took a last draw on his pipe and watched her face firm.

"Yes. He volunteered at the start of it all. There was little I could say to dissuade him."

"Flying? Many Americans are flying–"

"Ambulance Corps. He died in France."

After a moment, Crispin cleared his throat. "You never mentioned–"

"Not much point. We don't even have a word to describe a mother who has lost her son. A husband, yes. Parents, yes. But your child."

Crispin stared somewhere past the horizon. "But your home is–"

"We are somewhat adrift, you and I. After you have lost your son and husband, there is very little that tethers you to a place. He was our only child. I have no close relations." She looked at the men working on the planes before she continued. "But I can be of use here." She fingered the strand of jet beads. "At least that was what Doctor Rivers told me when he gave me these. They are from Whitby."

He leaned down and tapped out the dead ash on the edge of the tire. "Is that how you bear up? Work? Duty?"

"Life goes on, Lieutenant. In some odd way, nature wants us to survive. I think my family would expect no less of me. I still feel them with me." After a time, she looked at him. "I think sometimes that love is what drives us. Perhaps it is stronger than death, or hate or war. But it is less certain."

He frowned. "Doing one's duty—"

"I think you might confuse what you do with who you are."

Stowing the cold pipe in his pocket, he said, "Excuse me, but many men do define themselves by their occupation."

She put up her hand to stop him. "Soon, you will probably be teaching at Oxford, because that is what you want to do. And you are a very determined young man—"

"Yes, but—"

"Let me finish. But that is not who you are."

His eyebrow arched. "Sorry?"

"I think you are a good and kind young man who will meet some charming young lady. I believe that you can grow into a good husband and father, if you can capture your nightmares and dispel them. From what you've told me of losing your parents, you will make an added effort to be a good parent. You value it. But I think that will be the case if you teach or take up carpentry or astronomy."

"Gæð a wyrd swa hio scel."

She looked at him. "Which means?"

"'Fate will go where it must.'"

Chapter № 42
Wednesday
November 8, 1916
West of London, England

Crispin expected their driver to return when the door of the head-quarters building opened. Instead, a tall man in a leather flying suit trotted down the steps and crossed the grass toward the automobile.

The pilot's wavy chestnut hair had been cut recently at the sides and was far too long on top to have been trimmed by a camp barber. Crispin chuckled and wondered if it were a fashion homage to Rupert Brooke, the Golden Apollo fallen before Gallipoli. Crispin wanted to ask if he penned callow war sonnets imitating Brooke.

Crispin knew the type. Still tanned from the summer. The easy smile. He could just see him moving with grace on the cricket field, in his whites. The hair and pronounced ears were all too familiar from the portraits in the dining halls at Oxford.

Crispin motioned for Doctor Lee to remain at the car. "Best I meet with him alone." He gripped his cane handle firmly and walked toward the pilot, who had outstretched his hand. The signet ring on his little finger was old. Crispin knew it was a family crest without looking. Good grip. Not the fop one might have imagined from the signet ring or the silk ascot at his neck. Clever enough not to salute one out of uniform. Insignia on his collar was barely visible. A Major.

"Lieutenant Crispin?"

Crispin took his hand and shook it quickly. "Yes, Major."

"Charles Wickham. I'll be flying you today."

"Thank you, sir. Our credentials." Crispin presented his military identity card and Doctor Lee's passport. Crispin took their ages as similar, but when Wickham looked up to return the documents, Crispin searched the man's eyes and knew that he had not been to France. His war had been in England, as a desk-wallah. Pushing a pencil before flight school.

"May I have Director Kell's letter as well?"

After Crispin removed the letter from his interior coat pocket, Wickham read it with care and slipped it into his pocket. "Damned nuisance, these formalities."

"Kell would expect no less."

"Kind of you to say so. You've actually met him?"

Crispin looked at the airfield. "Of course. I trust that the arrangements have been completed for the closed observation plane?"

"They were, until we got bounced."

Crispin raised his voice more than he wanted. "Bounced?"

"Requisitioned earlier today, by someone that outranks even your Director Kell. I only have one craft available."

Crispin put on a brave smile. "I've flown in the Avro before. Quite serviceable, but a bit crowded for two observers, don't you think?"

Wickham pointed to an aircraft that made the Avro look like its pup. "We'll be flying the Handley Page over there."

"You cannot be serious. That behemoth?"

He grinned. "She is our newest bomber. Just off the line. They are outfitting her now. I need to get some air time on her to seat the seals and run in the engine before she goes into combat and those boys bang her about."

Crispin stared at the craft. Each of the wheels under the wings was almost waist high. Gesturing at the wings, which stretched over a hundred feet tip to tip and seemed to droop, he asked, "Is she fit to fly now?"

"I flew her from the factory myself. Quite frisky without the weight of the bombs. The Lewis machine gun fittings go in later in the week. The boys painted her markings on last night. Should be dry by now."

He looked for the antenna wire. "You do have radio communications, don't you?"

"Not yet. I had the lads cobble up a speaking tube, co-pilot to front gunner, just for the test flights. Damn thing is so bad, I can't hear a word they say without putting my ear to it."

"It seems like a recipe for disaster."

Wickham stood straighter. "I'm taking her up today. I've got to. So you can go with me or you'll have to take your chances on when the weather next opens up and there is a craft available for you. Could be weeks."

Crispin looked at the sky, trying to adopt the weather eye that he had seen in Meade. "Well, time and tide shall not wait for us, will they?"

"Afraid it's now or not."

Crispin stared at the massive engines. "I just needed to be convinced that something that large could actually fly before I would ever let the Doctor set foot in it."

"Good Lord, man. Those are twelve-cylinder Rolls Royce engines. She's the top of the line."

Crispin gave it another look, nodded his approval. "Well then, best we leave straightaway." He motioned for Doctor Lee to join them and made introductions.

As they walked toward the headquarters building, Doctor Lee looked up at the airplane and asked, "Where would we sit?"

Wickham pointed as he spoke. "There are spots for four in the Handley Page. Pilot and observer are together between the wings. Front gunner, in the nose of the craft, is ahead of me by ten feet and slightly below my line of sight. The rear gunner is just behind me."

She looked over the ship. "Who has the best view of the landscape?"

"Clearly, the front gunner, but that spot catches all the wind. When it is fitted, the machine gun deflects a great deal of it."

Doctor Lee asked, "Don't you have goggles for that, and a hat?"

Suppressing a smile, Wickham said, "Helmet. Of course we do, but at ninety miles an hour, it is quite brisk."

Doctor Lee paused a moment before saying, "Ninety! Imagine that! Couldn't I sit very low? Just pop up when needed? Don't you think that's the best spot for me, Lieutenant?"

"She has a point. I should sit next to you, unless you are having a co-pilot on this flight."

"Next to me would be grand. We have a glazed windscreen, so you can keep a constant watch and read the map. Do you have a flight plan in mind?"

As they approached the steps to the headquarters building, Crispin slowed and Doctor Lee walked very close to him as he went up the four steps, one at a time. "Yes, I do indeed."

Wickham opened a small door to the left of the main entrance to the building. "Good, we can go over it in the pilot's lounge while they pump the petrol into the plane."

Doctor Lee entered the small room. The interior door was on the opposite wall. A torn maroon sofa was against the left wall under a faded print of a fox hunt. She walked directly to the aviation map of England tacked to the right wall above a battered card table and two metal-framed chairs. Crispin stood in the doorway looking at the ten-by-ten rabbit hole which could have been one of the boardinghouse rooms of his youth or a farmhouse billet. Crispin and Wickham joined Doctor Lee at the map.

Crispin used his pipe stem to point to the aviation map. "Our mission is to survey the banks of each of these three rivers."

Wickham looked at Crispin. "May I inquire as to the purpose of your aerial survey?"

Crispin shrugged. "Regrettably, no."

"How far inland need you fly?"

"I, that is, we need to inspect the entirety of each river."

Wickham nodded and started tracing an elongated 'S' on the map with his index finger. "Would this sort of a flight serve your needs? Starting below the southernmost of the rivers?"

Crispin asked, "Specifically, what are you proposing?"

"I'll take a long loop out to sea, then fly west to the source of the southernmost river. Then I'll turn and fly east over the middle river to the sea. Turn, then fly west over the length of the northernmost of the three. Thence, home."

Doctor Lee said, "It would be most advantageous if we were over the rivers as late in the day as will allow us a return by twilight—"

"Which is about four. Just under an hour each way. Fifteen to twenty minutes over the rivers. Yes. Yes. We'll push off at two."

Nodding, Crispin said, "Splendid. Can you provide us with maps for the flight?"

"Of course. I'll be calling up the gun emplacements on the coast and advising them of our flight plan. We are a new profile. I have no intention of being shot down by our own coastal defense."

Crispin asked, "New security signs daily?"

"Yes. Can you signal for me? Simple flash of a hand torch."

"Certainly. I would be pleased to do so, just let me know the proper answer to the challenge well in advance and their location. I wish to have it clearly in mind." Crispin forced a chuckle. "I do not want to hesitate or get it wrong, lest they fire on us."

Wickham laughed. "No worry there. They would shoot off a colored flare before that. I'll tell you that signal sequence as well."

Crispin nodded and looked at Doctor Lee, who was staring at the map.

Wickham tapped it. "There is a gun emplacement here at Felixstowe. We will be within its range. They built Brackenbury Fort on the foundation of Walton Castle."

Crispin scowled. "Really?"

"Yes." Wickham turned to leave. "I'll have tea and some biscuits sent in for you while I attend to the ship."

Crispin smiled, but after Wickham left, he slumped into the sofa and folded his arms.

"What is it, Lieutenant?"

Crispin paused to remember that she was an American. "What he called 'Walton Castle' was built by the Romans as a fortress to protect access to both the Orwell and the Deben Rivers. Built before Christ was born. Later, invading Normans called it 'Wadgate,' meaning 'landing place.' They expanded the keep, you know the castle's inner tower, and added a bailey. Later still, Henry II confiscated it. He simply dismantled it in 1175."

"Lieutenant? What is it? I still do not understand why—"

"Quite possibly it was one of England's most important ecclesiastical sites. Many believe it to be the site that Bede called 'Dommoc.' That's the location of the first Christian bishopric in East Anglia."

She pointed to the wall map. "Can you show me exactly where? I want to see it for myself as we fly over."

Crispin pointed with care to a spot just south of the entrance to the estuary. "It's right here."

A crewman delivered a tray with two steaming mugs of tea and two folded maps. He placed the tray on the table, nodded without a word, and left. Doctor Lee handed a mug to Crispin and sat quietly. Crispin watched her unfold her map and read it.

"Now, Doctor Lee, I want to assure you that there's nothing to be afraid of when we are flying. It's going to be a bit breezy and loud up there, but Wickham is a seasoned pilot. He has assured me that the craft is sound. If you have any concerns during the flight, just ask me. We will be able to communicate, but our pilot will not be able to hear you. There is a temporary speaking tube that you and I will use."

She walked to the small window in the door and looked out to the airfield. "What are they doing out there?"

"They do quite a complicated pre-flight inspection. Wires and wings and things. Quite a bit of scurrying about." Crispin shifted his feet and wished he could pace. He turned to Doctor Lee. "Well, it seems that you are indeed the *tertium quid* of this lot."

"The third what?"

"The third *something*, literally. Meaning, an often ill-defined position. Such as, the odd man out. We stood on the edge of discovery that neither of us could have made alone. You found the bridge between my language and Meade's maps. For that, I thank you. Cumming was correct when he sent us to you, and I was an ass not to have seen that sooner."

"I understood."

"I know. That was in part what was frightening to me. How beyond my own control I had become. A puppet to noises and servant to dreams. But you helped me find my way again."

She paused a moment before patting his hand. "We did work well together, didn't we? It gets better, the better you get. And now you can help me." Doctor Lee opened her map again and scowled at it. "There seems to be a lot more on this map than on an atlas. Do you know what all this is?"

He stretched his neck as though his tie was too tight. "Theoretically."

"Well then? What are these added lines?"

"Grid lines and coordinates. That allows us a sort of shorthand, a code on the radio. In spite of all the map-reading courses the Army provided, I must admit that I never found them as interesting as the land itself. I am no Meade, who finds a fascination in cartography."

"What does fascinate you then?"

"I look at this map, and I see England. Not its hills and lakes. But the history of a people, its language, and its faith." He laughed. "I was not their best map reader. With all of history spread out before me, my mind wandered. In some ways, I feel that England is the family I never had."

Doctor Lee put on her reading glasses and flattened her map on the table next to the sofa. "Lieutenant, tell me what you see that I don't."

"I see an England before it had that name. Here, you see London, but I see a Roman town called '*Londinium*.'" Crispin let his finger glide on the map. "And this road to the north led to *Verulanium*, what we now call Saint Albans after England's first martyr. Much later, the Magna Carta was drafted there."

"I must make a point to visit."

Crispin did not hear her. "I look at the whole of this island, and time flows back and forth like a tide." Crispin laid his fingertips on the map and felt for England's pulse. "Where to start? In the time of Meade's map, England was seven kingdoms."

She watched his index finger hover over the map. "Northumbria in the north, all this above Hadrian's Wall. And Mercia, here, below it." Crispin pointed to the eastern coast. "Here's East Anglia, where we fly today. And below it, Essex, then Kent, and then Sussex. This long southern stretch is Wessex. Together, the kingdoms were known as the Heptarchy."

"But those names aren't even on this map."

He looked at the closed door and spoke very softly. "If I am right, today we will find the grave of the *bretwalda-*" He looked at her. "King Rædwald of East Anglia. It was his stepson, King Sigebert, who extended the reach of Christianity after his return from France with a monk who later would become Saint Felix."

"At the place called 'Felixstowe' now."

"Full marks, Doctor Lee. If you wish, I could tell you of some of the places we'll see from the air."

"Point them out for me now, please."

"Certainly, here we have…." He paused letting his finger rest on the chart.

"What is it?"

He sat back and looked directly at her. "My dreams. You know how visions of the men at the front were always with me, waking or sleeping? Now, I dream of other things."

She nodded.

"In actual fact, I believe I have constructed the story of the creation of Meade's map out of a tangle of dreams while I was feverish. Do you want to hear it?"

She nodded. He cleared his throat and sat straighter. He spoke in a hushed tone suitable for a bedtime story.

The candles gutter when the widowed Queen of East Anglia tugs open the heavy oak door to the monk's room in the castle's keep. Smoke spirals into the haze hovering at the vaulted ceiling. The hem of her raven dark cloak snags on the rough stone floor. She pulls the heavy wool around her bony shoulders and says, "Take up your quill."

While he readies a fine sheet of vellum, she closes her eyes and inhales the scents which had become a part of her husband's wool cloak. The richness of beeswax candles and sweet smudge of incense. The sharpness of ink and cloying bitterness of tallow lamps at the writing desk. The earthiness of yeast from bread and ale. The coarseness of wood smoke.

She points to the monk and says, "I shall bury my Rædwald as the Christian he became. But I shall honor him as the kings of Uppsala were buried with gold in their warship. Write this, Brother Felix. Helmet and mail shirt." The Queen's gaze goes to the sound at the door. A large man, all shoulders and chest, wearing a dark cloak over black leather breeches and high boots, marches into the room as if he owned it. Seeing the Queen, he drops to his knees, sobbing.

Her hand lingers on his shoulder. "I know, good Reeve. You were his North Star in battle, and now one last task I ask of you. Take the mapmaker back to Sweden and return with a burial ship." Her features had been set by age into a calm and calming face. The amber cast of candlelight behind her returned the coils of her braided white hair to their golden hue, brighter than the threads of gold encircling the amethyst at her throat.

He stands near her. "Honor me. Take my land." The Queen unclasps the amethyst brooch at her neck and hands it to him. "For your wife. My son will be king, fate willing. Hold this so he will know of your great service to his mother."

He bows deeply before he says, "Best I go alone for the ship. The Northman knows of such burials and can begin the digging before the ground is stone hard."

She asks, "How will you find your way?"

He says, "Have him make a map. Riddle the pathway for a new captain. I will give him the riddle's answer when the time is right." When the map was readied, the Queen looks at the men. "He was a war-brave man, a ring-giver to his knights, and a good king to his people. He was my winter's hearth mate." She hands each man a gold coin with her king's likeness on it. "The stone tower above him and the ship beneath him will honor his name. His memory shall outlast our own."

And that is the story of how the portolano came to be.

Doctor Lee grinned and patted him on the knee. "Well done. It could have happened that way. Very inventive of you."

"Thank you."

"Not at all. You know, I should tell you something that has been on my mind."

"Oh?"

"That you remind me so of my son when he was about your age. Not in looks, he was darker and stocky, but in your firm determination and intelligence."

"I take that as a compliment."

"And, I have been thinking that soon we will be going our ways and may not cross paths for quite a while; therefore, I would like to give you a remembrance."

"As though I could forget—"

"Hush." She reached to her collar and pulled a sturdy gold chain from under her sweater. Dangling from the chain was a large gold signet ring. "I want you to have a ring. It was my husband's. Stewart wanted to give it to Charlie for his twenty-first birthday. He was so attached to it,

I convinced him to have a copy cast for our boy, so they each would have one. Now it is somewhere...."

"I couldn't."

She unclasped the chain and placed the ring in his palm. "See if it needs sizing."

Crispin slid it on his ring finger where it fit perfectly. He looked at it carefully. Solid, square, manly, not a family crest, but a lone griffin, an eagle-beaked winged lion, cut deep enough into the gold face to be used as a seal. The corner above the griffin's flared wing was dented, rounded, possibly crushed somehow.

"That looks splendid on you."

"I cannot begin to thank you."

"Enough said. Now could we have a bit more tea?"

At one thirty, Wickham burst through the doorway and handed them leather helmets with goggles and leather dusters. "Sorry, but these will have to suffice. We haven't any added flying suits available." Crispin helped Doctor Lee put the long leather coat over her wool coat and carried his duster and the helmets to the plane. They walked out to the grass airstrip as Wickham ran ahead of them.

Crispin nodded as they approached the crewman holding the ladder, which leaned against the nose of the craft. Crispin helped her buckle the helmet and waited at the foot of the ladder while Doctor Lee unbuttoned the front of the apron skirt. As the breeze shifted the hem back, he saw that roomy tweed jodhpurs were tucked into her knee-high boots. She carefully climbed into the open gunner's nest in the nose of the plane. She stepped down onto the seat, looked down at Crispin, and waved.

As the ladder was pulled away, Crispin yelled up to Doctor Lee. "You are quite certain? It's an hour up and another back."

She nodded and slid down into the seat.

Chapter № 43

Wednesday
November 8, 1916
West of London, England

C rispin buttoned the neck of the duster and seated his goggles as Major Wickham signaled the crew to start the Handley Page. Both Rolls Royce engines popped to life immediately. A blue cloud of exhaust floated in front of the windscreen and over Doctor Lee, who was not more than ten feet in front of him in the gunner's cockpit.

Wickham tested the throttle. The roar and rumble of the engine shook the plane. Crispin had completed his silent prayer by the time Wickham engaged the linkage and the bomber jolted forward.

Doctor Lee glanced at her watch and then buttoned the neck of the leather coat. It was a few minutes after two. The bomber lumbered faster and faster until there was no more jolting. Doctor Lee turned and looked back at Crispin as the plane left the ground and the wings flexed. Once airborne, the engines took on a low growl. Crispin watched Doctor Lee test the wind on her face and then retreat to the lower position in her seat.

Crispin leaned down and yelled into the speaking tube, "Doctor Lee! Doctor Lee?"

She leaned down and shouted into the funnel end of the tube, "Yes, Lieutenant?"

"Good! You can hear me."

"I sure can!"

He tracked their progress on the map he clutched on his lap.

The first leg of the flight was the reverse of his night flight into

Hendon. They flew over the northern margins of London. Crispin smelled the bitterness of coal smoke and called into the tube, "London, to the right. Saint Albans to the left."

He watched her emerge from the shelter of the cockpit and stare over the edge like some mythical Valkyrie or some shield-maiden riding a winged horse. Looking past Saint Albans to the far north, he noticed a thin line of cumulus clouds on the horizon. He tried to count the number of puffs in the long row and not think about his prior flight.

They flew over Enfield. After half an hour, the plane swung to a north-by-northeast path over a brown and green quilt of farmland and small villages. The clouds were no longer on the horizon, but higher and moving south.

Crispin pointed to Chelmsford on his map. Wickham nodded verification as they flew over it and then turned to the east. The air was moist and smelled of pine pitch and salt.

Wickham pointed to the clouds. "The weather is developing faster than the meteorologists predicted."

"Can we get there in time to see shadows?"

"I'll push it to the red line to get there before the clouds get any thicker. Do you still want to start your survey at the harbor, and go west, up the River Stour? Can we cut it short?"

Crispin faced him. "No! We need to see it all."

Wickham increased throttle, and the engines pulsed deeper and louder. Doctor Lee turned to Crispin and put her hands up in a questioning manner. Crispin pointed down, to the speaking tube.

"Doctor Lee? I've asked him to press on. The weather!"

"I see. Thank you."

Crispin watched the villages and towns that were passing under their wings and a hundred stories filled his memory. As the coast came closer, Crispin shouted into the tube, "We're going out to sea now to line up on the River Stour!" He looked down as they passed over the bay near Jaywick to the open sea. To the east, the deep sea was cobalt with occasional whitecaps. The water lightened to azure at the coast.

Suddenly blocks of anthracite seemed to float in the pale sea. He looked up. Scattered high clouds cast random shadows on the sea and stole its brilliance. "Mackerel skies," Meade had called them. The higher clouds were then joined by lower and thicker cumulus. The weather was shifting. Crispin needed shadow to find the mound. Yet, he wondered if he should have Wickham turn for the aerodrome now that the craft was jolting and being buffeted by the changing weather.

Wickham scanned the sky above him and the northern horizon. He did not smile as he looked at Crispin and nodded. All of his charm had been replaced by a firmly set jaw.

Just off the coast of Harwich, Wickham slowed the plane, banked and flew inland over the short, wide River Stour. Crispin put the strap of the binoculars around his neck for fear of having them jolt from his cold hands. The late sun slipped through the occasional clouds and glinted on the water. Long shadows fell from the buildings and trees, but the fields were flat. Only the shadows of the clouds crawled over them. Crispin motioned down with his hand and Wickham slowed the craft.

Wickham shouted to Crispin. "About the right speed for your survey now?"

"Fine, thanks. Hold it under two thousand feet if you are able."

When the River Stour narrowed and disappeared into the land, the giant plane began to turn.

Crispin leaned down and shouted into the tube. "See anything?"

Doctor Lee lifted up and shook her head for him to see as the bomber completed its turn and flew east over the gentle hills and small streams that led to Ipswich.

Crispin found Ipswich on the map that was flapping in the wind despite being pressed against his thigh. As Wickham straightened from his turn, Crispin saw the sun break through the clouds and glint off stone roads hand-set by Romans.

The storm front continued moving toward them. As the airplane flew over the center of Ipswich, boys were playing soccer in a park. Crispin pulled his binoculars to his eyes and saw the boys stop and wave to the massive plane. The goalie in a red jacket held the ball for a moment and then kicked it toward them.

Crispin smiled, put down the glasses, and looked over the land, hoping for a wedge of shadow escaping from a mound. The altitude gauge hovered around fifteen hundred feet as Wickham flew a line above the river's course directly to the sea. The plane's shadow ran in front of them, like a cross floating over the river. It went gauzy and indistinct as the fog on the bank thickened. A small mound appeared in a field behind a row of homes. Crispin leaned toward the tube. "Look! To your right."

Doctor Lee craned her neck and then shook her head.

At the coast, Wickham swung a wide arc above the water and then flew north of Felixstowe over the small estuary of the River Deben.

Crispin looked below and saw the sea shift colors again as they approached the shore. Arcs of foam rolled between the sea and land. A low fog was building like steam at the reedy edges of the estuary.

Wickham shouted to Crispin, "Brackenbury Fort ahead!"

Crispin yelled into the tube. "Coming up on Walton Castle!" He pulled the signal light from its case and held it at shoulder height. Wickham tipped the wings, then straightened his course. Crispin saw the gun emplacement below signal with a light. Three Morse code letters were flashed as the challenge. Crispin picked out the letters easily, aimed his light, and flashed back as he had been instructed. He was relieved when there was no need for a flare.

Crispin put away the light and looked down again. He shouted into the tube, "The remains of the Norman walls of Walton Castle! At its base, see the Roman stonework?" Crispin looked at the orderly stone as it trailed from the gun emplacement into the sea.

The estuary began as a mud flat that mirrored the low sun and rippled red and gold. Swans flew below them and landed, cutting foam trails into the water. Reeds held the fluff of fog. Grasses appeared and turned the barren flat into a marsh. The scraggly marsh gave way to fields of brown wild grass and then to meadows. Further west were the dried grain fields gleaned daily by the swans.

The plane banked and the estuary disappeared behind them. Wickham adjusted his course to track the twists in the river. The frequent changes to accommodate the bends and turns in the river left the compass swaying. Crispin rotated his map to define the east banks. He turned to Wickham. "Slower, if possible. And hold your altitude under a thousand feet."

Crispin held his position on the map with his finger. Ramsholt on the right bank. Waldringfield on the left. The open land to his right showed low riverbanks and level fields. One field was darker than the rest with new furrow marks combed over it. Some clouds were shadowing parts of the field. Ahead of them were clusters of homes and warehouses. Docks and chandleries peppered the river banks at Woodbridge just as when Sir Francis Drake built his warships there.

The twists in the river matched Crispin's recollection of the clearly inked lines on the Baldwin portolano. The cove to the left was an exact match. Now the town of Woodbridge crowded down to the left bank of the river and ended in docks that ran along the low banks.

Crispin searched the speckled sunlight along the river's edge for the grain mill he had written about as a schoolboy. "Wickham? Can you see the mill? The tide mill?"

The pilot searched the foggy banks and then pointed left to a three-story building next to a large pond. Crispin glanced at the white planking and red Mansard roof before he scanned the open land along the river's right bank.

Across the river from it, an escarpment rose over a hundred feet. The fog had curled halfway up the cliff into a copse of oak trees which hid much of the fields beyond.

He waited a moment. The plane flew past the trees. A white three-story manor house was on the far side of the oaks and beyond it was open farmland. This field was bounded to the south by a plot of old pine trees. Rounded shadows of the scattered clouds crawled across the open field. He saw a chestnut horse pulling a plow at the edge of the field. The farmer tugged on long reins, stopped, and looked up as the rain began. Crispin used the man and his horse to find a scale on the land.

Crispin looked past him to the area near the pines and thought he saw four shadows spiking in long sharp wedges into the pale field. He ripped off his goggles and followed the long shadows to their source and counted four mounds on the earth. Binoculars to his eyes as the plane began to turn, he saw that one mound was taller than the rest. He shouted into the tube. "Look right!"

He put the binoculars to his eyes again and estimated the largest of the mounds at nearly thirty feet high and over a hundred feet across. As the plane pressed forward, the largest mound lost its first impression of being round. It became more rectangular and then narrowed into bow and stern, matching the outline of the ship mounds at Uppsala that Doctor Lee had drawn for him. He shouted. "Doctor Lee! Look to your right! Can it be the–"

Drops of rain splattered on the windscreen. Crispin let the binoculars drop on their strap as he leaned closer to the windscreen.

He glanced forward and saw Doctor Lee leaning on the rim of the cockpit, wiping her goggles with her hands. Her gaze was locked on the mounds just as a cloud erased the shadows. She looked back at him, pulled the goggles down around her neck, and stared at the field.

Wickham yelled. "Rain! Can I turn for home?"

"No. Straight on, until my signal." Crispin looked to where the river snaked under a bridge in less than a mile. The rain was melting the fog on the riverbanks and staining the fields. The shadow danced in and out of view.

Crispin turned to hold the sight of the mounds that rose gently from the field, like pillows lost under a brown blanket of winter grass. The smaller mounds were circular humps with even margins.

Crispin dared not hope that he had found the ship buried in the earth almost a thousand years before. He leaned down to the tube. "Near the trees, the largest mound! Did you see the outline?"

"It seems impossible— but yes!"

Crispin stretched up in his seat and looked aft of the wing until the stand of trees obscured the mounds. Only then did he thrust his hand in front of Wickham and point south. Wickham quickly turned the plane and increased their speed and altitude.

Crispin looked to the east, down the River Deben past the mounds now hidden in the rain-darkened field. He saw the smudge of the rain going to the sea, speckling the river. The outline of the coastal defense shimmered in the late light and then vanished behind the scrim of rain. He grinned, thinking that there been a day when King Sigebert and Bishop Felix stood atop the keep of Walton Castle and looked westward at the tall burial monument which had honored King Rædwald and that it was no longer hidden from history.

The leading edge of the storm caught them and rain slammed against the massive plane. Doctor Lee had disappeared from view.

Crispin yelled into the speaking tube. "Doctor Lee? How are you?"

She shouted. "I'll be fine! Just tucking in."

Crispin sat up and shouted to Wickham, "How does the Handley Page manage in the rain?"

"We'll know soon enough." Wickham pushed the throttle to its maximum and outran the downpour. Crispin looked at the clouds ahead and saw them thin as they flew south. A few minutes later, Wickham adjusted the throttle and reduced their speed slightly. "Can't run her at full throttle any longer, but we can still make the field before dark."

Crispin leaned down into the cockpit. "We'll be back by dark."

He looked ahead and watched Doctor Lee let the wind buffet her as she looked quickly over the nose of the craft, nodded, and then retreated. As the plane sped south into better weather, he turned toward the twilight where Mercury and Venus glistened next to the evening star in the slim strip between land and the sheet of clouds on the western horizon.

Wickham nudged Crispin and pointed ahead. The aerodrome was just visible. Crispin shouted into the tube. "Almost home!"

When they approached the aerodrome, and the nose of the craft tilted down slightly, Doctor Lee emerged from the shell of the forward cockpit and braced herself as Wickham landed.

When the engines had stopped, four men raced to the wheels with large wooden chocks. Wickham turned to Crispin. "Mission successful, Lieutenant?"

Crispin handed the binoculars to Wickham. "Yes. Although your report for the flight will omit any mention of your two passengers."

Wickham's mouth opened slightly as though to protest, and then he shrugged as the mechanics positioned the ladder against the nose of the craft. "As you wish. Can I assist you?"

"No. I'll manage from here. Thank you."

"Very well. See you inside." Wickham left the cockpit. Crispin followed him down to the grass. Crispin pulled his cane from his coat's sash and pushed his goggles back on his forehead. As he watched Wickham trot toward the headquarters building, he felt warm tears on his cheeks. He inhaled the fresh scent of crushed grass and gasped as he felt the hollow longing being replaced with something solid and full, a palpable sensation like the warmth of hot chocolate. He blinked and searched for the word. *Hāmcyne*, homecoming. Now he understood what Odysseus and Beowulf had known before him.

He brushed his gloves over his face as he walked to the base of the ladder and waited for Doctor Lee. The rain they had outrun twice before pelted them as she stepped off the last rung of the ladder. Crispin took her arm. Once they were several steps away from the crewman, Doctor Lee squinted against the rain. "Lieutenant? Your leg?"

"Never better. Did you see the larger mound?"

"Yes. It was so different than the others." She stuttered as she shivered. "A tower would account for that, as it collapsed and spread."

He slowed his gait and turned toward her. "And the smaller mounds?"

"Only time will tell." He noticed that she was still shaking and her grip on his arm had tightened. When she removed her helmet, he saw that her hair was soaked.

He steered her toward the headquarters building. "We need to get you dry and warm again."

As they walked, Crispin imagined a tower with a beacon above the river in a time long past.

Wickham, still in his flying suit, sprinted across the field. "Lieutenant Crispin! This just came for you." He passed a folded slip of paper to Crispin. "Highest urgency. They want you to call immediately." He took Doctor Lee's arm from him, and escorted her toward the building.

Crispin unfolded the paper. He recognized the number before the ink began to run in the rain. It was Kell's direct line.

Chapter № 44

Thursday
November 9, 1916
Stockholm, Sweden

The afternoon had the pewter dullness of the Swedish winter. When the driver from the Grand Hotel stopped at the main entrance, Meade made a show of carrying his new black briefcase with the gold-plated lock in one hand and his new black Borsalino fedora in the other. The uniformed bellman followed him with two tan suitcases on a gleaming brass cart as he crossed the deep red carpet to the reception desk. When Meade unbuttoned his black overcoat, his dark blue suit looked almost black in the subdued lighting.

A slim man with thinning sandy hair leaned over the marble counter and smiled warmly. "Herr Meade, good afternoon." Meade remembered the man's efficient manner and watery blue eyes. He was thinner than last year. The brass sign to the side of the blotter was engraved with the name: Herr Johansson.

"*Välkommen till Grand Hôtel.* It is our pleasure to have you as our guest again. If you will be kind enough to sign this registration card...."

Meade took the freshly dipped pen from him, skimmed the completed card, and signed it. He reached for his passport but left it in his jacket pocket when Johansson shook his head. "That will not be necessary for you, Herr Meade."

"Thank you, Mister Johansson."

"Your suite on the seventh floor is ready. As you requested, it has a view of the Royal Palace. May I make dinner reservations for you?"

"Please. Your smörgåsbord at seven tonight."

"Will you require any services before dinner, sir? Valet? Opera tickets?"

"No, thanks."

"Your usual breakfast at seven?"

"Make it six-thirty."

Nodding, Johansson placed a key with a brass fob on the blotter with care and put a square envelope next to it. "Herr Meade, a young woman left this note just before you arrived."

"What did she look like?"

The desk clerk leaned forward and said quietly, "Strikingly attractive, if I may say so. Deep blue dress."

"Thank you."

Meade stepped to the end of the reception desk, put his briefcase on the counter, and examined the envelope. Sealed. Cream-colored stationery. Ordinary. Not the hotel's. He dug in his pocket for his knife, slit the top of the envelope, and took out the paper. Small notepaper. Folded once. Not monogrammed. Meade read the scrawled handwriting.

"Opera Cellar, bar at 6 p.m. WBC."

Meade looked around the lobby quickly, wondering if Grimes was setting a new trap. He looked at the envelope again. Meade remembered seeing initials at the end of Crispin's journal entries. It did look like his handwriting. The flat line before the 'W' began. That sweeping curlicue at the end of the 'C.'

Meade looked at his watch and then at the clock above Johansson. Five thirty-six. Less than half an hour to the meeting. If he left now, and walked quickly to the Opera Square, he could just make it.

Meade returned the key to Johansson. "Would you have my bags sent up and unpacked? I feel like getting some air before dinner."

"Certainly, sir." Johansson nodded and motioned the bellman to the desk.

"And send a small bottle of aquavit to my room."

Johansson lowered his voice to a confidential whisper. "If you are entertaining the Prime Minister, we have his special reserve aquavit in the cellar."

"No. I'm not here to see Mister Hammarskjöld this trip. Your house bottle will be fine."

"Certainly, sir."

He took the briefcase with him and strode past the doorman, who opened the gleaming door and nodded slightly.

It was cold enough for snow. Meade tugged down his hat and walked briskly. The seawall and water were on his left and land was to his right as he set out for the Opera Square. He looked along the promenade. Men and women were walking quickly with the small, measured step used when iced patches hid on the stone. A few men clustered at the ferry stop, shifted from foot to foot, and pushed their hands deeper into their pockets. He counted. It was fifty-three paces to where Stallgatan branched off to the right and another twenty paces to the large white fortress of the Svenska Handelsbanken, where he would meet Grimes tomorrow. Dark window shades were drawn down over the glass doors of the bank.

Behind him, the ferry horn blew as it approached the dock near the hotel. He went to the steps of the bank and pretended to tie his shoe. He looked back.

The hotel's pale stone looked almost milky in the dim light, and the green copper roof seemed black. It hadn't taken five minutes to get to the bank. The ferry docked. The disembarking passengers fanned in different directions. Everyone waiting for it boarded in an orderly line. Several seagulls chattered and swirled above the ferry as Meade walked past the entrance to the bank and ducked into the courtyard behind it. When the small heavy oak door to the courtyard opened, Direktör Lund motioned to Meade. Once inside, Lund said, "A pleasure to see you again, sir. The vault is open."

Meade handed Lund the paper with all three signatures. "As we agreed. Any of these three will have signature access. The key will not be required."

Nodding, Lund said, "Your box is on the table in the vault." He waited in the dim lobby while Meade entered the bright vault, pulled the Baldwin and Hedeby portolanos from the pouch under his shirt, and dropped them beside the steel box. After slipping the Baldwin into the box, Meade returned the Hedeby map to the pouch and put it under his shirt again. As he began to close the metal lid, he took a last look at the Baldwin. He stopped when he noticed that a longer line extended from each of the asterisks. It had been such a rush at the hospital that he could not recall if Crispin had ever used the straightedge to extend those longer lines on the atlas.

Placing the Baldwin on the table, Meade carefully aligned the edge of the bank box to extend the longest line of the right asterisk up the map. It crossed all three rivers. He kneeled on the floor and used his eye to sight along the longest line on the left asterisk. He marked the intersection with his finger and stood slowly. His finger was just above the uppermost of the three large rivers before the second big bend.

As he put the Baldwin in the box, he called for Lund, who entered the vault immediately, returned the steel box to a slot in the wall, and locked it into place. He handed one key to Meade and retained the bank's master key on a chain looped over his belt.

Meade tossed the key in the air twice and handed it to back to Lund. "Send a courier, someone you personally trust, with this to my London office tomorrow. My secretary is expecting it and will have a handsome bonus for both of you."

"Certainly. Is there anything else I can do for you tonight?"

Meade shifted his briefcase to his left hand, opened the brass door over the five-by-five inch window, and looked out onto an empty courtyard. He nodded, and Lund unlocked the door. "Nothing else tonight. When I arrive tomorrow, make it seem as if you have not seen me for at least a couple of months."

Lund pulled the door open and Meade slipped through it. "Certainly. *God Natt.*"

As the door shut, Meade said, "Good night." He crossed the empty courtyard, returned to the promenade, and skidded on a patch of ice. He regained his footing and shortened his stride. There were buildings on his right. Then a bridge to the left, called 'Strömbron,' led to the old town. The bell tower of the old cathedral jutted above the roofs. Meade continued along Strömgatan and arrived at the Opera Square in a few minutes. Rather than turning toward the Opera, he walked a hundred yards past it, spun, and backtracked to the square. No one stopped. No one looked out of place. Then a man in a tan coat entered the doorway to a pharmacy. Meade tensed and then chuckled at himself.

As he crossed the square and walked toward the arches of the Opera, he watched the students, many in long leather coats, who chatted in an orderly queue near the ticket window and wondered if any were waiting to watch for him. But no one seemed to notice as he walked to the side of the opera building and down the stone stairs to the Cellar Restaurant.

The restaurant's vaulted ceiling had been retained in its original state of raw brick and mortar. The ornate walnut cabinet behind the bar extended to the ceiling and was embellished with etched mirrors. The dozen stools at the bar were empty. Meade was grateful that the meeting was before the performance. The bar would have been shoulder to shoulder during intermission or afterward.

Of the dozen tables for four, three were filled. Two men in leather coats were well into a second round of aquavit and beer, laughing at something. One had a pipe, but was blonde and outweighed Crispin by fifty pounds. The other two tables were occupied by middle-aged couples having an early dinner before the opera. The plates of meatballs in cream sauce with small boiled red potatoes were being pecked at with the regularity of ravens.

He sat on a stool at the center of the bar, carefully placed the briefcase on the stool next to him, and covered it with his coat. He looked at his watch. Four minutes before six. He ordered a coffee and waited.

At six, a woman with straight blond hair cut at chin level entered. The two men at the table stopped talking to watch her glide across the room. She was tall, lean, in her mid-twenties, and wore a dark blue dress. She carried her overcoat on her arm and walked directly to Meade, who was also watching her. She draped her coat over his and sat on the stool to his left. She turned her back to the room and opened her purse. In English as British as Crispin's, she said, "Smile. Pretend that we are acquainted."

"Great to see you," Meade said, louder than he intended. He whispered, "Who sent you?"

Smiling at him, she pulled a black enameled cigarette case from her purse. As she took a cigarette from the case, Meade lit a match and smiled. She cupped his hand, leaned over the flame, and said, "Lieutenant Crispin." She looked up from the flame and frowned, teasingly. "You expected that RLS thing."

"How do I know this isn't a trap?"

The bartender walked toward her. She ordered a coffee slowly in formal Swedish. He bowed before he turned to get her cup. She leaned closer to Meade. "Lieutenant Crispin thought you would want something more than the RLS."

Meade took a sip and watched her over the rim of the cup. "Okay. Convince me."

She patted his collar and smiled again. "He said he owes you a pint at his local."

Meade grinned. "Anyone else would have said 'local pub,' but not him."

She moved close to his ear and whispered, "Grimes is sending Stahl after you."

"The guy from Amiens? I thought—" Meade stopped when she raised her eyebrows. After the bartender delivered her coffee, Meade continued quietly, "I thought he was in custody."

She held the cigarette without smoking. "Had to exchange him for one of ours. Seems he is back in the game. He'll be going to your room when you are at the bank."

He whispered, "Why?"

She pulled back and smiled. "Just listen and keep smiling. To kill you. Too complicated to explain now."

"Great."

She touched his chin with her right hand. "Delay at the bank until the last possible moment. Engage Grimes in *persiflage*. Then–"

"What's persiflage?"

She chuckled. "He said you'd ask. It is banter, mocking banter."

Meade grinned. "That's my fellow."

"After you leave the bank tomorrow, do not return to the hotel. Get on the train to Uppsala. Track Three. At 13:45. Don't board until it's moving."

"I'll need a ticket."

She balanced her cigarette on the rim of a crystal ashtray, reached up, and slowly straightened his tie. "I have it. I'll put it in your jacket pocket in a moment."

Meade smiled broadly and nodded. "Okay. After I go to Uppsala, what–"

She tapped a gray ash into the crystal ashtray on the bar. "We will take you out of the country safely."

Meade pulled back and looked at her blue eyes. "Is Crispin there?"

She paused before saying, "He's been ordered to the hospital in England."

"Okay. I'll do it your way. Now what?"

She let go of his tie and smiled. "Stand up and embrace me. Keep your side to the bar."

He stood and wrapped his arm around her waist as though they were dancing.

"Lower. Be rude." She kissed his neck just under his ear. Meade felt her slip the ticket into his jacket pocket next to the bar. He lowered his hand past the small of her back.

She pushed him away and slapped his cheek.

The sharp sound of the slap echoed in the quiet bar. The diners looked up from their plates. Meade reflexively brought his hand up to his cheek and held it there. He watched in silence as she grabbed her purse and coat before strutting out of the bar. Meade shrugged to the diners who were staring at him and picked up her cigarette. After a deep draw on it, he ground it out, placed several bills next to the coffee cups, and left quickly. The cold air soothed his stinging face. He started to put his hand into his suit coat pocket to look at the ticket and then thought better of the idea. He carried the briefcase with extreme care as he walked back to the hotel. His eyes darted between the few people still on the street.

Meade marched through the lobby, retrieved his room key from the front desk without pausing, and got into the caged elevator. He turned to the attendant and said the difficult word for seven with care, "*Sju.*" He stood silently as the elevator operator rotated the handle and the elevator rose with a muted whirr.

At the seventh floor, he walked to the white and gold door of his suite and opened the gleaming lock with his key. The mechanism was smooth and silent. The door swung open easily.

Pushing the door shut behind him, Meade drew the small Smith & Wesson from his holster, looked around the sitting room, walked softly over the twenty-by-twenty foot Persian carpet in the sitting room, past the campaign desk under the windows, to the open walnut door into the bedroom. After glancing in, he entered and saw that his bags had been placed on the carved chest of drawers next to the mirrored wardrobe. The bed was turned down and a silver dish of chocolates was on the table next to it. The tiled bath past the bedroom was empty. He was alone.

He returned to the sitting room, grateful that Crispin hadn't seen his excess of caution. He locked the door and sat on the peach-colored velvet settee. On the marble-topped tea table, a round silver tray held two thimble-sized glasses and an ice bucket cradling a small bottle of aquavit.

Meade poured a glass and toasted the oil painting opposite him. The scene depicted a rearing white stallion about to carry his saber-wielding, blue-coated master into some battle in the seventeenth century. That was the way to do it. No slinking around in the cold. Mount up and charge.

As Meade dressed in his tuxedo, he added opal shirt studs, matching cufflinks, and secured his holstered gun on his belt at the small of his back. He took the small briefcase with him to the veranda on the ground floor and followed the maitre d' to a table overlooking the water and close to the buffet table, which was over twenty feet long. The candlelight shifted the burgundy velvet on the upholstered chairs to a deeper hue than he remembered.

Although he normally enjoyed the complexity and variety of the dishes, tonight he was eating, not dining. The waiter presented Meade with an iced glass of aquavit and a plate containing an assortment of black sturgeon and red salmon caviars, each served on a halved hard-cooked quail's egg. Meade looked over the buffet and plotted his strategy. He decided to forego the pickled herring and cold fish plates, the course of salads and cold meats, for a platter of hot meats and vegetables. He made a show of selecting the breast of pheasant with sliced truffles, reindeer filet with brown sauce, and meatballs in cream sauce with a lingonberry compote, accompanied by duchess potatoes, glazed carrots, and red cabbage cooked with apples.

He declined the proffered desserts and iced punch wine. He ordered a cup of coffee. Halfway through his coffee, he thought better of his decision and selected a flaky pastry covered with whipped cream and a golden cloudberry sauce. Each time he went to the buffet, he left the briefcase unattended against the wall and watched it in a calculated manner.

When he returned to his suite, he was startled to find the lights blazing and the curtain open. He started to close the curtain and then remembered that there was no blackout in Stockholm. Meade put the briefcase on the desk and went into the bedroom.

After he slipped the train ticket from his tuxedo trouser pocket into the jacket of his blue suit, he pulled his opera glasses from his suitcase, turned off the bedroom lights, went to the window, and looked over the waterway into the old town and then along the promenade. The lights in the Royal Palace glowed amber and etched golden lines across the water. Few people were out in the cold night air. Down at the seawall, the small ferry docked and exchanged passengers. Nothing seemed out of place.

Meade returned to the sitting room, closed the curtain, opened the briefcase on the desk, and unbuttoned his shirt. He wrapped the leather pouch containing the Hedeby map in the tissue paper and string which he had brought with him and hoped that it would make the map look as important as it was purported to be.

Taking the bottle of aquavit, Meade twisted out the cork stopper, walked to the bathroom, and poured the top third of the contents into the sink. He stood the closed bottle on the right side of his briefcase, placed the wrapped map on the left, and filled the center with crumpled pages of the *Dagens Nyhetter*.

When he held the case by the handle, the bottle remained upright. Once he removed the cork, tipping the case would spill the aquavit on the pouch and its contents. The threat of obliterating the ink or allowing Meade to put a match to it might impress Grimes. Before he retired, Meade put the packed briefcase at the foot of the wardrobe and his gun on the table beside his bed. For the first time in years, he found himself worrying about a meeting.

Chapter № 45

Friday
November 10, 1916
Stockholm, Sweden

By six twenty-five Friday morning, Meade had dressed in the trousers of his dark blue suit and starched white shirt. He checked his pistol and left it and the holster under a towel on the bed. He pushed back the heavy velvet draperies and looked through the double glazed windows toward the bank. A light snow sifted through the streetlights and made cones of silver along the seawall.

There was a light tap on the door before the waiter pushed a linen-covered cart into the room. On the cart were the morning edition of *Dagens Nyhetter*, two silver-domed covers, a silver coffee service, and cut-crystal dishes of sweet butter, raspberry preserves, and orange marmalade. The waiter poured the coffee. The room filled with its smoky scent. He pulled away the covers and placed them silently on the lower rack of the cart. Pale bone china rimmed with blue and gold held a selection of small pastries. Two soft-boiled eggs nested in china cups. When the waiter saw Meade looking in his direction, he nodded. "Herr Meade."

"*Tack.*"

"You are quite welcome, sir. Is there anything else I can provide for your meal?"

"No. Thanks."

After breakfast, Meade savored the last of the coffee. The contrast to the days of Crispin's insipid tea made the coffee seem even richer.

As he knotted his pearl-gray tie over the gold pin that linked the tips of his collar, he thought of the blonde fixing his tie and wondered how she fit into all this.

Meade paced, looked at his watch, and took his compact Smith & Wesson from under the towel. He snapped open the chamber and confirmed that the six rounds were still there.

After sliding the holster over his belt, he seated the pistol in it. He put on his suit coat, adjusted his tie, and tugged on his overcoat and hat. He looked at the bank again through the opera glasses and saw Grimes walking into the front door at ten before ten. Men and women were wrapped in overcoats and moved cautiously over iced walkways like penguins. The early morning snow had been churned into a gray slush on the sidewalk. No stragglers. He opened the briefcase, reached down, and uncorked the bottle. He slipped the cork into his coat pocket, turned off the lights in his room, and took the stairs to the lobby.

As Meade walked directly to the bank, he found the cold air refreshing. He paused briefly in the bank's gray marble lobby before Lund walked over to him with an outstretched hand. They shook hands and Lund said, "*God däg*, Herr Mead. It is good to see you after so many months." He bowed his head slightly and said quietly, "Your associate has arrived."

"What name did he give you?"

"He did not offer one. But he did give me a very substantial treasurer's check drawn against Credit Suisse to hold pending his further instructions. Would you like me to join you now or wait?"

"I'll meet with him first."

Lund opened the carved oak doors marked *Direktör – Privat*. Seated behind Lund's desk was Grimes, smoking a cigarette.

Meade placed the base of the briefcase on the large pale oak desk with care. He did not release the handle. "Hope I didn't keep you waiting too long."

Motioning to the case, Grimes said, "Let's see what you have in there."

Meade glanced around the room. The office was as he remembered it. The one door was behind him. A small high window showed only the dull gray sky. Oil paintings of former bank directors and a small seascape hung on the paneled walls. The light from the glass globes on the brass chandelier made the room starkly bright. The wall clock was just where Meade could see it without being too obvious.

Meade stared at Grimes without moving his hand from the case's handle. "Are your funds on account here now?"

The man's lips formed a practiced smile. "Bearer check, wasn't it?"

"That's the same as cash, and I'm not that stupid." Meade picked up the briefcase.

Grimes half-smiled. "You'd walk out on this kind of money?"

"There are always other buyers for interesting documents."

Grimes laughed. "Easy, Mister Meade. Put the case down. I gave your banker the treasurer's check drawn by Credit Suisse on its own account. He has already verified it and put it at your disposal." He motioned to a bank slip at the edge of the desk. "On my approval, that is."

Grimes stood, crushed his cigarette in the glass ashtray, and straightened his black double-breasted suit coat. He stretched his head to the left as though his collar were too tight and leaned on his overcoat which he had draped over the arm of the chair.

Meade opened the case slowly and grabbed the open bottle of aquavit as it started to tip toward a string-wrapped parcel. Grimes gasped and grabbed for the bottle as well. Meade brushed his hand aside, corked the bottle, and set it on the desk. Meade noticed that Grimes' overcoat was on the back of Lund's chair. He left his on.

Grimes watched Meade lay the parcel on the desk and push it toward him. Meade sat and put his hat on the desk before saying, "Open it. Gently."

As Grimes untied the string and peeled away the paper, a film of sweat covered his brow. He stared at the leather pouch and tried to suppress a smile. He opened it and removed the Hedeby map.

He looked at the outline of the shore, the Latin inscription, and nodded. A smile started at his eyes and was repressed. He took a large hand lens from his overcoat pocket and held the parchment. After glancing at the front, he turned it over and looked at the inscription on the rear and grinned. Then he placed it on the desk.

His fingers trembled as he removed the cotton wool that padded the seal. Lens to his eye, he tipped his head and read the rim of the wax.

Grimes put down the hand lens and smiled at Meade. "So. A chart to *Heidiba*, is it? Do you know what you have here?"

"Got a pretty good idea."

Grimes smirked. "Did you go there? To Hedeby"

"Yes. The harbor matched the map. Pristine. Couldn't find any record of an excavation. So? Do we have a deal?"

"Yes. We have an agreement."

Meade did not move from his chair. "Do you mind if I ask you something?"

Grimes padded the seal and slipped the map into the pouch without answering. Meade persisted. "How'd you know I had it?"

"I was the one bidding against you at the auction. On a rumor that there was something from the Baldwin collection hidden in that mess of worthless maps. I never knew it was such an old portolano. That's called collecting."

"But I got it. And for a lot less than you are paying now. That's called business."

Grimes stood. "Now, if you will excuse me, I'll sign the bank authorization and have the funds transferred." Grimes pulled a Parker Snake pen from his coat pocket and uncapped it. He signed the paper and blew on the wet ink. He placed the paper on the table in front of him and capped the pen. He handed the pen to Meade and stood to leave the room. "I believe this was yours."

Meade took the pen and slipped it into his suit's inner pocket with a smile. Grimes picked up the pouch and started to walk to the door. Meade stood in his way. Leaning back to the desk, Grimes placed the pouch on the edge of the desk in front of Meade and then left the room.

A few moments later Grimes returned with Lund. As Grimes sat at the desk, Lund handed Meade a half-sheet of paper. After Meade nodded to him, Lund left the office.

Meade pushed the pouch across the table.

Grimes slipped the pouch into his thin briefcase and snapped the chromed clasps. "Quite the clever chap, aren't you? First this little bottle trick. Then having my funds transferred to some trust, not your personal account. Pity we won't be doing business in the future. I've rather enjoyed this."

"Who knows?"

"Of this you may be assured: we shall never do business again, Mister Meade. Never."

Meade resisted the impulse to grab him. "Don't count on it. It's a small world."

Grimes stood. "Shall I leave first?"

"Go ahead. I want to talk to my banker on another matter. Send Lund back, will you?"

When they were alone, Meade wrote a draft against his personal account and handed it to Lund. "That's for a thousand U.S. dollars. I'd like the draw in American bills, if possible. I may be travelling soon."

"Certainly, sir. We can accommodate that easily."

Meade paced and looked out the window. It was snowing, and the light in his hotel room was glowing in the dullness of the day.

Chapter № 46

Friday
November 10, 1916
Stockholm, Sweden

Lund fanned the bills on the desk. "Herr Meade. As you requested."
Meade scooped up the stack of bills. Lund held the flap of the briefcase open, expecting Meade to put in the currency. Instead, Meade split the bills between the two front pockets of his suit jacket. "Keep the case and bottle. A present from me."

"Very kind of you, Herr Meade. May I call a taxicab for you?"

"No thanks. I need some fresh air." When Lund turned to go to the door, Meade slipped his pistol from its holster into his overcoat pocket.

Lund gave a half-bow and smiled as he held the office door for Meade, who was buttoning his coat. The lobby was almost empty. The guard opened the heavy front door as Meade tugged on his fedora.

The wind-driven snow felt like needles on his face after the warmth of the bank. Meade held his wristwatch almost at chest height. He squinted over it toward the Grand Hotel. All he wanted right now was to get his bags, a cup of coffee, and the first boat to France. Instead, he had to become invisible until the train left for Uppsala.

He went right down the Strömgatan promenade and turned up the collar of his overcoat. A few delivery trucks and horse-drawn wagons loaded with crates crawled over the slick cobblestones. Most of the pedestrians had vanished. After a few paces, Meade looked at his watch again. Quarter to twelve.

He needed to stay moving or tuck out of sight for two and a half hours. When he did not return to the hotel, they might come looking for him. He shoved his hands into his pockets and walked faster.

Meade recalculated the distances and travel times. The train station was on Vasagatan, past the opera. Ten minutes away, if he stayed near the Opera Square. Even if he strayed into Old Town, a quarter of an hour should be adequate for the walk. Five minutes, if he could find a taxicab. But in this weather, he couldn't plan on it.

Walking toward *Gamla Stan*, Meade wanted to look like a tourist in Old Town. He would duck in and out of antique shops for warmth and let the narrow twisted streets hide him. Maybe he would linger over a coffee in a small pastry shop.

He crossed the street and walked along the seawall toward the bridge. The ferry horn rattled against the buildings. Meade watched the gulls swoop over the water churning behind the ferry. The wind pushed foam against the base of the seawall and blew small flecks onto the gray cobblestones. Meade looked behind him. He was the only one walking next to the seawall. An old woman and a man walking ahead of her clung close to the buildings. White sailboats tugged at anchor. Small varnished sailboats bobbed like amber seabirds as the snow collected on their canvas covers.

As he neared the bridge, he heard the shrill squeal of locking brakes. He glanced toward it and saw a truck. Crates on the back of the truck clattered as the driver shifted, accelerated slowly, and passed him. A stocky man in a tan overcoat ran from where the truck had been to the ferry dock. He slid to a stop and looked at the schedule on the lamppost. Meade shook his head. He would have a cold wait before the next one arrived. He tugged his hat down and hunched his shoulders against the wind. Just before turning onto the bridge, Meade felt a hand on his left elbow. He tightened his grip on his gun.

The raspy voice came from behind his left shoulder. "No, Herr Meade. Just walk."

"What the–" Meade started to pull away and thought better of it when the pressure to his ribs increased.

"Do as I say, and you will not have any difficulty from me."

Meade kept a slow steady pace along the promenade, passing the first bridge. The man came even with his left side. Meade looked straight ahead. "What do you want?"

"Money."

"Sure. Let me give you my wallet." Meade started to remove his left hand from his coat pocket.

"Hands in pockets." The man slapped his palm against the small of Meade's back and hit the hard leather holster. "As I thought. You do have a gun."

"What—"

"I saw the *Direktör* take the stack of money into his office."

"Grimes send you?"

The man laughed and shoved Meade away from the seawall toward a small side street. "Go in there, now."

They had walked only a few paces up the empty street when the man shoved Meade into a closed doorway. Meade twisted. His shoulder crashed into the door. He barely kept his balance on the icy step.

The man tapped the shiny barrel of the small revolver against a braided leather button at Meade's chest. "Open your coat. With your left hand."

Meade unbuttoned his overcoat slowly and pulled back the left side of his suit jacket. The man reached toward the front suit pocket. Meade slowly pivoted, sliding to the side of the gun barrel pointed at his chest.

At the sound of tapping on cobblestone, Meade looked past the man's shoulder. Someone was coming up the alley. Slim, black wool overcoat. Nondescript hat pulled low. A cane in his left hand.

Crispin drew a small blued Beretta, took aim, and shouted, "Halt!"

The man spun and fired quickly. The bullet splintered a double glazed window above Crispin's head.

Crispin turned his side to the man like a duelist and returned fire.

The man grunted, grabbed his thigh, and fell to the cobblestone. He rolled once before raising his pistol toward Crispin.

Meade fired from his pocket. The slug ripped through Meade's overcoat and hit the man's shoulder, slamming him back on the cobblestones. Pulling his pistol from his pocket, Meade ran toward the man, who was struggling to sit up. The cane sliced through the air toward the man's forehead. Meade jumped back. The thud sounded like a dropped melon. The man crumpled on his side.

Crispin said, "He was quite fortunate that I was not a better batsman at cricket." He pocketed his pistol and shifted the cane to his right hand. "Best we press on before the authorities arrive."

Meade stood motionless.

Crispin pointed with the tip of the cane to the bills beside the gun on the cobblestones. "Pick them up." Meade slowly bent and retrieved both. As he stuffed the bills into his coat pocket, he looked at Crispin. "Glad to see you. Should you be here?"

Crispin took the man's small revolver from Meade and put it in his pocket. "Of course not. They think I am in transit to Birmingham University Hospital as we speak."

"I'll get a taxi and—"

"No." Crispin shoved him toward the promenade. "Walk with me—now. Am I making myself understood?"

"Yeah, we gotta go." Meade put his gun back in his coat.

"There's a good fellow."

When they were alone and halfway over the windswept bridge, Meade took Crispin's elbow and stopped him. He pointed to his left leg. "Your not in the splint—"

"But I am. Rather baggy trousers over Doctor Lee's newly revised splint."

"Why aren't you in England, getting better?"

Crispin grabbed the snowy railing of the bridge. "Kell's boys in London intercepted a cable that the Germans had set an ambush for you. Fearing that the RLS may have been compromised, Kell passed me over to Cumming to write a note that you would know to be legitimate to meet our contact."

"It worked. She warned me. You think he might—"

"That fellow? Just a common thief. Not at all their type."

"Why'd they want to kill me? They got what they wanted."

"You apparently present a liability to them."

Meade flung his hands out. "How? By black-marketing old documents? Half of Germany does it."

Crispin glanced down the promenade. "It seems that Grimes has political aspirations that might be derailed if you were to pop up as the source of his archaeological find."

"I hated letting that bastard go."

Leaning down as though to tie his shoe, Crispin placed his Beretta at his feet and stood. "We had no choice in the matter, although I would have preferred to have his guts for garters." He kicked the pistol under the railing and into the sea. "But at least he paid you well for it. Didn't he?"

"Already deposited."

Crispin shivered as he grinned. "Splendid!"

"You found it, didn't you? I can tell by that smile."

Laughing and barely able to speak, Crispin's hand drew a large arc as he said, "We saw these mounds—"

After motioning to silence Crispin, Meade said, "Don't tell me. The reeve's meadow was above the second bend on the upper river."

Slamming his hand against the rail and sending a clot of snow into the icy water, Crispin shouted, "Damn! You called Doctor Lee, didn't you! I so wanted to be the one to tell you."

"I haven't talked to her." He crossed his arms and let Crispin sputter.

"But! Then how—"

"In fact, you did show me where it was. You had the right idea by extending the longest line on the asterisks, but you used the wrong map.

I didn't know if they were meant to relate to the two Michaels or not, but when I followed the imaginary lines to where they crossed, it was the reeve's meadow that you discovered."

Seeing that Crispin was shaking in the cold, Meade asked, "So what do we do now, Professor?"

After Crispin had dropped the assailant's chromed revolver to his feet and kicked it into the sea, he turned toward Old Town and shouted over his shoulder, "Have lunch!"

Meade held on to the railing wondering if he had heard Crispin correctly and then ran a couple paces to catch up with him.

"Lunch? I can't eat now!"

"Well, I can't keep wandering about on this splint. Besides, we need to be remembered in a restaurant. Not back there. Who knows who might have noticed me lurking outside the bank waiting for you."

Within a few minutes, they had passed the Royal Palace and were in the center of Old Town. Crispin stopped at the door of a small restaurant. "Seems pleasant enough." Meade pulled the heavy door open. Crispin entered and took a table at the front of the restaurant. Meade took off his overcoat and folded it on the vacant chair, covering the gaping hole at the pocket.

"Meade? Would you be kind enough to order?"

"Why? I thought you spoke–"

Crispin unbuttoned his overcoat. "My point exactly. My Swedish is quite good. I'd be taken for a native."

Meade waved vigorously and called for the waiter. He proceeded to order in very poor but exceedingly loud and convoluted Swedish. Finally, the waiter said in English, "Very well, sir. That is aquavit, a platter of cheese, and hard bread to start. Then meatballs in cream sauce for you both with pilsners."

Meade said, too loudly, "That's it. Tack so much, buddy!" The waiter suppressed a smile at being thanked in the informal manner used between close friends– or when addressing small children.

The cheese plate and two glasses of aquavit arrived quickly. Crispin downed his aquavit in one sip and looked around the restaurant. Half of the dozen tables were occupied. They were far away from the other diners.

Meade whispered, "How'd you spot him?"

"When he left the bank, he looked the wrong way before crossing the street."

"What?"

Crispin sighed. "Think for a moment. In Sweden, as in Britain, one drives and walks on the left side of the road. It has been that way since oxcarts. As a pedestrian, you expect cars in the lane closest to you to be passing right to left, so you look to the right."

Meade interrupted him. "Of course. I'd normally do the opposite. So would a German."

As he put a slice of cheese on some flatbread, Crispin said, "Precisely. I noticed that chap when he looked the wrong way and stepped into the path of the truck."

"I'm sure glad you saw him when you did."

Crispin nodded but then was silent. He looked pale and a film of sweat covered his forehead. His eyes darted around the room.

Meade whispered, "The fever?"

Crispin nodded as he ran the cloth napkin over his face and looked around the small restaurant. "Meade, you need to talk."

"About what, Professor?"

"Anything! Just get us noticed."

Meade picked up a slice of cheese and gestured with it. "You know, the Grand Hotel makes its own aquavit. Can't get it anywhere else in the world."

"That's the stuff. Louder, if you please."

"They add cumin, anise, fennel, and even sherry to give it a special flavor."

Several diners cast discreet sidelong glances at Meade.

The waiter approached with their pilsners. Crispin tapped the table as though lecturing. "Did you know that means the 'water of life'? *Aqua vitae*. From the Latin. And further, did you know that they call Stockholm 'the Venice of the North'? It is composed of many islands."

The waiter shrugged as he returned to the kitchen for their plates. Crispin tried not to smile. "That's done it, Meade."

At ten after one, Meade overpaid the bill. Crispin reached for his cane. It slipped from his grasp. Meade grabbed it before it hit the floor. "Here's your, what'd you call the good sword? '*Hrunting*'?"

Crispin blinked sweat out of his eyes and took the cane. "Just so."

When they were on the windy street, Meade pulled on his coat and turned to Crispin, who had gone pale and leaned his back against the cold stone of a building.

"Meade? I think I need to rest for a moment. Isn't there a church near here? *Storkyrkan*? Built in 1200 something or another."

"Yeah. Next street over. Can you make it?"

Crispin lurched off the wall and staggered forward. Meade grabbed his elbow.

They walked less than a block before Meade saw the church's bell tower above the roofs. They turned toward it.

Crispin looked up at the sign in gold lettering "*Sankt Nikolai Kyrka*". He translated, slurring his words. "*Saint Nicolaus Church*, call it the 'Storkyrkan,' big church. You know there's a dragon in here. A real dragon."

Meade guided him into the dim church and steered him down the wide center aisle toward the gray marble railing in front of the altar of dark wood and silver. Tall gold candleholders and a plain gold cross reflected the light from candles and lanterns along the brick columns. As they passed the small side chapels, Meade looked for a place for Crispin to sit. The rows of pews were far too exposed. He needed to find a corner out of sight.

Meade smiled when he saw the larger-than-life statue of Saint George in mortal combat with a russet-winged dragon. The warrior was mounted on a dapple-gray steed. Both knight and steed were clad in gold armor. The dragon snarled with open alligator jaws and viper tongue at the rider and mount. The horse's hooves thrashed at its head, and the long sword was just starting the fatal arc.

Meade eased Crispin into one of the chairs in the church, near a secluded corner.

"Thank you, Meade. Sorry, I'm feeling a bit lightheaded. Did you see the dragon?"

"Yeah. Just sit there. I'll go for a doctor—"

"No. The blonde. She'll be watching for you at the train station. Send her back for me and go on to Uppsala."

"Is she one of Cumming's agents?"

Crispin nodded, looked past Meade, and watched the dragon as it seemed to move toward him.

Chapter № 47

Monday
November 13, 1916
West of London, England

Searching for a cool place on the smooth sheets, Crispin stretched, heard whispering, and held his breath. In a moment, he parsed the distant voice from the one in his dream and recognized Doctor Lee. She chuckled and rushed on with what she was saying. After a deep breath, he started listening to her words and Meade's responses.

As he turned his head on the pillow and squinted, Crispin saw them sitting at the far end of the stark white room. She was dressed in her brown suit and gestured broadly, "Oh, Mister Meade! It was simply spread before us, and the shadows just popped out from the mounds. I cannot tell you how exciting it was...and how disappointed we were that you were not there to share it with us."

Crispin fell back on his pillow, realized he was again in pajamas, and huffed.

Meade pointed at him. "Hey! Rip Van Winkle is waking up."

When Crispin heard the tapping of Doctor Lee's low heels against the wood floor, he propped himself up on one elbow and tried to focus. He noticed that Meade wore a casual black sweater and slacks. He looked at his attire again and discovered that he was not in hospital nightclothes. His cream-colored pajamas were silk and the dressing gown over the foot of the bed was of a fine wool in a deep claret with a crest embroidered in gold thread over the breast pocket.

In one seamless action, she took the thermometer from the alcohol-filled stand on the counter that could have served as a bud vase and shook the mercury down as she walked toward his bedside. "Good morning, Lieutenant Crispin."

"Are we at the vicarage?"

She nodded as she put the thermometer under his tongue. Meade chuckled as he approached the edge of the bed. "Kell's put us on ice here until Grimes takes the bait."

Crispin gave a dramatic groan and removed the thermometer. "On ice?" His hand brushed against the stubble on his chin, and he frowned.

She took the thermometer from him. "Like fish in a market!" She placed it again, and scowled at him when his hand started for the thermometer. He let his hands drop to the bed and watched her. Meade stood in silence until she took out the thermometer and said, "Now that you have joined us again, let's bring you up to date. Today is Monday the thirteenth. Late morning. You have been sleeping fitfully since your arrival here late Friday night."

Crispin's eyes widened, and he frowned in disbelief. "Monday? How could—" He felt his chin again and tipped his head as though performing some difficult calculation.

Meade stood at the foot of the bed. "Just to fill in the gaps, you passed out in the church, I got a cab, and the blonde got us out. By boat."

Crispin's head had fallen deeply into the pillow. "By boat? I had no idea."

Meade shook his head. "Hidden in the bilge—"

Raising his head he looked stunned. "In the bottom of the boat? I must have been as oblivious as Jonah."

"You were a pretty sick guy. Just barely awake enough to drink some broth and water and let me help you to the bathroom—"

"You did that?"

He shrugged.

She walked to the counter, read the thermometer, charted his temperature, and glanced at Meade. "I asked the cook to make up a good thick soup. I think Lieutenant Crispin is ready to graduate to it now.

Could you bring a large mug of it? Not a bowl, a mug."

Meade left for the nearby kitchen without a pause. When they were alone, she checked his leg and directed him to remain in bed.

Looking at the ceiling, Crispin sighed. "At least it's over."

Shaking her head, she said, "Not really. Seems they want us to stay at the vicarage until they know Grimes really believes the map to be genuine."

Crispin sat upright. "What? If I am in England, I need to be reassigned."

She helped him sit up. "They can order you to stay here, and have. Meade and I are not British subjects, yet we thought you could stand our company for a few more days." She chuckled. "It seems like paradise after that anatomy suite at the hospital." She rearranged the pillows to prop him up in bed.

"Being a prisoner in paradise makes it no less a prison."

After Meade had delivered the soup and departed, she watched as Crispin drank it and fell back against the pillows. She pulled a worn leather-bound book from her knitting bag and handed it to him.

"Something for you to read this afternoon."

Crispin turned the book so he could read the gold lettering on the spine. "*The Odyssey*! The Greek edition. I *have* read it."

"Not this one. It was my father's." Crispin opened it with care. "We would sit in the parlor after supper, and he would read a paragraph in Greek and then offer his simplified translation while I looked over his elbow. I stumbled through it again last year."

Crispin stopped fanning through the pages and looked at her. "I did not know you read Greek."

"My Latin is better. *Errare humanum est*."

He blushed as he muttered the translation. "To err is human."

As she walked past him, she patted his arm. "Sometimes I think it is what makes us human."

When she returned an hour later, Crispin had fallen asleep with *The*

Odyssey open on his chest. She took it, marked his place with a strand of yarn from her bag, and resumed her knitting. When Crispin stirred and grabbed for the missing book, she said, "I put it on the side table."

He blinked and squinted. "I had to stop."

"Fever again? Headache?"

He shook his head vigorously. "I had to think on it. I am seeing it in quite a different light than when I was in school." He propped himself up on one elbow and looked at her. "Why did you give me this to read?"

Without looking up from her knitting, Doctor Lee said, "When I worked in Edinburgh, after I lost my son, I wanted to understand what drew men to war. I found Homer's account of the Trojan War in *The Iliad* far too familiar. I understood that Odysseus, as a king, rose to the call and fought for a decade at Troy. Then I read the second half of the story, *The Odyssey*, and started to understand that the aftermath of war is not new to your generation, or my father's."

Crispin squinted at her and said, "I puzzled at why it took another decade for Odysseus to return to his wife and son in Ithaca." His voice grew faint and hoarse. She put down her knitting, brought him a glass of water, and held it as he sipped through the glass straw. He cleared his throat and said softly, "Thank you."

Doctor Lee nodded. "You are more than welcome."

He took a breath, exhaled and took a deeper one. "He was no longer just a king. He was Odysseus *et ux*, meaning 'and wife.' He feared their reunion as much as he longed for it. His journey was not just to return to Ithaca. Wasn't his quest to become whole again?"

She nodded. "He had changed– and so had his world. His son had grown to manhood in his absence."

He asked, "And his wife? What ever could she have thought of his delaying his homecoming?"

"She trusted that he would return. She spurned a hundred suitors, didn't she?"

Crispin arched an eyebrow. "So the story goes." Crispin gave her a shy smile. "Perhaps he feared letting Penelope know who he had become, who the war made him."

She nodded. "We all change. But we can decide *how* we change. The king has a real conflict. He wants to succumb to the forgetfulness of the lotus-eaters, the temptation of adultery in the siren's song, and unending challenges to avoid facing his fears. Yet, he knows those distractions would betray his duty and undermine who he wants to be."

He blurted, "Between Scylla and Charybdis!"

She nodded. "Between two equally difficult choices."

He shook his head forcefully. "No. You will recall that Odysseus has to sail between the monsters on either side of the Strait of Messina to go home. One gap-mouthed monster sucking in the sea and making a whirlpool that could pull down the ship. The other a six-headed monster. To avoid one, he had to sail too close to the other."

Doctor Lee said, "I thought you were making a modern reference to two equally bad choices."

Crispin said quickly, "But they are not at all equal. I, like Ulysses, would sail closer to Scylla, the six-headed monster and put only a few in peril. I would not risk the lives of the entire ship's company on Charybdis."

She looked at him in a way he had not seen. "I know that you are brave enough for any battle, man enough for any challenge. But only you can decide what to make of the sorrow of this bitter winnowing."

She turned and walked across the room, sat, and resumed her knitting. Crispin opened the book again and stared at the same page for a full minute before he began to read again. After another mug of soup in the afternoon, he excused himself, bathed, and shaved.

When she heard the sound of men in the kitchen, she looked past Crispin, who was reading in his hospital bed, and saw Kell and Meade striding through the doorway. She stood and held her knitting. "Meade? What's happening?"

Kell came into the room, unbuttoning his dark overcoat. He removed his bowler hat as he approached Doctor Lee. "I thought I'd pop in to congratulate you three personally."

Crispin came through the door behind them and walked toward his bed slowly. "Congratulations?"

Kell grinned. "Cable came in last evening. Grimes put together a team of diggers, and they began their excavation in the Hedeby harbor yesterday about noon."

Doctor Lee asked, "How could they ever launch an expedition so quickly?"

Kell chuckled. "It is wartime. All the niceties of permits and planning seem to go by the wayside. Already bringing up old bottles. Recent trash no doubt."

Crispin fell back on the bed, leaned his head back into the pillow, and laughed. Meade opened his mouth but no words came.

Doctor Lee looked at the men and nodded as her grin grew wider. "Isn't that something?"

"Indeed! When I informed His Majesty of the matter, he requested that I extend his personal appreciation to each of you. Sent along a gift from his cellar with me, as I told him I was retrieving the seal personally."

Meade walked past him saying, "I'll get it for you."

When he was almost to the door, Kell said, "And the map, as well."

Meade stopped. Crispin sat up and said, "I think not. Even if it were here, it is Mister Meade's personal property."

Kell stared at Meade. "The map is not here?"

Pausing slightly, Meade said, "Correct."

Kell grinned. "Oh, I see. That is what you had McLean running off—"

Crispin said firmly, "McLean had nothing to do with it."

"But he went to Barclays Bank in Oxford and—"

Doctor Lee nodded as she finished for Kell. "Made a deposit of a wrapped parcel containing a blank of used parchment to Crispin's bank box. It was *not* the parchment which he assumed it was."

Veins were now visible on Kell's neck. "Then where is—"

Crispin answered sharply. "The Baldwin Portolano is where any of the three of us can secure it and deposit it with the British Museum when our conditions are met."

Kell arched his neck and almost shouted. "*Conditions?* Are you expecting the government to *purchase* it?"

Meade frowned. "No!"

Crispin waved his hand for Meade to be silent. "We shall proffer it immediately after the mounds at Sutton Hoo, as I believe it should be called, are excavated and its treasures are secured for the British people."

Doctor Lee added, "And the scientific community."

Crispin continued. "Those are our conditions." Meade folded his arms over his chest. Kell exhaled loudly. "I will advise His Majesty." He shook his head and smiled. "You three!" He turned and followed Mead into the dining room. When Meade pulled the velvet bag from the map case and handed it to him, Kell examined the seal before he put it in his pocket. "Thought it best to be sure you three hadn't pulled some other feat of legerdemain and passed off a replica to me." Kell stood at attention and said quietly to Meade as he extended his hand, "It has been an honor to have assisted you, sir."

Meade looked taken aback, but then shook Kell's hand.

Kell lowered his voice to a whisper. "The P.M. spoke to me quite out of school. Your endowment of the medical trust at Ipswich was pure genius and—"

Meade said very slowly, "You will never mention that again." Kell nodded rapidly as Meade stepped closer to him and whispered, "Ever!"

Kell sniffed before he said, "My associate, Cumming, has adopted a motto for the foreign branch. *Semper Occultus.* 'Always secret.' That shall be my personal pledge to you, Mister Meade." Kell reached into his suit coat pocket and drew out three envelopes. "Downing Street sent these along for each of you. I shall wait for them here, as I must return them to the Prime Minister."

Meade shook his head and reached for them. "No. Tell Asquith that

I'll burn them here. You have *my* word on it."

Kell compressed his lips into a pale line and his nostrils flared as he stared at Meade. After a moment, he forced a small laugh and pushed the velvet bag deeper into his coat pocket as he turned for the door.

As Meade passed through the kitchen on the way to the infirmary, McLean was chipping shards from a block of ice and placing them into a Champagne bucket. "I'll bring it in when it is properly chilled."

When Meade joined Doctor Lee and Crispin in the infirmary, he said, "The King sent over a vintage Champagne. McLean is chilling it now."

Doctor Lee glanced at Crispin and nodded approval. Crispin sat up, threw his covers back, and announced, "This room is entirely unsuited for the moment. We should remove ourselves to the study."

McLean was placing the faceted Waterford Champagne glasses on a silver tray as Crispin marched past him, wearing a robe and using a cane. "We shall be in the study."

Crispin took the chair by the fire and let his cane fall to the red carpet.

Doctor Lee put the footstool under his ankle and sat on the sofa. After Meade joined her there, she patted his arm. "Well, I don't know whether to be grateful for our fellowship or sad at losing you both."

Meade said, "I don't think you can get rid of us that easily."

After McLean delivered the tray of glasses and the cook carried in a silver bucket with the Champagne surrounded by ice, Crispin nodded to them and they departed, closing the door behind them. Meade looked at the label, whistled, opened the bottle, and carefully poured three glasses.

Crispin glanced at his colleagues and then to the ceiling. He raised his faceted glass and watched the light fracture into rainbows as he recited, "*Sio gehaten is, geong goldhroden, gladum suna Frodan; hafað þæs geworden wine Scyldinga, rices hyrde, ond þæt ræd talað, þæt he mid ðy wife wælfæhða dæl, sæcca gesette.*"

Meade sighed. "What now?"

"*Beowulf*, about line two thousand fifteen, a toast to peace. Far too long a passage to translate."

Doctor Lee touched the rim of her glass to Crispin's. "Well then, to a peace that comes soon and lasts long."

Meade raised his glass took a small sip, savored it, and took another. "Have to admit, George has great taste in wine!"

Shaking his head, Crispin corrected Meade. "*His Royal Majesty* has excellent taste in—"

She laughed at Crispin's reprimand. "Well? What's next for us all after the war, do you suppose?"

Meade looked at Crispin and a smile escaped before his laugh. "The Professor's got to start his teaching career and write huge books with lots of footnotes."

Crispin sat straighter. "Of course, I will be publishing my translation of *Beowulf* and an Old English dictionary. Perhaps a glossary of new terms related to the war."

Meade shook his head as he pulled three sealed envelopes from his pocket. "Kell dropped these off with me. One for each of us." Meade looked at the names written in ink with a broad nib. "Under the condition we burn them after reading the contents. Agreed?"

Both nodded quickly. After fanning the three envelopes on the small table, Meade said, "Ladies first."

Doctor Lee put her glass down carefully and ran her finger over the embossed address on the envelope. "It's from 10 Downing—"

Crispin examined his envelope. "Why is the Prime Minister writing to us? Cannot imagine this is an easy time for him."

She pulled her glasses from her pocket and paused before she opened her letter.

Crispin asked, "What is it, Doctor?"

"Wherever fate takes us next, I hope that we shall remain in contact over the years. You two have become quite special to me."

Both nodded before she read her letter and sat back into the velvet-covered settee. The men watched her as she blinked quickly. "I am offered the Directorship of the new clinic at Ipswich."

Crispin slapped the arm of his chair. "Perfect!"

She nodded to Crispin, who held his envelope toward the light of the fire and tapped the letter to one end. He tore the other end, slid out the letter, and read it twice. "I have an interview at the OED after I muster out. Temporary work while they sort out the teaching positions at Oxford."

Meade frowned. "OED?"

Crispin sighed. "Meade, that is the *Oxford English Dictionary*. They are still writing it!"

Meade pointed his unopened envelope at Crispin. "Really? If anyone knows words, it's you."

Doctor Lee looked at Meade. "And you, Mister Meade? What's in yours?"

Meade opened his envelope and read his letter. A second sheet of paper, a half page with a purple stamp on the corner fell to his lap. He picked it up quickly and slipped it into his jacket pocket. He smiled, tossed his letter and envelope into the fireplace, and watched the paper curl. He waited until the others passed their letters and envelopes to him and theirs too had gone to embers.

She watched his face and saw his eyes crinkle at the edges. "You are going back to France, aren't you?"

"Might."

Doctor Lee grinned. "I knew it! Well, she can't notice you here. Can she?"

Meade feigned surprise. "What?"

"Mister Meade, this isn't a Sunday school. You are a very attractive man, and she is a widow. If you want to see her, go to Cannes."

Meade held up his hand. "But—"

"You told me she turned her chateau into a hospital. Going to help her, aren't you?"

Meade smiled at her. "Did you always get your way with Stewart, too?"

"Only on important things." Doctor Lee looked into her glass and then held it up in a toast to Meade. "And thence to France we shall convey you safe, and bring you back, charming the narrow sea to give you gentle pass." She blinked and forced a smile. "Can anyone tell me who said that?"

Meade said, "Shakespeare."

Doctor Lee looked up from her glass and winked at Crispin. "Yes, in his *Henry V*. That's what he said to his army in another war. Odd that. 'Band of brothers' he called his troops. Not much changes, does it?"

Crispin laughed. "Well, Meade, back to France, is it? Need anything, a pocket dictionary, English to French. I might have an extra." Crispin patted the pockets of his dressing gown theatrically.

"No, thanks. But I'd like to borrow your ring. Professor?"

Tipping his head, Crispin asked, "My new ring?"

Meade winked at Doctor Lee and pointed to Crispin as though catching him in a joke. "The ring of Gyges."

Crispin looked surprised. "You know Plato's fable?"

"Not when you first mumbled about needing your ring of Gyges when we landed back in England. I thought you'd gone off your nut. But I looked it up when we were at the hospital and found out that it is from Plato's *Republic*."

"Right you are, Meade. Full marks. Do you know the story, Doctor Lee?"

"I'm sure I must have read it, but I can't say I recall it."

Smiling, Crispin lowered his voice. "The ring was magic. It seemed to be an ordinary ring until you turned the bezel. Then, the wearer became invisible. Plato used this power to pose several questions. What would we do if we had that power? Would our ethics or behavior change?"

She nodded. "Oh, I see. Would we steal if we knew we never would be found out?"

"I believe that the Anglo-Saxon proverb put it right. *Man dep swá hé byþ þonne hé mót swá hé wile.*"

Meade looked up, waiting for Crispin to translate.

"Oh, yes. It means 'man does as he is when he may do as he wishes.' So you...."

Meade interrupted him. "Well, are you gonna give me the ring or not?"

"Oh, Meade, I would, were it mine to give, but...."

"But what, Professor?"

"I suspect you wouldn't change a whit."

Meade sipped his wine. "Kind of you to think so."

"Not at all. Simple truth."

McLean tapped on the door before opening it. He spoke to Meade. "Your cases are in the Panard, sir."

Doctor Lee looked shocked. "So soon?"

Meade nodded. As she hurried from the room, tears welled in her eyes. Meade finished his Champagne, which seemed to have gone bitter.

Crispin looked at the empty doorway. "All that remains is for me to lead them to the site, when the time is ripe after the war is behind us. I may cage another airplane ride out of it if I am lucky."

Meade stood up and clapped Crispin on the shoulder. "Never thought I'd live to see the day when you wanted to fly."

"Nor did I. However, if no one is shooting at you, it is quite interesting. I just flew to set an example for her."

"Doctor Lee? She's tougher than both of us put together. It has been a pleasure working with you."

Crispin stood and leaned against the arm of the chair. "And you."

Meade's smile went crooked. "If you ever decide that teaching isn't for you—"

"Are you offering me a position with your firm?"

"If you ever change your mind, just go to my London office—"

Crispin adopted his best stern look. "Promise that you will visit."

"And how would you explain me?"

"Rich Americans never need explaining. They just do as they will. I'm planning to pass Doctor Lee off as someone I met in the hospital. Without added details, it is almost true."

Meade turned toward the door of the study. "I'd better go find her."

After glancing in the study, dining room and walking past the kitchen, he found her in the infirmary, looking into her knitting bag. "I wanted—"

"Here it is." She pulled a six-foot long charcoal muffler from her bag and handed it to him. "I made one for each of you. Thought I'd be sending yours to your office in London."

Meade draped it over his neck and tossed the tasseled end over one shoulder with a flourish. "Just what I needed. Thanks."

"Do I see your fine hand in all this?"

Meade put on a guise of schoolboy innocence. "All what?"

Doctor Lee gave him a quick hug and hooked her wrist around his elbow. "Let me walk with you."

"My pleasure."

Crispin had gone ahead and stood like a coachman, leaning on the Panard's open rear door. He extended his hand. "Godspeed, my friend."

Meade shook his hand and ducked into the car.

Crispin shut the door firmly and nodded to McLean, who drove down the long graveled entrance. He walked to the marble bench by the front door, tugged his robe tie tighter, sat, and watched the car crunching slowly over the gravel toward the roadway. Doctor Lee sat beside him and stared at him with the look by which mothers elicit confessions. "Did he tell you what was in his envelope? Did I guess right?"

"I think so. I am almost certain that was a letter of transit that he slipped into his jacket."

The Panard turned and circled back to the marble bench. As it slowed to a stop, Meade grinned through the open window. "Remember our motto. *Semper Occultus.*" He laughed as McLean drove away.

Crispin turned to Doctor Lee and whispered, "Always Secret."

A Note to Readers:

I hope you enjoyed this book and will find the following Reader's Guide of value.

The author's blog at SharonOLightholder.com is a resource to print Reader's Guides for your personal use or that of your book club, share your thoughts on the book, and see what's happening next. You can also visit my Facebook page: Sharon O. Lightholder.

Acknowledgements:

Any book is a collaboration of the thoughts and energy of many. Maureen O. Shanahan continues to be a tireless reader of seemingly endless drafts, purveyor of wise counsel, and all around great sister. My brother-in-law, Dennis F. Shanahan, M.D., M.P.H., graciously brought accuracy to the aviation and medical aspects of this book.

The historical records and artifacts preserved by visionaries in museums and libraries are key to anchoring fiction in fact. Particular thanks are due to the staff for access to the collections the Bibliothèque nationale de France, (Paris, France); the Bodleian Library, (Oxford, England); Uppsala Universitetsbibliotek Carolina Rediviva, (Uppsala, Sweden), The Sutton Hoo Society, British National Trust, the Smithsonian National Air and Space Museum, and the San Diego Air and Space Museum. My ongoing appreciation goes to the librarians and archivists at the California State University system, the San Diego City Library, and the Carlsbad City Library.

About the author:

Sharon O. Lightholder, author of *The English Rendition*, was raised on both American coasts, lived in Asia and Europe, and attended universities in the United States and Sweden before completing her legal education while working as a probation officer. She worked as a public policy, fiscal and legislative analyst and program manager for a public entity before moving to San Diego where she now writes.

A Reader's Guide

The Baldwin Portolano
By
Sharon O. Lightholder

1. How is daily life during World War I different from your life today? How is it similar?

2. There is a significant difference in age and experience between Dr. Lee (a woman in her late 60s), Mr. Meade (about 50) and Lt. Crispin (just 21). How does age and experience influence their view of the world and their actions?

3. Taking the novel as a whole, what are the best and worst character traits of Dr. Lee, Mr. Meade, and Lt. Crispin?

4. Did Dr. Lee help Lt. Crispin address and manage his shell shock? How is the shell shock experienced by soldiers in WWI different from or similar to today's Post Traumatic Stress Disorder?

5. Did you discover something about the WWI era that you did not already know?

6. Before the United States had entered WWI, many Americans volunteered as ambulance drivers and worked in hospitals in the battle zone. Others volunteered to be pilots. What compels such voluntary acts?

7. Although from divergent backgrounds, what created a bond of friendship between the three main characters?

8. How was Dr. Lee's life as a professional woman in her era different from today's professional woman? How is it similar?

9. Will these three have other adventures together or drift apart after the war ends?

10. What other aspect of the time, place or characters was important to you?

www.ingramcontent.com/pod-product-compliance
Lightning Source LLC
Chambersburg PA
CBHW020920020726
47495CB00002B/266